Reach For Tomorrow

Jessica Blair

D1392076

PIATKUS

PIATKUS

First published in Great Britain in 2006 by Piatkus Books
This paperback edition published in 2007 by Piatkus Books

Copyright © Jessica Blair 2006

This edition published 2007

All the characters in this book are fictitious and any resemblance to real
persons, living or dead, is entirely coincidental

The moral right of the author has been asserted

*All characters and events in the publication, other than
those clearly in the public domain, are fictitious
and any resemblance to real persons,
living or dead, is purely coincidental*

All rights reserved
No part of this publication may be reproduced, stored in a retrieval
system, or transmitted in any form or by any means, without the
prior permission in writing of the publisher, nor be otherwise
circulated in any form of binding or cover other than that in which it
is published and without a similar condition including this condition
being imposed on the subsequent purchaser

A CIP catalogue record for this book
is available from the British Library

ISBN 978-0-7499-3743-0

Set in Times by Pamlimpsest Book Production Limited
Grangemouth, Stirlingshire
Printed and bound in Great Britain by
Mackays of Chatham Ltd, Chatham, Kent

Piatkus Books
An imprint of
Little, Brown Book Group
100 Victoria Embankment
London EC4Y 0DY

An Hachette Livre UK Company

www.piatkus.co.uk

First published in Great Britain in 20.. by Sphere Books

Copyright © Penny Vincenzi

For a very dear friend, Jill
with grateful thanks for your love in friendship.

NORTH AYRSHIRE
LIBRARIES

02206831

CANCELLED

Bertrams   24/03/2010

            £6.99

HQ

Acknowledgements

There are many people involved in the production of a book and I thank all who worked on this one, in particular those at my publisher's,. and especially my editors who brought it to its final version.

I must give heartfelt thanks to my daughter Judith who vetted this book in all its early stages and did much of the background research. Without the support of all my family, throughout the trying time of moving house, this book would never have been completed.

Chapter One

Colette Clayton straightened from her camera and surveyed the Whitby scene she had photographed – oh, she couldn't remember how many times since she had been given a camera thirty-four years ago for her eleventh birthday.

The view, looking upstream along the River Esk towards the bridge that joined the crowded East and West Sides of this busy Yorkshire port, had come to mean a great deal to her. She had photographed its many moods at all times of the year. It was not just one picture to her but many, never two the same. The cool, sharp light of an early-winter morning today lent the scene a restful atmosphere though overhead, out of the frame, were glowering clouds, driven by the furious wind and sent skidding overhead, possible portents of doom and disaster. Perhaps she loved this scene best when the sun was lowering to the west, saturating the scene with a tranquil light over the town's ships and buildings, a day's work done, she decided.

There were many such pictures, admired and praised by friends or bought through the photographic business she had built into a successful enterprise. But Colette was never satisfied with her own work as she strove in vain to match the atmosphere of a painting of the same scene that hung above the fireplace in the drawing room of her house on the West Cliff. It was signed, *Arthur Newton 1889*.

Every day for two years since its unexpected arrival she had stood in front of that picture and seen in it, not only an atmospheric depiction of her favourite view along the river but also an expression of the love she and Arthur Newton had once shared, a love that she had long believed to have been cauterised by his

1

betrayal of her. But the surprise arrival of that painting after Edward had made his acquaintance and unsuspectingly taken him home to tea with his mother had made her realise she had always retained a deep affection for her first love, despite a happy marriage to another man. Bernard Clayton had loved her devotedly until his tragically early death and had died without realising that their son Edward had been fathered by another man.

Nor had Edward known that Bernard was not his real father until the surprising arrival of Arthur Newton's painting and a sketchbook. Although both were addressed to Colette, his mother had told Edward to unwrap the smaller package while she removed the wrapping from the canvas. On finding the sketchbook he had flicked through its pages and been surprised to discover a sketch of his mother dated 1866. Startled and surprised that she had known Arthur Newton so long ago he had studied it intently, slowly realising from the care that had been lavished on the portrait that artist and model had been deeply in love. Then the answer to something that had always puzzled him dawned: he knew at last from whom he had inherited his own talent as an artist.

Edward's immediate desire to find his real father again, after meeting him purely by chance on the quayside without realising who he was, was curbed by his affection and respect for Colette. 'Too many lives would be stricken,' she insisted. 'Your father is married and has a daughter.'

Edward had complied, but Colette knew that his desire to make contact, especially now that he knew he had a half-sister, would never falter and she could only hope that when he made the effort to find Arthur Newton and his daughter, there would be no unfortunate repercussions.

Colette remained still, casting her eyes across the scene, judging the play of light that would result once the clouds had moved away from the sun. One more photograph . . .

She patted the fair hair she always tied loosely on top of her head when working outside. She was simply attired in a plain brown dress that, though well fitting, allowed her freedom of movement to manage her equipment. Her actions, even when making minor adjustments to the settings on her camera, were graceful, not to make any contrived impression but coming naturally to her. Her blue eyes were alert, always judging views and people in terms of their appearance before the camera. She drew a handkerchief trimmed with lace from her pocket, dabbed her nose absently and watched cloud shadows, pursued by sunlight, race across the red roofs of Whitby that climbed the cliff towards the ruined abbey. The river, on its way to the sea, sparkled like a trail of diamonds caught by the light.

Now! She thrust the handkerchief away and swiftly made the exposure. Afterwards she gave a contented sigh, approving of what she knew would be a good photograph. She dismantled her equipment with the help of her sister Adele, two years younger than herself, who had taken a few hours away from her family to help as she used to when Colette first began her study of photography. These were precious moments the sisters enjoyed. They chatted amicably as they made their way back to Colette's house on the west cliff.

Marie Newton's eyes brightened with excitement. It replaced the doubt that had been there but moments before when she'd opened the letter which had arrived as she and her father were about to start breakfast. Arthur had guessed who had sent it and had watched with an anxious expression as his thirty-two-year-old daughter slit the envelope open. When he saw her eyes light up his anxiety evaporated. He guessed the letter contained the news she had been eagerly awaiting. Although it would mean a parting for them, he would not stand in the way of her furthering her artistic career.

'Papa, Monsieur Bedaux has accepted me to study under his tuition!' The joy in her voice revealed Marie's intense excitement. She thrust the piece of paper across the table at him.

He took it with trembling fingers.

He had privately doubted the wisdom of her widening her artistic experience and technique in Paris but it was only natural that her thoughts had turned there; the city was the shining light for art students of all ages. Its reputation was far-flung and exciting. Paris pulsed with life in every shape and form. The students who flocked there hoping to find fame and fortune created an unrivalled atmosphere in the boulevards and cafes of Montmartre and Montparnasse, filling them with hectic *joie de vivre* and constant talk of drawing, painting, fabulous sales and intriguing commissions. And besides all this the city dwellers ceaselessly pursued their own pleasures in a celebration of women, wine and wit.

Small wonder then that Arthur had some misgivings about Marie venturing into such a world; after all she was an attractive young woman. She had an engaging personality, could readily be at ease with people, had a sharp mind and was particularly engaging on the subject she loved most – art. Her growing talent as an artist had been inherited from her father, her looks from her maternal grandmother, particularly her eyes which were beautiful and languid, but with an ability to shine with pleasure and excitement as they were now. Arthur loved and admired her. He could not hold her back. There were many who ventured into the Parisian throng and survived. Why shouldn't his daughter do likewise? He should trust her, give her his love and let her go. She would love him all the more and return time and time again. Besides, it was possible she would not be living alone in Paris . . .

'I wonder if Lucy has been accepted?'

'You've voiced my very thought,' he replied. 'We'll walk over to Cherry Hill after breakfast.'

'I hope your recommendation drew attention to the work she submitted.'

Arthur nodded. He hoped so too for it would mean that the two friends could live together. He cast his eyes over the letter from Paris again

Marie and Lucy Wentworth had first met in London in March of the previous year when attending an art lecture. They had become close when they discovered that outside the capital they lived within two miles of each other, near Deal on the south coast. Six months later, after they had become almost inseparable, Lucy had confided in her friend that she had been married.

Taken aback, Marie had remarked, 'But you wear no wedding ring?'

'Nor do I bear his name,' Lucy had offered with bitterness in

4

her tone. She had gone on to reveal that in 1884 she had been the envy of many young women when she had married the handsome, dashing Army officer, Giles Langley-Clift whose family had estates in Northumberland. The following year she had accompanied him on his posting to India but after three years and three miscarriages the marriage had turned sour. She became aware of whisperings among other wives but paid little attention to them until it was revealed that for a year her husband had been having an affair with a wealthy young Indian woman. Scandal broke and stuck with such intensity that it resulted in a double suicide pact which rocked the Army in India and even had repercussions in England. Back in her own country Lucy could not escape the implications her unusual married name conjured up so sort anonymity by reverting to her maiden name of Wentworth and living with her widowed mother, Isobel, at the family farm now run by a competent manager. Lucy rekindled with great vigour her old love of painting, which had been stifled by her husband, and on meeting Marie was grateful for her father's advice and encouragement.

Arthur looked up from the letter and said with all sincerity, 'Wonderful news, Marie, just wonderful. Bedaux may not be at the forefront of the Parisian art world but he's a competent artist who sells regularly. I'm told he's also a good teacher, especially of portrait painting in which you say you wish to specialise. You should progress well with him but are likely to meet with opposition, maybe even contempt, from some of the male fraternity, especially the young pretenders.'

'Don't worry, Papa. I'll manage. I've met opposition to female artists in London, Scarborough and here in Deal.' She gave a little chuckle. 'Paris hasn't reckoned on Marie Newton.'

'I'm so proud of you, and I know your mother would have been too.'

'Would she, Papa?' There was a hint of doubt in her voice.

'Of course she would. You were her much-loved daughter. I know what you are thinking, and I agree. She never really understood the hold of art upon us even though in time she did cease to oppose my career as an artist and lent me her support.'

Marie saw sadness cross her father's face then and knew he was thinking of what might have been. Though Arthur was only in his mid-fifties, the tribulations of earlier years had lined his otherwise distinguished face, and worry over his wife's final illness had greyed his hair prematurely. Otherwise he was still a strong, upright figure and as she watched him Marie hoped she would have such vitality when she was his age. Though he lacked inspiration now and painted very little, Arthur's bright eyes never ceased to search out and appraise scenes he would once have transferred to paper and canvas.

'Mother was never really in favour of my following in your footsteps.'

'She saw it as an obstacle to what she desired for you – a happy marriage with children for her to dote on. But she never once forbade you to strive for the career you desired.'

'I think you were very persuasive there and tempered all her objections.'

Arthur shrugged his shoulders. He made no comment and instead said, 'I know she would have been very proud of you, Marie, don't ever think otherwise.'

She left her chair as he was speaking, came to him, knelt down and hugged him. 'I owe it all to you. You taught me, guided me, but most of all I inherited my ability from you – what more could you give me?'

He stroked her head with the tenderness of a father's deep love. 'But by doing so, did I deprive you?'

'Deprive me?' She looked askance at him.

'Of the love of a man who would make you a good husband and give you the joy of children. Did my encouragement of your art take that chance away from you? You grew from a shy young girl into a self-confident, very beautiful young woman whom many men have found attractive. You've had many suitors.'

'If I had wanted any one of those men I would have married.'

'Perhaps I did fail you by encouraging your talent.' He gave a little shake of his head.

She raised her hand to his cheek then stopped the movement. She looked deep into his eyes. 'You did not. Don't ever think that.'

'You are thirty-two, Marie. Time does not stand still for any of us.'

'I know, Papa.' She pushed herself to her feet. 'Now, no more of this! Be happy for me.'

He gave a forced smile. 'I am happy for you and I know you will make the most of your opportunity.' In a way Arthur envied the good fortune presented to his daughter. It had been a chance he had never had. His own natural ability had been recognised and encouraged through a casual meeting with an art dealer, Ebenezer Hirst, in Leeds. Arthur's family had shown no such interest in his talent, only in the sound steady job they had found for him at the railway offices which they believed would provide comfort and an assured future. The same attitude was shared by his wife, Rose, and their marriage sailed into dangerous waters when he threw in his job to paint. She eventually gave him an ultimatum that she would tolerate his whim only if the standard of life that she had experienced during his work with the railway was never allowed to slip.

Working under such a stricture forced him to tackle only subjects that would be good sellers. There was no inspiration for him there. That only happened after he had met and fallen in love with a Whitby girl ten years younger than himself. His affair with Colette Shipley had had a tremendous impact on his work and Arthur became nationally known as a result, especially for his paintings of Whitby and Leeds. What he had looked on as an ideal situation ended abruptly when Rose and Colette came face to face. Rose realised she was married to an unfaithful husband and Colette learned she was in love with a married man. It was only then that Arthur appreciated the depths of his own folly and deceit. Shaken and remorseful, he resumed his fidelity to his wife, finding common ground in their love for their child. He learned that Colette found solace in her marriage to a childhood sweetheart, though there was little joy for him in that fact.

Arthur's work had slipped back into the realms of the ordinary. His true inspiration, the one person who could raise it to glorious heights, had been missing from his life, until one day on a nostalgic visit to Whitby he saw her again and realised that, even throughout a happy marriage, she had never relinquished that final remnant of love for him that dwelt in her heart. Buoyed up by this knowledge,

Arthur had once again painted with a sureness and passion that he knew were guided by Colette. This return to form continued until Rose's illness took them from the Yorkshire coast to the shores of southern England where she had made only a partial recovery before she faded away.

Father and daughter had remained together after she died but now they were faced with a parting that could take on the mantle of permanency. That prompted Marie to put a question to her father as they walked to Cherry Hill.

'Would you like to return to the North? To Leeds where you were brought up or to Whitby for which I know you have great affection? Maybe even Scarborough where we were happy and which I always regard as our family home.'

Arthur stopped and turned his gaze across the waters of the Channel, now calm under the caress of a gentle breeze. Marie saw a faraway look in his eyes and wondered what thoughts had been prompted by her questions. His lips tightened. She knew a decision was coming. He turned his eyes slowly away from the sea and said as he started to walk again, 'We talked of this when your mother died, but chose to remain here. I think the same applies now.'

'But things are different, Papa. With your blessing I am leaving. Then I was not.'

'I know, but I shall remain here, I couldn't face the upheaval of moving north again.' It was a thin excuse but he knew it would suffice to satisfy his daughter. He could not tell her the truth. If he returned to Yorkshire perhaps the love he and Colette had shared, which he knew still remained deep in their hearts, could blaze again. But fanning those flames would shatter lives. Marie and Edward would have to know of the past and the unfaithfulness of their parents; all respect and love would be gone. His love for Colette was too great for him to subject her to the torment of a rift between her and her only child. He gave a little nod and confirmed with conviction in his voice, 'I have a good cook-housekeeper here and an efficient household staff. I have my love of art to occupy my time and mind so I will remain here. Mrs Wentworth and I will be able to exchange news of you both, and living here will mean less travelling when you and I visit one another.' A lame excuse he knew but it helped to still Marie's concern.

'If that is what you want, Papa.'

'It is. So that is settled.' Arthur gave a little pause to emphasise his decision then said, 'Of course I will accompany you to Paris and see you settled.'

'There is no need, Papa, I am perfectly capable of looking after myself,' protested Marie. 'Besides, hopefully Lucy will be with me.'

'I know, but for this first time you must have an escort. I will be easier in my mind if I know you have arrived safely. I will be able to see where you are living and where you will be studying, and satisfy myself that everything is to your liking and benefit. I'm sure that Mrs Wentworth also would like to know that her daughter is settled.'

Marie knew her father. That determination in his voice, when he had set his mind on a particular course of action, was familiar to her. She knew it was no use objecting further.

They were still two hundred yards from the large farmhouse, standing on a hill with a line of cherry trees to its left from which it took its name, when the door was flung open. A laughing Lucy ran to meet them, waving a piece of paper in the air.

'She must have been accepted!' cried Marie joyfully, and started to run towards her friend.

All decorum was thrown aside as they flung their arms round each other. Laughter rang through the air.

'I've been accepted!' cried Lucy. 'I can't believe it.'

'So have I, so have I!' shouted Marie as she swung Lucy round. 'We're going to Paris! We're going to Paris!'

Arthur, smiling at the joyous enthusiasm of the young folk, congratulated Lucy in his turn.

He was pleased that this pretty young woman would be with his daughter in Paris. He had locked her story in his mind, never to be mentioned. He was pleased the laughter lines around her eyes had returned along with her naturally happy, friendly nature. Her dark, shoulder-length hair framed a round, rosy face that reflected much time spent out of doors, as was only to be expected having been brought up on a farm on the western side of Deal.

'Oh, Mr Newton, I'm sure your recommendation did the trick,' cried Lucy, her expression brimming over with thanks.

'That would not have been enough of itself. Monsieur Bedeaux would look first for talent.'

He glanced beyond them and saw Lucy's mother coming from the house. Isobel Wentworth was a fine woman, tall and erect with an air of natural authority though she did not let that appear unless it was necessary. In the year since their daughters had met and he had come to know Isobel, Arthur had learned that there was a kind tender heart behind her exterior. He also knew that she was not a woman to take any liberties with; cross the line and their friendship would be destroyed, and in his lonely hours Arthur valued that friendship. He slipped past the two friends and went to meet Isobel.

He admired her black gored ankle-length skirt. A white blouse could be glimpsed beneath a reefer jacket that emphasised her slim waist and showed that this was a lady who cared about her figure and appearance. Her copper-coloured hair was straight but drawn back in an attractive way to frame her oval face and reveal her lively hazel eyes.

'Arthur!' Her voice was soft, gentle and full of pleasure.

'Isobel.' He removed his hat and made a little bow when he reached her. 'This is good news.'

She gave a little grimace along with her smile. 'Is it?'

'You know it is. It's what our daughters want, and if we let them go they will succeed,' he returned quietly in a tone that was meant to reassure.

'But Paris?'

'They will be all right there. They are sensible and old enough to cope. We still tend to think of them as younger than they are, and believe we should be looking to their every need when really they are easily able to be independent.'

'I know you are right, Arthur, it's only a mother's natural concern.'

They started to stroll to the house, leaving their daughters to enjoy their news together.

'Isobel, I am proposing to accompany Marie to Paris to see that she is settled. I have no doubt that they will want to travel together so, if you approve, I will escort Lucy too.'

Isobel stopped and looked at him with gratitude in her eyes. 'Please do. I should be a lot happier knowing that you were there.' She laid a hand on his arm as she was speaking, a sure sign of her appreciation.

The girls reached them.

'Mr Newton is going to be your escort to Paris,' announced Isobel with relief in her voice.

'There you are, Mother, I told you not to worry. Mr Newton will see us safely there and bring you news of where we are settled. It's all so exciting!'

Isobel smiled at her daughter. 'Come along in. We'll have some hot chocolate.'

Time rushed by and before any of them realised it the day of departure for Paris was upon them.

Arthur had fussed over Marie's preparations. She had let him, knowing that it eased the prospect of his having to face life without her.

As the coach that would take them first to Cherry Hill and then to Dover pulled away, Marie looked back at the house with sadness. Except for the loss of her mother, she had been happy there. Moving away from it marked a break, a change in her life which, from now on, would chart a different course. She dabbed a tear from her eye, swallowed hard and bit her lip. Her father would not want to see her sad but would prefer to see a determined young woman, eager to look at the future firmly and seize the opportunities that came her way. He would also want her to enjoy the adventure that lay ahead, and she regarded the unknown life before her as such. She resolved to do well for his sake as well as fulfilling her own ambition to become a good portrait painter and breach the walls of a male dominated citadel.

Her reaction was not lost on her father. He reached out and patted her hand comfortingly. 'Enjoy the journey,' he said quietly.

Marie gave a wan smile, nodded, drove back the tears. By the time they reached Cherry Hill she was genuinely looking forward to the new experience she would share with Lucy.

The warmth and pleasure in their eyes when Marie and Lucy

11

greeted each other matched the day's sunshine. As Isobel came forward to greet them, Arthur could tell that her outward brightness was forced and hid deep regret that her daughter was leaving. He gave her a reassuring look as he said, 'I know it is easy to say, but don't worry. Lucy will be all right. I'll report as soon as I get back.'

'Thank you.'

He waved away her thanks and said, 'We shouldn't linger.'

Isobel nodded, hugged her daughter and said goodbye with last words of advice, 'Look after yourself and write often,' she instructed.

'I will, Mama.' The words choked in Lucy's throat. She returned her mother's affectionate embrace, turned and stepped quickly into the coach. She shut the door behind her, leaned out of the window and reached out to make contact with her mother's hand in a last gesture of love as the coachman sent the horse forward.

In a few moments more excited chatter filled the coach and this continued until they reached Dover. There they were swept up into the bustle and activity that preceded the sailing of any ferry for Calais. Arthur ushered the two young women past the port officials. Once on board he found them a comfortable seat on deck, giving way to their wishes to remain in the open as the weather was so fine.

The clop of hooves, and creak of carriages and wagons bringing passengers and goods to the dockside, were swallowed up amid the shouts of command and answering retorts of sailors bent to their tasks so as to have everything ready by sailing time. The young women were fascinated by such seeming confusion and did not have one boring second as they waited for the ship to sail. This was preceded by a momentary lull, with activity on the dockside diminishing as preparations were finalised and a last check was being carried out.

Then orders came from the bridge, answering shouts from the quay. Smoke belched from the stack, bells clanged. Marie and Lucy jumped from their seats and, holding on to their hats, even though they were tied by ribbons under the chin, hurried to the rail. Mesmerised by the activity on shore, they saw ropes unwound from capstans, friends and relations waving goodbye to loved ones, eyes dabbed with handkerchiefs. Children ran in chase of the stately motion of the boat or were held tightly by their mothers and cajoled to wave to their fathers. Slowly the ship was eased from the dockside and the excitement of being underway thrilled them. Any apprehension that they had had beforehand about being seasick disappeared. They did, however, bless their luck that they were faced with a smooth crossing.

So it proved and they enjoyed the exhilarating salt air and the throb of the ship's engines that seemed to tell them that their lives were changing and that, unusually for young women of their class at that time, they were stepping into an unknown wider world. They thanked their own interest in art and their understanding parents for this opportunity to step out from under the strictures of the society in which they had lived. Freedom beckoned.

Reaching Calais, much of the activity they had witnessed was repeated in reverse as the ship was brought skilfully to the dockside. With only a smattering of French from their schooldays in England they understood little of the exchanges here, but once the gangway was run out and passengers were allowed ashore Arthur lost no time in ushering them through to the Paris train. They were fascinated by the countryside they saw as the train huffed and puffed its way to the capital where once again Arthur soon hired a cab to take them from the noise and clatter of the Gâre du Nord to a residence on the edge of Montparnasse.

Marie and Lucy exchanged excited chatter over everything that caught their attention on the way through the city. Arthur smiled at their enthusiasm, which blossomed as if they were still schoolgirls. He remembered his own reaction when he'd first visited Paris after his wife had died and Marie was studying in London.

People strolled along the grand boulevards, stopping to exchange a passing remark with acquintances or, if they were friends, lingering longer. There was elegance in their dress and posture, and they seemed oblivious to the rush and bustle around them and the noise that characterised these thoroughfares. Whirling wheels followed smart carriage horses; vendors' carts rattled and hawkers cried their wares; a double-decker omnibus, drawn by huge Percherons, swayed past taking passengers to various parts of the city; customers in the pavement cafes were attended to by white-aproned waiters. People strolled in the open spaces past flowerbeds ablaze with colour, or tried to calm their excited children as they hurried to the puppet show or the colourful, magical carousel. The streets of Paris were bathed in warm sunshine that gleamed on polished harnesses, shining leather and newly painted coaches, landaus, fiacres and phaetons.

Taking it all in, Marie decided, I am going to love it here, though she kept the thought to herself.

When they dismounted from the cab she and Lucy gazed at the building they had reached, wondering with some trepidation what lay before them. It was so unlike the attractive ornate buildings they had seen on the way, imagining that the place where they were to study would be the same. Instead they found themselves standing in front of a building that had little character and was similar to the rest of an undistinguished row.

They placed their bags beside the front door and Arthur struck it sharply with the brass knocker. Their sense of disillusion heightened when the door opened to reveal a sharp-featured lady of medium height who gazed haughtily at them as if they had no right to use the knocker in a way that had disturbed the peace of the house. Her black dress, without any relief in the way of a brooch or lace trimmings, and straight hair drawn tightly towards the back of her neck, added to a formidable appearance. She turned a cold gaze on Arthur as much as to say, What are you doing here? then swept her eyes over Marie and Lucy.

'Well, young ladies, what is it?' she snapped. Though her English was good it had a marked accent.

'Er . . . We are expected,' Marie spluttered.

'Oh, you must be Mademoiselle Newton and Mademoiselle Wentworth from England.' Marie felt a slight relaxation in the woman's attitude though she still held an air of unflinching authority.

Seeing the woman's eyes turn questioningly to Arthur, Marie quickly informed her, 'This is my father.'

The woman gave a curt nod and said, 'Come in, don't stand on the pavement.'

14

Marie, wondering what sort of a world she was stepping into, did as they were bidden, feeling distinctly relieved that her father had insisted on accompanying her.

'You are here to learn from Monsieur Bedeaux. I will take you to him in a moment. Follow me.' The woman started towards a door on the right but made a brief pause to say, 'Leave your bags there.' She indicated a spot beside a small table at the bottom of the stairs and then carried on. They left their bags and hurried after her. They found themselves in a square room, heavy with dark furniture. 'Sit.' The woman indicated three chairs but she remained standing when they meekly sat down. 'Monsieur Bedeaux is a man devoted to his art. He wants no domestic disturbance but leaves everything to me, Madame Gerard. It is really up to you to find your own accommodation but I have made enquiries with a friend of mine, Madame Foucarde, who is responsible for some properties in Montparnasse belonging to a wealthy lady who lives in Senlis. I will take you there after you have seen Monsieur Bedeaux'

Marie was thankful for the woman's consideration though could not say she had warmed to her exactly.

'Well, any questions?' snapped Madame Gerard, as if she was astonished that none had been forthcoming.

Marie and Lucy gave a slight shake of their heads.

The housekeeper grunted, 'Very well, follow me,' and sped towards the door again. Marie exchanged a querying look with her father as, not wanting to incur the wrath of this formidable woman, they all followed quickly.

Madame Gerard knocked on a door in a passage that led from the hall. She swung it open and announced, 'Monsieur, Mademoiselle Newton and Mademoiselle Wentworth are here.' She gave a brief sweep of her hand to indicate that they should enter the room.

Marie, followed by Lucy, stiffened her back and strode purposefully past Madame Gerard, determined to throw off the deference that the housekeeper had striven to impose. She would not present a submissive front to Monsieur Bedeaux whom she was sure would be as overbearing as his housekeeper. But Marie received a shock when she entered the room. The man who turned from his easel was of medium height and slightly built. Some would have called him small. Marie's immediate reaction was, How does he cope with her? but she had her answer when she saw the stern light of authority in his eyes. She knew immediately that he was not a man to be crossed but also realised there was a sparkle behind those sharp eyes that promised kindness and understanding towards those he liked.

'Mademoiselle Newton, Mademoiselle Wentworth, it is a pleasure to meet you.' He stepped towards them and, taking their hands in turn, raised them to his lips. His smile was friendly and engaging. Marie judged him to be in his early fifties, though it was hard to tell in a person who had few care-lines to mark his features. His cheeks carried little flesh and his nose was thin and pointed, but it was his eyes which would command people's attention, no matter what emotion they were expressing.

He turned to Arthur. 'It is a pleasure to meet you, sir.' He held out his hand.

'And a pleasure for me also, Monsieur Bedeaux. I have seen some of your work and particularly admire your portraits.'

'Ah, if only *all* Paris appreciated them.' He gestured with his hands and grimaced with regret. 'Now, Monsieur, as much as I would like to chat with you about art and where it is going in these days when the Impressionists are being pushed to the fore, I would like first to speak with these two young ladies alone.'

'Of course, I understand,' replied Arthur, though somewhat disappointed.

'Madame Gerard, please make Mr Newton comfortable.'

She gave a slight nod and started for the door.

Monsieur Bedeaux immediately halted his housekeeper. 'Some refreshment, please, Madame Gerard, I'm sure the young ladies will be a little travel-weary. After our talk, I believe you are going to take them to Madame Foucarde's?'

'I am, Monsieur.'

As the door closed behind her and Arthur, Monsieur Bedeaux indicated two chairs. 'Sit down, please.' He waited a moment then slumped into a chair opposite theirs.

'I am sorry if we have arrived at an inopportune time and interrupted your work,' said Marie, indicating the canvas on the easel.

Bedeaux gave a dismissive wave. 'You did not interrupt anything, Mademoiselle. Knowing you would be arriving today, I did not allow myself to become absorbed in anything. I was merely experimenting.'

As he was speaking Marie and Lucy had been taking in his studio. Two easels supported canvases; the one at which he had been working was positioned so that light from a large window overhead was cast across the canvas. A table was littered with pots of powders, brushes, pencils, pestles and mortars. The bare floor-boards were splattered with paint, while canvases of various sizes stood against the walls on which hung several portraits. The whole room seemed to be in a state of chaos but the girls reckoned it was organised chaos; Monsieur Bedeaux would know where every-thing was, and no doubt this was the state in which he could work best.

Noting their curiosity, he said, 'You are wondering if this is where you will be studying. It is not. This is my private studio, conveniently in my house. You, along with the other students, will attend classes in the large building at the end of the street – my teaching studio. You will be there at nine o'clock tomorrow morning. Now you must tell me something of what you have been doing.'

Before Marie could start, Madame Gerard appeared with a tray set with cups, saucers and plates. She was followed by a maid carrying a tray on which there was milk, sugar, a teapot and some biscuits.

A look of horror crossed Bedeaux's face but, before he could speak, Madame Gerard explained in a tone that would brook no criticism from him, 'I thought tea for our young ladies from England would help them settle in more quickly. You can educate them about wine tomorrow at luncheon.'

Bedeaux pulled a face at her.

Marie smiled to herself. She reckoned these two were on good terms and got along well, no matter what the outward signs were.

'Thank you, Madame Gerard.' Marie relaxed. Maybe the house-keeper was not so formidable and unbending as she appeared; she had put some thought into this welcoming gesture.

Madame Gerard gave her a thin smile that disappeared almost immediately as if she was saying she was not yet sure of this young woman. She turned to Bedeaux. 'Ring when you are finished, and I will take the young ladies to Madame Foucarde.'

He merely nodded.

When the door closed Lucy said, 'Would you like me to pour?'

'For yourselves. I want none of that rubbish,' he grunted.

'It's very refreshing, Monsieur.'

'Poof!'

Lucy smiled to herself as she poured the tea. Although she had only been here a short while she sensed she was going to like it. Madame Gerard might seem a little stern and aloof and Monsieur Bedeaux somewhat eccentric, but she instinctively felt that here she would find understanding hearts when everyone had got to know each other better. She took a sip of the tea and immediately experienced its soothing warmth. At least Madame Gerard knew how to make a good cup of tea, English style, something she had not expected in France.

'Now, Mesdemoiselles, tell me something about yourselves, your art and ambitions.' Bedeaux made his voice soft and gentle, intentionally. He wanted them to feel at ease so that he would get to know more about them than he would if he merely fired questions at them. He was pleased when he saw them both relax.

'I had a natural talent for drawing from an early age,' began Marie, 'probably inherited from my father. I was encouraged by my parents, particularly my father who, as you know, is a well-recognised artist in England. He has had his ups and downs but when inspiration visits has achieved some excellent work. He is a good teacher too.'

'His work is chiefly landscapes, I believe, but you want to concentrate on portraits? Very well, but my tuition will also take in broader aspects of art. I insist that you try other genres, and drawing must form a vital part of this. Why have you come to me?'

'My father thought that the development of my ability might proceed better under a stranger's tuition. You were strongly recommended, so here I am.' She saw him give a little hitch of his shoulders at her flattery and knew she had a useful weapon here that could help her keep on the right side of Monsieur Bedeaux in the future.

He turned his eyes to Lucy.

'There was no artistic talent in my family unless way back in ancestors I do not know of, but I remember liking to draw as a child. Other things got in the way and, though I did keep it up, I could never get the time to do as much as I liked. But when my husband died, I was able to devote more time to my studies. I became friendly with Marie who encouraged me to do more, and then she kindly introduced me to her father who offered to give me some tuition. Because Marie was doing more portraits, she suggested that I took the opportunity to make use of the model too. I did and enjoyed the work.'

Monsieur Bedeaux nodded. Now he had a clue to the sadness behind Lucy's eyes. 'Good! For now, I must tell you that my tuition will mean hard work and long hours for you. I want you to become absorbed in your painting.' He gave a small pause then added, 'Don't look so downcast, Mesdemoiselles, it isn't that I don't want you to enjoy yourselves as well.'

'I always enjoy myself painting,' replied Marie. 'We both do.'

'Ah, but you need contact with other people in order to observe, to study faces and characters. You cannot shut yourselves in a studio all the time and expect to develop as a portrait painter. You have to learn something of both worlds – work hard when you are in the studio, but also get out and about and enjoy yourselves. Paris is a city in which you can find anything you want. I must warn you that many of the artistic fraternity frown on women attempting to enter what is regarded as a man's domain.'

'And you, Monsieur, what is your opinion?'

'Would you be here now if I thought like that?' He snorted and waved his hands in a gesture of disgust. 'They are dolts who think as they do. If talent is there in a woman, I say, foster it. Why shouldn't a woman draw and paint as well as a man? Now, an end to this! Have you brought any work with you? Let me see if you are worthy of my time.'

'I have my sketchbook and two small portraits by way of

introducing my work to you. Travelling precluded bringing any larger works. I thought that you would see from these my current preoccupations,' said Marie and, with a nod, Lucy indicated she had done the same

'Then away, bring them.' He waved his hands in the direction of the door.

Marie and Lucy put down their cups and hurried from the room. Returning, Marie gave him her sketchbook but held back the small oil painting of her father she had completed a month ago.

Monsieur Bedeaux turned the pages without comment, merely making the occasional grunt from which Marie could deduce nothing. As he closed the book he said, 'The painting.'

Marie, who had kept the portrait out of sight, turned it round.

The moment's silence was charged with worry for Marie. Her hands trembled. She nervously dampened her lips.

'Two paces forward,' he ordered curtly. Marie did as she was told. 'Good. That is the position from which this painting should be viewed. That is where it makes its impact. Further away it would be lost; nearer and the viewer would not take it all in and you would lose the point you wanted to make.' He fell silent, studying the painting for a few minutes, then said, 'Good. Now you, Mademoiselle,' he ordered, glancing at Lucy.

He took her sketchbook and went through the same procedure as he had with Marie. When he had viewed her portrait he paused thoughtfully for a few minutes then said, 'I expect when you received my letter you both thought that it meant you had been accepted for tuition by me. It did not.' Marie and Lucy exchanged quick glances of doubt and despair. Did this mean that Monsieur Bedeaux was not going to teach them? He couldn't just take one of them, surely. Lucy feared that if that were so, it would be the daughter of an artist who would be the lucky one. It was only natural. She was beginning to feel a tightness in her throat and tears welling in readiness. Then she realised Monsieur Bedeaux was speaking again, 'All it meant was that I would consider you after I had seen you . . .'

Marie couldn't hold back. 'And?'

'. . . Happily I like what I see. I will teach you both.'

Relief surged through them. They started to splutter their gratitude which only stopped when he silenced them with a gesture.

'Bring your work tomorrow when we will begin in earnest.' He rang a bell and a few moments later Madame Gerard appeared. 'The young ladies are ready now.'

'Very good,' she returned, and her glance at Marie and Lucy told them to follow her. Arthur joined them at the front door and Madame Gerard led them through the streets of Paris without comment until she stopped at a large wooden door set in a long plain wall that had four rows of identical large double windows opening inward with small railings in front of them forming iron balustrades. At three of these young people stood observing them.

It was a plain building with nothing about it that was inviting. Both Marie and Lucy had inner misgivings. Neither voiced them though each could read the other's reaction in her set expression.

Madame Gerard tugged hard on the iron bell-pull and a few moments later one section of the door swung back with a rumble and squeak. They were confronted by a young girl whose initial suspicion evaporated when she recognised Madame Gerard.

'Madame Foucarde will be at home?' Madame enquired.

'Yes, Madame.'

'Then we shall see her.'

The girl stepped to one side and then, after they had all moved into a cobbled courtyard with similar buildings to this visible on each side, scurried in front of them to lead the way. Entering the opposite section, she knocked on the first door on the right. At the call '*Entrez*' she indicated to the others to wait. She entered the room to return a moment later and say, 'Madame Foucarde will see you now.'

From the exchanges between Madame Gerard and Madame Foucarde, Marie deduced that they knew each other very well. Madame Gerard made the introductions and left with an order to Marie and Lucy to be with Monsieur Bedeaux by nine o'clock the following morning and not to be late.

Madame Foucarde smiled as the door closed behind her and indicated to the young women and Arthur to be seated.

'She is not as formidable as she appears to be. You'll find her good-hearted when you get to know her, if you keep the right side of her.' She glanced at Arthur. 'You'll find she will look after your two young ladies, as will I if they choose to take one of the two apartments that are available.'

'Thank you,' he replied. He had been studying Madame Foucarde and saw her to be a lady of medium height and build with a slim figure, attractively clothed in a well-made bright dress that he was sure was carefully chosen to match her personality – one that was affable and outgoing. He felt certain that she would be party to Paris's reputation for having a good time but would not condone the behaviour of any of her young tenants who stepped beyond the bounds of decorum as she saw them. She would be scrupulously loyal to the person for whom she supervised the four blocks of apartments.

'I have two apartments available, both in this block. When I knew the young ladies might be coming, I did not let them after they had been newly decorated two weeks ago. We will have a look at them now, then, if you decide to have one, we can talk about other matters relating to it.' She rose from her chair and, telling them to leave their luggage where it was, led the way to the fourth floor.

She took them first to an apartment that overlooked the courtyard. Its three rooms, bedroom, sitting room and kitchen, were well appointed. The second apartment was similar but each room was bigger and both the bedroom and sitting room, this one with a balcony, had a glorious uninterrupted view across Paris. Both girls knew this was the one they wanted but feared it might be too expensive for them. However, when they returned to Madame Foucarde's apartment and she told them the cost they were pleasantly surprised and, with Arthur's backing, the matter was soon settled.

'Before you sign the agreement, I must tell you that male visitors are strictly forbidden. It is not I who sets the rules but my employer, the owner of these apartments. I would be instantly dismissed if anything untoward happened, so I must be strict about this.'

'You will have no trouble from us,' Lucy hastened to say.

'I am reassured. You can have your fun elsewhere. Paris is so gay and loves the young and young at heart.'

'Madame,' Arthur began as the papers were being signed, 'is there a hotel nearby where I could stay?'

'There is one a few blocks away. It is not one of your grand hotels but it is clean and comfortable and friendly.'

'That will do me. Direct me there and I'll let my daughter and her friend settle in before I return to take them out for a celebratory meal.'

'And I shall tell you the restaurant where you will get the most exquisite food at a reasonable price. It looks nothing from the outside but don't be put off as I know many people are and walk away. Inside – ah!' She raised her hands and flicked her fingers wide in a gesture of ecstasy that was reflected in her expression.

As Arthur closed the outside door behind him, Marie and Lucy grabbed their bags and hurried up the stairs without pausing for breath. They were too excited by their own good fortune. Immediately they entered the apartment, they dropped their bags and ran to the glass doors, flinging them open to stand on the balcony.

'Paris! What a view!' cried Marie. There was laughter in her eyes and on her lips as she turned to her friend and saw the same joy on her face. They flung their arms round each other and then, with arms still linked, turned and gazed across the city, wondering what future it had in store for them.

Chapter Two

Colette pondered the changing September light for a few moments. Was it going to enhance the scene? Could she capture the subtle shadows cast by the pointed arches of Whitby Abbey's ruined nave? Should she wait? Record it as she visualised it might look in a few moments and it would be a sure seller to many of Whitby's visitors next summer.

'Hello, Mother.'

Colette swung round. 'Edward.' She smiled affectionately to see her twenty-four-year-old son. 'Have you finished your sketching?'

'Yes.' He nodded and held out his sketchbook. While his mother had been taking her photographs, he had been adding to his studies of the town; a view across the river to the West Side, aspects of the abbey, and one he especially liked taking in the piers that protected the river and harbour from the rigours of the North Sea. He would work some of them up into paintings in a room that his mother had had especially converted into a studio for him at the house.

She looked at what he had done. 'A good day's work.' Though they were rough sketches, she appreciated his talent, recognising it as coming from his father.

'What about you?' he asked.

'I too have done well. There's just one more I'd like to take if this light develops as I hope it will.'

He glanced in the direction in which she had set her camera and realised what it was she wanted from the photograph. They lapsed into silence, watching the shadows develop.

'Good day, Mrs Clayton.' A deep voice intruded on their thoughts.

They turned, already recognising the tone.

24

'And you, Edward,' a tall gentleman of about Colette's age added. He raised his hat in acknowledgement of the lady. His brown eyes were bright, expressing pleasure at seeing her. He was smartly dressed in grey trousers fashioned to the present-day style and showing below a thigh-length jacket of dark brown. A yellow cravat was tied neatly at his throat, emphasising the whiteness of his shirt. He carried a silver-topped cane.

'Mr Robinson,' Colette returned politely.

Edward nodded.

'Matthew, please. We have been friends long enough.'

It was a friendship between two married couples that had built up over six years, having started when Matthew Robinson and his wife called at Colette's studio and shop and revealed that he had a photographic business in Scarborough. Since both spouses had died, Edward had detected Matthew's deepening interest in his mother and, after learning that she still felt love towards his real father, would have preferred that Mr Robinson did not intrude on her society.

'Your visit to Whitby, Matthew, is it business or pleasure this time?' Colette enquired politely.

'Not business certainly, Colette. I'm taking a little time off. I've been so busy this summer and feel the need for some relaxation now. I can always find it in Whitby, and especially so when I can share your charming company. Would you do me the honour of dining with me this evening?'

Colette's reply was not instantly forthcoming.

'Please don't say no,' Matthew put in quickly, in a tone it would be hard to refuse.

'That is kind of you,' she acknowledged with a little nod of assent.

'Splendid.' He beamed. 'I will call for you at six-thirty. We can dine at my hotel.'

'I will be ready,' she replied.

'Thank you for doing me the honour. Until this evening.' He smiled, raised his hat and left them.

Edward watched him for a few moments and then, when he was out of earshot, turned to his mother. 'Why did you accept?'

'It would have been unkind not to do so. He's an old friend and is always most attentive when he comes to Whitby.'

'With an ulterior motive!'

'And what might that be?'

'You know very well, Mother. He would like your business and would marry you to get it.'

'He's never given any indication that . . .' started Colette indignantly.

'One day he will.'

'Stop, Edward! I'll have no more such talk. My life's my own.'

'Well, I think you should examine your feelings very carefully, and refuse to make any commitments to him. I know where your true love lies.'

'And you know that will get me nowhere. Your father is married. If I can find some happiness and comfort elsewhere, why shouldn't I take it?'

He hesitated then said quietly, 'I beg you not to be hasty, Mother.'

'Lucy, do hurry up! We don't want to be late on our first day,' Marie called to her friend as she smoothed her ankle-length black skirt and adjusted the collar of her white blouse, viewing herself in the mirror that hung close to the main door of the apartment.

'Coming! Coming!' came the reply, and almost instantaneously Lucy appeared, trying to adjust her hat while holding a bag and her jacket.

Marie grinned at her friend's dishevelled appearance. 'Come here! Let me put you right. You shouldn't have turned over in bed. You should have got up when I did.'

'I feel better for those extra few minutes,' countered Lucy, surrendering her bag and jacket to Marie who placed them on a table.

Within a few moments she had Lucy's appearance to her liking. 'There you are,' she approved. 'Now, come on.'

'A pity you couldn't see your father off this morning,' commented Lucy, picking up her bag.

'He didn't want it. I think he would have felt the parting. Besides, he understood why Monsieur Bedeaux wanted us early on our first day. Let's go!'

26

There was laughter on their lips as they emerged into the autumn sunshine. It felt good to be alive, here in Paris, heading for their first art class with an unknown future stretching ahead. There seemed to be movement everywhere in the street; a whirling mass of bodies with students prominent amongst them, gripping paint boxes as if their very lives depended on them. Which perhaps they did. Greetings were exchanged, laughter rang out, arrangements quickly made for the evening, but there was no stopping now, they were all bent on reaching their art school, studio or atelier.

'What a bustle,' commented Lucy.

'So many students,' mused Marie as they set off along the street. 'No wonder, with Paris the art centre of the world.'

'Isn't it fun to be part of it?' The excitement in Lucy's eyes was matched by the smile on her lips.

Marie was pleased for her. Life had not been easy for her friend and there was a time when Marie had thought that Lucy's mother might not approve of her daughter's desire to study in Paris and even refuse to let her go. Thankfully that had not happened. Here they were on a fine golden day, a spring in their step and hope in their hearts, on their way to Monsieur Bedeaux's art school.

Students were flowing eagerly into the barnlike building. A few feet inside the doorway, Marie and Lucy, bewildered by all the activity, looked around wondering which way to go.

'Young ladies from England?' A small man with a short Van Dyke beard delivered the question in a thickly accented voice. His eyes were bright and busy as he appraised the newcomers.

'Yes,' Marie informed him shortly, not liking the way he openly assessed them.

'*Bien*. Follow me.' He led the way to a passage on the right, exchanging greetings with a number of people as they went. 'Monsieur Bedeaux told me to be on the lookout for you. I am Monsieur Verner and I organise the running of his studio.'

He led the way to two large doors. In the centre of each, at waist height, was a large, highly polished brass knob. He paused and turned to the girls.

'Here you will find the last of Monsieur Bedeaux's intake for the coming year. The other new students have assembled over the last four days. There will be seventeen newcomers in this room when you join them. Monsieur will be along in a few minutes after I have let him know that his group is all assembled.'

He opened the right-hand door, allowed them to enter and closed it behind them.

Marie and Lucy found themselves in an average-sized room, its walls painted a neutral colour. Seats were arranged in the centre facing a dais on which stood a small table and chair. Traditional paintings adorned the walls but nobody was giving them a second thought, on this the most important day of their lives. The ten men and five women already present were of many nationalities. Marie's quick assessment put them mostly in their early twenties, making her and Lucy the oldest members of the group. They were sitting in twos and threes, no one sat on their own, and Marie was glad that Lucy was with her.

As they crossed the room to the nearest chairs they were aware of curious glances cast in their direction. As Lucy was later to remark, it was as if the men were questioning their age and wondering why older persons, and female at that, were bothering to join them.

They sat down feeling ill at ease and, attempting to lighten that, fell into a desultory exchange of whispered remarks. They sensed a quickening in the atmosphere when the door opened once again and Monsieur Bedeaux, followed by Monsieur Verner, entered the room and strode to the dais. The students had risen to their feet. Bedeaux signalled them to sit down in a manner that seemed to indicate he wanted no such formality. He himself sat down and Monsieur Verner stood to one side of the dais.

'Good morning, everyone! I am pleased to see you are all on time. Keep it that way whenever a particular hour is stipulated during your stay at my school. You are here to receive tuition in art in order to develop the skills you already have or else you would not have been accepted. For the first six months you will examine the broader aspects of art. Only after I am satisfied that you have reached a certain standard will you be allowed to specialise and receive specialist tuition. To assist me in that aim I bring in some of the leading artists of Paris. Heed them well. You will be split into small groups and each will have its own atelier in this building.

'The naked body is the standard on which all artwork is based. Draw the naked body to make it alive and you can draw anything. Females were formerly barred from such drawing and therefore barred from accomplishing anything of consequence because art's ruling elite frowned on their being in the presence of nudity. Ideas change, fortunately, but only very slowly. Many institutes and art schools still do not allow females into their life drawing sessions, thus negating the point of women attempting to study in the first place. Thank goodness there are more enlightened private schools and ateliers amongst which I am proud to number my own.

'I make no distinction between men and women. In my eyes you are all artists, whether male or female. You will use the same models for life drawing, but in the first year will not work at the same time. So much propriety we shall observe, for form's sake, for one year only. After that I shall expect you to be beyond such concerns.'

He cleared his throat and went on, 'My fees are forty francs a month for five half-days a week. That covers your tuition. The rest of the time you will use your atelier as you wish. This way I keep a flexible timetable, and it gives you time to develop your own individual tastes and styles. I do not restrict you to indoor work. There are times when you will have the opportunity to work outside, and there will be excursions to the countryside when there will be the chance to paint alongside your tutors and other artists of note.'

He cast his eye over his audience so that they felt he was scrutinising their reactions to what he had said.

'I expect you to work hard – draw, draw, draw, paint, paint, paint. It is the only way to succeed. But I do expect you to enjoy yourselves as well. There is life out there and you as artists should be free to depict it in whatever style you choose to develop. Now, your ateliers have already been allocated. Monsieur Verner will conduct the two English ladies to theirs. I will see that the rest of you know where you will be working. Follow me.'

The students sprang from their chairs and were only a step or two behind him as he flung open the door.

Monsieur Verner came over to Marie and Lucy. He led them across the entrance hall to a passage. It had no windows and was only dimly lit, but when Monsieur Verner opened a door on the right they stepped into a room with five big windows that allowed a sea of light to flood in.

Four females were busy setting up their easels. They all stopped when the door opened and turned to make their appraisals of the new arrivals.

'Good day, young ladies,' declared Monsieur Verner.

'Good day, Louis,' they chorused, laughter in their voices for they knew he did not like them to use his Christian name, yet he relished their teasing which he encouraged.

'Are you going to be our model today, Louis?' someone queried.

'You know that is not possible, Charlotte,' he replied indignantly, though he savoured the possibility in his mind.

'I'll bet you would like to!' The words caused a ripple of laughter among the students, and brought spluttering protests and reddened cheeks from Monsieur Verner who managed to say, 'I have brought Madamoiselle Marie Newton and Mademoiselle Lucy Wentworth who are from England and will be sharing this room with you,' before hastily retreating.

The four students looked a little taken aback. They had been told by Monsieur Bedeaux that he was placing two new students with them and had expected them to be about their own age, not two women who were older and, judging by their clothing, decidedly prim and proper. However there was nothing they could do about it so they would make the best of it. Better to be friendly right from the start. Time would dictate any change of attitude.

They came over to Marie and Lucy, everyone talking at once until Charlotte held up her hands and called a halt. 'Let us introduce ourselves properly,' she said, bringing order to the group. 'I am Charlotte Claris from Lyons, and this is my cousin Yvettte Durand also from Lyons.'

Both women were tall but with graceful bearing. Marie reckoned that they had a distinguished ancestry, but if so it made no difference to the unpretentious friendliness that showed in the warmth of their eyes and in their touch as they shook hands with the newcomers.

'This is Adelina Mornardt from Switzerland.'

The Swiss girl smiled, showing two perfect rows of white teeth. There was a friendly light in her pale blue eyes. 'Welcome to our group.'

'And last but by no means least is Gabrielle Hoetger.'

'I am very pleased to meet you,' she said as she took first Marie's hand and then Lucy's in a strong grip. She was a well-built young woman who made no attempt to disguise the fact that she was amply endowed. Marie reckoned that, although her features were hard, there was a kindly side to her nature.

Marie duly introduced herself and Lucy.

'So this is your first year with Monsieur Bedeaux?' asked Charlotte.

'Yes. And our first time in Paris, or in fact outside England.'

The other girl rolled her eyes and cast a mischievous glance at her three friends. 'Ah, now, that is something. I expect you will want to see the sights of Paris?'

'Yes,' said Lucy eagerly. 'You've all been here a while?'

Laughter broke out among the students.

'Oh, yes,' replied Yvette, a twinkle in her eye. She glanced at Adelina as if to say, You tell them.

'This is our second year,' she said.

'I wondered when I saw you setting up your easels. We were not instructed to . . .'

'You wouldn't be. You see, Monsieur Bedeaux would not let us move on to our second year. I'm afraid we did not put in sufficient work. We were all too keen to enjoy Paris, having escaped our families for the first time. Ah, the freedom!'

'And Monsieur Bedeaux allowed you to stay?' queried a surprised Marie.

'Yes. He said he saw a promise in the work we had done that he could not allow to be overlooked. And he needed to encourage females, especially as we would find it difficult to be admitted elsewhere when it was known we had been with him for only a year. He said he would give us another chance if we started at the beginning again. We assured him of our resolve to work hard this time. He warned us two new female students from England would join us. Maybe he thought you would be a sobering influence on us.' She gave a little laugh. 'I don't think you'll be that! I'd guess you aren't as prim and proper as he thinks – or you appear,' she added, noting the severe cut of their skirts, jackets and blouses. 'Maybe we'll be a bad influence on you. If you wish, we'll show you the sights of Paris.'

'We would value that,' replied Marie. 'I can assure you that our age won't cramp our style, will it, Lucy?' Marie wanted to get on friendly terms with these younger students as soon as possible; with their experience of Paris they could prove an asset.

'We certainly won't,' replied Lucy with a bright smile that embraced them all.

Before any more could be said, the door opened and in strode Monsieur Bedeaux. He gave the door a slight shove and allowed it to click shut behind him.

'Good morning, young ladies.'

'Good morning,' they returned in unison.

His eyes had taken in the room. 'Ah, I see my four wayward students are already prepared to work.' He raised his hands and shooed them away with a dismissive motion. 'Off with you, off! You know what I want of you – the painting you were working on at the end of last term. Off!'

With knowing smiles at each other they filtered away to their easels.

Monsieur Bedeaux turned to Marie and Lucy. 'Now, young ladies, this is where you will work while you are with me. Over here,' he led the way across the room, 'there are some easels, paint boxes, palettes, pencils and paints. Chose what you want. If you are not comfortable with any of them, purchase your own. Above all, be comfortable with your equipment.' He paused and cast them an enquiring look, one that seemed to signify he knew the answer but had to put it nevertheless. 'Have you drawn or painted from life?'

'No, Monsieur,' they answered together, a tremor of embarrassment in their voices.

He threw up his hands and raised his eyes to heaven in despair. 'Then you shall do it soon and without any embarrassment on your part. You will have to get used to viewing the naked body. These other young ladies have already done so but, alas, they find themselves having to start all over again or else leave my studio for good.' He paused, drew breath and said, 'So there you are. Choose your equipment, find a space and start drawing and painting in earnest.' He did not wait for any further reaction from them but swung round with a flourish and walked briskly from the room.

As the door clicked shut behind him the other four young ladies put down their brushes and left their easels to gather round Marie and Lucy again.

'Let's get you two fixed up and work out your floor space,' said Charlotte.

Within ten minutes Marie and Lucy had chosen their equipment and the six easels had been arranged to take the best advantage of the available space.

When that was done Adelina said, 'I suggest we have a break now for a drink. We have facilities beside the sink over there,' she pointed out to Marie and Lucy. 'We can get to know each other better.'

In a few minutes they were all sitting in a circle, mugs of coffee in their hands.

'Have you accommodation?' asked Gabrielle.

'Yes,' replied Marie. She went on to explain where their apartment was situated. 'It is wonderful and is supervised by a Madame Foucarde.'

'Ah, I know the place,' cried Yvette. 'I was taken there by a friend once who was in her last year as a student. You are lucky to get an apartment there.'

'I thought we were,' commented Lucy. 'You'll have to come round and see it.'

'Yes,' enthused Marie, seeing this as an opportunity to get on friendlier terms with the students with whom they were going to spend so much time within the atelier. 'This evening?'

The other four girls agreed enthusiastically.

'Seven o'clock.' Marie suggested. 'That will give us time to get some food in.'

'We'll bring the wine,' said Adelina.

'That's arranged then,' said Charlotte. 'Now, I think we had better get something done to show Bedeaux that we mean business this year.'

'What will he expect from us?' queried Lucy.

'An extension of whatever it is that you have been doing,' called Yvette over her shoulder as she went to her easel.

'Figure drawing,' replied Marie.

'Then draw one of us,' said Gabrielle. 'I'll pose first.' She drew a chair into a position that suited Marie and Lucy.

They fell to work with an eagerness that betrayed their delight at having pencils in their hands again. Their enthusiasm was contagious and by the time Charlotte called a halt they had the satisfaction of knowing that the work they had left unfinished at the end of the last year was imbued with a new life.

It was only when Charlotte said, 'It is time we ate,' that they all realised they were hungry. 'We'll take you to a cafe nearby – cheap but good food, plain, nothing fancy.'

'Sounds just right,' approved Marie.

Over lunch they got to know each other better and Marie and Lucy were sure they were going to get on well with the younger women. They in their turn realised the Englishwoman were going to place no constraints on them because they were older.

'Where did you do your art training in England?' Gabrielle asked.

'My father was my mentor,' explained Marie.

'And he helped me too when I became friendly with Marie,' added Lucy.

Gabrielle looked curiously at Marie. 'Newton,' she said, recalling Marie's surname. 'Your father wouldn't be Arthur Newton?'

Marie looked at her with curiosity, wondering how she knew of her father. 'Yes, he is.'

'We have two of his paintings at home,' Gabrielle cried.

'You have?' Marie was surprised.

'Father had to go to Hull on business. He took Mother with him and they had a holiday on the Yorkshire coast, visiting Scarborough and Whitby. There they bought two of your father's paintings: night scenes of a harbour. They are wonderfully atmospheric. We love them.'

'Do you paint landscapes too?' asked Yvette.

'Yes, but I've come here to concentrate on portraits.'

'Why, if you have inherited the talent for landscape from your father?'

'I wanted to branch out into a wider field. I have always been interested in people's physiognomy and want to reflect that on paper and canvas.'

'Then you have come to the right person in Monsieur Bedeaux. He may not be among the elite Parisian artists but he is one of the best teachers. Take note of him even if he seems to be leading you down paths that appear to bear no relation to what you want to do. It is all part of his technique and it will be reflected in your work which will be better for it. He is a very shrewd judge. Thank goodness he saw something in our work and enabled us to stay on even though it meant starting all over again.'

'I'm so glad he did. It has enabled us to meet you and I feel we are all going to get on well,' said Marie.

The friendship was cemented that evening when the four friends came to Maria and Lucy's apartment. They all declared themselves jealous that the newcomers had found such a splendid place to live. The view across Paris brought gasps of admiration and continued to do so as darkness fell and the city became a kaleidoscope of shimmering light, dazzling and alluring and full of promise.

'You will have to taste it all,' said Charlotte to Marie as they stood quietly together, absorbed by the spectacle.

'I'd love to, and I'm sure Lucy would too.'

'Then so shall it be, but first you must get settled in, become absorbed in your work, see all the usual sights by day. You must get to know your way around before sampling Parisian night life.'

Two days later Marie received a letter from her father informing her that his journey home had not been too tedious.

But I missed your company as I do your presence in this house. Don't have any deep regrets at leaving but make the most of the opportunities Monsieur Bedeaux's school offers you and enjoy life.

Take care.

Marie wrote back:

My Dearest Papa,

Thank you for your letter. I was pleased to have it and to know that you had reached home safely.

I miss you and miss home too but I am gradually settling here while at the same time feeling glad that I have Lucy with me. I am sure I will be happy here. We share an atelier at the school with four other young ladies. They are younger than ourselves but we get on well and they are very friendly: Charlotte naturally takes the lead. She and her cousin Yvette are both from Lyons. Then there is Adelina who is Swiss and Gabrielle who is Dutch.

Gabrielle's father and mother purchased two of your paintings of Whitby at night when they were visiting the town. When I learned that it seemed to bring you close again. I was glad that someone here knew you.

I must thank you for giving me this opportunity. I think that I know something of what you felt when you decided to take up painting as a career. You protected me from the many prejudices shown against women artists in England but I was aware of them, as you know I must have been. Here, in spite of opposition from some quarters, there is a greater sense of tolerance and freedom. In the short time I have been in Paris I realise that there are so many opportunities for individuality in the way we express ourselves. Paris offers the realisation of my most cherished dream, that of being able to work towards becoming the artist I want to be. It is something I will cherish and I can never thank you enough for giving me the opportunity to experience this newfound freedom.

Love and regards from your daughter,

Marie

Chapter Three

Colette stopped at the open door to the drawing room. Her son, his attention concentrated on the painting above the mantelpiece, did not hear her. She studied him and realised from his attitude that he was thinking about his father. She was thankful he had respected her wishes when the painting had arrived nearly three years ago. During recent weeks she had detected a restlessness in him, a clear need to try to find his father. She knew she could not hold him back much longer.

She stepped into the room.

Edward heard her footsteps and turned. The serious expression disappeared from his face and he smiled as he held out his hands and said, 'Mother.' She came to him and he kissed her on the cheek. 'Did you sleep well?'

'I did, thank you.' She glanced at the painting. 'Do you learn every time you study it?'

'Indeed I do. The technique of the brush strokes, the use of light and dark, the creation of atmosphere, the scene as the artist sees it. I also see something of the man who painted it but he remains a shadowy figure despite our brief meeting. He must have been a wonderful person for you to have loved him for so long.'

Colette slipped her arm through his. 'Come, let us go to breakfast.' There was a catch in her voice and Edward knew he had touched a nerve. He said no more, allowing her time to settle her thoughts as they walked to the dining room.

He was halfway through his porridge when he looked up and said, 'Mother, I don't think I can respect your wishes much longer. The desire to find my father has grown too strong to resist. I have to begin my search.' He met his mother's gaze squarely. He saw worry there and went on quickly, to reassure her, 'I promise that if at any time I believe I am going to cause anyone pain, I will give up.'

Colette knew from the sincerity in his voice and the pleading look in his eyes that he meant what he said. He wanted her approval and blessing.

She hesitated. Had she the right to forbid him? If she did she knew he would respect her decision but, by not fulfilling his yearning, would his love for her be damaged? She bit her lip and said quietly, 'Very well, I release you from the undertaking I rightly or wrongly imposed. I thought it best at the time but I see I have no right to keep you from your father or he from you. But I do not want other people hurt.'

'I have made you a promise, Mother. I will keep it.' Edward rose from his chair and came to kiss her on the cheek. 'Thank you. Can we talk about him a bit more now?'

She nodded. She had gathered her thoughts by the time he returned to his seat. Before he could put a question, she spoke. 'Your father came originally from Leeds. He worked in the railway offices there but gave that up after he was married in order to become an artist. He had a mentor in a man called Ebenezer Hirst, an antiquarian bookseller and art dealer. Arthur and his wife Rose had a daughter called Marie. They came to live in Scarborough.' Her voice faltered.

'How did you meet?'

'He had come to Whitby to do some sketches for future paintings. I was taking photographs. One day we met by chance and, through what we saw as our common interest in form, struck up a friendship.'

'And it developed from there?'

She nodded.

'You did not know he was married?'

'No. I only found out when his wife and some friends called at the house he had taken in Well Close Square. It was a terrible shock' Her eyes dampened at the recollection of that day.

'So you saw no more of him?'

'No, nor knew anything of him until you brought him to our house by chance though you did not know who he was.'

'Why did you not tell me then or tell him that I was his son?'

'Because he was married, with a daughter. Too many wounds would have been opened. We wanted to protect you and Marie from the hurtful judgement you might both have made about your parents.'

Edward decided he should change tack. 'Where did he sell his paintings?'

'Ebenezer Hirst in Leeds was what you might call his agent as well as his mentor.'

'Would he still be alive?'

'I have no idea but if he is, he must be in his eighties.'

'Do you know where he ran his business?'

She shook her head. 'No.'

'Father did paintings of Whitby. Did he sell through somebody here?'

'Yes. Mr William Redgrave.'

'He had the shop in Skinner Street, the one that is now a dress shop?'

'Yes. But Mr Redgrave died a few years ago.'

'Was there no one else connected with it?'

'He had a wife but she moved to her sister in Northumberland when her husband died. There was a brother, Mr Richard Redgrave. I don't know what happened to him when his brother died and the shop was sold.'

'He didn't want the business?'

'He wasn't deeply involved in it. I never really knew what he did.'

'I don't suppose the present owners will know anything about him.'

'I doubt it.'

'It might be worth an enquiry. I may as well start there. Did anyone in Scarborough sell his paintings?'

'I don't know.'

'Do you know where he lived in Scarborough?'

'No. He never told me and certainly never invited me there. Maybe I should have been suspicious then but I was blinded by love.'

'We know the painting he sent you did not come from Scarborough, but it gave us no other clue as to where he might be now. It seems I may not have the easiest of tasks unless Mr Hirst can help me.' Edward saw that his mother had had enough questioning for now so merely added, 'Do you want me to keep you informed of my discoveries as I make them?'

Colette met his questioning look firmly. 'Of course I do.'

'And will you please remember what I said about Mr Robinson?' She gave a little smile. 'You're worried?'

'I don't want you to make a mistake. You have had a very happy marriage but I know for whom you have felt the strongest love.'

She did not respond to his comment. After breakfast she heard him go upstairs and come down a few minutes later. Standing at the drawing-room window she watched him leave the house, feeling fiercely proud of the young man he had become. Arthur would be proud of him, too, and be pleased to have passed his talent on to his son. But, frightened of the hurt it might cause, she did not know whether she wanted Edward to succeed in his quest. She sighed and turned from the window, knowing he was bound on the first step of his mission.

Edward reached the dress shop in Skinner Street from which Mr Redgrave had once conducted his art business. He gave a moment's thought to the approach he would take, then pushed open the door and entered a spacious room in which several of the latest fashions were displayed. One wall was occupied by oak drawers of various sizes. In front of them was a long counter behind which two young ladies were giving their attention to a customer. On seeing Edward, one of them came over to him.

'Good day, sir. May I be of assistance?'

Edward had noticed the name of the owner above the door and now replied, 'I would like to see Mrs Boltby, if that is possible.'

'I will see, sir. Who shall I say wishes to see her?'

'Mr Edward Clayton.'

She nodded and said, 'I won't be a moment, sir.' She hurried to the back of the shop and disappeared through a door.

A few moments later it reopened and a middle-aged lady appeared, immaculately attired in a well-fitting black dress. She held herself erect, presenting a formidable first impression, but as she came closer to him Edward saw that her expression was pleasant.

'Good day, Mr Clayton.'

'Thank you for seeing me, Mrs Boltby.'

'How may I help you?'

'I am trying to trace an artist whose works were sold by Mr Redgrave. I believe he owned these premises before you?'

'Alas, Mr Clayton, I know nothing of Mr Redgrave's business. It had been closed by his wife after his death well before I bought the building.'

'Presumably she would take all the records with her?'

'Yes, or else destroy them before she left. Went to Northumberland, I believe.'

'Then unless she actively took part in the business it would seem she would be unable to help me?'

Mrs Boltby nodded. 'It would seem so. But if you wish to trace her I have the address to which she went. Whether she is still there, I do not know. Would you like it?'

'Please. It might be worth an enquiry. I count myself fortunate that you have it.'

Mrs Boltby smiled. 'I requested it when I came here in case any mail came for her. That ceased some time ago, but I'm a methodical hoarder, Mr Clayton. I won't be a moment.'

When she returned she handed him a piece of paper. He glanced at it and put it in his pocket. 'Oh, and I believe Mr Redgrave had a brother. Do you know anything about him?'

She shook her head. 'I'm sorry, I don't. I never met him. I was told he left immediately after his brother died. Some difference of opinion with his sister-in-law, but over what I don't know.'

'You don't know where he went?

'No.' Then a thoughtful expression crossed her face. 'If I recall correctly, though I did not pay much attention because it did not concern me, I seem to remember three names being bandied about at the time. Ruswarp, London . . .' she gave a little laugh '. . . and that's a contrast if ever there was one!'

'And the third one?'

41

'A place called Ampleforth, a little village across the moors near Helmsley. I'm sorry I cannot tell you any more than that, except that if he survives he must be ninety or more. I believe he was older than his brother.'

'I am deeply grateful, Mrs Boltby,' Edward said, rising from his chair. 'It was most kind of you to see me.'

'Not at all, Mr Clayton. I hope you are successful in finding the artist you seek.'

As he walked back home, Edward realised he was not much further forward except that he had two new possible lines of enquiry, but if the people concerned still existed he did not hold out much hope that they would be of any real help. The man behind the business itself, the man who might have been best able to help him, was dead.

Colette was sorting some of her latest photographs when Edward reached home.

'I guess where you have been,' she said. 'You look disappointed.'

He gave a grimace. 'I really shouldn't have expected to meet with success straight away. I saw Mrs Boltby. She knew little except that Mrs Redgrave went to Northumberland, and Mr Redgrave's brother left as soon as his brother died. She was only able to tell me that rumour had it he had gone to Ruswarp, to London, or to a village called Ampleforth, near Helmsley.'

'It may be worthwhile enquiring at Ruswarp and Ampleforth,' Colette said, believing she should show an encouraging interest. 'To trace him in London would most likely be an impossibility.'

'There was one other possible lead. Mrs Boltby had Mrs Redgrave's address in Northumberland.' He pulled a piece of paper from his pocket. 'Here it is. She's with her sister in a place called Longframlington.'

'Will you go?'

'Possibly, but I think I'll try Ruswarp first, it's the nearest, and then Ampleforth. I can ride to both those places but if I go to Northumberland it will be by coach.' Though he had come home feeling somewhat disappointed, talking about the leads had sharpened his enthusiasm again.

'When will you go to Ruswarp?' his mother asked tentatively.

'I have that commission to finish for Major Donovan. I must get on with it so probably won't get to Ruswarp until the end of next week or maybe the week after, depends how the painting goes. With winter approaching, I might leave Ampleforth and Northumberland until next year.'

Colette nodded but wisely made no comment. She was privately thankful that Edward was not going to set everything else aside to pursue a quest that might lead him nowhere.

Arthur strode purposefully towards Cherry Hill Farm. It had become his practice, whenever he received a letter from Marie, to visit Lucy's mother and exchange news of their daughters. But today there was some news in Marie's letter that he thought it better not to pass on; in fact, that news had given him some cause for concern, though he chided himself for being over-protective. Besides, that urge to protect was to no avail. Marie was in Paris and he could not watch over her from this distance. He must trust her. If Lucy had mentioned the same news to her mother, he hoped Isobel would not be distressed.

Marie and Lucy had settled in to their new life and by all accounts got on well with the four students with whom they shared their atelier. Arthur was pleased about this for it meant that there would be no disruptive atmosphere to affect their work. It also appeared that the six of them shared a good social life.

The younger students had introduced the newcomers to the city, taking them to see all the usual sights: the Eiffel Tower, Notre Dame, the Seine, the Bastille, the Place des Voges, the Sorbonne, the basilica of Sacré-Coeur, and many more. Marie's letters were always full of enthusiasm for what they had seen and it had always been a pleasure for Arthur to impart this to Isobel, filling out what Lucy had told her, and receive in return the other girl's impression of the sights.

But in this latest letter Marie had shown excitement about a promised introduction by her fellow students to Parisian nightlife. 'It will open a door to so many possibilities for drawing many different characters,' she had written, feeling that she had to make some justification for an outing she had sensed her father wouldn't approve of. She knew she could have said nothing but felt that was not right when he always showed so much interest in what she was doing.

Nightlife in Paris? he reflected. Well, maybe it would be best if Isobel did not know of her daughter's expedition, albeit as one of a group of six.

'Are you ready?' Charlotte put the question as Marie admitted her, Adelina, Gabrielle and Yvette to the apartment. There was laughter in the air and they were filled with anticipation of an enjoyable evening as greetings were exchanged.

'Waiting for Lucy as usual,' replied Marie with no malice in her tone. She was used to Lucy always bringing up the rear.

'It's a beautiful evening,' commented Adelina, going to the window to look out across the city. 'Just right for our excursion.'

'How warm?' asked Lucy coming from the bedroom.

'A shawl will be sufficient,' replied Yvette, shaking the blue one she had just slipped from her shoulders.

Lucy disappeared back into the bedroom to return a few minutes later with a multicoloured shawl. 'Ready,' she announced proudly.

Everyone gave a little cheer. Lucy pouted, miming offence. Everyone burst into laughter and in this joyous mood they followed Charlotte from the apartment. It had been their automatic assumption that she would be the leader.

'The city takes on a different atmosphere at night,' she said as the stepped outside. 'You can just feel the beginning of the change – it's much more relaxed, as if the whole place is relinquishing the bustle of the day when the need to make money predominates.'

'Where are you taking us?' asked Lucy.

'Well, I think of the city as being in three parts. There is the shady part with its strong associations with the underworld. I am not taking you *there* and I recommend that you avoid it. Then there is the highly respectable area, the place for the affluent, for men in prominent positions, the aristocracy, politicians and people of note. An interesting area to study architecture and see the latest fashions as people parade them, each trying to outdo the other.'

'And the third area?' prompted Marie when Charlotte gave a momentary pause.

'What I call in between; where you can mingle with people of all kinds, rich and poor, notable characters and nondescripts, people who have made it and people who are trying to make it, writers, artists, musicians, politicians, clerks, merchants. Oh, all manner of people, seeking whatever entertainment takes their fancy. It is a place of numerous cafes, cheap and expensive. You can sit in one and see the world go by. That is the area we will go to this evening.'

They were soon swept into the gaiety of the crowds that flowed this way and that with a constant motion only interrupted when a group would strike out towards another destination. The roadway was a stream of horse-drawn vehicles, never stopping, never ending.

'Goodness, they look too precarious for their own good,' cried Marie, pointing out the smartly dressed females and their gentlemen companions on top of a swaying coach, driven by an elegantly dressed man.

'A party, no doubt heading for a night out at some theatre or club driven by their host.'

Swirling wheels, flashing whips, clattering hooves, all added to the excitement. Many lights were already on, and, as they were joined by more and more in the gathering darkness, became a string of jewels spread over the night-time city. The friends passed shops and restaurants at one of which they paused to observe the well-to-do clients descending from several coaches to enter the building, no doubt anticipating a convivial evening. Outside several cafes people were relaxing with their wine, forgetting the cares of the day.

'Let's stop at the next vacant table we see,' suggested Yvette.

'Good idea,' agreed Gabrielle. 'We've walked far enough, we deserve a rest.'

Two blocks on they saw four people leave a table. As one they rushed forward and it was only after they had settled that they took stock of their surroundings. They were outside one of the larger cafes, the front of which appeared to have been newly painted. The tables and chairs were well appointed and there was a buzz of talk from the occupants. Yvette took on the role of expert by ordering wine from a smart waiter who hastened to attend them.

Marie glanced around, taking in the other people, wondering if here was her opportunity to do some sketching, but the light-hearted banter of her companions made her decide that the sketch-book should remain in her pocket. She did not want to destroy the carefree atmosphere. There would be plenty of opportunities to come on her own or with Lucy to sketch the people of Paris.

She became aware that there were five young men sitting at the next table. She paid them little attention as she joined in conver-sation with her companions. It was only when she was halfway through her second glass of wine that she became aware that the five young men were in the process of loudly expressing their opinions of female artists. Those opinions rankled with her. She picked up her glass, drained it and held it out to Yvette who picked up the bottle and was about to pour when she hesitated and cocked a querying glance at Marie. She knew the young woman from England was not used to a lot of wine. She had only ever seen her consume one glass whenever they had been together before. But now Marie ignored Yvette's querying look. She poured. Marie nodded her thanks, still without speaking. She was concentrating on the conversation from the next table. Her eyes flashed in annoy-ance. She swallowed half of her wine and, with anger beginning to burn in her eyes, leaned forward and said quietly, 'Did you hear that?'

Her companions looked sharply at her.

'Hear what?' asked Lucy.

'What they said.' Marie threw a glance at the next table.

'No,' answered Adelina. 'What was it?'

'One of them said females should be banned from all art schools.'

'Just talk!' said Charlotte.

Marie shook her head in annoyance. 'It's not. Another agreed and said that females were taking up places that should go to males. The general opinion seems to be, what is the point in any of us studying art because we will never be as good as the least able man.'

'Big-heads!'

'Bigots!'

'They'll learn!'

'I'm going to teach them now!' Marie started to rise from her seat.

Lucy grabbed her arm. 'No, sit down, Marie. Don't make any trouble.'

'I won't. I'm only going to tell them they are wrong.' She shook her arm free and in one swift movement drained the rest of her wine as if that would give her the courage to face five total strangers she thought were maligning them. Before anyone else could stop her she had left the table and faced the young men.

They glanced up when they were aware that Marie was standing over them; their conversation stopped. They looked questioningly at her.

'Your opinions are wrong and utterly bigoted,' she snapped, eyes flashing angrily.

For a moment there was silence as if they were wondering to what she was referring.

'Wrong,' Marie emphasised. 'I can draw as well as any of you.'

A fair-haired young man glanced round his companions with amusement in his eyes. When his gaze came back to Marie there was mockery in it. 'That's your opinion and you are welcome to it.'

'As are you to yours,' Marie seemed to agree, then added, 'but you should be sure of your facts. Besides, if you were a gentleman you would not be so bigoted. Or do you think it's the fashion to deride lady artists and so assume your stupid attitude because it appears to be the thing to do?'

He smirked and glanced round his companions. 'Ignore her, it's the wine talking. Not used to it, I expect.'

All except one chuckled and agreed with him.

'Ignore me? Don't you dare!' Marie stormed. 'Can't you think for yourselves? Can't you form your own opinion without following the bigoted attitude of people who think they know best? If you are tutored by such people you'd be better leaving them.' She became aware that the one man who still had not spoken was staring at her.

Marie was a little uneasy under his gaze. She felt her colour heightening. Chiding herself for this reaction she tightened her lips, but even in her confused state she took in his appearance. His clothes were typical for an art student, but she recognised that their quality was good. His brown hair, parted at the left side, was neatly cut. His eyes were sharp, with a keenness that brought out the depth of their blue. She half turned as if to escape his gaze and in doing so stumbled. Lucy was out of her chair in a flash to support her. 'Come and sit down, Marie,' she advised, steering her in the direction of their table. 'They are not worthy of your attention.'

'Another one!' mocked the fair-haired young man. He glanced at their table. 'And four more over there. All taking up places that should be occupied by male students.'

'Hey, steady on. Don't be so hard on them,' the young man who had been staring at Marie broke in.

'You keep out of it,' one of his companions admonished, 'you haven't been here as long as us.'

'Maybe, but times are changing.'

'Then it's up to us to put up a united front,' snapped the original speaker. 'We have to hold out against the introduction of females. The number of poverty stricken would-be artists walking the streets is mounting.'

'If they had the necessary talent they wouldn't be doing that,' countered Marie sharply.

'More likely they couldn't compete with the charms you flaunted at your examiners.'

Marie stiffened. With fire in her eyes she glared at the young man who seemed to be the leader of this group. 'I don't care for your insinuation,' she snapped.

'Guilty conscience, no doubt,' he countered.

Marie made a movement towards him but was restrained by Lucy. Realising the situation could get out of their control, Charlotte had risen to her feet. She shot a glance at her three friends that indicated they should leave and came over to Marie. 'These louts are not worth bothering with, Marie. I presume they call themselves gentlemen but are in fact far from that.'

Marie let Charlotte and Lucy escort her from the table but was aware that a pair of deep blue eyes were still intent upon her.

They had gone about fifty yards when Marie stopped. She swayed a little as she brought her hands to her head. 'Oh!' She gave a little moan.

'Are you all right?' Lucy asked with concern. She glanced at the others. 'She's not used to wine.'

'She drank it too quickly,' said Adelina. 'She'll be all right after we visit a cafe nearby. Coffee's best for curing a hangover.'

Adelina proved right and Marie felt much better by the time they reached the apartment. She tumbled straight into bed, slept well and rose the next morning to be reminded of her confrontation with the young men at the next table.

'Did I embarrass you?' she asked Lucy.

'No. We were ready to back you but thought it was probably wiser to retreat. You had made the point.'

Marie nodded but said no more, her mind still on that young man with remarkably blue eyes.

49

Chapter Four

'I'm going,' Marie called out as she picked up her sketchbook and bag and headed for the door.

'All right,' came the sleepy acknowledgement.

Marie let the door slam behind her, hoping it would rouse Lucy. As she left the apartment and stepped into the sunshine and crisp air, her mind was occupied with thoughts of her friend. Lucy had taken to sleeping in. She had always been a poor riser but this last month was always late for the first session. Marie's berating had had little effect on her. She hoped her friend was not going to let slip this opportunity that had been presented to her. She definitely had talent and it had emerged strongly, even after this short period of Monsieur Bedeaux's instruction and advice. Marie must have another word with her. She was toying with the idea of how to approach Lucy without offending her when she heard her name called out.

'Marie!'

She glanced round but saw no one she knew. She must have been mistaken.

'Marie!' Again, a little more urgency in the voice.

She stopped and turned round to see who, among the flow of students hurrying to their schools, called her name. An arm was raised and a young man burst past three young people to confront her.

'I thought you hadn't heard me,' he gasped, showing signs of relief.

She looked at him with curiosity. Her mind was confused. She did not know him and yet there was something about him – the eyes! The depth of their blue was lit by obvious pleasure to see her.

Those eyes had rested on her and caught her attention before. Now there was no doubt in her mind. It was the same young man who had made her feel uneasy when she'd confronted the sneering students two weeks ago.

'I thought I would never see you again,' he said quietly. His voice was low and gentle as if he did not want to frighten her. 'I hoped I would, but Paris is a big place.'

She drew herself up, assuming an attitude of indignation. 'Why, with your views of women artists, you should want to see me I don't know, unless it is to insult me again. And how dare you use my Christian name?'

He smiled disarmingly. 'It is the only name I know you by; it was the only one I heard when we last met.'

'Some meeting!' she snapped. 'I must go.'

'No, wait! I want to explain.'

'There's nothing to explain. Your views were made perfectly clear in that cafe.'

'Were they?'

'Yes.'

'Are you sure? Did you hear me agree with the others?'

The intonation in his voice cast an element of doubt into Marie's mind. She hadn't heard him speak during the last brief meeting; he had just stared at her. 'Er, well . . . I'm . . .' she spluttered.

'Apparently you didn't, and it would seem that you did not hear me try to modify their ideas,' he said firmly. 'The views of my companions are not mine.'

'Then why do you associate with them?'

'They are my friends.'

Marie gave a little grunt of disapproval.

'Let me walk you to your school. I presume that is where you are going?'

Marie's immediate instinct was to refuse but she hesitated. She remembered she had felt an attraction to him that evening and had thought about him since. Now, face-to-face, she felt that attraction once again.

There was an earnestness about him that foretold joy if she accepted and disappointment if she refused. She liked that inability

51

to disguise his feelings. And could she deny that his open ingenuous features had attracted her? There was a vigour about him, foretelling eagerness to succeed in anything that caught his fancy. She wondered how that would appear in his artwork. Was he a painter? A sculptor? Did he concentrate on oils or watercolour, and was he adept with a pencil? She found herself wanting to know. She met his enquiring gaze. Could she deny the hope in the depths of those deep blue eyes?

She nodded. 'Monsieur Bedeaux's.'

He fell into step beside her. 'I'm George Reeves and I'm with Monsieur Paillette, not far from you. Now, let me explain. I am in my first year. The companions you saw me with I knew from schooldays back in England. They are all in their second year. We had just met up for the evening. I am not in constant touch with them. Might never see them again. I was surprised they were so strong in their views. Believe me, they are not mine. I'm sorry if they insulted you.' His voice and attitude were so sincere Marie could do nothing but believe him.

'Thank you for your explanation. I am pleased you do not share their opinions.' She stopped beside an open door. 'This is where I must leave you.'

The flicker of disappointment that crossed his face was not lost on her. 'Will you allow me make amends by taking you for a glass of wine or coffee this evening?' The words came out quickly as if he did not want to hold them back. She hesitated so he added even more quickly, 'We can talk art. I'd like to exchange ideas.'

She wanted to say yes, but shouldn't she have a chaperon at this first meeting with a young man she did not know? First meeting. It wasn't really, was it? Well . . . She was away from home; she had her own life to lead, and as for a chaperon, there was Lucy, but Marie wasn't going to have *her* play gooseberry. 'All right. That would be nice, thank you.'

'Where can I meet you?' he asked.

'Why not here?'

'Excellent.'

'In the afternoon we are very much left to our own devices,

though of course there is a certain amount of work expected of us. I can finish any time after four o'clock.'

'Good. I will be here at quarter-past. At that sort of time we'll both be wanting something to eat. I know a nice small cafe. We'll go there.' Before she could make any comment he added, 'Until this afternoon,' and was gone.

Marie stood watching him go, struck by his confident step and bearing. He must have felt her gaze for he looked back and waved. Automatically she raised her arm. As she turned to go into the school, she realised that there had been a certain intimacy in their gestures, as if they were already special friends.

Throughout the day Marie's mind kept wandering to her meeting with George Reeves. She recalled especially his attractive eyes. They'd seemed to search to her very soul and yet were gentle and understanding and filled with a desire for friendship. He was good-looking with fine-cut, well-proportioned features.

She had been ready to scold Lucy for being late but that desire had vanished with the thought of the young man and their coming meeting. When she arrived mid-morning Lucy cast a sheepish glance in Marie's direction and was surprised not to be met by sharp words. No doubt they would come, in the meantime she got on with her work. Half an hour later, when Marie stood back to view her painting and then came over to Lucy, she thought the telling-off was about to happen. Instead, after a few moments viewing Lucy's work, Marie said, 'That's one of your best yet. It is coming on well. I'm sure Monsieur Bedeaux will think so. I'm pleased for you.' She gave her friend a hug and returned to her own easel.

Lucy shot a surprised glance at the other four students as much as to say, 'What was all that about? What happened before I got here?'

All she received in reply were looks of surprise and expressions pulled to show, We don't know.

Surprised looks were exchanged again when at four o'clock Marie started to tidy up; unusual for her as she frequently worked late, saying that she was here to paint and not to waste her time on frivolity.

Satisfied that she had left everything as she wanted, Marie called out, 'I'm off, see you at the apartment, Lucy.' She hurried to the door, wanting to be out before anyone could ask questions.

Everyone was so astounded by this unusual behaviour that Marie was gone before they realised it.

Marie paused at the doorway and from the step surveyed the scene, searching for a tall young man with a mop of brown hair among the people hurrying home or lingering in earnest conversation. Others were content merely to be in each other's presence as they strolled hand-in-hand.

Marie wondered what George's hands would feel like. Rough? No, his would be the hands of a painter, gentle, sensitive, desiring to make the brush do his will. She started out of her reverie as four young people, laughing without a care in the world, passed close to her. George? Where was he? Maybe he wasn't coming; maybe he'd forgotten. But surely not? He hadn't struck her as being the forgetful type; his earnestness had belied that. Something must have happened to him. All sorts of ideas raced through Marie's mind. Maybe he had changed his mind about her. A little wave of despondency and disappointment washed over her. How long had she been waiting? How long should she wait? Feeling let down, she started to turn away. She didn't want any of her friends to come out and see her.

'Marie!' She stopped. Joy surged through her at the sound of his voice. Her broad smile was met by one of equal pleasure. 'I'm sorry I'm late,' he panted as he reached her. 'Monsieur Paillette had something extra to say to us.' He gave a little chuckle. 'Not that I can remember much of what he said! I was concerned that you might not wait.'

'I was beginning to wonder, but now you are here . . .'

'We'll go to a little restaurant I know. Nothing pretentious, but the food is good and the wine is excellent. It's on the edge of Montmartre.'

'That sounds interesting,' she replied as they started off.

They chatted amiably, if with a certain wariness, as if they were feeling their way around each other, not sure what reaction their words might bring.

Then George pointed out, 'I don't know your surname. I only know you as Marie.'

'Newton, Marie Newton.'

George stopped, his eyes intent on her. 'Newton?' He gave a little doubtful shake of his head and said, 'No, he couldn't be.'

'Who?' Marie prompted when he hesitated.

'Your father wouldn't be Arthur Newton, would he?'

She smiled at his perplexity and nodded. 'Yes, he is.'

'Good heavens! I don't believe it.'

Laughter tripped from her lips at the sight of George's dumbfounded gaze. 'It's true. I am Arthur Newton's daughter.'

A sudden doubt attacked George. 'I mean, Arthur Newton the artist?'

Marie nodded. 'Yes, my father is the man you think he is.' She glanced round. 'I think we had better start walking again. We are blocking the pavement.'

George started and automatically took hold of her arm to guide her back into the flow of people. 'I've admired your father's work ever since I became interested in art and found what I thought was some talent in myself. His night scenes are exceptional.' There was no mistaking the enthusiasm in his voice.

'Thank you,' she replied. 'I'm pleased you like his work.'

'If yours is anything like your father's then you must be very talented.'

Marie gave a little laugh. 'I couldn't pretend to be as accomplished. As you know, my father's work has been mainly concentrated on landscapes and seascapes. It was natural that under his tuition I should follow suit but I am really more interested in portraits. That is why my father decided I should come to Monsieur Bedeaux.'

'I've heard he has a reputation for portraiture. You are lucky to be with him.'

They turned off the main thoroughfare into a side street where George guided her into a small restaurant.

As soon as they entered a thin waiter dressed in black trousers and waistcoat over a white shirt and with a white apron tied at the waist came to meet them. 'Good evening, Monsieur Reeves, a table for two?'

'*Merci*, Henri.'

The waiter ushered them to a table close to the right-hand wall. Four of the ten tables were already occupied by young people who cast the new arrivals cursory glances without interrupting their conversations. Henri held the chair for Marie who smiled while she made her thanks.

'You are known here?' she asked quietly as she leaned towards George.

'I discovered this place shortly after arriving in Paris, liked it and saw no reason to look elsewhere. Oh, I will do one day when I decide to explore further.' He made a slight hesitation then added quickly, 'Maybe we could do that together?'

Marie met his earnest gaze. 'That could be nice but maybe after this evening you'll change your mind.'

'I think not. I have not got you out of my mind since the first time I saw you.'

Marie blushed. 'But you do not know me.'

'Then give me a chance to do so.'

Before she could reply the waiter returned with the glasses of wine that George had discreetly ordered when they entered the restaurant, and with a marked flourish presented each of them with a menu.

They studied them, discussed what was on offer and made their choices. Time passed pleasantly. They were not rushed and, as the late afternoon moved into evening, their conversation drifted on.

Marie learned that George came from a family with a small estate in north Norfolk who had encouraged him in his desire to become an artist.

'I was thankful I had understanding parents who recognised that there was something in me that had to be given expression. If it did not develop that would be an end to it. They realised I had to try and encouraged me to do so from my time in school.'

'If there was no artistic talent in your family then you had very understanding parents.'

'I appreciate that, and it has made me all the more determined to succeed.'

On leaving the restaurant they enjoyed an easy companionship as they strolled along the boulevards, taking a circuitous route to Marie's apartment.

'Here we are,' she said, coming to a stop.

George eyed it. 'Imposing,' he commented.

'I share the apartment with my friend from England, Lucy Wentworth. We have wonderful views across Paris.'

'You are very lucky. My two rooms are small but clean with no view at all.'

'Thank you for a most pleasant evening,' said Marie.

'May we do it again sometime?'

She smiled. 'Of course.'

George's heart beat faster when he saw the pleasure in her eyes. 'Thank you. I'll look forward to it.'

'What about Sunday afternoon?'

George had not expected her to make the suggestion, nor had he expected their next meeting to be so soon. Only two days away! 'I'll meet you here at two o'clock. What would you like to do?'

'Stroll, watch the world go by, see all the latest fashions.'

'And we'll follow it with some scrumptious cakes.'

Marie was on air as she hurried up the stairs to the apartment. She had had a splendid time in the company of a young man with whom she had felt at her ease. The empathy between them had grown and she had felt very happy just to be with him. She looked forward to sharing more time with George Reeves.

Immediately she entered their apartment Lucy was on her feet, dropping the book she had been reading.

'Where have you been? What made you leave the studio early? I was beginning to worry. Have you eaten? I waited an hour for you.' Irritation and indignation had entered her voice as the questions poured out.

Marie laughed at her friend's concern. 'I've been perfectly all right. And I have eaten.'

'Where?'

'A nice little restaurant somewhere on the edge of Montmartre.'

'Indeed. On your own?'

Marie shook her head. 'No,' she replied lightly, knowing her friend's curiosity was mounting.

'Oh!' Lucy's lips tightened when Marie offered no more explanation. 'You left the studio earlier than usual. You must have been meeting someone special.'

'Yes.' Marie knew that her friend was seething with curiosity and delighted in teasing her by holding back any information.

'Well?'

'Well, what?'

Lucy gave a grimace of annoyance. 'Who were you with?'

'A friend.'

'Do I know her?'

'Him.'

Lucy's eyes widened. 'Oh!' She gasped as if all the wind had been driven from her sails.

'Him,' Marie repeated.

'Who?'

'George Reeves.'

'Who's he?'

'A student with Monsieur Paillette. If you had got up early you'd have met him too, though you have already done so, of course.'

'What?' Lucy was mystified.

Marie laughed. 'He was one of the students I took to task about female artists.'

'You couldn't take up with one of *them* after what they said?' Lucy showed her disgust.

'He was the one who spoke out against the others.' Marie went on to tell her more about George and the evening they had spent together.

'Are you seeing him again?' Lucy asked when Marie had finished her story.

'Sunday afternoon.'

'Oh. So soon?'

'I'm getting a lot of "ohs" out of you,' chuckled Marie.

'Well, you're a bag of surprises. Mmm.' Lucy looked thoughtful. 'If this George is going to take up your time, I'm going to have to find myself a beau.'

As the end of their first term in Paris approached, Marie and Lucy were looking forward to spending Christmas in England.

Marie wrote to her father giving him the timetable for their journey then went on to say:

Thank you for offering to meet us at Dover. George, whom I have mentioned before, will escort us from Paris. He is looking forward to meeting you and thanks you for the offer of a room for the night before continuing his journey to Norfolk.

I am sure you will like him, Papa. He is kind and considerate, generous, and oh, so handsome.

Arthur smiled to himself. Since the shock of that first letter, telling him that his daughter had met a young man, George had figured in every subsequent missive. He went to his desk and took out a bundle of letters neatly tied with white ribbon. He took out one in order to refresh his memory before meeting George Reeves in a week's time.

I am so carried away on an enormous tide of happiness that I am neglecting to tell you all about him. He is ten years younger than me, tall, handsome, with brown hair and striking blue eyes. He is English, coming from a family who have a small estate in North Norfolk. He has an elder brother and two sisters, all of whom are married and live in that area. His brother will take over the estate but George and his sisters have had ample provision made for them by their parents when the time comes. Free from the responsibility of running the estate, in which he had little interest, he has his parents' support in pursuing an art career. He is good, Papa, and everyone here believes he has a great future.

To find such talent in a man who is interested in me is

wonderful. To fall in love with such a person and find he reciprocates that love is even more wonderful.

Be happy for me, Papa.

Arthur's eyes dampened as he recalled the day that letter had arrived. He had stared at the words, loath to believe the implications they were carrying. He had sensed he was losing his daughter. Life would never be the same for him. He faced a future bereft . . . At that point he had had to pull himself up sharply and chide himself for entertaining such thoughts. Nevertheless, suspicions had lingered. What did Marie really know of this man ten years her junior? Doubts remained until he had confided in Isobel Wentworth and she had pointed out that age made no difference when two people were truly in love and reminded him that interfering parents often caused more damage to relationships than they were aware. He would not be losing a daughter but gaining a son, had he looked at it like that?

Now, in a week's time, he would be meeting this man who had captured his daughter's heart.

Arthur donned his top-coat and hat, picked up his walking stick, shoved the latest letter in his pocket and left the house to walk to Cherry Hill. It was a bright day but chilly and he found the fresh air exhilarating. He hummed lightly to himself, joyous in the knowledge that his beloved Marie would soon be home.

Reaching Cherry Hill he was admitted immediately according to the instructions Isobel had given to her staff. His outdoor clothes were taken and he was shown to the drawing room.

Isobel rose from her chair and laid down her embroidery to greet him. 'Arthur, what a pleasant surprise.' She held out her hands to him and allowed him to press a gentle kiss on her cheek. 'Tea?' She gave a little chuckle. 'Something a little stronger?'

'Well, that would be pleasant.'

Isobel was already crossing to the decanters on a sideboard. 'Another letter?' she asked, noting the paper he took from his pocket.

'Yes.'

'You know you don't have to wait for the arrival of a letter in order to pay me a visit.'

'I know but . . .'

'You are a considerate man, Arthur, but there is no need to consider our reputations, we are both free.'

'I know, Isobel, you are most kind.'

'Then accept my kindness more frequently.' Her eyes were fixed intently on him as she handed him his glass.

'I will, thank you.'

She sat down opposite. 'Well, what does your daughter have to tell us this time?'

'About their arrival at Dover. I will meet them with the carriage.'

'Thank you.'

She also tells me that they will be escorted from Paris to Dover by the young man I have mentioned to you before.'

'Splendid! It is good to know they will be looked after. You'll be looking forward to seeing him?'

'I knew this was likely to happen when they came home for Christmas so I have invited him to stay the night before continuing his journey to Norfolk. Marie tells me he has accepted.'

'Excellent. You will see more of him and get to know him. You must all come and dine with me that evening. Let's make it a joyful first homecoming for our daughters. And the first of our Christmas celebrations.'

'Thank you, Isobel.' Arthur raised his glass. 'Here's to us and to them.'

As he walked home Arthur found his thoughts turning to Isobel. She was a fine woman, attractive and with a tenderness that was captivating. She was a person who cared deeply about her daughter, her home and her land. She had taken an encouraging interest in her daughter's artwork that had helped through the trying time after Lucy's husband's death. Arthur's own lonely hours had been brightened by thoughts of her. Maybe he should take up her hint that he should visit more frequently, especially when their daughters returned to Paris in the New Year.

He was deep in thought and not totally aware that he had taken the right-hand fork in the path until he realised he was close to the cliff edge. He stopped and concentrated his mind. There was nothing untoward in the fact that he had come this way except that the intention to do so had not been in his mind. He had used this path before and enjoyed it but it was a walk that always took his thoughts back over the years to the small town on the Yorkshire coast that held a special place in his heart – Whitby. The memory of it had always been there and throughout the intervening years it had never dimmed for with it came reminders of Colette; private thoughts that he cherished.

He strolled on. The sea broke in leisurely waves far below on the rocks at the foot of the cliffs. His gaze swept across the waters of the Channel, in his mind seeing them as the North Sea running fast to the cliffs on which stood a ruined Norman abbey. He had shared that sight with Colette. He wondered how she was and if she had ever told her son the identity of his real father.

Chapter Five

'Mr Robinson to see you, ma'am,' the maid announced when she had come to Colette's bedroom where she was sorting dresses.

'Very well, Tess, show him to the drawing room and tell him I'll be down in a moment.'

'Yes, ma'am.' Tess hurried from the room.

Colette turned from the clothes laid out on her bed and went to her dressing table. She sat down on the stool and examined herself in the mirror. She adjusted the neckline of her dress, and made sure the jet brooch in the shape of a whale was securely fastened. She put two mischievous wisps of hair back into place and patted the hair at the nape of her neck. Satisfied, she stood up, smoothed her dress and walked slowly to the door.

She wondered about Matthew Robinson. He was attentive, pleasant and generous. She had enjoyed his company in the past, still did, but was not sure whether she wanted the relationship to move any further. She was aware of Edward's view of Mr Robinson's intentions; though she did not fully agree with it a doubt had been cast in her mind which she found persisted whenever she was in Matthew's company.

As she walked down the stairs she wondered what brought him here on this early-December day. When she entered the drawing room he turned eagerly from the window.

'Matthew.'

'Colette.' He stepped quickly towards her, his face alive with pleasure. He took her hand and raised it to his lips as he bowed his greeting.

'What brings you here?' she asked as she indicated a seat to him.

He went to it but waited to sit down until she was seated opposite him.

'I've really come to see Edward.' He gave a slight pause then added, 'Ah, I see that surprises you.'

'Well . . .' She met his gaze with enquiring curiosity.

'Although it is Edward I want to see, I could not miss the opportunity of asking you if you will do me the honour of dining with me at the Angel on Boxing Day.'

'That is kind, but I'm sorry, I cannot. Edward and I have been invited to my sister's for the whole Christmas season. It will be better if we leave dining at the Angel until another time.'

'Certainly.' He embraced her decision with grace but made no attempt to hide his disappointment.

Not wanting the invitation to be pursued at this time, Colette put in quickly, 'You want to see Edward?'

'Yes, is he at home?'

As he offered no further explanation, Colette rose from her chair and went to the bell pull. When Tess appeared she said, 'Mr Edward is in his studio, tell him that Mr Robinson would like to see him.'

After the maid had left the room, Matthew informed her that he had a proposition to put to Edward and hoped he would like it.

When the young man appeared a few minutes later Matthew rose to his feet and greeted Colette's son with a warm benevolent smile and a firm handshake.

'Good day to you, sir,' returned Edward politely. 'You wished to see me?' There was curiosity in his voice and eyes. He sat down beside his mother.

'I'll come straight to the point,' said Matthew, leaning slightly forward in his chair, his eyes intent on Edward. 'I would like to commission two paintings of Whitby.'

Mother and son looked taken aback by the unexpected request. Colette shot a sideways glance at her son, hoping his decision would not be influenced by the fact that it was Mr Robinson offering the commission. She was relieved when she saw his initial surprise overtaken by excitement.

'Certainly, sir,' replied Edward with enthusiasm. 'What exactly do you want?'

'The choice of scenes is up to you so long as they are of Whitby and recognisably so. I would like one of them to be a moonlight scene.'

'Very well.' They went on to discuss size and media.

'You must charge me the full amount,' Matthew instructed. 'There must be no special rate because I am a friend of your mother. That would be no way to do business. These two paintings are birthday presents so I must have them by the beginning of March.'

'That will give me no problem.'

'Very well, that's settled.'

'Thank you, sir.' When Edward stood up, Matthew rose as well. They shook hands on the deal.

'Thank you, Matthew,' said Colette when the door had closed behind her son. 'Edward appreciates your coming to him.'

'He is a talented young man whose work, I am sure, will be sought after in the future so that makes these paintings an investment for my twin sisters as well as objects that will bring them pleasure.'

He stayed a few minutes longer and then politely took his leave.

When she had seen him out of the house Colette hurried to Edward's studio. 'That's wonderful,' she cried. 'I'm so proud of you.' She flung her arms round him and hugged him tight.

'Two commissions at once! Marvellous!' He gave a chuckle and eased his mother away so he could look into her eyes. 'You don't think he's done it to get closer to you?'

'Edward!' she chided. 'Fancy thinking such a thing!'

He laughed out loud and turned to his easel. 'You never know.'

Colette ignored his teasing. 'How is this one coming along?' She positioned herself to study his work in progress.

A ship was running for harbour before a storm. White sails stood out against dark ferocious-looking clouds. The sea was beginning to seethe and the activity of the crew revealed their anxiety to reach safety.

'Edward, that's splendid,' cried his mother in admiration.

He glanced at her and knew this was no idle praise. She stood transfixed. He said nothing, let her enjoy her absorption.

The silence was broken when she said, 'Are you doing much more to it?'

'No. I have that area of sea to touch up, it needs to be a little angrier. And I will balance it with a touch here on the sky. Then I think I will be satisfied, if ever an artist can be satisfied.'

'I don't think I ever saw your father really fulfilled by one of his paintings,' said Colette wistfully.

'That's interesting.' He nodded at the painting. 'This has taken longer than I expected. As you know, I had hoped to visit Ruswarp and Ampleforth before now.' He gave a shrug of his shoulders. 'And now with two more to do, I'm going to have to delay my search even longer. I hope that by March winter will be over, but it can linger on the moors and if we get heavy snow the track to Pickering can be blocked for some time.'

Colette made no comment but felt a touch of relief that Edward was not going to be able to root into the past just yet.

'Papa!' Marie rushed to her father waiting on the dockside as soon as the passengers were allowed on shore at Dover after the crossing from Calais.

Arthur's face broke into a broad smile at the happiness that shone from his daughter. He held out his arms to her and they embraced each other with deep affection. 'Let me look at you,' he said, easing her away but still holding her hands at arm's length. 'You look radiant and happy.'

'I am, Papa, I am.' She half turned from him to see Lucy hugging her mother. 'I'm so glad, for Lucy's sake, that you brought Mrs Wentworth.'

'Welcome home, Lucy.' Arthur accepted her kiss.

'It's lovely to see you, Mr Newton.'

Marie exchanged greetings with Lucy's mother and then turned back to her father. 'Papa, I want you to meet George.' She took him by the hand and moved to the young man who had stayed a few paces away. 'George, this is my father.'

He smiled and took Arthur's hand in a friendly grip as he said, 'It is an honour to meet you, Mr Newton.'

'And I am pleased to meet you, George,' Arthur returned. 'Thank you for escorting Marie and Lucy from Paris. Now, meet Lucy's mother, Mrs Wentworth.'

66

With introductions over, they took their places in the hired coach and it was a joyful party that made its way to Arthur's home.

'Dinner will be at half-past six,' Isobel informed them when Arthur, Marie and George left the carriage. 'But come as soon as you are ready.'

Marie ushered George into the house while Arthur went to make sure that the coachman would return with a smaller vehicle for them at five o'clock.

As he followed them he assessed his first impressions of George. He liked him, admired his manners. The young man was not shy but did not push himself forward or try to impose himself on others. He had a gentle air and Arthur liked the way he was attentive to Marie. His startling blue eyes enhanced his finely cut features – no wonder she had fallen for him. But Arthur knew that first impressions could sometimes prove false, though he judged that the impression he had formed of George in this short time would be true.

When he reached the house he found that Marie had taken the situation in hand. She had introduced George to her father's housekeeper who had escorted him to his room, leaving Marie to give him a tour of the house later.

When they had prepared for the evening they found they had half an hour to spare and so settled in easy chairs in the drawing room.

'Papa, George has been an admirer of your work for quite a while,' began Marie.

Arthur cast a glance at the visitor.

'Yes, sir, ever since I saw one of your paintings in the house of friends in Burnham Market.'

'Which one was that?'

'*Abbey Night*, sir.'

'Ah, yes, I remember it. I tried to create an impression of ghostly monks among the ruins.'

'You certainly did that, sir. I distinctly remember how you hinted at them through the way you layered your paint.'

'Thank you.'

'Do you paint as much now?'

Arthur gave a slight shake of his head. 'No. Marie is always pressing me to do more but I'm satisfied with life as it is. I'm comfortable, quite content that I've dropped out of sight, though of course I was never as well known as many of the painters of my time. Some day I may paint in earnest again but I feel at the moment that I want a little more freedom to do other things.'

Their conversation turned to technique and Arthur saw that George was absorbed by it. He liked the earnestness of this young man, and also his willingness to pick up tips and hints and not be afraid to ask questions. The half-hour flew by and it was with some regret for all three that this conversation had to be curtailed.

The evening air had a distinctly chilly feel to it so they wrapped up well for the carriage ride to Cherry Hill where Lucy and her mother gave them a hearty welcome. They were ushered into a large room where a log fire burned merrily in a large grate. A maid appeared carrying a large bowl of steaming punch. Glasses were charged and soon everyone was feeling warm inside and out.

From then on the evening passed in a relaxed atmosphere over a simple meal cooked to perfection. Conversation flowed over all manner of subjects from life in Paris to the bleak north Norfolk coast, Queen Victoria to the architecture of Notre Dame, pencil sketching to working in oils, superstition to the latest fashions.

It was midnight before the guests left after offering their sincere thanks for a splendid evening celebrating the homecoming of the students from Paris.

On the way home Arthur eased himself against the seat and said, 'When we left for Mrs Wentworth's we had to break off a most interesting conversation and I believe you two were picking up tips from me.'

They both acknowledged his observation.

'How about carrying it on tomorrow?' He gave a slight pause and then added quickly, 'Ah, no. That would be intruding on your parents' time, George. You must be home.'

Buoyed up by this unexpected invitation to spend another day with an artist he admired, he was quick to reassure Arthur. 'I told my parents I didn't know when I would be arriving, so I could stay another day if that is all right with you, sir?'

'Of course it is.' Arthur smiled to himself. He had cast the bait and the fish had duly bitten. Now he would have a better chance to assess George Reeves. He had liked what he had seen so far; tomorrow would make or mar his opinion.

The following night when he went to bed Arthur heaved a sigh of relief. It had been a demanding day; George had wanted to know so much about his techniques and the direction he thought the art world would take next. But he had enjoyed it all and he had had the opportunity to assess whether his first opinions of George Reeves were correct. He was pleased to find that they were. He liked the manner in which George was attentive to Marie, and was delighted to see her so happy. He realised Isobel was right, age difference need not matter.

The next morning after breakfast Arthur left the young couple to themselves. It was only when the trap was ready to take George to the station that his host reappeared.

'Thank you, sir, for all your hospitality and kindness.'

'Think nothing of it, young man, it has been a pleasure meeting you and talking with you.'

'Sir, with your permission, I will return two days before we are due to leave for Paris so that I can escort Marie and Lucy safely to their destination.'

'That is very considerate of you,' approved Arthur. 'You are welcome any time.'

'Thank you, sir.' George turned to Marie, took her hands and kissed her lightly on the cheek as decorum required, though their memories were of more passionate kisses exchanged a short while ago. 'Take care of yourself, Marie.'

'You too, George. I look forward to your return. Have a safe journey.'

Marie slipped her arm through her father's as they watched the trap roll down the short drive and into the highway. George waved and father and daughter responded. As they turned back into the house, she said, 'Thank you for being so kind to him, Papa.'

He patted her hand reassuringly. 'He's a fine young man. You could do a lot worse.' To save his daughter's blushes he paused on the step and turned to survey the sky. 'I think it as well he is on his way today, there are menacing clouds about.'

Arthur's prediction proved correct. Late that afternoon it started to rain and continued to do so for two days. The next day was calm, skies cleared, the temperature dropped and, later on, the sky darkened from the north-east. The first snowflakes fell shortly before midnight and all over the country people awoke the next day to a covering of snow.

Though the snow fall did not lie deep in Whitby it did on the moors that isolated the town from its hinterland. Any thoughts that Edward had nursed of visiting Ruswarp or Ampleforth in his quest to find his father had to be set aside until the weather changed. Frustrating as it was, he tempered his urge to investigate by concentrating on the commissions for Matthew Robinson and enjoying Christmas and New Year with his mother, aunt and her family.

Arthur enjoyed having Marie at home, though he knew she thought of George in Norfolk all the time. They wrapped themselves in their warmest clothes and stepped into the snow on Christmas Day to enjoy themselves with Isobel and Lucy at Cherry Hill. It was a resplendent feast that Isobel's cook had provided, and after the midday meal a pleasant afternoon and evening were spent in relaxing conversation with tongues and thoughts loosened by the excellent wine Isobel had provided for the occasion. The snow had not been thick along the south coast and on New Year's Day Isobel and Lucy had an exhilarating walk before spending the day with Arthur and Marie.

In north Norfolk, George enjoyed his time with his family but his mind was constantly on the girl he had left behind.

'George, who is she?' He was startled one day by his mother's question. They had braved the sharp wind that swept across the low-lying coast. There was nothing to stop it on its journey from the Arctic, but it had been merciful to those living along the open coast and George and his mother had decided to seek some exercise.

'Who, Mother?'

'The girl you have been mooning about throughout Christmas.'

He gave a small smile. 'Was it so obvious?'

'To me, not your father, but that's men for you.'

'Her name is Marie Newton.' He went on to explain everything about her and once in full flow there was no stopping him.

'I can tell you are very much in love. I pass no judgement now but cannot wait until I meet this wonderful person and see for myself how she really is and not how you want her to be. You must bring her to meet us the next time you are home. I long to meet the girl who can steal my son's heart.'

'You shall, Mother. I know you'll like her.' He kissed her on the cheek. 'Thank you for being so understanding.'

When it was time for the students to return to Paris the weather had relented. Seeing them go left Arthur in the deep pit of loneliness. His heart ached. A void had been left by his daughter's departure, but more so perhaps by the thought that he would now come second to another man. He knew that was a different love, one in which he could not share, but despite realising it was inevitable this would happen one day he felt bereft. The last rumbling from the carriage as it disappeared from sight seemed to draw another line through the past and herald another beginning. Was that what was meant when he felt Isobel's hand slip into his?

He had gone over to Cherry Hill where George and Marie had collected Lucy. He would walk back later. Now he was glad of this arrangement for it meant that he and Isobel could ease the pangs of parting from their girls together.

'Let's have a cup of tea, Arthur,' she suggested.

He nodded. 'Tea, the cure for all ills.'

They walked into the house. She still held his hand. He found comfort in her touch.

They were cosy together, warmed by the tea, comfortable in easy chairs in front of a crackling log fire. Time slipped away in pleasant conversation, each enjoying the company of another in a way they had not done since the loss of their respective spouses.

It was only when there was a knock on the door and Tess came in to ask if she should draw the curtains and light the lamps that

71

they became aware of the passing hours and that they had been drawn into a shared enjoyment of the light from the fire's dancing flames.

Arthur watched the maid perform her task, and when she had left the room stood up. 'I should be going.'

Isobel rose gracefully to her feet

'It will not be a pleasant walk, Arthur. Stay to dinner. Stay the night.'

He raised one eyebrow. 'But . . .'

Her laughter stopped his words. 'I'm offering you the guest room. We are two mature adults, surely we can share the same house for a night and be sensible about it.'

'Well . . .'

The way he drew out the word told her that he would like to take advantage of her offer. 'Then that's settled! Come, I'll show you the guest room. You can tidy yourself and I'll tell Cook that there'll be another for dinner and breakfast in the morning.'

She led the way from the drawing room, up the curving flight of stairs and turned left at the top. The room into which she directed Arthur occupied the south-west corner of the house. It was large and comfortable, papered with the latest floral pattern and furnished tastefully in mahogany.

'A maid will be in to turn the bed clothes down while we dine. In the meantime I'll send someone with a ewer of hot water.' As she was speaking she had gone to what Arthur thought was a cupboard let into the wall but when she opened the door he saw it was a walk-in closet in which there was a washstand with a marble top on which there stood a ewer and basin with towel and soap laid out beside it. 'I think you will find all you need here. Make yourself at home and then come and relax in the drawing room.'

'Thank you, Isobel, I appreciate what you are doing. I would have been lonely on my own – missing Marie terribly.'

'And contemplating a future when she will belong to someone else. I know, I went through it when Lucy married. Don't dwell on it, Arthur, and if ever you want to share your thoughts, I am here. We females see things differently from you men.'

Their eyes met and held for a moment. An understanding sprang between them. He stepped forward and kissed her on the cheek. 'You are a good friend.'

'Good gracious, you up already?' Marie made her astonishment marked on seeing Lucy already in the kitchen with the table set for breakfast.

Her friend smiled, a twinkle of delight in her eyes. 'I thought that would surprise you.'

'So is this . . .'

'To be a regular habit,' Lucy finished for her. 'I made a resolution when I was at home to discard my lazy morning habits and get to our atelier on time.'

'I'm pleased to hear it.'

'I don't want to let people down, most of all my mother and your father.'

'Good. You've talent. I think you improved more than anyone last term. Keep it up in future.'

'I intend to. Now, come on, let's get our breakfast and be off.'

Twenty minutes later they left their apartment and stepped out into weak sunshine that could not warm the chilly morning.

When Marie commented on the cold, Lucy replied brightly, 'It's not cold, it only makes you move faster.' She stepped out briskly.

Marie gave a grimace of surprise. 'Goodness, your holiday at home has done you good.'

'Ah, yes, and I've made another resolution.'

'And that is?'

'I'm going to find a young man. You've got George, I'm not coming along as a gooseberry, and I'm not going to sit around on my own. I'll find someone and then we can be a foursome.'

'Are you ready for it yet?'

'As I've said before, life has to go on.'

Much to their surprise their four friends were already at the atelier, setting up their easels.

Excitement broke out in the room as greetings and news were exchanged enthusiastically. The four students revealed that they had all come to the same decision as Lucy: the rest of the year was going to be devoted to painting.

73

'We are not going to work to the exclusion of all pleasure,' explained Charlotte, 'but we aren't going to let pleasure intrude on our work as we have done in the past. There is going to be a time and place for both. So this evening we are going to celebrate our new resolution and drink to the start of a new term! You two must come along. Get word to George, Marie.'

She laughed at the enthusiasm in Charlotte's voice. 'I had arranged to meet him so we'll be along. Where and when?'

'Six o'clock, our usual place.'

Lucy knew such gatherings always attracted other students and sometimes other young folk. Maybe her second resolution would be fulfilled sooner than expected.

'Our usual place' was one that Charlotte and the other three had introduced Marie and Lucy to during their first term: Restaurant Renard, which like several other establishments aimed itself at the students of the many art schools throughout Paris. It had modelled itself on the grand cafes catering for the boulevard set, but in less ostentatious ways. It had become justly popular and, though talk there was chiefly of art, the students also discussed many of the subjects of the day. Wine and good food would loosen their tongues but Monsieur Renard who owned the property had a strict code of conduct that the diners had never broken, no matter how good a time they were having. Students would come here to meet friends, renew acquaintances, or make new contacts.

The premises consisted of one large room and several smaller ones. A bar stretched along one wall and four barmen worked it while a dozen waiters attended the tables. The furniture was solid without being overwhelming and tables and chairs were spaced so as to allow freedom of movement. The walls were painted a light green and were decorated with many paintings that students, having finished their courses, had presented to Monsieur Renard in appreciation of his services.

Diners were beginning to drift in when Charlotte and Yvette arrived early, had a word with the manager and commandeered two large tables, one that would take twenty and the other ten. Though this was more than big enough for their own group they knew that before long, when friends and non-friends realised there was a party going on, every place would be taken and re-taken as fellow students arrived and passed on if they were not staying very long.

Marie arrived with George, Lucy with Gabrielle and Adelina, but within a few minutes they were joined by friends from various art schools and others whom they did not as yet know but soon would. The table was kept supplied with food and wine as the students all contributed to the bill.

Conversation flowed, spirits were high, this was the start of a new term and everyone was determined to get it off to a good start.

'Your eyes are drifting,' Marie whispered in Lucy's ear.

'Do you blame me?' she replied with a knowing smile.

'No.' Marie gave a slight shake of her head. In fact she approved. She thought it right that Lucy should give serious thought to her future. 'But don't press it too hard. It's often best to be the hunted.'

Lucy made no reply, just gave a slight nod. Her eyes had caught sight of a young man who had just entered the room. He stood tall in the doorway, surveying the scene as if he was looking for friends or deciding whether he should go to the bar. His clothes were immaculate, the clothes of a man who cared for them and the effect they had on his appearance. His short grey jacket was left undone to reveal a pearl-grey waistcoat of fine material fastened with pearl buttons. His trousers were a perfect fit, coming to the laces of his highly polished black shoes. A pale blue cravat, that seemed to enhance his dark eyes, was tied neatly at the collar of a white shirt. A black top hat that had been carefully brushed was tipped at a jaunty angle and revealed a quiff of black hair pressed down on his forehead. She saw his eyes scan their tables and then look away. Disappointment touched her when she saw him head for the bar. She turned to speak to Gabrielle. So intent was she on their exchange that she did not notice that a chair opposite her had become vacant until someone spoke.

'May I sit here?'

When Lucy looked up her heart missed a beat for she was looking at the man she had last seen heading for the bar. 'Er, no.'

'It's someone's seat?' he asked.

'No.'

He smiled at her confusion. 'That's two negatives – does that make a positive?'

'I . . . well . . . yes, do sit down.'

'You are sure that I can?'

'Of course.' Lucy had got a grip on her confusion by now and chided herself for her reactions. He must think her an imbecile.

'Good.' He sat down. 'Now, let me introduce myself. Philip Jaurès, born in Switzerland of a Swiss mother and a French father, a distant relation through my mother's side of the family of Adelina Mornardt. I was told I might find her here. Does either of you know her?'

'Adelina!' they both said at once. 'We certainly do.'

Lucy added quickly, 'We share the same atelier.'

'My goodness.' He glanced round. 'Of all the people in this room I pick two who not only know her but paint with her. Is she here tonight?'

'Yes, somewhere around, it's probably best if you wait here.' Lucy quickly suggested. 'She'll be back soon. It is our table, we're celebrating our return to schools. I'm Lucy Wentworth.'

'Ah, an English rose!'

Lucy blushed under the penetrating gaze of his dark eyes. 'And this is Gabrielle Hoetger.'

'Dutch, no doubt.'

'Indeed.'

'Are you a student here?' Lucy asked.

Philip laughed. 'Goodness me, no, I couldn't paint a picture to save my life.'

'I doubt that,' said Gabrielle stolidly.

'It's true.'

'What do you do?' asked Lucy.

'I'm in the financial world. A family firm, operating only in Switzerland until now. I'm opening an office in Paris.'

'That must be interesting.'

'Exciting. I arrived yesterday. When I heard Adelina was coming today I thought I would welcome her. Seems I've wandered in on a celebration.'

All the while, Lucy had been studying Philip. He held himself upright, projecting the forceful manner of one who wants to be noticed. She reckoned he had no need to adopt that manner, for his lean figure, strong jawline and the perfect symmetry of his face would have drawn attention. And if they didn't, his eyes certainly would. They were pools of dark mystery, tempting and challenging anyone to explore their depths. The thought gave Lucy a moment of apprehension but it was gone in a flash when she saw them sparkle with interest in what was going on before focusing on her, giving her the impression that she was the only one who mattered at that moment. She was drawn by them.

'So,' he said, 'tell me, is Adelina a good artist?'

With Gabrielle's attention occupied by the person on her left, Lucy found herself answering his question. 'Yes, she is, but I think she could be much better if she would apply herself more seriously.'

'Ah, that's Adelina from what I hear.' He took a sip of his wine. 'And you? Are you a good artist?'

'That is not for me to say.'

He smiled. 'Don't be modest.' His soft voice, the way his eyes held hers, drew an answer from her.

'I'm not as good as any of those with whom I share the atelier.'

He laughed, and his eyes sparkled. 'I think you are being far too modest. I'll have to see for myself.' He would not call the young lady sitting opposite to him a beauty but there was an attractive air about her that kindled his desire to know more abouther. He judged her to be about five years older than himself, but what did age matter? She was well dressed so she was not short of money even though she was a student. She wore no rings, her only ornamentation being a rose-shaped brooch pinned at the neck of her white blouse. 'You are English?'

'Yes, from near Deal in Kent.'

'Near Deal?' he prompted.

'Yes, my parents had a farm.'

'Had?' Once more he pushed for information but it went unnoticed by Lucy as she continued to explain.

'Well, we still have. My father is dead but my mother resolved to keep the farm going.'

He raised an eyebrow. 'I'm sorry to hear about your father.' He gave a little pause as she acknowledged his sympathy with an inclination of her head. 'So does your mother run the farm?' He had put a note of surprise in his voice.

'Not really, although she keeps a check on everything. She employs a manager to see to its everyday running.'

Philip locked this information away in his mind. It was obvious that the farm must be good land which seemed to indicate that the family had money.

'Does any of your family help her?' he asked casually.

'I have no brothers or sisters.'

'So will you take over or is it to be a career in art for you?'

'Who knows what the future holds?'

'Indeed.' Philip changed subjects. He must not seem unduly curious. He already had some information that might come in useful. 'Have you been to Paris before?'

'Not until I came last September.'

'Have you done much exploring?'

'A little, soon after we came.'

'We?'

'My friend Marie Newton lives close by in England. She's at the end of the table.' She indicated Marie. 'And that's her young man next to her, George Reeves.'

'Maybe I'll meet them later.'

They chatted about a range of subjects while enjoying the food and wine and the exchanges with others who kept the busy tide of people around the two tables flowing. Lucy was pleased that he seemed in no hurry to leave in order to seek out Adelina.

When her friend did appear, Philip was on his feet immediately. 'My dear Adelina!' he exclaimed enthusiastically, extending his hands to her.

Lucy was surprised to see Adelina look taken aback but the reason why came a moment later.

'Philip, good heavens, I haven't seen you in years. What are you doing here?'

He took her hands and kissed her on both cheeks. 'Opening an office in this wonderful city so I had to look up my dear Adelina.

My enquiries led me here where, while waiting for you, I have been ably looked after by your friend Lucy.' He gave her a ravishing smile and then turned it on Adelina as he said, 'You look wonderful as always. I fell for you when we were children and I do so all over again.'

'Flatterer! You always had a quick tongue.' Adelina cast a glance at Lucy. 'Beware of it.'

'I'll cope,' Lucy replied.

'Is that a challenge?' His eyes darkened as if imparting a dare.

Though she felt impelled to rise to what she saw there, she merely shrugged her shoulders as if she thought the challenge not worth taking. In doing so she knew that she had teased him further and that his interest in her would be heightened.

He turned and, seeing a vacant chair, pulled it to the table. 'Sit down, Adelina. Let me get you some wine.'

She thanked him and sat down. When he had gone to the bar she said, 'That was a surprise. We spent some time together when we were children as our families lived near each other, but then they moved away we lost touch and I haven't seen Philip for about ten years.'

'You did not know he was coming to Paris?'

'No. He's a distant relative on my mother's side.'

The rest of the evening passed off in a pleasant carefree atmosphere. Philip had learned a lot more about Adelina's friends without seeming to pry. Realising from this that Adelina, Charlotte, Gabrielle and Yvette already had their own escorts to see them back to their apartments and that Lucy would not want to intrude on Marie and George's company, he sought her permission to see her safely home which she was only too eager to give.

He was the model of decorum but when they reached her apartment and he raised her hand to his lips, she thought she saw a flash of desire touch the dark depths in his eyes.

'Lucy, because of some work that was transferred with me I will have to go to Calais for three days, but when I get back would you do me the honour of dining with me – say, next Thurday?'

'That is most kind. I am pleased to accept.'

79

A broad smile broke across his face. 'I am honoured. I will be here at seven.'

He doffed his hat as he gave a slight bow, then turned and walked away.

Lucy's steps were light as she hurried up to the apartment. She flung her coat aside as she went through the entrance hall and burst into the sitting room.

Marie spun round from the window. 'You look pleased with yourself,' she commented, seeing the exuberance on her friend's face and sensing the joyful energy that filled her.

'Isn't he just gorgeously handsome?' cried Lucy, rapturous laughter on her lips as she did a dance in the middle of the floor.

'I suppose you are referring to Philip, seeing that he escorted you home and you spent most of the evening with him?'

'Who else? And he's asked me to dine with him next Thursday.'

'And you've said yes?'

'Naturally.'

'Don't be swept off your feet too easily.'

'Don't put a dampener on me!' snapped Lucy.

'I'm not. All I'm saying is, be careful.'

'You mean, he's not your type?'

'He's not.'

'Then you shouldn't pass judgement on mine. I have never criticised your choice of George.'

Marie knew she maybe shouldn't say more but felt she had a duty to her friend. 'Adelina told me that he used to be regarded as a bit of a black sheep in the family.'

'Did she tell you that the families lost touch and she had not seen Philip for ten years?'

'No.'

'Well, that's what she told me! If he had a reputation then, he could have changed in the meantime.'

'Reputations stick, often with reason. I'm only thinking of you. You have only recently got over the loss of your husband, I don't want to see you hurt again.'

Chapter Six

Edward made a final adjustment to the painting he would simply call *Moonlight Over Whitby*. He touched the brush to the silvery glow behind the ruined abbey. He had taken his viewpoint from the West Cliff looking across the river, showing the moonlight spilling across the roofs of the houses climbing from the river towards the ruins.

He stood back, looked hard at the painting for a few moments, then gave a grunt of satisfaction. He laid his brush down and walked to the window, assessing the prospect for good weather tomorrow.

Throughout the winter, while he had been working on the two paintings for Matthew Robinson, his mind had constantly turned to his father and the search he would have to conduct. He had made enquiries by letter from several galleries around the country, but with little success. Though Arthur Newton was known, particularly in the north, no one knew of his whereabouts. There were mentions of purchases of his work made from Ebenezer Hirst so it seemed a visit to Leeds might yield some information, but with Ruswarp and Ampleforth nearer he would try to find Mr Richard Redgrave first.

A knock on the door brought his mother into the room. 'You said you might finish it today,' she said. 'I wondered if you wanted to delay our evening meal?' Colette crossed the room as she was speaking so that she could view the painting that stood on an easel with its back to the door.

'I've just finished.'

Colette took her son's arm as she swung round to view the painting. She did not speak for a moment but drank in the beauty and technique displayed in the picture. 'Very, very good.' She gave her assessment with a sigh.

'You like it?'

'It's one of your best.'

'You really think so?'

'I wouldn't say so if I didn't mean it. Matthew will be delighted with it – with them both.' She glanced at a second painting leaning against the wall across the room. Edward had painted ships tied up at some of Whitby's quays along the east bank of the river for the other part of his commission.

'When will you deliver them to Matthew?'

'This one will need to dry. I thought, if the weather is good, I would visit Ruswarp and Ampleforth first and then deliver the canvasses to Mr Robinson.'

Colette began to worry and it showed in her expression.

'Mother, you have known since you revealed that Arthur Newton was my real father that I would have to make enquiries. If my visits to Ruswarp and Ampleforth yield nothing then I will go to Leeds.'

'I know, Edward. It's just that I don't want anybody to be hurt, especially you.'

'I've told you, if I think that is going to happen, I will call the whole thing off.'

Colette knew she could not hold her son back.

Edward spent the next day arranging his visit to Ruswarp and the following day found his mount ready for him when he arrived at the White Horse in Church Street.

It was a pleasant March morning and he enjoyed the ride along the bank of the Esk to the tiny village of Ruswarp. His enquiries there revealed nothing, however. Though two people knew of the Redgrave brothers who had dealt in paintings in Whitby, neither knew of Mr Richard's whereabouts and were adamant that he had never lived in Ruswarp.

It was a despondent Edward who reported back to his mother. She knew she had to offer some sort of encouragement.

'You can't expect to succeed immediately. Maybe Ampleforth will yield something.'

Two days later he set out on this mission that would take him across the high and desolate moors to Pickering and then westward along the Vale of Pickering to the market town of Helmsley. It was here that he had decided to find accommodation for the night, maybe longer if his enquiries led to anything positive, as he deemed it a more likely place than the tiny village that was his final destination five miles further on.

Odd pockets of snow still lay in the north-facing hollows of the high moors and a chill breeze blew across the heights. Edward had come well prepared and was thankful for the heavy coat that came to his ankles. He took a break at the lonely Wagon and Horses, nestling under a rise in the terrain that was steep enough to make the trackway loop on its course to the top. Fortified by a tankard of ale, bread and cheese and a slice of ham, he was not sorry to be on his way again. He had met with sullen and suspicious stares from the pub's four occupants who were huddled round a table as if hatching a plot. Edward was wary for the next three miles but eventually relaxed when he judged he had not been followed.

He did not stop in the market town of Pickering but pressed on along the vale to arrive in Helmsley by late-afternoon. He brought his horse to a halt on the edge of the market place with its old stone cross. Several people were hastening about their business, eager to be home before long. The only people to take any notice of him were three old men leaning on their sticks. He had seen them emerge from one of the inns and pause before making their parting remarks. That pause was extended when they observed the stranger on the horse. Edward figured they would not move until they saw what he was going to do.

He cast his eyes over the surrounding buildings and, judging that the Black Swan looked the more salubrious inn, turned his horse in its direction. When he swung to the ground and tied his mount to the rail he saw the men nod their heads, as if they had agreed on something, and then shuffle off in different directions.

Within a few minutes he had obtained a room, ordered a meal for later and seen his horse taken by the ostler to be settled for the night.

His room was comfortable if sparse, the full Yorkshire meal ample enough for two, and after three tankards of ale and some pleasant exchanges with the landlord and two of his regular customers, Edward slept well. He made a hearty breakfast the next morning for he did not know how the day would unfold.

He eyed the sky as he led his horse back into the market square. It did not look promising; thick grey clouds covered the sun, but they were moving before a west wind. Maybe it would keep rain away. Edward swung into the saddle and headed out of Helmsley in the direction indicated by the landlord of the Black Swan. He crossed the River Rye on the edge of the town and climbed the rise beyond it. Recalling that the landlord had told him to keep to the left-hand fork in the track, he rode into a small depression before turning right to ride through woodland that climbed a spur in the hill. Reaching the top, he paused to look down into a valley running east-west, and far beyond it could see the distant Pennines. But he had no desire to stay to admire the view for he was eager to learn if there were answers to his questions in Ampleforth.

The track descended gradually into the village that straggled along the hillside overlooking the shallow valley. Cottages in various states of repair lay to either side of the rough roadway. Smoke rose from some chimneys to be whisked away eastward by the wind. A man leading a horse and cart came out of a gateway and turned ahead of Edward. A woman in a black dress, its spreading skirts worn at the hem and a soiled white apron tied at her waist, swept a doorstep with a broom that had seen better days. Two young boys, yelling in chase, ran out of a cottage only to pull up short and gape at the stranger who rode past.

Negotiating a dip in the roadway, he found himself confronted by the White Swan, a dour stone building which looked sturdy enough to have weathered several centuries and to last several more. He halted his horse, swung from the saddle and eased his limbs, then went inside. The stone slab floor was strewn with straw; a fire burned brightly in a large grate and gave the place a welcoming atmosphere.

There was no one to be seen but Edward heard voices coming from somewhere at the rear. He went to the counter at the bar and rapped hard. A few moments later a man of just under six foot appeared. He was broad of shoulder and hard of muscle. His square head resting on a broad neck made him seem distinctly formidable, so that a stranger might be apprehensive about accosting him, but his eyes belied this impression. They were bright and brown, and Edward detected friendliness there. He judged it was not merely because he was a potential customer but would be extended to anyone who encountered this man. At the same time he did not look like the sort of man to cross, ready smile or no.

'Good day, sir,' the landlord greeted him amiably.

'Good day to you too, landlord,' Edward returned affably. 'I'd like a tankard of your best ale.'

'Yes, sir.' As he was drawing the beer the man glanced at Edward. 'Ridden far, sir?'

'Only from Helmsley this morning, but from Whitby yesterday.'

The landlord nodded and placed the tankard in front of Edward who fished in his pocket for some coins.

'Stay at the Black Swan, sir?'

'Yes.'

'You'd be well looked after there.' The landlord leaned on the counter as if he was settling in for a conversation. No doubt he was curious about this visitor he had never seen before.

'Indeed I was.'

'Good. My brother and his wife run that hostelry.'

'I'll mention that I've seen you if I stay there tonight. It depends how long I am in Ampleforth.'

'So, you've come here especially then?'

Edward could tell from the man's tone that he thought it a strange thing to do. 'I've business here. Maybe you can help me.' He saw the landlord's curiosity heighten. This was a man who liked to know what was going on in his village. 'I'm looking for a man called Richard Redgrave – used to live in Whitby. Must be getting on in years, I believe he knew my father.' Before he had finished speaking Edward knew from the glint in the landlord's eyes that he had struck a chord.

'He came here a few years ago. Lodges with Aud Nellie Sykes at last cottage from here on the left, at the east end of the village.

Cantankerous old man, though. Aud Nell, as we calls her, can handle him. Seems she's a very distant relation. Don't know how you'll get on with him. Get Aud Nell on your side and you might glean what you want, though.'

'And what's the best way of doing that?'

'She likes a drop of whisky.'

'Then give me a bottle, please.'

When the landlord had handed over the bottle, Edward asked, 'Will my horse be all right left here if I walk to the cottage?'

'Certainly. I'll have it rubbed down for you, if you wish?'

'That's most thoughtful, thank you.'

Edward's rap on the oak door of the cottage was soon answered to reveal a small woman whose age was hard to judge because of her smooth rosy complexion but he reckoned she was probably in her mid-sixties. Her black dress was simple, without any adornment. She wore a white apron tied over it at the waist. Hair that was still dark was drawn back into the nape of her neck.

'Sir?' she said in an enquiring tone.

'I'm Edward Clayton, looking for Mr Redgrave.'

'Then you have come to the right place,' she said with a smile. 'But I'm afraid he's gone for his daily walk.' Seeing the look of disappointment on Edward's face, she added quickly, 'He won't be long now. Would you like to come in and wait?'

'I would if it's no trouble? I've ridden over from Whitby on purpose to see him, though I must admit it was a shot in the dark. I'd heard a rumour that he might be in Ampleforth.'

As he was speaking Nell had stepped to one side to allow him to enter the cottage. He found himself in a large square room with two doors leading off it, no doubt to a kitchen and scullery. An oak table and chairs stood in the centre of the room, a sideboard against one wall. Two battered armchairs stood one on either side of a black kitchen range which had been painstakingly cleaned and polished.

'Do sit down.' Nell indicated one of the chairs. 'Would you like a cup of tea?'

'That is kind of you.'

She went to the kettle sitting on a trivet on the hearth and placed it over the fire.

'Maybe you would rather have a drop of this,' added Edward, withdrawing the bottle as if by magic from his pocket.

Nell's eyes sparkled at the sight as he handed over the bottle. 'Maybe later,' she said. 'And it wouldn't do to let Mr Redgrave see it.' She chuckled and secreted the bottle in a wall cupboard. 'You've been making enquiries at the inn, no doubt.' She busied herself with cups and saucers as she added, 'What's your business with Mr Redgrave, if you don't mind me asking? I might be able to tell you something that would help.'

'I don't mind at all. I'm trying to trace an artist called Arthur Newton. I believe he once sold pictures through Mr Redgrave's shop in Whitby.'

'Ah, that would be his brother William's shop. Richard, the one who lives here, only had a minor interest in it.'

'But he might know of Arthur Newton.'

'Indeed he might. He left the business and Whitby immediately his brother died so I don't know . . .' Her words were interrupted when the door opened and a man of medium height came in. He was well wrapped up in top-coat, scarf and hat. His gloved hands held a walking stick.

'It's cold out there,' he said in a tone that indicated he thought the weather had no right to be severe. He turned from closing the door and pulled up sharp with an exclamation of surprise on seeing a stranger sitting in one of the chairs near the fire.

'Richard, this is Mr Edward Clayton from Whitby who has made a special journey to see you,' said Nell as she started to pour water into a large teapot.

'More fool him on a day like this,' grunted Richard Redgrave, propping his stick in a corner and peeling off his gloves before flinging off his coat and hat. He stood and stared at Edward. 'Well, young man, what do you want with me?' He pushed past the younger man and plonked himself in the chair from which Edward had risen to greet him.

Nell noted the action with embarrassment and looked apologetically at Edward. 'I'm sorry, that's Richard's chair . . . I never thought when I told you to sit down. Have mine.'

'Thank you but no, ma'am, I'll not take your chair. If I may

I'll have one of these?' He pulled out a chair from under the table.

She nodded her approval.

'Come on then, young man, why do you want to see me?' Richard asked irritably, holding out his hands towards the fire and then rubbing them to get the circulation going.

'Well, sir, I wondered if you could tell me anything about an artist whose works you used to sell in your shop in Skinner Street?' As he finished his enquiry Edward took a cup of tea from Nell and thanked her.

Richard accepted his with a grunt and didn't even look at his landlady. He fixed his eyes on Edward. 'Did some very good work, and some mediocre work. Could have been outstanding but something got in the way.'

Edward was taken aback by this bald statement presented with a no-nonsense air. He automatically asked, 'What got in the way?'

'How do I know? These things are private but I'd guess a woman. They're always at the root of every trouble.'

Edward was ready to spring to his father's defence but thought better of it. An argument with Richard Redgrave would not be to his advantage. He shrugged his shoulders and said, 'Well, that's as may be. It's not what I am interested in. I want to contact him and wondered if you knew of his whereabouts or what happened to him?'

Richard ignored Edward's question and instead countered it with a query of his own. 'Why do you want to get in touch with him?'

Edward had to think fast. He did not want to disclose the real reason or anything that might raise suspicion in the old man's mind. 'I'm doing a series of articles about English artists and he is on my list.'

Richard grunted. 'Can't help you. When he left Whitby his paintings were delivered to the shop by carrier but he gradually sent fewer and fewer until they stopped altogether. He never let us know why or where he went.'

Still Edward clung to hope. 'Would your brother's wife have any information?'

Richard gave a contemptuous groan. 'Not her. The house

became hers on my brother's death. I knew she wouldn't want me there – she had only tolerated me because of William – so I got out straight away. She didn't even offer to sell me William's share of the business.'

'You wouldn't have wanted it then.' Nell felt she had to give her assessment of the family history. 'And you aren't and never were an easy person to live with. It's a wonder Genetta tolerated you as long as she did.'

Richard shot her a withering look.

'Do you think it would be worthwhile my contacting her? Might she have kept any records?'

'Knowing her, she would destroy all matters relating to the business. She wouldn't want to be cluttered with any of that when she moved.'

'I'm afraid that would be so,' put in Nell. 'And I can understand that. Genetta was a great help to her husband because she was a good judge of an artist's ability.' She ignored Richard's contemptuous sniff and went on, 'But she was not interested in the everyday running of the business.'

'He had a long association with an art dealer in Leeds . . . oh, dear, what was his name?' Richard was annoyed with himself for not remembering.

'Ebenezer Hirst,' Edward prompted.

'That's him,' approved Richard. 'Try him. If he's still alive,' he added with a gloomy look.

'I mean to find out,' said Edward. 'I had hoped I'd find the information nearer home but I haven't, so Leeds it will have to be.' As there appeared to be nothing more to be gained here he stood up and made his thanks and goodbyes

As his enquiries in Ampleforth had not taken very long, he decided to spend the night in Pickering. He was grateful for fine weather for his ride to Whitby the following day. Reaching home, he quickly apprised his mother of the outcome of his visit to Ampleforth.

'I know it's disappointing when you expected your mission to find your father to be easy. Maybe it's not meant to be,' Colette told him.

'Mother, don't say that. I mean to find him and the next step will be to go to Leeds.'

But with another commission proposed by Matthew Robinson, who had been more than delighted with Edward's two previous paintings, the opportunity to do so did not arrive for over a month.

Lucy swung round from the window of their apartment. 'Another glorious day,' she said with unbridled joy and hugged herself as she did a pirouette across the floor. 'Isn't Paris just so glorious at this time of the year?'

Marie had to agree; the burgeoning beauty of the tree-lined boulevards had thrilled her, too. They added magic to the city and with the warmer weather the promenaders matched the colours of the blossom above in their own new outfits.

But Marie realised that it was more than the attractions of the capital that had captured Lucy's enthusiasm. She knew her friend had met Philip Jaurès several times in between his frequent visits to Calais. He had brought a new outlook on life to Lucy. With Philip's captivating vitality each day took on a brand new aspect, to be enjoyed to the full, and that included her work at the atelier. She painted with a new enthusiasm and was making rapid progress in her development as an artist. Monsieur Bedeaux assessed and praised her efforts, though he was careful with his enthusiasm, believing that showing too much fervour too soon could be counterproductive. Her fellow students were delighted for her and felt that her undoubted progress rubbed off on their own work in a way for they saw her achievements as a challenge to be met.

Marie was pleased and happy for Lucy but there were times when she worried for her nevertheless, usually the nights when she had trouble sleeping. Why should she doubt the relationship when it seemed to have brought so much to Lucy's life? In the light of day she would push aside the doubts and put their persistence down to the unholy hours of the night. Yet they would rise again. She wished she had someone with whom she could share her worries but knew her fellow students would not understand her misgivings. When she mentioned her uncertainties to George, who was usually a sympathetic listener, he warned her about meddling in affairs of the heart and Marie swiftly took the hint.

After being absent from the city for four days, Philip returned in a wildly enthusiastic mood. He sought an audience with Madame Foucarde.

Her smile was welcoming when he was shown into the room she used as an office but before he could speak she held up a warning hand. 'No, Monsieur Philip, I cannot allow you to go to Mademoiselle Lucy's apartment.'

'But, Madame, I have something important to tell her. It cannot wait!' The baleful look in his eyes and the persuasive tone of his voice was his first attempt to breach her rule about male visitors to any of the apartments.

She gave a little shake of her head. She had experienced Philip's charm on a number of occasions but had resisted it. Oh, she liked this young man. Who wouldn't? He was handsome and captured a woman's attention immediately. He had a soft, caressing voice that compelled people to listen. But more than anything it was his startling dark eyes that drew the attention.

'Oh, come, Madame Foucarde, am I not your favourite visitor? Please, you cannot deny me, not when I have such good news for Mademoiselle. It just can't wait.' Those eyes pleaded with her.

'If I let you go to her apartment, I stand the risk of losing my position,' she said firmly.

'Oh, I don't think that would happen. You are too good a concierge.'

'Flattery will get you nowhere.'

'I mean it, Madame. You are too valuable to lose. Besides, who would know? The owner of this block lives far away.'

'Someone might talk.'

Philip gave a little knowing smile. 'Who in Paris would betray an affair of the heart?' He threw up his hands in horror at the thought.

She was of the same mind but . . .

He seized on her moment of weakness. 'Madame Foucarde, you have been young, you no doubt loved, you would have had

91

obstacles to overcome and found ways of doing so.' He saw the light of fond memory in her eyes. 'Ah, I see you truly loved with all your heart. So how can you deny the growing love I have for Mademoiselle Lucy? Please, please, remove the obstacle that confronts me.'

Her eyes were intent on him. Her thoughts had travelled back in time. Oh, her love life had been tempestuous with a father's strictness to overcome. She saw in Philip a similar charm to that which she had once used to get her way. Who could deny the charm of such a handsome man? Who could deny the aspirations of two young lovers? She had bathed in the glow of Lucy's love and marvelled at the change it had wrought in the English girl. She was thankful for it because it reminded her of her own young days when she too had experienced a love that would not be denied. Could she in her heart of hearts deny the pleading of this young man?

'If I allow you to go then I am going to have to allow Mademoiselle Newton's beau to visit too.'

'So you would be bringing joy to four people! Both he and I will be the height of discretion and, I assure you, will not abuse the privilege you extend to us.'

Madame Foucarde's lips tightened as she considered her options. She was tempted to allow his request but pulled herself up sharply; her position here would be in jeopardy. 'No, no, Monsieur. It's more than my job's worth. Now, off with you.'

'Madame, if I write a note, will you please deliver it?'

She gave a small smile. 'Ah, Monsieur, that is different. Who am I to spoil a lover's tryst? It will be a privilege to be the bearer of such a note.'

'Madame, you are an angel.' Philip looked around as if searching for something.

'Monsieur, here you are.' Madame Foucarde opened a drawer and produced a pencil and paper.

'Madame, you are an angel twice over. Prepared as you are, I think you must have done this before.'

A mischievous glint came into her eyes. 'There are other young ladies in this block, they too have lovers.'

He wrote a brief note and Madame Foucarde went quickly to the girls' apartment.

The loud knocking on the door startled Marie and Lucy who were relaxing with their latest reading. They exchanged looks and Lucy pushed herself to her feet and went to the door.

'Madame Foucarde!' she exclaimed.

'A note, Mademoiselle.'

Lucy took the piece of paper, unfolded it, and gave it a quick glance. She met Madame Foucarde's knowing smile. 'Tell him I'll be right down.' She turned back into the room as Madame Foucarde left. 'Marie, Philip wants to see us.'

'Me as well?' Marie was surprised and curious.

'Yes, come on.'

They hurried over to find him waiting outside Madame Foucarde's rooms.

'Philip, what is so urgent?' asked Lucy, her concern vanishing when she saw laughter in his eyes.

'I'm going to teach you to ride a bicycle!'

'What?' Both girls stared at him in amazement.

Philip's voice was charged with enthusiasm as he went on, 'While I was away I learned. It's simple, just a matter of balance and steering. You'll learn in no time. I thought it would be good for us. We could get about more, enjoy the countryside. You'll find more subjects to draw and paint. Go and get ready and then we'll go for George.'

It was an excited trio who left the apartment block. Madame Foucarde saw them go and envied them their freedom, but she was happy in her heart to see young love blossoming.

Chapter Seven

From her bedroom window Isobel saw Arthur coming up the driveway to Cherry Hill. She viewed herself in the mirror, patted her hair, hurried downstairs and slipped a shawl round her shoulders as she left the house.

Arthur quickened his step when he saw her. His visits to Cherry Hill had become more frequent for he found Isobel's company eased the loneliness after Marie's departure. There had sprung up between them a natural rapport that he thought might promise more. Undoubtedly she was a fine woman with many attributes he admired; her self-assurance was no doubt born in her but further honed when she had to deal with the aftermath of her husband's death. Though that had brought sadness and a certain reserve also, these qualities disappeared when she knew she could trust people. She had made it plain to Arthur that she trusted and had confidence in him, and the implication behind that delighted him.

He always looked forward to the next time he would be with her. He had not looked for anything more but seeing her now set his mind racing, and he realised his heart had quickened too. For one startling moment he found himself comparing his present feelings with the love he had had for his wife, and for his lost love, Colette. He pulled himself up sharply. He should not be making comparisons. This was Isobel, an individual in her own right, and he should treat her as such; his feelings for her should be set apart from his flawed and guilty past.

Yes, Isobel was a fine woman. Her own face was lit by the joy of the moment. He felt at one with her.

'Arthur.' She held out her hands to him.

He dropped his cane, swept his hat from his head in polite

acknowledgment of his respect for her then let it fall beside his cane. He took her hands in his. At arm's length they gazed into each other's eyes. The silence between them held so much meaning that there was no need to speak. He drew her gently to him and kissed her. He felt her relax in his arms, her body soft and supple. Something told him that she too wanted this moment to go on. Their respect for each other had quietly turned to admiration, devotion, and a love that now expressed itself in the way they both wanted.

Isobel reluctantly broke the kiss. 'I think we'd better move,' she said huskily. She tried to step out of his arms but he held her without any force.

'Isobel, will you marry me?'

For a moment she did not speak. Then tears filled her eyes. 'Yes.'

Time stood still for a few fleeting seconds before Arthur swept her back into his arms and their kiss expressed the joy they were both feeling.

'You have made me a very happy man,' he said, and kissed her more gently.

Isobel ran her fingers down his cheek as she looked deep into his eyes. 'You are a lovely man, Arthur Newton, and I am honoured that you have asked me.'

'No, it is you who has done me the honour.'

'I think we should walk.'

He nodded. 'There is much to talk about.'

'Yes, but not today. Too many mundane things will intrude on what should be a happy day, one for us to remember the rest of our lives.'

Laughter glinted in his eyes. 'You are right. Nothing should mar today.'

As they started to stroll she slipped her arm through his. She had done this before but now the contact seemed much more intimate and it thrilled her. She had never expected to feel this way again about a man; she had never thought that anyone could measure up to her husband. She had not expected to honour his last request to her: 'Don't mourn for me. Miss me and then find someone else.' Now she had done so and she knew her husband would approve.

'There is just one thing I would like to say today,' she said.

Arthur glanced at her. 'And that is?'

'A request really. I would like this kept just between us for a while.'

'What about Lucy and Marie?'

'We'll tell them later when you and I have sorted a few things out. Don't ask me any more now. We said we would keep today free from mundane things.'

'Just as you wish. You tell me when you want us to inform our daughters that they are to become step-sisters.'

Isobel laughed. 'So they will! I hadn't thought of that.'

'Happy?' George shouted as they pedalled down a country lane five miles from Paris.

'Delirious!' cried Marie with uncontrolled zest. She had loosened her hair to allow it to stream out behind her.

'Look at us,' called George, steering nearer to her. 'Two weeks ago we couldn't ride. Now we are the best in the world.'

'Hurrah for Philip!'

'I'll second that!'

The day was warm and promised to combine having fun with some serious sketching. While they were working their pencils Philip would, he said, be content to laze in the sun reading. Marie considered his friendliness, his zest for life, his consideration. And that day a few weeks ago when he had taught them to ride . . . It had been a time of great amusement as they struggled to get their balance, wobbled, and fell off amid much laughter and hilarity. Each wanted to be the first to succeed and so the challenge spurred them all on. When Philip, helpless with laughter, had shouted instructions they had taken no notice, convinced that what they were doing was the best way to achieve their objective.

Now here they were riding like veterans, rolling along at an unimaginable speed that sent a thrill through them. Ahead, Philip and Lucy had set the pace and their gaiety swept back to embrace George and Marie. In the past few weeks Marie had overcome her first doubts of Philip. She had once advised Lucy to be cautious, but now she saw no reason to remind her friend of that. Lucy seemed so happy and Philip had shown her only kindness and consideration. Maybe Marie's first judgement had been wrong. George and their friends were happy with the relationship. She should be too. Today was certainly not the time to entertain negative thoughts about the man who was making her friend so happy.

Two miles further on they saw their companions slow down and stop. Philip quickly propped his bicycle against the hedge and then did the same with Lucy's. As Marie and George slowed down, he called, 'Picnic time.'

'Good,' agreed George enthusiastically, 'I'm famished after that ride.'

'Where?' asked Marie

'There looks to be a good place here,' answered Lucy, indicating a spot through the gate in the hedge. 'We spotted a level area beside the stream.'

They found the place and amid much teasing and joking laid out the delightful array of food that the two girls had prepared. Philip went back to his bicycle and returned flourishing two bottles of wine that he had secreted in a basket tied behind the saddle.

'Nectar! Nectar!' he cried, holding the bottles high. 'Fit for our two goddesses!' He held the bottles close to his chest and waltzed the last remaining yards with a dreamy look on his face as if he was in love with the wine he held in his arms. He passed the bottles to George with a gesture of regret and turned to Lucy. Encircling her waist with his hands, he said, 'Come, replace the love I have just surrendered.' He drew her close and began to waltz as he hummed a tune close to her ear. The merriment vanished from her face to be replaced by dreamy ecstasy, a world she always entered when Philip danced with her. He was so light on his feet, an expert at every step, with a gentle guiding touch that directed her effortlessly. Then that dream world was shattered when he stumbled over a tuft of grass and they tumbled to the ground together in fits of laughter. Their eyes met. Laughter disappeared. Hers became adoring; his filled with love and desire. Lost in a world of their own, Lucy's and Philip's lips came together.

'Come on, you two, picnic's waiting!' George's shout shattered the moment.

Laughing again, they scrambled to their feet and came to sit beside their friends. Light-hearted conversation accompanied good food and wine until Lucy and Philip stretched out on the grass and Marie silently indicated to George that they should leave. They drifted away to walk beside the stream.

Lucy and Philip, fingers gently entwined, lay side by side looking up at the canopy of blue that enclosed their silent world of contentment. Completely relaxed, Lucy was startled when eventually Philip broke the silence.

'I have to go to Calais on Tuesday.'

She sat up and twisted round to face him. 'Not again! How long this time?'

'I'll be back on Friday.' He saw disappointment in her eyes and added quickly, 'I'm sorry, my love, but it's my job. The firm needs me to keep my eye on some recent investments there.'

Lucy shrugged her shoulders. 'I suppose it can't be helped. But I'll miss you.'

'I'll miss you too.' He reached out and pulled her gently to him. He kissed her and said, 'Don't think about it any more. Enjoy the rest of the day.'

She smiled wanly, kissed him and lay down on her back to stare at the sky and wish that his work kept him in Paris all the time.

'Unless there are any other avenues to explore in Leeds after seeing Mr Hirst, I should be back in a couple of days.' Edward embraced his mother, picked up his bag and left the house for the station. With a sketchbook and a copy of *The Master of Ballantrae* by R.L. Stevenson in his pockets he was prepared for the train journey that would take him to Scarborough, York and finally Leeds.

The weather deteriorated the further away he moved from the coast. Though it was not raining when he emerged from Leeds station, he hoped the prevailing gloom was not a portent of his mission. He paused to scan the immediate area. Spotting a line of cabs, some of which were already being commandeered by train passengers, he hurried to join the queue.

He was soon being whisked through the busy streets. Observing people going about their daily lives, he wondered if any of them had ever been on a mission similar to his. He guessed there would be some who had never known their father, possibly were not even interested in tracing him, but he needed to know the man from whom he had inherited his artistic talent.

The cab began to slow and, glancing at the row of buildings on his left, Edward realised they were near his destination. The cab came to stop in front of a shop that had a couple of paintings displayed in the window. He dismounted, paid the driver, and, as the cab drove away, turned to survey the building. It was in need of repainting. The letters above the window were faded and the only word he could make out was the name 'Hirst'. He had difficulty deciphering that, but it was sufficient to tell him that this was where he wanted to be. He looked in the window which was badly in need of cleaning. The two paintings were only mediocre and displayed as if nobody much cared about them. Surely this was not the place where his father had sold his paintings? Surely those surroundings would have been more salubrious to attract potential customers to the calibre of works he knew his father produced? Yet there was the name Hirst, and this was the address he had been given. There was only one course of action to take. Edward pushed open the door and stepped inside. A bell tinkled as he shut the door behind him.

He found himself in a gloomy room with a counter on the left that needed dusting. Several paintings hung on the wall but they were not displayed to the best advantage; some hung crookedly, others had frames that did nothing to enhance the work within. He felt a qualm of disappointment flood over him.

He heard voices in a room above and then footsteps clattered down the stairs that led into the shop. A man appeared whom he judged to be in his late-forties whereas the man he wanted to see, the man who had handled his father's paintings, would be much older. The man's clothes were worn and his expression sullen. Edward reckoned customers would be put off even if they had got beyond looking in the window.

'Good day.' He made his tone pleasant, hoping to gain the man's interest.

His reply was little more than a grunt while he waited for Edward to continue.

'Mr Ebenezer Hirst?'

'No,' the man replied sharply. 'I'm Benjamin. My father's Ebenezer.'

'Is it possible to see him?'

'What for? I can sell you a painting if that is what you want. I run this business now.'

Not very successfully, thought Edward. It must have been better in my father's day. He said, 'I am making enquiries about a painter whose work your father used to sell.'

'Who might that be?'

'Arthur Newton.'

Benjamin looked to the ceiling in despair. 'I'm sick of hearing his name. My father goes on and on about him.'

'Then he may be able to help me.'

'It will help me if you talk to him and it gets Arthur Newton out of his system!'

'Then I can see him?'

'I'll fetch him.'

Edward waited patiently as he heard Benjamin inform his father that there was a man to see him. He heard Ebenezer protesting but when his son mentioned the name Arthur Newton, Edward heard a shuffling across the floor in the direction of the stairs. Benjamin appeared first regulating his pace to that of the man who followed him, a precaution lest Ebenezer slipped.

Edward watched a bent figure negotiate the stairs with a walking stick in one hand. He grunted as if there was pain for him at every step. He reached the floor safely and straightened as much as he could in order to see Edward better. He peered through narrowed eyes as if trying hard to pierce the gloom and bring the man who had come to see him into focus. He shuffled nearer.

'You ask about Arthur Newton?' His voice was strong in contrast to his physical appearance. His clothes, worn and soiled, hung on him. When they were new they must have fitted a bigger man and now gave the impression that Ebenezer Hirst was wasting away, from either illness or neglect. Edward would take a bet that it was largely the latter. He would normally have berated any man who neglected his father so but it was not in his interest to speak up now.

'Yes, sir. I am Edward Clayton and I come from Whitby.' He saw a flash of interest in the old man's eyes at the mention of Whitby.

'You knew him?' The eagerness in the old man's question was only momentary. Ebenezer gave a little irritated shake of his head. 'How could you, you are too young.'

'I would like to know anything you can tell me about him.' Edward had not yet decided how much he should reveal about himself.

'A great deal.'

'I'll leave you two to it,' Benjamin put in, and glanced at Edward with a look that showed he thought him a fool for getting his father started on a topic that was close to his heart. 'I've heard it all so many times.'

Edward gave him a curt nod and watched him leave.

Ebenezer said nothing until he heard a door close upstairs. Edward sensed the old man relax then. 'Come.' He shuffled towards a door at the back of the shop. He opened it and Edward followed him into the room beyond. Three walls were covered with paintings. Ebenezer pointed at two, drawing Edward's attention to them.

'Arthur Newtons!' Edward gasped.

'Aye.' The old man gave a nod of satisfaction that Edward had recognised Arthur Newton's work. Pride shone in his eyes. 'Two of his best paintings! The last two I had from him. I didn't know at the time that they would be, of course, so I'm more than pleased that I bought them myself. Yon scallywag,' he pointed to the ceiling with his stick, 'has wanted to sell them oftentimes but I'll not let him. That's one thing I've put my foot down about and I'll not move it.' Determination and defiance had come into his voice.

'They are wonderful,' commented Edward, his tone full of admiration. 'You say that these were the last two you had, why were there no more?'

'Let me say briefly that Arthur was born and bred in Leeds. I discovered his talent – it's an interesting story if you ever have time to return – he married and had a daughter. He gave up his job on the railway to paint and the family moved to Scarborough. Arthur continued to supply me with paintings, all of which I was able to sell. He remained loyal to me, keeping a promise he made when I sold his first one.'

'Then why were there no more after those two?'

'I can only think that he stopped painting.'

'Why would he do that?'

'I can't be sure, I can only speculate. The family left Scarborough because of his wife's ill health. They went south.'

'Did he not tell you where?'

'No. It seemed he wanted to disappear. I did receive several paintings after the move but they were always sent by carrier. Arthur never brought them himself. When these two came I had a premonition there would be no more so bought them.'

'Did you try to get in touch with him?'

'Aye, of course I did, but it was no use. I could never find out where he was.'

'And you don't know what happened to his family?'

'No.'

'You don't know whether they are alive or not?'

'No.'

'You say they moved because his wife was ill. How serious was it?'

'I don't know. All I know is that they were advised to move to a warmer place than the Yorkshire coast. Somewhere that didn't catch the cold northerlies.'

'You have not mentioned Whitby, sir.'

'Ah, Whitby! The family never lived there but it was the inspiration for some of his best paintings, not just of the town itself but others that he was painting at the same time. When his association with the place waned, his paintings lost that touch of brilliance, became workmanlike, mundane . . . a great shame. I tell you, my boy, that there was a period when Arthur Newton's immense talent shone from every painting.'

'But why didn't it shine from every one?'

'Young man, there are all sorts of things that can affect a man's artistic output and the disruption of domestic harmony can be a very big factor.'

'You are saying there was upheaval in his family?'

Ebenezer raised his hands. 'I don't know and it is wrong to speculate. Now, what of you? What is your interest in Arthur Newton?'

With Ebenezer's final observation, Edward had decided not to reveal his true reason for being here. 'I'm writing a series of articles about today's artists. Arthur Newton is on my list. I haven't been able to trace him and, hearing that you once handled his paintings, I thought you might know where he is.'

'I'm afraid I don't, but I can tell you a lot about him. Maybe that would help with your article.'

'I'm sure it would,' said Edward, seeing a chance to learn more about his father. 'I can stay in Leeds for a few days if necessary. May I come back tomorrow and talk to you?'

'Of course you can. I'll be pleased to tell you what I know.'

Edward sensed the old man was delighted to have found someone interested in Arthur Newton. There was excitement in the way he called to his son and told him that Edward would be returning tomorrow at ten o'clock.

'Now I have someone who is really interested and will listen to everything . . .'

'All right, Father. Don't go on so. Calm down.'

'But you don't know what this means to me. I discovered Arthur Newton. Mr Clayton is going to write about him. I'll be shown to be his mentor and Arthur will receive recognition as the great artist he is. Maybe it will spur him on to paint again.'

'You don't know that he's stopped, Father.'

'Of course he's stopped,' snapped Ebenezer. 'If he hadn't, he would still have been sending me pictures.' He turned to Edward. 'Don't be late, young man, I've a lot to tell you.'

By the time Edward approached the shop the next morning he had decided he would keep his word and write an article for a newspaper or magazine. It might result in his father revealing his whereabouts, especially if he was able to quote Ebenezer.

This decision put him in a buoyant mood as he tried the shop door only to find it locked. Puzzled, he stepped back and surveyed the frontage but detected no sign of life either downstairs or upstairs. He knocked harder and was relieved when a few moments later he heard bolts being drawn and a key being turned. When the door swung open a sombre Benjamin met him.

Sensing something was not quite right, Edward's 'Good morning' was tentative and querying.

'Come in.' Benjamin's voice was a monotone as he shuffled to one side to allow Edward to step inside. He closed the door and turned to his visitor. 'I've bad news. Father died during the night.'

Shock rendered Edward speechless. This couldn't be true; only yesterday he had spoken to Mr Hirst . . .

'Heart attack,' Benjamin went on. 'He got too excited at the prospect of talking to you about Arthur Newton.'

'I'm devastated,' said Edward. 'Truly sorry if I played any part in the tragedy. Maybe I shouldn't have asked for his help when I saw he was a frail old man. I don't know what . . .'

Benjamin stopped him. 'I don't blame you in any way. Father should have been able to control his excitement at the age of eighty-four. I am only sorry you haven't got your story.'

'Maybe I'll find someone else who knew him,' Edward answered lamely. He started to turn away when Benjamin spoke again.

'Mr Clayton, you are obviously interested in Arthur Newton and no doubt my father showed you the two paintings we have of his.'

'Yes, he did.'

'Would you be interested in buying them?'

For a moment Edward was speechless. His father but a few hours dead, and already Benjamin Hirst was grasping this opportunity to make some money. He was on the point of showing his disgust when he reminded himself that here was a chance that might not come again, for he was sure Benjamin would sell the business as soon as possible; it had been obvious from Edward's visit yesterday that he had no interest in it. 'Yes, I would,' he replied.

'Then there's no time like the present,' said Benjamin.

Within twenty minutes Edward left the shop carrying the two paintings.

'What have you got there?' Colette asked curiously when her son arrived home with what were obviously canvases that had been carefully wrapped for transportation.

'A present for you, Mother.' He carried the paintings into the drawing room where they were unveiled with care. The first one was *Roundhay Park, Leeds*. They both stood admiring it for a few minutes and then turned to the second; this was entitled *Mending the Nets, Whitby*. There was a special spark about its execution that raised it above the level of the first one. Something he had not initially noticed in the gloom of the shop but which was now immediately obvious in the afternoon light.

'Wonderful,' said Edward quietly.

Concentrating on the picture, he did not notice his mother determinedly wipe a tear from her eye in the aftermath of the memory the painting had brought flooding back. She recalled the day when she had photographed this very scene though in a different context to Arthur's interpretation. It had been a happy day they had shared. A day of dreams, rudely shattered and destroyed so soon afterwards. As those bitter memories welled inside her she almost told Edward to get rid of the painting but pulled herself up short. That would be unkind and would need further explanation. She was not prepared to do that and destroy her son's good opinion of his father. She would bury the bad memories and keep the better ones.

Colette kissed her son on the cheek. 'Thank you. Now tell me what you learned.'

Edward did so while they enjoyed a cup of tea.

Colette was shocked to learn of Ebenezer's death and sorry that Edward felt in some way to blame. She assured him that no stigma could be attached to his actions. 'So what is your next move?' she enquired, knowing full well that her son would continue his search and there was no use trying to persuade him otherwise.

'Well, we know he moved his family to the south coast.'

'So you are thinking of going there?' He nodded in reply. 'But where will you start?

'I don't know yet, Mother. I was hoping there might be a clue in what Mr Hirst was going to tell me, but that hope has vanished. I'll have to give some thought to my next line of enquiry.'

Chapter Eight

Philip stepped from the coach, adjusted his jacket and smoothed the lapels as he surveyed the scene; a sea of people hurrying, sauntering, standing, gossiping, studying, searching. Different voices, different accents, different tones mingled to rise and fall and be swept away on the gentle breeze, leaving behind the unmistakable atmosphere of people determined to enjoy themselves on a day out at the races. He cast his eyes over the array of fine clothes, appreciating especially those adorning the attractive females.

The bright blue sky dotted with white clouds over Longchamps had brought out a colourful display of the latest fashions. The English taste for gored skirts was beginning to predominate and Philip approved of the extra freedom it gave to the wearers, enhancing their movement in a way that, generally, they were not slow to exploit. Cotton, muslin and silk predominated in shades of red, pink and blue. Here and there splashes of green added variety. Colourful parasols were carried unfurled with equal impact, protecting delicate complexions against the sun. An atmosphere of relaxed enjoyment permeated the whole scene and, as Philip weaved his way among the milling crowd, he acknowledged acquaintances, recognising them as regular racegoers. He paused to talk to more intimate friends and exchange tips for the forthcoming races. All the time his eyes were searching though this was not obvious to those to whom he was talking. Then, his gaze resting on a particular group of four young men, he made his excuses to his latest companions.

He moved through the crowd with a suave nonchalance, pausing only to have a quick word with Monsieur Magalon, a racehorse owner with whom, over the past two years, he had cultivated a friendly relationship.

'Good day, Philip, thought you weren't coming,' was the first remark when he eventually greeted the four young men who were all about his age.

'You escaped the little lady's clutches then.'

'What would she say if she knew you weren't really in Calais?'

'Why don't you bring her along sometime?'

The banter from his four friends ran along the usual lines.

'What, and put her at the mercy of wolves like you?'

'We'd gobble her up.'

'And I'd lose the love of my life.'

'Oh, what are all your other paramours going to say to that?'

'They can say what they like. I'm a reformed character.'

That raised a roar of laughter. 'What? *You*, reformed?'

'Certainly.'

'Don't tell me you weren't flirting with Madame Magalon?'

'That's all in the line of business. Please Magalon's wife and you please him. Then he'll more readily part with information, or she'll wheedle it out of him and pass it on.'

'So what did you learn?'

'Bonhomie will be running in the two o'clock. Lady of Aquataine in the three o'clock. Bonhomie is a certainty, the other less so but worth a place bet.'

'Then let's get down to the serious business of the afternoon and find a few more runners we fancy.'

The afternoon went well for the five friends. They ranged around the stands with a *joie de vivre* that was familiar to many of the race-goers. These young acquaintances of Philip's lived on the fringe of the racing world, well connected and liked. They were not averse to placing large bets and were equable in temperament whether they lost or won. Philip was a bit wary about trying to match them in this. He knew they were all from wealthy families and that their fathers made them generous allowances – more than his, certainly – but he managed to put on a front when he was with them that eased when he won. As win he must!

Lucy would have money when she inherited the farm and, though that had been foremost in his mind when he first met her and learned she was an only child with a widowed mother, he counted himself lucky that he had genuinely fallen in love with her and she with him.

Shortly before the fourth race, Emile, one of his friends, felt a touch on his arm while he was studying his card in order to place a bet.

'Blanche!' His surprise, evident in his expression and voice, attracted the attention of his companions.

They found themselves staring at someone they would one and all have described as the most exquisite creature they had ever seen. Her oval face was filled with a glowing smile that embraced them all yet each man there felt it was meant for him alone. Her eyes, nose and mouth were classically beautiful and enhanced by a delicate complexion. Her black dress was in marked contrast to the many bright colours around the racecourse, but its severity was eased by the fine circular bands of cerise velvet that ran its full length from the high neck to the hem of the skirt flaring slightly from a tight waist. The sleeves, with only the slightest of puffs at the shoulders, ran tight to the wrist. She wore white gloves and carried a long-handled parasol. Her hat was large and flounced with feathers but she had positioned it so that it did not detract from her copper-coloured hair and enhanced her beauty by framing her face. Her only other adornment was a heart-shaped pendant suspended on a long silver chain at waist length. Philip realised she wore black because it made an elegant counterfoil to her figure and posture.

'My dear Blanche, I did not expect to see you here.'

Emile's glance at her dress was not lost upon her and she realised his inference. 'Emile, my period of mourning is over. Black becomes me, it's one of my favourite colours, so here I am.' She spread her arms as if to embrace them all as she revelled in the effect she was having then cast a questioning look at Emile. 'Aren't you going to introduce me and then these poor boys can relax?'

'Oh . . . Oh . . . Yes, of course,' he spluttered. 'Gentlemen, Blanche Daudet, a cousin on my mother's side. Blanche, my friends Auguste, Jules, Victor and Philip.'

She accepted each bow with a slight inclination of her head. 'I am pleased to meet you all,' she said in a soft caressing voice. Each man felt that he came under close scrutiny as he was introduced even though the moment passed quickly. Blanche's hazel-coloured eyes shone with tempestuous challenge.

Philip's mind was racing with admiration for this beauty that confronted him and at the same time trying to set the fascination aside in order to concentrate on her identity. Daudet? The name tinkled a bell in the back of his mind. Faint though it was, it was there. He needed to know more. 'Emile, where have you kept this wonderful creature hidden?' he asked.

'Blanche lives in the South of France, close to Marseilles, where her husband ran a large trading venture with the Eastern Mediterranean and beyond.'

That identified her for Philip. He recalled reading of the death of Monsieur Daudet eighteen months ago. His widow must be a very rich woman.

His thoughts were interrupted by Blanche herself. 'And you, Philip, what do you fancy for this race?'

'Er . . .' He forced his mind back to the present and realised the others were on their way to place their bets. He glanced at his card. 'Moon Wind.'

She gave an approving chuckle. 'That's what I told the others but at thirty-to-one they wouldn't have it. So, let's you and I place our bets and show them whose right.'

On their way to do so Philip asked, 'What makes you so sure, with odds like that? Or is it just the gambling streak in you?'

She gave a little shake of her head. 'I have no inside knowledge, if that's what you are thinking. If I get a hunch, and that's all this is, then I follow it. What about you? Why did you choose it?'

'Like you, intuition, and I like the odds.'

'You like a gamble?'

'Yes.'

'Are you a winner or loser?'

'In the long run a winner.' He wasn't going to tell her that at times his situation was precarious.

'Cards?'

'Yes, and the tables. But I prefer the races. I don't like the confines of the card tables. And with the horses you can study form. Cards, well, there's always that element of blind luck.'

'Isn't there in all gambling?'

'I suppose so but I like to shorten the odds.'

She gave a little laugh. 'What of the odds on Moon Wind?'

'Well, they are shortened in our favour – we are both following our intuitive streak.'

When Philip was placing his bet she studied him. Her initial impression upon first joining the group was confirmed. This certainly was a handsome man. And his clothes, of the best quality, did not hide an athletic body. He had the air of a man who knew how to handle himself and generated an aura that drew people's attention. She had also been struck by his manners as he had escorted her through the crowd. He rejoined her and they were about to set out to find the others when Blanche placed a hand on his arm and stopped him.

'I'm in Paris for a week. Would you like to show me the gambling tables?'

Though he was a little taken aback by this direct approach Philip did not show it and answered quickly, 'That would be my pleasure and privilege.'

'Good. I will be in Paris the day after tomorrow. I'm staying with friends, Monsieur and Madame Mercier, at their residence on the rue de Chaillot. Call on me the day after that. And not a word to the others.'

Seeing Emile approaching, he gave a nod of understanding.

'Placed your bets?' asked his friend.

'Yes,' replied Philip. 'Moon Wind.'

'What? You followed Blanche's idea?'

'Why not?'

'Relying on feminine intuition! Good grief, what will you do next?'

'Walk away with some winnings.'

Emile laughed. 'You would if you made a bet for it to come in last!'

The exchanges stopped when the shout of 'They're off!' swept through the crowd.

For one moment doubt came into Philip's mind and anxiety gripped him. He had bet every franc he had. Excitement swept through the spectators as they called out the names of the horses on which they had placed their money. They urged them on, gesticulating with their arms as if they could push the horses into a faster pace.

Philip's cajoling stopped and turned into a moan of despair. Emile was right. Moon Wind was at the back. Blanche, standing next to Philip, heard his moan.

'The jockey will make his move in the next furlong,' she whispered close to his ear.

Hooves thundered on the turf; the crowds roared.

'There he goes! Come on, Moon Wind! Come on!' Blanche's call sharpened Philip's attention.

The horse had come wide from the back and was answering the jockey's call to become the sleek personification of released energy. It seemed to flow across the turf without touching it. Aware of its movement, the other jockeys urged their horses to respond, but Moon Wind would have none of it. One by one it overhauled the others until there were only two horses left, racing neck and neck for the finishing line. Philip and Blanche were shouting at the top of their voices, their bodies tense even though they were jumping up and down, all decorum banished for a few minutes in the roar of the crowd and the pulsating beat of the hooves. For one moment Philip feared he had lost all his money but then he was leaping in the air. As he touched the ground he grabbed Blanche and swung her round. 'We did it! We did it!'

She threw her head back and laughter rang from her lips.

'You should have followed feminine intuition,' grinned Philip at the sight of his friends' gloomy faces.

'They'd better look happier tonight when they dine with me,' smiled Blanche. 'You won't say no to that, will you? Seven o'clock at the Restaurant Rose. Come on, Philip, *we'll* go and collect our winnings.' She cast a mischievous glance at the others as she emphasised that word. 'Did you make a killing?' she asked as they walked away.

He grinned. 'I did. I put everything I had on it.'

Blanche raised an eyebrow. 'That was a bit risky, wasn't it?'

He shook his head. 'No. I had every faith in you.'

'Let's hope that faith, or rather mine in you, continues at the tables when we test our luck again.'

Blanche insisted on entertaining the five young men lavishly. Like all gamblers she did not disclose the amount of her winnings but it was obvious that it had been substantial.

Philip found her fascinating and intriguing, with a charm that could be woven tightly around any man she chose. Victor and Auguste she teased and they loved her for it. Jules, who was closer to Emile, she charmed to the point where he swore to himself that he was in love with her and felt disappointed when she, recognising the stage his feelings had rapidly reached, held him at arm's length in a way that did not wound him. She sensed that Emile was pleased that his cousin had come back into his life and determined that she should never drift out of it again.

The mood around the table was relaxed and convivial in the presence of good company, good food and exceptional wine. Blanche sipped at her wine and let her eyes come to rest on Philip. He intrigued her. She prided herself on being a good judge of men but there was something about this handsome young gentleman that she had been unable to put her finger on. He was good company, charming, thoughtful, maybe a little too suave and gushing . . . as if he was frightened of offending? She had noticed that sometimes his attention on what was happening around him drifted away and, at such moments, a dreamy thoughtful haze covered his eyes. She wondered where he went then. Intrigued, she wanted to know more about him, but she would not pry. She had found that knowledge of a person had a way of revealing itself to her.

She had learned earlier in the day from Emile, without direct questioning, that Philip was working in Paris for the family investment firm with headquarters in Switzerland. If he was able to live in the style he projected he must be well paid or else a successful gambler. That supposition heightened her interest in him because she, in her heart of hearts, was a gambler not only at the races and tables but also in life.

When she had married she had had little and her husband was

only a small-time merchant. Ever ready to trust her instincts, Blanche had persuaded him to gamble first in the spice trade. Everything they had had been invested in one shipload. They had never looked back and their empire had built up quickly. Too quickly for her husband, for the work and responsibility that came with it brought on a devastating heart attack. A few days later the vultures hovered. Blanche played one off against the other and when she finally sold the business she was a very rich widow. Now, her mourning period over, she had emerged from her cocoon of sorrow to do what her husband had always insisted they do – enjoy life. And part of that enjoyment was gambling, something she would do without being reckless. Her money had been too hard won at a terrible cost to go down that road.

As her eyes rested on Philip she wondered if she had found a kindred soul? But caution tempered her thoughts for she sensed that he might be reckless, particularly if he had to chase money to pay for his lifestyle. His lifestyle? She wondered if that might be a front too, and what lay behind the dreamy look that had just passed across his face. Love? She was curious. Who could capture the heart of such a man? What kind of woman?

She would have received a jolt had she been able to see that person now: Lucy, hair askew, her painter's apron daubed by splashes as she vigorously applied paint to the large canvas standing on her easel in the atelier.

Marie, who had chosen to stay behind with Lucy that evening in order to finish her own painting, smiled to herself but reckoned she might be feeling the same if George was leaving Paris as often as Philip was lately.

Lucy had complained to Marie about it and, as exasperation grew into annoyance, painted with yet more venom.

'Does that help?' Marie asked after a while.

Lucy, dashing a broad streak of red across the top half of the painting, as a prelude to working it into a sunset, was only then aware that Marie had spoken. She started. 'What was that?'

'I asked if it helped?'

'If it helped what?'

'Painting with such force. Does it help to get Philip out of your system?'

Lucy stared at her friend for a few moments; the implications of what she had been doing dawned on her. She grinned sheepishly and then began to laugh. 'I hadn't realised I was venting my annoyance. But I was.'

Marie smiled. 'I thought not. So let's see the result.' She left her painting and came to view Lucy's. They stood side by side in silent study. The minutes passed and then Marie said, 'I think you have found a new method if you want to bring the power of upheaval into a painting – have strong feelings about something you want to get off your mind and then start your picture.'

'Mmm,' said Lucy thoughtfully. 'I wonder what Monsieur Bedeaux would say to that.'

'Ah, Mademoiselle,' Marie imitated their tutor and spread her hands in a hopeless gesture, 'the work of a frail temperament. Control and technique – they must be your watchwords.'

The friends burst into hysterics and that was the end of painting for the day.

As they walked back to the apartment Lucy brought up the question of the forthcoming Easter break. 'Are you going home?' she asked.

Marie gave a thoughtful grimace. 'I suppose I should, Father will be expecting me.'

'But it's such a short break.'

'I know. In some ways it would be wiser to stay here. We'd be able to get on top of our work and it would save money. George has almost made up his mind to stay.'

'Doesn't that sway you to do the same?'

'I suppose it does, but then I think of Father.'

'I'm sure he would understand. I feel the same way about Mother but . . .'

'The pull of Philip is much stronger?' Marie finished for her.

'Yes.'

'Then let's decide, here and now, we'll stay,' said Marie with finality.

'It's settled,' agreed Lucy with equal authority. 'We'll write to them straight away.'

114

She might have tempered her decision had she known that at that very moment Philip was back in Paris and calling at an imposing residence on rue de Chaillot.

Following protocol, he had sent a note earlier in the day to Madame Daudet seeking her permission to call on her. He knew that she would infer his real intention was for her to accompany him to the gambling tables. With this in mind he had hired a Victoria and driver for the evening and now, seated comfortably, was being driven to the Merciers' residence.

He was expected and the butler who admitted him showed him to a small drawing room where guests could be received. It was tastefully decorated and furnished without being elaborate. He was admiring two watercolours on the wall when the door opened. He swung round and only just succeeded in stifling a gasp of surprise that would have been regarded as bad manners, but Blanche had been aware of the effect she had had on him and was pleased.

Her dress of black surah had a high neck from which fell a jabot of white lace. Matching lace adorned the cuffs of the tight sleeves that swept unhampered from the shoulders. The skirt fell from the tight-fitting waist, shot with white embroidery that gave way to a more elaborate pattern as it neared the hem. She had draped a lace shawl over her copper-coloured hair and flung its ends around her shoulders to frame her face. The simplicity of this presentation directed the onlooker's attention to her elegance and beauty.

'Philip,' she greeted him, holding her hands out to him.

'Blanche,' he replied in a tone that was scarcely above a whisper, so stunned was he by the charisma of the woman he would be proud to escort to the gaming tables tonight. He took her hands and raised them to his lips. 'May I say how beautiful you look?'

She inclined her head in acknowledgement and gave a little smile but her eyes sparkled. He was not sure if there was a touch of amusement in their expression. 'Monsieur and Madame Mercier send their apologies but they had a prior engagement. However, they hope to meet you and, if you are free the night after tomorrow, you are invited to dinner.'

'Please thank them for me and say I will be delighted to accept.'

The rapport he had struck up with Blanche at the races was helping him move into circles from which he might profit. The Merciers were well-known property dealers. Could he not make discreet use of their expertise to advance his own funds? Well, he would see.

'After that you will have only another full day here?' he commented.

'Ah.' Her eyes twinkled. 'You are keeping a check on my time.'

'Who wouldn't on such a beautiful vision?'

'You are a flatterer. But to answer your question – yes, that is when I return home. But if all goes well this evening we can have another night at the tables tomorrow, and again the evening before I return home.' She turned towards the door and said over her shoulder, 'Who knows? Maybe it won't be long before I return to Paris.'

He dwelt on that hint as he escorted her to the Victoria. As attractive, glamorous and sophisticated as Blanche was, a woman who could turn heads and hearts, Lucy's simple, down-to-earth enjoyment of life and love of people, especially him, were foremost in his mind. The fact that she could invade even these moments revealed Philip's true love for her.

When the driver saw that they were comfortably seated he took his place and sent the 'night horse' on its way. He had already received his instructions from Philip and was delighted to be driving such an elegant, eye-catching couple. A beautiful lady and a handsome man were sure to catch the attention of the other drivers bringing gamblers to the tables of Château Royal, four miles out of Paris.

As she stepped out of the Victoria, Blanche eyed the building with a critical eye. Though it was almost dark by now she was able to make out the ornate Empire Period façade.

'It once belonged to the Laroche family, rich landowners beheaded during the Revolution. The remodelled château eventually came into the hands of an unsavoury character who saw his chance of pandering to the nouveau riche in search of excitement. His reputation at the time could have spelled rigged tables but he saw that would not pay in the long run. He reformed and is now the most charming of hosts and attracts people not only from Paris but a much wider area, especially when there are race meetings in the vicinity.' While he had been offering this explanation Philip had escorted Blanche towards the imposing entrance.

An immaculately dressed footman opened the door, greeting Philip with a touch of familiarity though he was the model of decorum when Philip introduced his guest.

'It is a pleasure to welcome you, madame. I hope you will have a pleasant evening.' He turned and gave a signal to one of three young women, attired in close-fitting, ankle-length black dresses. The only relief to their severe attire was a white heart-shaped brooch pinned at the right breast. Each woman's hair was drawn up from the back of the neck and piled on top of her head with not one hair out of place.

'Follow me, madame,' the young woman said politely. 'I am Renee. If you need anything throughout your visit please ask for me.' She escorted Blanche to the powder room where she freshened her make-up, little though she wore, for she really had no need to enhance her beauty.

When she returned to the entrance hall she found Philip waiting for her. 'You look exquisite,' he said quietly. 'I'm sure heads will turn when we make our entrance.'

She made no comment but felt a charge of excitement as they walked towards the imposing double doors flanked by two footmen. She could already feel the atmosphere of the gaming room and felt an urge to chance her luck.

'Good evening, madam, sir,' the footmen greeted them as they opened the doors which, in spite of their size, swung easily.

The large room was awash with the quiet buzz of conversation though it was kept to a minimum as people concentrated on their cards or the roulette wheels.

'We'll walk around and observe for a few minutes,' advised Philip quietly, sensing the eagerness in Blanche to start gambling. 'Then make our choice.'

He escorted her round the tables, pausing at each one to note the state of play and the amounts being risked by the players. He nodded a greeting to friends and acquaintances without speaking, not wishing to break their concentration, but it did give him satisfaction to see that not one of them ignored the elegant lady he escorted.

After ten minutes Blanche indicated that she had made up her mind. 'Let's get our chips, we'll play the central roulette table.'

'Ah, the biggest returns,' smiled Philip.

'Why not? Let's go for a killing. I feel lucky.'

'If you are then I will be.'

They collected their chips and within five minutes were taking two places vacated by a man and his wife who were down on their luck.

Philip made no comment when he saw where Blanche had placed her bet. He followed suit, keeping to the same small amount. That was a fortunate move for the ball did not settle right for them. He saw Blanche was not deterred and followed her next bet which again was lost. He raised a questioning eyebrow at her but she merely gave him a whimsical smile in return and placed her bet on the same number then proceeded to place a substantial bet on red. He hesitated a moment, trying to decide if he should spread their bets by placing his elsewhere but followed her just as the croupier made his final call.

His eyes were transfixed by the ball as it rolled around the spinning wheel which slowed and allowed it to make its final bounce and settle. Philip's eyes, still on the ball, widened. It had nestled exactly where they wanted it. Excitement surged through him. He turned to Blanche and saw that she showed no emotion – the mark of a true gambler. Who had he latched on to? He liked to gamble but had never been able to control his emotions like Blanche. She appeared ice-cool and was proceeding to make her next selection as if to say, That bet is over. Now we make another.

So the evening proceeded; the small bets were losers but the larger brought their rewards. It was after one of the latter failed that Blanche called a halt. 'Our luck here has changed,' she whispered. 'We'll try the cards.' Once again she studied the tables before making her choice. She waited while one gentleman finally gave up chasing his losses then took his place. She looked over her shoulder at Philip who bent to hear her whispered words: 'I'll play for us both, doubling the bet I would have placed so we'll be in it together. Unless you don't trust me?'

'My faith in you is implicit,' he replied. 'How could it not be after that roulette?'

She smiled and patted his hand which he had rested on her shoulder to reassure her that he approved of whatever she did.

He watched, fascinated by the way she played her cards, manoeuvred and bluffed. She seemed to have an uncanny knack of knowing when to make a low bet or a more ambitious one and when the cards would fall in her favour. By the time she withdrew she had doubled their money.

'Your intuition is amazing,' commented Philip as he escorted her from the table.

Blanche smiled. 'I've always been lucky. Now, I noticed a dining room when we arrived. I think we can afford dinner.'

He laughed. 'We certainly can, and champagne to celebrate.'

'Why not?' she agreed.

'That was a wonderful evening,' he said as the Victoria stopped at the Mercier residence. 'Thank you for being my companion this evening.'

'It is I who should thank you. Without you I would never have found the Château Royal and made a very nice profit.'

'You previously suggested that we should do it again tomorrow. Do you still want to?'

'Yes.'

'The same place or another?'

'You know of more?'

'Oh, yes.'

'Then let us see if we can do the same elsewhere.'

As Philip lay on his bed his mind dwelt on the amazing woman with whom he had spent the evening. Lady Luck certainly dwelt on her shoulders, but would she always do so? There was a small fortune lying on his bedside table. What might it be tomorrow at this time? More or less? He couldn't bear to contemplate the latter. With Blanche beside him, it must be more. But what would happen when she returned home? His talisman would be gone. Something might come out of the Merciers' dinner party . . . but maybe he had better not bank on that; maybe the land in England that Lucy would inherit was the better bet. It was she he truly loved, but Blanche fascinated him.

Chapter Nine

Arthur picked up the letter from the mat inside the front door. He recognised Marie's writing and tore open the envelope, eager to read her latest news. He counted himself fortunate that he had a daughter who wrote regularly and kept him up to date with her art studies and her life in Paris. No doubt this letter would be just as chatty. He hoped it contained her plans for Easter. He liked to have something to look forward to, and this year they would celebrate the news he and Isobel would break to Marie and Lucy.

He started to read, devoured the news of her painting progress, chuckled at the latest bicycle escapade, and was pleased that she was enjoying a life in which George was still playing an important part. But disappointment overwhelmed him when he read: 'Papa, it is such a short break at Easter that it does not seem worth the expense of coming home. Lucy feels the same so we have decided to stay here. It will also enable us to get ahead with our work. I am sorry and I will miss you but I hope you will understand.'

He wandered slowly into the drawing room and sank on to a chair. Dazed by the news, he was unaware of the sunlight streaming through the window. Before the letter's arrival he had sat here seeing its brightness as a symbol of the joy of having Marie at home when the house would come alive. This would be the very first Easter without her. He felt bereft. How long he sat there staring without seeing he did not know, but he was shaken out of his stupor by a thought that struck him sharply. He was being selfish. Marie had her own life to lead. He should not expect her to travel home whenever she was free from work. He had encouraged her to go to Paris. The city had its attractions. She had always enthused about how much she liked it and wanted to explore more of it. This would give her the opportunity. What of George? He glanced at the letter again and realised he had not finished it. The final sentences told him that George was staying in Paris too. Now he knew there was an added incentive for her not to come home. He dismissed the pang of jealousy, annoyed with himself for feeling it. He should be delighted that his daughter was happy.

But what of the plans he and Isobel had made for breaking the news that they were going to marry? They had decided to tell the girls over a special dinner at Easter that they would marry in the summer when Marie and Lucy were home again. But what now? He pondered a moment then stood up. He must see Isobel.

The walk to Cherry Hill, skirting the boundaries of fields lush with grass, nearing the cliff edge with views over the sea that took his mind to imaginary faraway places, was always a pleasure but today that was tempered by the disappointing news from Marie.

Negotiating the last twist in the path that revealed the house, he saw Isobel sitting on a garden seat placed to the right of the terrace so that it caught the sun for most of the day.

She saw him, raised a hand, rose from the seat and came to meet him. Even from this distance he could sense her despondency. She was not holding herself as she usually did; her shoulders drooped a little and her step did not have its habitual briskness. He knew she also must have received a letter from Paris. As they drew closer he saw the disappointment in her eyes and sorrow in her weak smile.

'Hello, Arthur,' she said quietly, without the usual briskness to her tone. 'No doubt you have received one of these?' She held up a sheet of paper.

He kissed her lightly on the cheek and then answered. 'If that is from Lucy saying that she is not coming home for Easter, then yes, I have received the same message from Marie.'

'And no doubt you are as deeply disappointed as I am?'

He nodded. 'Yes, particularly after what we had planned.'

'Do we write and tell them we want them home for a special reason?'

He took her arm and they started to stroll towards the house. 'I thought we might do that but dismissed the idea. I understand

121

their reasons and I would not like them to think that we are making decisions for them. We let them go, we must let them stand on their own two feet.'

'I suspect that there are young men in the offing.'

'No doubt that has something to do with their decision. After all, Marie and George do seem to be getting along well, and from what you have told me Lucy seems smitten by this Philip.'

'So what of our plans to break the news to them?'

'I've given it some thought. I would still like to tell them face to face. What about you?'

'I most certainly would prefer that.'

'Then we shall go to Paris. That is, if you can spare the time?'

'Of course I can. My manager is capable of looking after things. He has my trust and has little need to consult me.'

'Good. Then we shall go.'

As an expected guest, Philip was quickly admitted to the Merciers' residence. He had been in the small room for receiving guests only a few moments when the door opened and Blanche appeared. Though dressed similarly to the style she had worn the previous evening, this dress was sufficiently different to emphasise her exquisite taste in clothes and colour, everything combining to accentuate her figure.

'Philip.' She extended her hands to him and offered her cheek for a kiss. 'Madame and Monsieur Mercier would like to meet you. They will be here in a moment.'

The door opened and a small dignified lady entered, bringing with her an aura of peacefulness that immediately permeated the room. It put Philip at ease even though he felt himself come under the scrutiny of her piercing eyes. He realised that here was a concerned and attentive hostess. He received the same impression from the man who followed her. Slightly built, he held himself erect and the hair that was greying at his temples emphasised his air of distinction. Having done some checking, Philip knew Monsieur Mercier was in his late sixties. He bore his age well and still showed how handsome he must have been in his younger days.

'Monsieur Jaurès.' Madame Mercier gave him a smile that was warm but a little wary as if she held something back that might turn the smile into one of real approval.

'Madame.' Philip bowed as he took her hand and raised it to his lips. 'It is most kind of you to receive me.'

'Ah, Monsieur, we do so out of curiosity. We take a deep interest in our dear dear friend Blanche.'

Before she could say any more her husband stepped forward. 'Greetings, Monsieur.' His handshake was firm but his eyes were keen and Philip knew that he shared his wife's curiosity to know who was escorting their guest. Maybe they felt some responsibility for her while she was under their roof.

'Monsieur, it is a pleasure to meet you. And may I thank you both for the invitation to join you tomorrow evening?'

'After returning from Longchamp, Blanche spoke highly of you and, as she had no partner for the evening, it seemed the natural thing to do. The guest list was compiled before we knew we would have Blanche with us and comprises mostly my business associates, though there will be some friends who share our interest in opera.'

'Are you interested?' queried Madame Mercier.

Philip raised his hands in despair. 'Alas, I am not very knowledgeable,' he added quickly. 'But I am interested in art.'

'Ah, very commendable.' A twinkle came in to her eyes. 'We must discuss the modern trends. I will be interested to learn your opinion. Now, we must not keep you two young people any longer. Do enjoy your evening.'

Philip noticed that neither of the Merciers had asked where they were going. He wondered if Blanche had told them. If so, did they approve of her gambling? His curiosity was so strong he could not resist putting his questions to Blanche once they were seated in the carriage.

Laughter spilled from her lips. 'Oh, yes, they know I like to gamble, but they also know that I'm sensible about it. Though they are not gamblers themselves, they don't disapprove of it. Who could amidst the gaiety and love of life that permeate Paris?' She cocked her head. 'They wanted to cast their eyes over you to make sure that I wasn't being accompanied by an unscrupulous gambler who might be leading me astray or trying to part me from my money.'

'Do you think I passed with flying colours?'

'Without a doubt, after the way I built you up.'

'Thank you for that.'

'Oh, by the way, are you really interested in art?'

'Well . . .' He drew the word out and she knew the answer.

'I had better warn you that Madame Mercier will seek you out tomorrow evening for that discussion.'

'Oh, dear, then I've chosen the wrong subject.'

'You'd better do something about it.'

'I will.'

'Maybe I'd better hover and rescue you, if you give me a signal.'

'That would be appreciated. I'll pull my left ear, like this.'

She laughed. 'Don't use it frequently if she corners you more than once. It will look suspicious if I have to keep breaking into your discussion about modern art and all its trends.'

All thoughts of art, of which Philip knew very little, were banished in the excitement of another night at the roulette and card tables where once again Blanche showed her luck and skill. But once he had taken her back to the Merciers' a problem arose in his mind. He must have a crash course on art with Lucy tomorrow.

The following morning Philip was waiting outside Lucy's and Marie's apartment when they came out to go to their studies.

'Philip!' Lucy ran to him. 'I didn't know you were back in Paris.'

He smiled and kissed her on the cheek. 'I only got back late yesterday.'

'What are you doing here at this time?' She wiped the curiosity from her face. 'What a silly question! You are here to let me know you are back. Walk with me. Tell me we will meet later?'

'I'll go on.' Marie broke in.

'Oh, sorry, Marie,' replied Philip. 'Hello.'

She smiled. 'No need for apologies from lovesick people. See you later, Lucy.'

'Well, what about later on?' asked Lucy as she and Philip set off.

'I need your help right away.'

'Help?'

'I have been invited to a function tonight and I let it slip that I was interested in art.'

'You, keen on art?' Lucy gave a little laugh, for in their association, although he had shown interest in her work, he had never displayed the slightest enthusiasm in art itself, either generally or specifically. 'But what's the problem?'

'Well, when I let that slip it was heard by an elderly lady who wants to hear my opinion of modern trends.'

'And you think she might raise the matter with you at this function? Why not tell her the truth and take me along?'

'I can't. It's a private party and my invitation is as a representative of my firm.'

'So you want me to take the day off to coach you?'

'Yes.'

'It's a vast subject about which people have wildly differing opinions.'

'Give me just enough to get by.'

'I'll do my best.' Lucy was willing if it meant a day spent with Philip.

'Thanks.'

At five o'clock Lucy called a halt to her tuition while they were sitting in a small cafe. She had enjoyed spending this time with him. He was a good listener and a quick learner due to his nimble brain and retentive memory. 'Now, you should relax for at least an hour and think no more about what I have told you.'

'But . . .'

'You'll be all right. The information will come back when you start to talk. I believe you are skilful enough to direct the conversation in the direction you want. Besides, this lady is not going to commandeer all your time; she'll have to talk to other people. I look forward to hearing how you got on when we meet tomorrow.'

'Oh, I'm so sorry.' Philip looked downcast. 'I have to go to Calais again.'

Lucy looked dejected.

'Don't look so disappointed, love. We'll be able to meet the day after. I'll make sure I'm back.'

Though her smile was wan she took heart from this promise. And after all she had had a full day with him today.

Philip was welcomed graciously by Madame and Monsieur Mercier and taken in charge by Blanche as other guests were arriving.

'Did you manage to learn anything about trends in present-day art?' she asked quietly with an amused lilt to her voice.

'Oh, I did,' he said with a twinkle in his eye as he met her enquiring gaze. 'You might be surprised.'

'So you may not need rescuing?' said Blanche in a dismissive tone.

'I wouldn't say that. After all, how do I know where Madame Mercier might take the subject?'

'So there are quicksands in your knowledge?'

'Let's say pitfalls. I won't be buried.'

Any further reference to the matter was quashed when guests began to circulate. Monsieur Mercier had seen that excellent wines were available and soon tongues were loosened as the atmosphere relaxed. The Merciers were perfect hosts making sure that none of their guests was neglected after they had introduced everyone. They had given equal thought to the placement at the long table in the oak-panelled dining room. Philip was pleased that he had been seated next to Blanche, but with his charm and good looks he had quickly attracted the attention of many of the guests, especially the females. Some of the men showed particular interest when they learned that he worked for the family firm of Jaurès Investments, a small but influential firm based in Switzerland, and had come to Paris to establish a base here.

Fortified by good food and wine, the guests retired to the large drawing room to circulate and carry on their conversations in a convivial atmosphere.

Blanche and Philip were talking to brothers Paul and Armand Debois, who were interested in Philip's role in Paris for his family's

126

company and whether he was empowered to make loans for a project in which they were interested, when Madame Mercier interrupted them.

'I hope you will allow me to spirit Philip away, I want to hear of his interest in the modern movements in art.'

The brothers bowed to Madame Mercier. 'Certainly, Madame. We can carry on our conversation another time.' They glanced hopefully at Philip.

'Of course, gentlemen, may I call on you the day after tomorrow?'

'We will be delighted. Here is our card. Shall we say ten o'clock?'

'Admirable.' Philip turned to Madame Mercier. 'Now, I am all yours, Madame.'

'Good. Let us claim another glass of wine and find a seat where we will not be disturbed.' She glanced round and, catching the eye of one of the waiters who were constantly in circulation, led the way to a seat in a window alcove, unaware of the knowing glance that was exchanged between Philip and Blanche.

'I am interested in what the young think of art in the modern world.' She paused to take a glass of wine offered by the waiter. After Philip had done likewise and they had settled in their seats, she continued, 'You may have noticed the paintings on the walls and deduced from them that I am a collector. It is because of that that I am interested in the opinions of the young for I believe their tastes will embrace the sought-after works of today and tomorrow.'

'I had noticed them and thought you must be a collector. I noted your Impressionist paintings, an excellent collection and a wise choice when there has been much of a derogatory nature aimed at these artists who, I believe, are real geniuses.' He saw interest and relief sparkle in her eyes.

'I'm so glad you believe I did the right thing.'

'Most certainly.'

'But what about the prejudices of the French academic tradition? Won't that bring about the demise of the Impressionists?'

'Madame, if you believe that then you misjudge the power of art. Impressionism will survive all the criticism the traditionalists throw at it. I believe it is well worth continuing to purchase the works of the new Impressionist painters – Monet, Pissarro, and in particular Renoir and Degas.'

'Ah, most interesting! You have singled out the very painters I have had my eye on. And beyond that?'

Philip gave a little shrug of his shoulders. 'Who can tell? There'll be trends. Some will survive, some will fall by the wayside. But there will be another major movement. It is a matter of what will develop out of one of those trends.' Philip was rather enjoying this conversation. He felt he was coming over as an expert, though what he was saying had only general connotations. 'We have to keep our eyes and ears open and hope we recognise the right track, and therefore the explosion, before it happens. However, there is one thing I am certain of. No matter what its critics say and how much people try to deride Impressionism, it has and will continue to have an influence on art and its development, even if only to bring out counteractive work. And there may be further opportunities for investment in that development.'

Madame Mercier gave a little nod. 'Most interesting, Philip. I'm pleased to have your assessment. It will help me when I make other purchases.'

'I'm pleased my views have been of some use.' He pulled at his ear. He had got away without having Madame Mercier quiz him further. Now was the time to break off this conversation.

A moment later Blanche appeared at his side. 'May I interrupt this tête-à-tête?' she said with an apologetic smile. 'I have someone who wants to meet Philip.'

'Of course, my dear,' replied Madame Mercier.

Philip stood up. 'Thank you, Madame. I have enjoyed your company. Maybe another discussion, another time?'

'I look forward to that.'

As they moved away Blanche said, 'You've made a hit there. It must have gone well.'

Philip smiled. 'It did. I thought I was going to be quizzed by an expert but she isn't. I talked generalities and she lapped it up.'

Blanche looked at him with surprise. 'But all the paintings on the walls?'

'Bought without any real knowledge. She's a lucky collector. Maybe latching on to things she overheard.'

'Really?'

'Oh, yes. She had the impression that I was an expert and, as soon as I realised she wasn't, I made a few general hints appear to be specialist knowledge.'

Blanche chuckled. 'You're incorrigible.'

'Now who have you that I should meet?'

'No one! That was an excuse because of your signal.'

He smiled. 'So let's talk to someone.'

'You're enjoying yourself.'

'I am. There are influential people here, maybe some who are looking for financial backing that I can put their way.'

By the time he was ready to leave Philip had made another two potential clients and from those contacts hoped he would pull off some business to his own advantage. As he walked home he felt highly satisfied with himself, and tomorrow he had another evening of gambling accompanied by Blanche.

That evening proved successful as well. Although they did not win as much as on the two previous visits to the tables, they were highly satisfied and in high spirits when the cab took them back to the Merciers'. Reaching the house, Philip helped Blanche to the ground and dismissed the cabbie. He took her in his arms. She did not resist and returned his kiss with equal fervour.

'I'll miss you tomorrow,' he whispered, close to her ear.

'And I'll miss you too,' she replied.

Still holding her, he leaned back so that he could look her in the eye. 'When will you be coming back to Paris?'

'Maybe sooner than I'd anticipated,' she replied with a teasing note in her voice. 'Will you ever come south?'

'Maybe I can dream up some business that impels me to do so.'

'One way or the other it looks as if we shall meet again.'

'I cannot let my talisman slip away forever.'

'We cannot let distance mar our lives.'

'Nor shall it.'

Their lips met and passion flared. When the kiss ended she

turned quickly from him and went to the door. There she paused and said quietly, 'Don't forget me, Philip.'

'I won't.'

Blanche was gone, leaving him staring at a closed door but still seeing a vision of the loveliness he had held in his arms.

He turned slowly and walked home, aware that Paris had settled for the night and in her apartment Lucy would be asleep.

The thought jolted him. Now there were two women in his life when a week ago there had been only one. They were so different, each attractive in her own way, and each with potential riches. Lucy would inherit money that he could invest. Blanche was already rich and he had no doubt that she would willingly take up any investment suggestions. And with the connections he was making, further opportunities to do so were fast presenting themselves. But . . . Philip thrust the dilemma from his mind. Now was not the time to make a decision. Events might occur that would do that for him. And he had the Debois brothers to see tomorrow.

The day was bright and enhanced Philip's good mood. Life in Paris was turning out well and had become much more to his liking than he had envisaged when told he was to open and run an office here. He was determined that the Debois brothers should be his first clients and that he would keep his ears and mind open for any investment tips he might turn to his personal advantage.

From the brief conversation he had had with them at the party, plus the little research he had done this morning, he knew they were land developers, shrewd in their assessments of possible trends in the rapidly expanding city.

Philip came to the building he sought and paused to eye the façade before entering. It was not imposing but the inside came as a surprise. He took in its brazen opulence. The patterns of the marble floor echoed the elaborately carved banister of the elegant curved staircase. Large oil paintings were displayed to best advantage on the plain walls. At one side a bulky reception desk was occupied by a steward who stood up as Philip approached him.

'Good morning, sir. May I help you?' His tone was respectful.

'Good morning,' returned Philip pleasantly. 'I have an appointment with the Debois brothers.'

'Yes, sir. Monsieur Jaurès?'

Philip nodded.

'I was ordered to send you straight up.' He tapped a knob on his desk and in a moment a livery attired boy appeared. 'Take this gentleman to the office.'

'Follow me, sir,' the boy said briskly, and started for the stairs.

Philip followed him to the first floor where they quickly gained admission to a suite which was again a surprise. A young lady sat behind a desk in an outer office that was tastefully furnished and papered in delicate colours.

'Monsieur Jaurès, I presume,' she said with a welcoming smile. 'Come this way, please.'

She led Philip through a door leading into a corridor that was flooded with light from a large window at one end. There was a door to either side but she knocked on the one on the right where a plaque indicated that this was Armand Debois' office. After a slight pause she opened it and walked in, announcing, 'Monsieur Jaurès, sir,' as she held the door open for Philip to enter.

He flashed her a smile of thanks that set her heart fluttering and caused her to make a hasty retreat.

The brothers had obviously been awaiting his arrival. No doubt, he speculated, discussing what they required of him. They both rose to their feet, Armand from behind a large oak desk and Paul from an armchair. They greeted him with firm handshakes and friendly smiles and indicated a second armchair positioned so that he was able to view both men at the same time.

With the niceties over in a few minutes Armand came to the point of the meeting. 'As you probably know, my brother and I are land developers and that requires financial backing, borrowing on reasonable terms. We hope that we might talk business.'

'We know the sound reputation of Jaurès Investments in Switzerland and when we learned that you were opening an office in Paris we thought that there might be an opportunity for us to develop a working relationship,' explained Paul.

'Gentlemen, let me say right from the start that I hope this will

131

be the beginning of a long and successful collaboration. I am empowered to make loans up to a certain amount. Above that, authority has to come from my head office in Geneva. Generally there will be little difficulty. There is a stage in any negotiation when I will have to inform my superior in Geneva what is entailed, but that is merely a matter of head office knowing what is going on so that it can be related to other commitments.'

'That is perfectly understandable,' agreed Armand.

'Your principal interest is in land and its development, I understand, so I presume that any loan we are able to make you will be to further that?'

Armand glanced at Paul who took over the explanation. 'Yes, our chief concern is land that we believe will increase in value as Paris develops.'

'So you really need to know in which direction that might occur?'

'We have our sources.'

'Reliable?'

Paul raised his hands as if to quash any further questions in that direction. 'I am not at liberty to disclose our source but we do not rely entirely on that. We have made our own careful study of the areas around the present city boundaries and have assessed where we think expansion might take place.'

'And you want backing to buy that land and then develop it in those areas?'

'Yes. We are looking well ahead. We already have land in various areas very close to the present boundaries and, though there are some similar areas available, we are now looking further afield.'

'I see,' said Philip thoughtfully. 'Of course I would need to know where these sites are in order to assess whether it is in my firm's interest to pursue the matter with you.'

'Naturally. That is what we would expect. In return we take it that you would treat our ideas as strictly confidential?'

'Oh, Messieurs, that goes without saying. You must have sought financial help for previous land purchases. May I ask why you have now come to Jaurès Investments?'

Armand gave a little smile. 'Jaurès Investments have an

132

extremely sound reputation in Switzerland. They have never previously appeared to be interested in opening offices outside their
native country but now we find them opening an office in Paris
and took it as fortuitous that you were at the Merciers' party. We
liked what we saw and realised that it might be advantageous to
meet you on a business footing.'

Philip inclined his head in acknowledgement. 'Thank you,
gentlemen. Do you wish to talk business in more detail while I
am here or would you rather make another appointment after you
have had time to consider whether you wish to proceed with
Jaurès?'

The brothers exchanged a quick glance. Finally Armand said,
'We have no need for any further consideration. If your terms are
suitable we will go ahead. There is no time like the present. So
you will need to know where our interests lie?'

'Indeed,' replied Philip.

Armand started to rise from his chair and said at the same time,
'Would you like to come this way?' He made for a door to the
left of his desk.

Paul gave way to Philip who followed Armand into an adjacent
room. A long oak fitting with a sloping top at waist height occupied one wall. Armand opened one of its full-length drawers of
shallow depth, extracted a map and laid it on top where it was
prevented from slipping to the floor by a strip of oak.

Philip was quick to identify the northern boundary of the city
and saw that the map was chiefly concerned with land beyond
that. He noted that there were several pencil marks on the map
but they meant nothing to him.

'This is the area we are interested in at the moment.' Paul pointed
to a section on the map.

'Why that particular area?' asked Philip, taking in the details.

'We believe the city will expand in that direction with residential
properties.'

'What type?

'You note that it is convenient to the area of Paris that has
become the residential area of the rich. We believe that is the
direction in which similar properties will be built. We would like

133

to buy the land now, and develop it with similar houses when the time is right.'

Philip saw their reasoning and had no doubt, from another study of the map, that they were right, but he held back from agreeing at once. 'You could be right and this would be the time to get that land. Before I come up with any figures I will have to have a look at the area and maybe have a survey done. Have you already done so?'

'No,' replied Paul, aghast that Philip even entertained such a thought. 'We know the land, and to have a survey done would only alert other people to what might be going on. We would like to make this purchase without our rivals knowing that we are thinking about it.'

'Rivals? Do you know if they have made any move towards obtaining this particular land?'

'As far as we know they have not, but that could change at any time. We are anxious to make our purchase.'

'Have you approached the owner of the land?'

'We have. He is very interested in our offer. He was a friend of our father so would be more inclined to sell to us. He knows that we will not renege on the criteria on which he is insisting.'

'I notice that you have other areas marked in a similar way. Are you interested in those too?'

'Some maybe, others no.'

'Why not?'

'Well, we think that those areas, and that one in particular,' Paul tapped the map, 'will have to be developed to provide homes for manual workers.'

'But wouldn't there be money to be made there too?'

'Oh, yes, there can be if the growing industrial movement brings factories nearby, but we prefer to develop the more salubrious sites where the rich are likely to settle.'

'To go back to the land which you want to purchase immediately, can you assure me that it is suitable for what you want?'

'We would not have gone this far with you if we weren't certain,' said Armand. 'Dismiss any doubts you may entertain.'

Philip looked thoughtful for a moment. 'I think my father, who is head of the firm, would advise caution.' He saw the brothers exchange a glance of disappointment. 'However, I like what I see. I know of your business and you have convinced me that you need to move quickly. Therefore, gentlemen, I suggest we discuss the financial arrangements now.'

Two hours later they shook hands on the final agreement and the Debois brothers, highly satisfied with the terms Philip had offered, suggested that they adjourn to their favourite restaurant for lunch.

Walking back to his office, fortified by excellent wine and good food, Philip felt that all was well with the world. He had negotiated a good deal and reckoned his father would be pleased with his first achievement in Paris. His thoughts turned to the markings on the map and in particular the two areas in which the Debois brothers had declared no interest. Maybe he could turn that knowledge to his own advantage.

Chapter Ten

'Ma'am, Mr Robinson is asking if you are receiving visitors?'

Colette stopped her embroidering and glanced at Edward. 'Certainly, show him in.'

The girl left, closing the door behind her, to reopen it a few moments later to admit Matthew Robinson.

'Colette!' He beamed with pleasure as he crossed the room. 'Thank you for seeing me.' He took the hand she offered and raised it to his lips, meeting her gaze with friendliness. 'Edward, how are you?' He turned to greet the young man who had risen from his chair.

'Very well, thank you, Mr Robinson,' he returned.

'Do sit down, Matthew.' Colette indicated a vacant chair to her right.

'Thank you.'

Edward waited until he was seated before resuming his own place.

'What brings you to Whitby?' asked Colette. 'Taking more photographs?'

'Oh, my dear,' he gave a little shake of his head, 'I would not presume to venture into what I consider to be your territory unless I had a special commission. No, I have come on purpose to extend an invitation to you and Edward.'

'Invitation?' Colette was curious.

'Yes. I have organised an exhibition in London of my photographs of Scarborough and the surrounding district. I will be setting it up next week. There will be a preview the following Monday evening. I would like you and Edward to be my guests.'

Taken by surprise, a moment passed before Colette replied. 'Oh, Matthew that is very kind but we . . .'

He stemmed the protest he could see coming. 'I will make all the travel arrangements and book the accommodation.'

'No, Matthew, that is too much!'

'Not at all. It would be my pleasure.'

'We couldn't impose on your generosity and time.'

'You wouldn't be. I see it working this way. I go to London to supervise the hanging next Monday and return to Scarborough on Tuesday. You and Edward come to London with me on the Saturday.'

'But wouldn't it be easier for you to stay in London after the hanging rather than return to Scarborough? Edward and I could travel to London on the Sunday or even on the day of the preview.' Colette looked at her son. 'What do you think, Edward?'

Part of her was excited by the prospect of seeing London but she was cautious, wondering if there was more to Matthew's invitation. She did not want to feel under any obligation to him. Well, she would abide by Edward's decision.

'I don't think we should refuse Mr Robinson's kind invitation. It is most generous and thoughtful of him.' He turned to Matthew. 'But I think Mother is right, there is no need for you to do all that travelling.'

'I don't mind.'

'I know but I can easily escort her.' Edward was adamant.

'Very well, but I insist you come to London on the Saturday and make the stay a holiday.'

'That is most generous of you, Matthew,' accepted Colette.

'Splendid! Splendid!' He beamed with delight. 'I will make all the arrangements immediately and let you know as soon as they are finalised. Now, I have taken up too much of your time.' He rose from his chair.

'Won't you stay for lunch?' asked Colette.

'That is kind of you, and nothing would give me greater pleasure, but I have another appointment in Whitby, a short one with a solicitor, and would like to catch the noon train back to Scarborough.'

Colette and Edward accompanied Matthew to the door where once again they made their thanks before he left.

'You did astonish me, Edward,' Colette commented as they returned to the drawing room.

'Why?' he asked, feigning surprise.

'Accepting Matthew's offer so readily.'

'I knew you would like to go. Besides, it gives me the opportunity to enquire about my father at some of the London galleries I haven't yet contacted.'

'I see,' was all the comment she made.

They realised that Matthew Robinson had spared no expense when, after they'd travelled first-class by train to London, he met them with a hired cab to take them to Claridge's on Upper Brook Street. After Matthew had announced their arrival they were fussed over in reception and escorted to their rooms by three bell boys immaculately turned out in carefully brushed uniforms. Colette and Edward had rooms next to each other on the first floor while Matthew, not wishing to impose his presence, had taken a room on the floor above.

Colette stood in the middle of her luxuriously appointed room. Her thoughts dwelt on Matthew's generosity. A cursory glance out of the window registered nothing of the bustle on the street. She had to admit she liked Matthew, a feeling that had grown from the friendship of two married couples with similar interests, drawn together by the profession of photography. She recognised that since the loss of his wife he had experienced loneliness just as she had done after Bernard's death. That lonely feeling had taken on a different aspect with the passing of time, when they had each come to terms with the loss of their loved one and begun to feel the need for close companionship. In that respect she valued Matthew's friendship. That was how she saw their relationship at any rate, but now she worried that he was taking it more seriously. With that thought came the recollection of her first love, the one that had ended in hurt and pain and almost destroyed her trust in men. Although unknown to him, Bernard had rebuilt that trust. She had come to a more forgiving view of Arthur's behaviour. Now she wondered what he would think if he could see her sitting in Claridge's as Matthew's guest. With that thought came the partial hope that Edward might turn up some news of what had happened to him.

Throughout the succeeding days Matthew gave them every attention; showing them the sights of London, escorting them to the theatre, dining them in the sumptuous surroundings of Claridge's, and taking pride in escorting them to the evening preview of his exhibition.

Though Colette already knew Matthew had talent as a photographer, this exhibition showed that it was exceptional. She was particularly struck by the way his eye for composition had developed and had nothing but praise for his dark-room work.

With Matthew's time being taken up with other guests to the exhibition, Colette sought out Edward's opinion. He had to admit he was impressed by Matthew's talent and declared there were a couple of photographs he would like to interpret in colour on a large canvas.

'I think Matthew would be flattered. We will ask him, and if he agrees I will purchase those two photographs for you in memory of this visit.'

'That is most generous of you, Mother. Will you ask him? He is rather tied up at this moment and I want to slip away. I have said nothing about what I have been doing when I have been out on my own. I did not want to spoil your enjoyment by giving you my findings in dribs and drabs. After this appointment today I might have something more definite. I'll see you back at Claridge's.'

Colette nodded, feeling distinctly uneasy. Did she really want to know? Would it be better if she did not? But she could not deny Edward his right to know his father.

When Edward left the gallery, he buoyed his thoughts with the hope that one of his two appointments would yield the news that had so far eluded him.

He walked briskly to Bond Street and the Abbey Galleries. He felt no interest in the two paintings displayed in the window. Another time maybe, but now there was a much more important matter in his mind. His enquiries at six other private galleries had drawn no news of his father. Two had heard of him, one had handled the sale of two of his paintings for a private collector, but none was of help in his quest. It seemed as if his father had wanted to disappear. Now as he entered the Abbey Galleries Edward's hopes rose a little as they had done at every other place he had made his enquiries. Would they be dashed again?

He entered the reception area where a young woman was sitting behind a desk dealing with some printed notices. She looked up and smiled as Edward approached her.

'May I help you, sir?'

Edward made a quick decision. If he made a direct query about his father he would probably receive a negative reply, the receptionist was too young to have known him, so he made out that he was interested in seeing some paintings.

'Very well, sir. If you will take a seat, I will get someone to help you.'

As Edward sat down she opened a door to her right. A few moments later she reappeared followed by a young man who oozed confidence and knew that his smart appearance impressed customers.

'Thank you, Jane,' he said to the young woman, and then to Edward, 'Good day, sir. You wish to see some paintings?'

Edward quickly sized up the situation. He felt he would be better dealing with someone more senior but did not want to dent this young man's eager-to-oblige attitude.

'Yes.'

'Anything particular, sir? Or a particular artist?'

'Seascapes and night scenes.'

'Very good, sir, will you come this way?'

Edward followed him through a door and found himself in a large room with several paintings displayed on its plain walls.

'I can be showing you some paintings which may be of interest, but you would be better dealing with our Mr Wiston who has specialised in night scenes for many years. He is busy at the moment in another room,' he indicated a closed door, 'with a customer. I don't think he will be long. In the meantime I can show you some seascapes.'

'That would be kind.' Edward wondered if his luck had changed. Someone who had dealt with night scenes for many years must surely have heard of his father.

The young man who had left him returned with a portfolio which he laid on the large table that occupied the centre of the room. He unfastened the ties at each side and opened the cover. For the next ten minutes Edward examined the paintings, showing interest as if he was a genuine buyer but wishing all the time that the man he wanted to see would appear.

Another five minutes passed. The young man apologised for the delay. 'I'd expected Mr Wiston to be finished with this customer before now.'

Edward dismissed his apologies.

A few minutes later a door opened and two men appeared. They went through to the reception area and a moment later one of them reappeared. Immediately the young man attending to Edward greeted him with, 'Mr Wiston, this gentleman is interested in seascapes and night scenes. I have been showing him some seascapes but said that you were our expert on night scenes.'

Edward could almost see this man, whom he judged to be in his late-fifties, pull his shoulders back with pride at the praise.

'I will gladly talk to you, sir. We have only a few night scenes in the gallery at the moment but I keep my eye on the market and receive an idea of what might be coming up for sale. You are . . . ?'

'Mr Clayton, I come from Whitby. I must be honest with you, at this moment I am not interested in purchasing a painting.' He saw a slight flash of annoyance mixed with curiosity and suspicion in the man's eyes. Edward went on quickly, 'I am interested in a particular artist who was noted at one time, particularly in the North of England, for his night scenes and seascapes, though he did other work as well. I wondered if you had dealt with any of his works recently and whether you know of his whereabouts? I would like to get in touch with him but so far all my attempts to trace him have failed.' He saw the slight hostility that had arisen vanish as he prolonged his explanation. It had been replaced by a definite air of interest.

'Who is this artist?'

'Arthur Newton.'

'Ah.' Mr Wiston raised an eyebrow. 'That *is* interesting.'

Edward's hopes soared. There had been no immediate denial; this man obviously knew of his work.

'We did handle some of Mr Newton's work many years ago. We commissioned some work from him through a dealer in Leeds. People here wanted paintings of country scenes to remind them of the open spaces beyond London. We handled a few night scenes as well. They were very good. Some were of Leeds, which I liked better than his paintings of the countryside. There was a lot of atmosphere about them, they caught the essence of city life at night. I believed there could be a great future for him if he concentrated on that type of painting. I never saw any of his seascapes.'

'Do you know where he is now?'

'No. We have not handled any of his paintings for many years.'

The hopes that had risen as Mr Wiston had been speaking were dashed. 'Do you know anybody who has?'

Mr Wiston shook his head slowly as he said with a thoughtful expression, 'No. Mr Newton seemed to disappear. Certainly he did from our dealings, though of course you can't keep track of every artist whose work you handle, especially when you are not dealing with them directly.'

'Quite so. I understand perfectly. I'm just hoping to find some clue, no matter how small, that will give me a lead to follow.'

'I'm sorry I can't be more helpful.'

Edward thanked him again and started to turn away.

'Just a moment, sir.'

Arrested by his tone of voice, Edward turned his attention back to Mr Wiston. He saw the other man looking thoughtful. Edward did not speak; he did not want to interrupt whatever it was that preoccupied Mr Wiston.

The man gave a little nod as if to confirm to himself that what had come into his mind was correct. 'I've just recalled that a few years back I heard Mr Newton had moved from the north and settled somewhere on the south coast.'

Excitement gripped Edward. It was a slim clue though it helped to confirm what he had heard before, but there were so many places his father could be.

'Do you know where?' he asked hopefully.

Mr Wiston shook his head. 'Sorry. Mr Newton's name happened to be mentioned in passing when I was attending a dealers' conference. I heard the south coast mentioned but no specific location.'

Edward, in exasperation, gave a little shrug of his shoulders. 'Well, it can't be helped. Thank you for your time.'

As he walked back to Claridge's he tried to formulate a plan for his next course of action. By the time he had reached the hotel he had decided that, because he was already in the South, he might as well go to the coast rather than return directly to Whitby. But that decision was dashed when his mother and Matthew returned.

Edward had taken a seat in an advantageous position from which he could see the entrance.

He jumped to his feet when he saw them. 'Mr Robinson, I must offer you my apologies for leaving your exhibition of wonderful photographs early. There was a gallery that I wanted to call at.'

Matthew waved the apology aside. 'My dear boy, that is perfectly all right. I know that you had given the exhibition your full attention and if you had a call to make there was little point in hanging about. I hope all went well?'

As they were talking they had wandered to a group of chairs and sat down.

'Reasonably so.' He saw a look of query momentarily cloud the excitement in his mother's eyes and sensed something had happened, but what? His mother and Mr Robinson . . . ? Surely not? Alarm sounded in his mind but further words intruded on his thoughts.

'You tell him, Colette.'

Edward was embraced by his mother's broad smile. 'Matthew has got you two more commissions!'

Edward stared at her dumbfounded by this unexpected news; so different from what he had been expecting. Relief swept through him and then surprise burst through. 'What?' He glanced from his mother to Matthew and back again, seeking an explanation.

'One of those paintings you did for me was a present for a friend in London, Mr Abbas Fontaine, who was influential in arranging my exhibition,' said Matthew. 'I gave it to him after you had left. He was delighted with it and immediately wanted to order two more. When I told him he would be able to meet the artist for himself and describe what he wanted, he was delighted.'

'We've arranged for him to take tea with us here tomorrow,' said Colette.

Edward had gathered his thoughts by now, 'This is marvellous. Thank you, Mr Robinson.'

'I had nothing to do with it. It's your talent that has gained these commissions.'

'Ah, but if you hadn't thought your friend would appreciate a painting you would never have given him such a present, so it is all down to you that I have gained two further commissions. Thank you.'

Matthew rose to his feet. 'Should we meet here for dinner this evening?'

They agreed and he left them.

'Now,' said Colette, 'tell me what happened?'

Edward quickly related his experience at Abbey Galleries. 'So I've narrowed the area of search but it is still enormous. I was going to suggest I went to the south coast from here but maybe I'll have to come home to get on with those paintings. We'll know tomorrow.'

The man who came to tea was small and dapper, buzzing with energy. He knew exactly what he wanted and was pleased when Edward made certain suggestions that enlarged on the ideas he put forward. He posed a time limit as one of the paintings he wanted was for a friend.

'I will start on them as soon as we are home,' said Edward. 'I would not wish to be late. And I will deliver them personally to Mr Fontaine.'

Colette knew her son would then continue to search the south coast.

*

'Letters!' cried Lucy as she came into the kitchen. She threw one down on the table in front of Marie.

They recognised the writing on the envelopes, and, knowing they were from home, ripped them open quickly. They were always excited when mail came from England for it brought their homes closer. Although they liked Paris and enjoyed the busy life of the capital they were always glad to have news from England. Since making their choice to stay in Paris for Easter they had developed guilty consciences and almost changed their minds. The sight of these letters, which they knew would contain their parents' reaction to the decision, pricked them again.

Their usual practice was to cast their eyes quickly over the letters' contents and then read them again more slowly but that was abandoned immediately as they read the opening sentence of Arthur's letter: 'We are coming to Paris!'

They both looked up, wide-eyed.

'They are coming here!' gasped Lucy.

Then, in the wake of their immediate surprise, they both let out a shout of joy.

'Read on, read on,' urged Marie.

They both did so and were soon in possession of their parents' plans. They would arrive three days before Easter and remain in Paris until three days before the start of the new term.

'They are going to be here for two weeks,' cried Lucy. 'How splendid.'

'And staying at the Continental on the Rue Castiglione. How grand.'

'And we are invited to dine with them that first evening.'

'I'm going to need a new dress!' Marie's words were not only to convince herself but also to seek Lucy's approval.

'So will I. We must look our best,' she agreed.

Marie turned back to the letter. 'It's just us who are invited. They say they will meet our friends later.'

They read the rest of the news in silence then looked up, bright-eyed, and immediately flung their arms round each other, joyously anticipating the visit.

*

The iron and glass structure of the Gâre du Nord, with its soaring arches forming a canopy that kept out any inclement weather, was today a hive of bustle and activity. The buzz of conversation, calls of porters, chiding of parents whose children were overexcited by all that was going on around them, hiss of steam and rumble of trolley wheels assailed Marie and Lucy as they entered the station. Swept up in their own excitement at the occasion they were almost oblivious to the cacophony of sound around them: last-minute advice, tears, desultory conversations to avoid deeper emotions, orders, good wishes, laments, enquiries; the station was filled with them all.

With plenty of time to spare the two friends focused their attention on the scene. Soldiers were saying goodbye to their sweethearts. A little girl clutched hard to her doll lest she drop it in the haste imposed by her parents. A little boy who did not want to be kissed by someone who was probably his maiden aunt. A stern father who wagged a finger at his errant son. There was plenty to amuse them besides their usual interest in the differing styles of female attire promenaded along the platforms.

Time passed and then they were aware of a train huffing and puffing its way into the station and gradually slowing down. Passengers flooded on to the platform from the carriages, some hurrying to leave the station, others delayed while a porter sorted their luggage or they greeted friends there to meet them. Marie and Lucy strained to catch a glimpse of their parents.

After a few moments Lucy called, 'There they are!'

'Where?'

'There.'

Marie searched, did not see them and was irritated by the ridiculous side of their exchange of words.

'Where?' she asked again.

'There!' replied Lucy. It was silly. She could see them; why couldn't Marie? She glanced at her friend and, realising she still hadn't seen them, repeated, 'There!' She turned her attention back to the passengers approaching them and started waving. Almost at the same moment she heard Marie shriek with delight and knew she had finally seen them.

A few moments later everyone was being hugged in the sheer excitement of the moment. Questions were fired, answers were made.

'Yes, we have had a good journey.'

'No, we weren't seasick.'

'The crossing was smooth.'

'Yes, I like being on the sea.'

'You've chosen a grand hotel.'

'Why not? This is a special trip to Paris.'

'George not with you?'

'No, he thought you would like us to yourselves.'

'Thoughtful.'

'We are looking forward to meeting Philip.'

'I'm sure you'll like him.'

All the while they had been making their way out of the station to find a cab. The porter in charge of their luggage had been following them but now he swept past and indicated to them to follow him. He was pleased to show his skill in getting them a cab quickly. Arthur admired his astuteness and tipped him liberally.

It was not long before the cab door was opened by a colourfully attired commissionaire outside the Hotel Continental. He snapped his fingers and immediately two boys attired in hotel livery ran forward and dealt with the luggage while Isobel, Arthur, Marie and Lucy were escorted to two rooms on the first floor.

'I'm so pleased you have come,' said Marie when, alone in his room, she gave her father an extra hug.

'I'm delighted to be here. Easter would have been very dull without you,' he replied.

'You would probably have shared it with Mrs Wentworth.'

'No doubt, but it would still have seemed strange without you. When Isobel expressed the same feelings about Lucy, we decided we'd come to you.'

'And live in the lap of luxury?' teased Marie surveying the room.

'Why not?'

'Exactly. Why not?'

'I ordered tea while Isobel and I were checking in. Should we go now?'

'You said in your letter that we would be dining with you this evening so Lucy and I came prepared for that and thought you would allow us to use your rooms to freshen up before the meal.'

'So you shall. I'm looking forward to this evening, just the four of us together. We'll meet your friends tomorrow as I suggested in my last letter.'

'They are looking forward to it.'

They sat back in their chairs, satisfied by the splendid food attractively presented and pleasantly served by waiters who fussed over them. With wine glasses replenished to accompany the selection of cheeses, Arthur caught Isobel's slight nod signalling that this was the right moment to make their announcement.

He leaned forward, took a sip of his wine and said, 'We have something important to tell you.'

In the slight pause that followed Marie caught Lucy's eye. Neither of them had any idea what this was about.

'Apart from wanting to see both of you, our visit here has a special purpose,' went on Arthur. 'We would have said what we have to say if you had come home but, as you chose to stay in Paris, we knew we would have to come here otherwise our timing would have been wrong.' He began to realise he was waffling so plunged into the matter. 'We plan to marry in the summer.'

The announcement came so suddenly that the two girls were taken by surprise. For one moment they started incredulously at him. Then the realisation hit them and they sprang out of their seats. Lucy hugged her mother, Marie her father, each saying how delighted she was. Then, in a rush, Lucy was hugging Arthur and Marie was congratulating Isobel.

The excitement attracted the attention of the other diners and the waiters. A few people frowned at the disturbance but most realised it marked a celebration and smiled at the enthusiasm and joy emanating from the usually reserved English people.

Marie and Lucy showered their approval on their parents and were eager to know how far their plans had gone.

'We have decided to marry during your summer vacation,'

explained Isobel. 'The exact date we want to discuss with you while we are here. And I want you both to be bridesmaids.'

'Heavenly,' cried Lucy, already anticipating new dresses.

'Love to,' said Marie, appreciating having been asked.

'Good,' said Isobel, delighted that they had accepted the whole situation so readily.

Though she had never voiced her thoughts to Arthur she had wondered if Marie would see her father's marriage as a betrayal of his wife even though she had been dead for some time. If that thought had crept into her mind again, it was banished when she heard Marie saying, 'I'm so happy for you both. And I want you to have a long and happy life together.'

'Thank you, Marie.' Isobel reached out and took hold of her hand. 'I appreciate that thought.'

'I'll do all I can to make your mother happy, Lucy. I'll take good care of her,' promised Arthur.

'I know you will.' Lucy leaned closer to him and kissed him on the cheek. Her eyes were damp with joy. Then they sparkled with laughter as she turned to her friend. 'Marie, we'll be sisters!'

'So we will,' laughed Marie. 'A few moments ago I was an only child. Now I have a full-grown sister.'

Arthur ordered a bottle of champagne so that the celebrations could go on.

With glasses charged, Lucy offered a toast to the couple who were to marry. 'Where are you going to live?'

'Well,' her mother took up the explanation, 'how would you feel if I sold Cherry Hill?'

For a moment Lucy did not answer and Isobel began to think that her daughter was hurt by this suggestion.

'I wouldn't mind, Mama,' she said slowly. 'It has been my home for so long but my marriage took me away from it. I know I came back but coming to Paris has made another natural break for me. Sell it by all means if that is what you want.'

'I see no sense in keeping the place when it necessitates employing a manager. I don't suppose you would want to run it eventually?'

'No, thank you. You sell it and enjoy the money.'

'Arthur and I have discussed this aspect of things, naturally. We have both decided to draw up new wills that will take care of you both with what should be rightfully yours when either of us dies. Those wills will become binding on the day we are married.'

'I would not want you to stipulate a certain sum and then leave yourself unable to enjoy the fruits of the sale of the farm. You and Papa worked so hard on it.'

'I will see to that, you can be certain. Neither of us intends to limit ourselves but nor do we intend to be extravagant and leave you nothing.'

'Enjoy it,' said Lucy firmly.

'And I want you to do the same, Papa. Don't hold back on my account,' said Marie. 'I want you to be happy.'

'Isobel has agreed that we should keep my house and she will come to live there.'

'I hope that does not upset you, Marie?' she said with concern. 'I don't want to usurp your place.'

'You won't be,' replied Marie sincerely. 'I am sure you will make my father happy there.'

'I will do my best,' returned Isobel, with tears in her eyes. 'Thank you for being so understanding.'

Chapter Eleven

I'll see you two downstairs,' said Isobel, picking up her silk wrap and making for the door.

She and Arthur had spent the day with their daughters visiting the Eiffel Tower, Notre Dame, strolling by the Seine, and taking refreshments at one of the tables outside a high-class restaurant, watching the rest of the world go by. They had returned to the hotel where Isobel had allowed the girls to use her room in preparation for the evening.

She found a chair from which she could observe the entrance, ordered a vermouth and settled to watch the coming and going of guests. Receptionists answered their queries, gave directions, supervised the recording of arrivals and departures; the concierge directed pages who, with a brisk step, went to help guests with their luggage or deliver a message on behalf of a visitor. The hotel swirled with orderly activity and Isobel, sitting still in the midst of it all, was enjoying it.

A few moments later a movement on the wide stairs caught her eye and her attention became riveted on Arthur who was strolling down slowly, viewing the activity. Her heart gave a little skip as she thought how distinguished he looked in an evening suit of the deepest black that enhanced the whiteness of his dress shirt. How lucky I am to have loved twice in the same way, she thought. No, not exactly the same way for each person commands a different love to any other, but each can be powerful in its own way. Both have and do make my heart sing with joy. I am lucky indeed.

'Hello, love,' said Arthur, 'the girls not down yet?

'No. You know what they are like, primping themselves for their beaux.'

'I do indeed,' smiled Arthur. 'But you didn't take so long.'

'I started sooner.'

'So you primped as much as they did?'

'I did.'

'There was no need in your case; you would have been just as lovely without any primping.'

'Are you flattering or flirting?'

'Both.'

She gave a coy smile as she inclined her head in acknowledgement, feeling younger than her years, delighted that she could still hold the interest of a man. Then the spell was broken; she saw Lucy and Marie coming down the stairs.

'Don't they look wonderful?' whispered Arthur, making no effort to disguise his admiration.

'So pretty,' agreed Isobel.

Marie and Lucy were revelling in making a sweeping entrance in such a grand hotel, so different from their usual student haunts.

Lucy's almond green skirt was topped with a pink blouse, while Marie wore a blue skirt and lemon blouse. The leg-of-mutton sleeves were wide at the shoulder and came tight to the wrist, while their full skirts fell from a narrow waist. They had piled their hair on top of their heads and secured it with pins and ribbons to match their blouses.

Arthur stood up and held out his hands to them, kissing them both on the cheek. He revelled in their radiant smiles, thankful that they both looked so well and happy. They sat down and Arthur signalled to the hovering waiter that now was the moment to bring the drinks he had previously ordered.

He glanced at his watch; ten minutes before the expected arrival of their two guests.

Apprehension coloured their conversation which grew stilted and trivial. Each knew the others were wondering how Philip would measure up to their expectations. Lucy hoped that he would impress her mother, while she hoped her daughter had chosen wisely. Marie was anxious for her friend for she knew she would be going through the same torment she had experienced when George was going to meet her father for the first time. Arthur hoped that the young man about to enter their lives did not disappoint Isobel.

'Here's George!' Marie sprang to her feet, relieved that the uneasy atmosphere had been broken.

He came towards them with a broad smile that spoke of his pleasure at seeing them again. He greeted Marie and then turned to the others in turn, making his felicitations first to Isobel.

Although he had met George in England and had liked him, Arthur still studied him with a critical eye and was thankful that, in these few moments, he reckoned this young man still measured up to his first assessment. He seemed to be right for Marie. George's arrival brought a fresh turn to the conversation and, having sensed the apprehension among them, he turned their exchanges to England and home.

Five minutes later Isobel drew in a sharp breath. Her attention had been drawn to a handsome, well-dressed young man who had paused in the doorway to survey the room. His clothes could not disguise his tall athletic figure but it was his handsome features that most caught her eye. His dark hair was well groomed. There was an air of confidence about him that was reassuring. Isobel's mind whirled. Twenty years younger and she would have . . . She pulled her thoughts up sharp. The young man's gaze had settled on them. He smiled and started towards them. Surely this couldn't be Philip? What had her daughter found?

Lucy was on her feet, stepping to meet him and escorting him to them, her arm through his.

Her smile was radiant as she brought him to her mother and made the introduction.

'Madame Wentworth, I am so pleased to meet you.' He took her proffered hand and raised it to his lips without his eyes leaving hers. Each knew they were sizing each other up. 'I have heard so much about you, I feel as if I know you.'

Isobel smiled. 'I hope it was all good. I too am pleased to meet you, and like you I have heard nothing but praise from Lucy.'

'I hope she did not flatter too much.' Philip knew that whatever Lucy had told her, this woman would make up her own mind about him. He realised that he must tread carefully, but also that his

153

good looks had touched a chord here. He was amused that she was still so affected by a man's attractiveness, but then why shouldn't she be?

On Lucy's bidding he turned to be introduced to Arthur and knew instantly that nothing he did would pull the wool over this man's eyes.

Throughout the evening the two young men were the height of courtesy. They were there to impress their prospective in-laws without appearing to push themselves forward. Modesty was the order of the evening and when queried about his work Philip was careful not to overstate his prospects. Arthur and Isobel already knew George's ambitions as an artist and it was inevitable that he, Arthur and Marie should get into a discussion for which Isobel was thankful. It enabled her to get to know Philip better.

With the evening drawing to an end George and Philip offered to escort Marie and Lucy home. Thanks were made, goodbyes were said, and an invitation from the two young men to join them at a notable restaurant in two days' time accepted.

The air was balmy; a few clouds moved sedately across the dark sky from which the moon bathed Paris in its magical light. Even though it was late, the city was still alive.

Marie and George, walking a little ahead of the others, slid their hands together. She felt love in his touch to which she responded. Philip's arm came round Lucy's waist, sending waves of desire through her.

'I think you made an impression on Mother,' she said.

'I'm glad,' he replied. 'I liked her.'

'Good, that will make things easier.'

'And I'm sure Marie's father was impressed.'

'I tried my best.'

'I'm sure you succeeded with him.'

'Was that so essential?'

'Yes.'

'Why? Why Mr Newton?'

'Let's catch the others up.'

Surprised by her reply, he could do nothing but respond to her urging.

'Marie, are we going to tell them?' asked Lucy, excitement in her voice.

'Why not? responded Marie with enthusiasm.

'Now what are you two up to?' asked George.

'Nothing,' replied Marie.

'It's not us,' laughed Lucy, 'it's our parents.'

'Your parents?' queried a mystified George.

'Yes,' went on Marie. 'They came to Paris because we weren't going home. They had planned to tell us there but as we decided to stay in Paris they came here to break the news to us – they are going to marry during our summer holiday.'

'What?' both young men gasped together.

'It's true,' said Lucy, emphasising each word.

'We'll lay on something special when we meet in two days' time,' said George enthusiastically. 'Won't we, Philip?'

'Er . . . of course.' Though stunned by this news he managed to hide this reaction. 'We certainly will. What a wonderful thing, for them to find love again.'

'Isn't it?' enthused Marie. 'We are both delighted.'

'We'll be sisters,' Lucy pointed out with delight.

'Of course,' said George. 'This is turning out to be an exciting holiday. It's quite making up for not going home.'

'It really is,' agreed Lucy. 'Mother's decided to sell the farm. She will live at Mr Newton's, though I think they plan to travel a lot.'

'Lucy is encouraging her mother to enjoy spending the money from the sale.'

Philip made no comment. Already he could see his own plans shattered.

After parting from Lucy and Marie, he and George needed to take different routes to their respective homes.

Philip's was a thoughtful walk home. Lucy's mother getting married, selling the farm, enjoying the money . . . What would her daughter inherit? Probably not as much as it had first appeared, or worse still – nothing. Could he love where there was no money? Philip chided himself for such a thought, yet . . . His mind turned to Blanche. A rich widow with whom he had struck up a special relationship; a very attractive woman with a magnetic personality. But didn't all those who enjoyed a risk attract? They had taken risks together and had made money, could that happen again? How far would she go to make more? But maybe if he used the information gained through the Debois brothers for his own ends he would have no need to turn elsewhere and then his love for Lucy would prevail.

The following morning when Marie and Lucy reached the atelier the other four students were already there, anxious to complete their paintings before Monsieur Bedeaux's inspection the following day, the one before their holidays. They still had another term before he made his decision about allowing them to continue their studies in another academic year, and realised it was vital to impress him now. Even though they were preoccupied they all sensed an air of excitement when Marie and Lucy arrived, and laid down their brushes.

'Come on, tell us,' said Charlotte.

'Tell you what?' replied Marie, feigning ignorance.

'You can't fool us. Something's happened,' prompted Adelina.

Yvette and Gabrielle chorused their agreement.

Lucy eyed Marie. 'Should we tell them?' she asked in a voice meant to tease.

'I'm not sure we should,' replied Marie with a grimace that expressed doubt about doing so.

Their attitude brought shouts of protest from the others. Yvette and Gabrielle grabbed Marie and Lucy's brushes. 'No painting 'til you tell us,' they cried triumphantly.

Marie looked at Lucy and shrugged her shoulders. 'I suppose we'll have to.'

'Our parents are getting married!' Lucy announced.

For a brief moment there was silence and then a stream of congratulations and questions erupted.

'To each other?' asked Yvette.

'Of course,' replied Lucy, in a tone expressing her surprise that there could be any other arrangement.

'Well, they could both have been marrying someone else.'

'We'll be sisters,' said Marie.

'Step-sisters,' corrected Gabrielle, always one for being precise.

At three o'clock that afternoon the door opened and to their surprise Monsieur Bedeaux walked in, accompanied by Arthur and Isobel.

'Ah, I'm glad to see you young ladies still here working hard. I was returning to the school and ran into Monsieur Newton and Madame Wentworth. I invited them in to meet you all. I can't stay, I have a meeting two minutes ago.' With that Monsieur was out of the door, leaving everyone to make themselves known.

Marie immediately took charge of the introductions which, quickly made, turned into a resounding cacophony of congratulations. Arthur and Isobel were caught up in the girls' joy. It meant an end to work, though the students took the opportunity to quiz Arthur about their work and were ready to take on board the useful tips he offered. Though no artist, Isobel showed interest and was particularly taken by Adelina's work.

Lucy noticed her mother discussing the painting with her friend and came to join them. 'Don't you think she's good, Mama?' she queried.

'I do indeed. I so like her interpretation of Notre Dame that I'm going to offer to buy it after her assessment.'

'What?' Adelina gasped. Her eyes widened in disbelief. 'You don't mean it?'

Isobel smiled. She glanced in the direction of Arthur who was preoccupied with Yvette and Charlotte. 'But not a word,' she whispered. 'I saw how taken Mr Newton was with it. I would like to buy it as a surprise for him, a remembrance of our visit to Paris that I know will mean much to us in the future.'

'Madame Wentworth, what can I say?' Adelina could hardly get her breath as she fought to keep her feelings under control. 'You must let me make a gift of it to you.'

'Not at all, my dear. That is very generous of you but I could not accept. We will get Monsieur Bedeaux to put a price on it and that is what I will pay you otherwise it will not be my gift to Mr Newton.'

'Philip will be pleased,' commented Lucy.

'Why Philip?' asked Isobel.

'He is a distant cousin of Adelina's.'

'Is that so?' Isobel tucked the information away as Arthur came to them.

'My dear, I think we should invite the four girls to join us for a meal at our hotel on Friday evening.'

'A splendid idea,' agreed Isobel. She had taken to the four students and was pleased that Lucy and Marie had found such likeable friends.

'Will that suit you all?' Arthur asked.

A chorus of thanks rang round the atelier.

Philip had spent an hour that same morning poring over maps of Paris. He had a retentive memory and had soon marked out the areas he had seen on the Debois' maps. He ignored the area in which the brothers were seeking to invest and concentrated on two sections in which they had declared they had little interest. It was a question of which was the most likely to yield a substantial profit. He decided he would take a cab to visit them.

As he rode the lanes and walked the fields he was alert to the potential each area had, noting the accessibility for road development and the possible use of the River Seine. He saw the Debois' point of view, that these were likely areas for houses for workers at the factories that were supposedly to be built in the vicinity but on which site exactly? If only he knew where the factories were likely to be placed he could make a killing. He needed to find out.

He played with this thought on his way back to Paris, and when they reached the city told the cabbie to take him to the street in which the Debois brothers had their office.

Armand rose quickly from his chair when Philip was shown into his office. Although his smile was welcoming there was a hint of curiosity and doubt in his eyes. He shook hands and said, 'Please do sit down.' He indicated a chair and resumed his own behind his desk. 'I do hope we have not encountered any snags in what we talked about yesterday?'

'No, no. Everything should be approved without any bother. I am sure that head office will back my recommendations.'

'Good, good.' Armand sank back in his chair with relief.

'I am here, if you will forgive me, to ask your advice. Or even to seek a favour.'

In the pause that came, Armand gesticulated with his hands as if to say, Ask and I'll do my best.

'As you know, I am new to Paris. I am getting settled here and have established my office but I think it would be beneficial if I was a member of an appropriate club.'

'It certainly would be. And you want me to recommend one?'

'It would be most kind if you could.'

'Well, you won't want the Royale – too exclusive. The Jockey is a sporting club. It has Baccarat tables but if you don't use them you are expected to resign. There's the Agricole and the Travellers . . .' He paused, looking thoughtful for a moment, then continued, 'You would meet the people you are thinking of at any of them but I believe you would be wise to join the Auberon. Most businessmen are members. Of course, many of them will also be members of some of the other places I have mentioned, but I think this is the one for you.'

'Thank you, that does clear my mind. I am most grateful.'

'Not at all. I'll go one better if you wish. That is my club and I could introduce you.'

'That would be splendid. It is most generous of you.'

'Why not dine there with me on Friday evening? You can get the feel of the place, and if you think you would like to join then I can make the necessary introductions.'

'This is more than I expected,' said Philip gratefully. 'Now, I am taking up too much of your valuable time.' He rose from his chair.

'It has been a pleasure. Friday then. Be at my house for six forty-five.'

'I will.'

'Oh, by the way,' added Armand as he escorted Philip to the door, 'it is evening dress if you are dining at the club.'

Philip felt highly satisfied as he walked back to his office where he found a note from George awaiting him.

'I have been trying to contact you all day but as I could not I went ahead and booked the restaurant we discussed for tonight.

159

I will see you at the Continental at six-thirty. Will you order the carriage?'

When Philip arrived at the hotel he found George already there and everyone enjoying a drink. 'Sorry I am a little late,' he apologised. 'I had some important business to attend to and it took longer than I expected.' He politely refused the drink Arthur offered, saying that it would take time and their carriage should be arriving within the next five minutes.

It was a happy party that was transported to the restaurant George and Philip had chosen on the outskirts of the city, and that mood continued throughout the evening. They enjoyed the food, the wine, the conversation and the company. The two young men knew they were coming under close scrutiny, without its being obvious, from Arthur and Isobel.

The carriage arrived at the prearranged time and their joyful mood continued on the ride to the Continental where they all enjoyed one last drink before George and Philip walked Marie and Lucy to their apartment. Neither couple wanted to play gooseberry to the other so by unspoken consent they separated and each went their own way.

The air was warm and still; the moon shone bright from a cloud-mottled sky. Philip slipped his hand into Lucy's. She squeezed his, a gesture of loving closeness. She deliberately slowed the pace. He did not mind and, with no one else about, gently took her into the shadows. His arms came round her waist and he drew her close. Their lips met and held, bringing passion sweeping through them.

'I love you, Philip,' she whispered when their lips parted.

'My love,' he returned, and kissed her again.

Marie felt comforted and protected by the love expressed in George's gesture when he slipped his arm round her waist. They strolled slowly, not wanting these moments of being together to end. No word was spoken. There was no need. They came to the river, stopped, leaned against the railing and looked along the moonlight shimmering on the water.

'Beautiful,' he whispered, then straightened and turned her into his arms. She looked up at him, love shining like the moonlight in her eyes. His lips came to hers and she responded. They were oblivious to those who walked past, smiling and nodding their approval – after all, this was Paris, a city devoted to love, especially on a night like this.

'Marry me?' he whispered close to her ear.

There was only the slightest hesitation from Marie as the words sank in. Then: 'Yes, yes,' she answered and, sliding her arms around his neck, looked at him with adoration and love.

Their lips met again to seal a pact that would endure.

When they started to walk, Marie spoke. 'George, please can we keep this to ourselves for the time being? I don't want to steal any of the attention from my father and Isobel.'

'Anything you wish, my love. Whenever you like we'll tell them – you say.'

'Would you mind if we waited until after they are married?'

'I would wait forever for you.'

She stopped and kissed him. 'You are wonderful. Thank you for being you.'

They walked again.

'So, we tell no one at all?' he said.

'Please, no one. Speak one word and it's surprising how quickly it gets around.'

'My lips are sealed.'

'Except when mine touch yours.'

The following evening Marie and Lucy arrived at the Continental early and went straight to the rooms occupied by their parents.

'You've timed that right, Lucy,' said Isobel who was sitting at the dressing table. 'Fasten this necklace for me, please.'

Lucy took the silver chain from which hung a heart-shaped locket, embossed with a single ruby surrounded by eight diamonds. 'This is new. I haven't seen it before.'

'Arthur bought it for me today. A memento of this visit to Paris and its meaning for us.'

'It's beautiful.' The next words slipped easily from Lucy's lips. 'I hope one day Philip buys me one.'

Isobel, who had been watching her daughter in the mirror, turned round on her stool. Taking her daughter's hands in hers she asked with concern, 'Do you really, my dear?'

'Oh, yes. I love him, Mama.'

'Lucy, don't rush into anything. You haven't known him long. Be wary of losing your heart.'

'Mama, of course I'll be careful. I want to finish this course – I think I am making good progress. Monsieur Bedeaux said so when he made his assessments.'

'He's told you already?'

'Yes. He examined our work yesterday and asked us to go into school today to hear his opinion. He gave me high praise.'

Isobel was on her feet and hugging her daughter. 'I'm so pleased for you. Now, the necklace!' She sat down again and as Lucy fastened it, asked, 'What about the others?'

'I think I'll let them all tell you themselves.'

Marie was breaking her own news to her father. 'Monsieur Bedeaux was delighted with my work. He was quite satisfied with all the genres I had covered and says that next term, while keeping in touch with other techniques, I can concentrate on portraiture.'

Arthur placed his hands on her shoulders and looked deep into her eyes. 'I am so proud of you.' He kissed her on the forehead. 'Your mother would have been too, and I know Isobel will be.'

She returned his smile and then her gaze became more serious. 'Are you sure about this marriage, Papa?'

Surprised by the question, Arthur looked bewildered as he said, 'Yes, of course I am. What makes you ask that?'

'Nothing. The thought just came to me when you mentioned Mother.'

He nodded his understanding. 'You've seen how happy we are. Nothing can mar that, just as nothing can mar what I shared with your mother.'

Happy with his reassurance, she smiled and kissed him on the cheek.

'I think we had better go down, our guests will be arriving.' As they went to the door he asked, 'How did Lucy do in her assessments?'

'You must wait and see. We all agreed that we would tell you everything this evening and then it could turn into a celebration for some while others might need shoulders to cry on.'

'Should I take a supply of handkerchiefs?'

Arthur tapped on Isobel's door and a moment later it was opened by her.

'You look lovely,' he said and kissed her on the cheek. As he turned he saw Marie had seen the necklace and locket. 'Do you like it, Marie?'

'It's beautiful,' she whispered, trying to keep a note of jealousy out of her voice.

'I'm so glad you like it,' said Isobel, turning back into the room.

Arthur ushered Marie after her. He closed the door behind him and brought two packages from his pocket. He handed one to Marie and one to Lucy.

They both looked mystified.

'Open them then,' he prompted.

They did as they were told and, eagerly anticipating the un-expected, each revealed a small box. Opening them brought gasps of wonder. In each box nestled a silver chain and crucifix with a diamond at the intersection of the cross.

'Gorgeous.' They poured out their thanks as they hugged Arthur and showered him with kisses.

'I knew the other day when we visited the atelier that you would both get good results so decided you deserved a present.'

'Going to wear them now?' asked Isobel.

'Of course,' they chorused.

'Quick then, let's get them fixed. Your friends will be here soon.'

Marie's and Lucy's happiness showed as they all went down-stairs and found a group of comfortable chairs. Drinks were ordered and had barely been touched when the four other girls arrived. Greetings were quickly exchanged.

'It is obvious from your high spirits that you all received good reports from Monsieur Bedeaux.'

'We did,' they agreed with wild excitement.

'Another term like this and he'll have to accept us for the rest of the course,' put in Adelina. 'We've proved ourselves!'

Arthur called for champagne to toast their success.

The evening was a joy for them all. Conversation flowed and, though it was inevitable that much of it was related to art, Arthur guided it successfully on to other topics and allowed individual conversation between neighbours at the table.

Isobel, seated at the foot of the table, had Adelina on her right and, when the time was right, slipped Philip's name into the conversation.

'A likeable young man,' commented Isobel. 'Most charming.'

'He certainly is,' agreed Adelina. 'And he knows it.' Catching the raised eyebrows and taking up the question that flashed in her hostess's eyes, she added quickly, 'I do not mean that in any detrimental way. He has always exuded charm, even as a child. He captured many hearts then. I do not believe he would use it for his own ends, but he likes the attention it brings.'

Isobel experienced a sense of relief though would not admit that openly. 'It must be nice for you to have him in Paris.'

'I don't see much of him, I think he sees more of Lucy.'

'I believe he does. She writes about him.'

'I was surprised when he sought me out. I did not know he was coming here and we had not seen each other for many years. We were close as children and played together. Our two families lived near each other. Then, when he was about thirteen, they moved away and we lost touch. It was good to meet him again.'

Isobel had no chance to pursue the conversation further as Arthur called for silence and then said, 'I want to raise my glass and say how lucky I consider myself, one man with seven of the most charming and beautiful ladies in Paris. To you all – and may the future bring each of you what you most desire.' He drank from his glass and then added, 'I have enjoyed this evening so much and the delightful company has made me feel young again. Mrs Wentworth and I return to England next Wednesday. We are going to visit the Louvre on Monday. Would you all like to join us?' His gaze swept over them, hoping for the answer he wanted.

He need not have worried. Charlotte answered for them all. 'We would be delighted to do so.'

The other girls all voiced their agreement and added their thanks.

'And afterwards we will take you to the best patisserie in Paris.' The others greeted Charlotte's invitation with emphatic approval.

'Scrumptious cakes,' whispered Adelina, recalling past visits.

'Good. I look forward to them. I'll not think about my figure for once,' said Isobel.

Across Paris, Armand Debois was rising from a chair at his club. 'Shall we go into the smoking room?'

Philip agreed. 'My thanks for a wonderful meal.'

Armand dismissed this with a wave of his hand. They found two chairs in a corner from which they could view the rest of the room. The small table between them was no barrier to quiet conversation. They were hardly seated when a waiter placed glasses of brandy in front of them, and another man appeared with a box of cigars. He flipped open the lid, offering it to Philip who declined the invitation to pick one. Armand made his choice and leaned back in his chair with a sigh of contentment.

'Good food, good wine, good company and a playful partner awaiting you, what more could you want from life?' he chuckled.

Philip suppressed his surprise at such an admission from a happily married man. After all, this was Paris, city of mistresses.

'Well, Philip, have you liked what you have seen so far? Do you think you'll want to become a member of this club? I'm sure with your family background there will be no objection to your application but you will need someone to vouch for you. I can do that.'

'That would be kind. I would like you to do so.' He leaned forward and lowered his voice a little. 'You pointed out one or two members when we were dining. What about the gentlemen in here now?'

Debois smiled. He knew full well that Philip would be eyeing potential customers. 'See the bewhiskered man who has just come in?' Philip nodded. 'Comte de Lespinasse, one of the richest men in Paris and with a strong influence on its development.'

'Is he in favour of the industrial expansion about which we hear so much?'

'That is a very thorny question at the moment. There are those who want factories close to Paris so the city will benefit from the increased revenue, and there are those who think it would be better to create a new town solely for that purpose a few miles away. They want to keep Paris a city of open spaces, of fashionable promenading in good clean air, a city of gaiety without the noise, grime and dirt that factories and their workers would bring.'

'And where does the Comte stand on this?'

'Ah, he's not standing; he's sitting on the fence.' Armand gave a little chuckle. 'He may sit too long and others will steal his thunder. See that sandy-haired gentleman taking his drink from the waiter? Monsieur Floquet will buy land at the drop of a hat. When he gets his heart set on something he's like a terrier, determined to hang on and get his way. Could be a potential customer for you.'

Philip's mind was ticking over, absorbing information. Maybe Armand was right. Monsieur Floquet could be more than useful if Philip managed to move first.

'Oh, now there's a man to avoid if he comes to you with ideas he wants financing. Monsieur Taine has his head in the clouds and all his ideas are pie in the sky.'

Philip cringed. How many more clichés was Armand going to use? He'd have to tolerate them; he did not want to offend him by passing any derogatory remark. The evening went by in similar fashion for the next forty minutes until Armand looked at his watch and said, 'Well, Philip, I am afraid I will have to leave you. Time to pick up my little ballerina, can't keep her waiting.'

He rose from his chair. 'I thank you for a most enjoyable and enlightening evening.'

'My pleasure,' returned Armand. 'I'll put in that recommendation immediately. I'm sure there are lots of people here who will contact you on a business level once you get known. Whether you develop any of those contacts in a social way is up to you.'

They had reached the lobby where they collected their capes and hats and bade each other good night.

*

When Marie and Lucy were leaving their apartment to spend Saturday with their parents, Madame Foucarde presented Lucy with an envelope.

'It was left half an hour ago by your young man. I was caught by a visitor otherwise I would have brought it to your apartment.'

Lucy thanked her. As they left the block she slit the envelope open. She glanced at the note and then stopped to read it properly.

Marie saw disappointment cloud her friend's face and knew it was not good news. Seeing Lucy's eyes dampen, she waited for her to speak.

'Philip's going to be away, possibly until Tuesday,' she explained with a catch in her voice.

'Oh, dear, does he say why?'

'Just that it's important and he's sorry.'

'Can't be helped. Try not to let it spoil your day.'

'He won't know about our parents' invitation for him to join us for the evening on Tuesday. I'll have to leave him a note.'

'George will deliver it for you.'

'I hope he's back in time. It's the last night of their visit.'

'I'm sure he will be.' Marie tried to sound comforting.

At that moment Philip was on his way to the racetrack at Chantilly. His hopes were high. He had been studying the form of the runners and had picked out three that he reckoned had a good chance of making him some money.

Reaching the course, he was swept up into the usual atmosphere that heightened his desire to gamble. He took little persuading therefore when, once he had contacted his four friends, it was suggested that after the races they should head for the card tables at a casino Emile knew of in the vicinity. Their winnings on the horses could be improved at the tables.

By the time the last race had finished that general hope was that their losses could be recouped at the tables. It was imperative that Philip should do so. He was startled when he heard a voice call his name and swung round.

'Monsieur Mercier! How nice to see you again.'

'You were looking a bit glum. Not had a good day?'

'Afraid not.'

'You've not had your lucky talisman with you – Blanche.'

'She certainly brought me luck.'

'Or her skill.'

Philip gave a wan smile. 'Yes, she is skilful,' he repeated. 'I must hurry, my friends will be wondering where I am.'

'One moment, please. I was going to come to see you on business but now we've met we can make an appointment. I have something I would like to invest in but do not wish to use my own money in the venture. I would rather borrow, at least for a short while until I saw the way things were going.'

'And you want to do it through my firm?'

'That's the idea. Monsieur Debois told me how helpful you had been to him.'

'You know Armand?'

'And Paul. Now, I'm holding you up. Come and see me on Tuesday. Eleven o'clock.'

'I'll be there.' He had planned to return to Paris late on Tuesday afternoon but this sounded like an opportunity not to be missed.

'You look much brighter,' commented Victor when he'd rejoined his friends. 'Did you get some good tips for next week?'

Philip gave a shake of his head. 'No, it was business.'

'I hope it gives you a better return than the horses did today,' said Auguste.

'The cards might do that.'

'You need Blanche with you,' suggested Jules.

'You're the second person today to make that comment.'

'Maybe there's something in it,' prompted Emile.

Philip began to wonder if that was true when by the end of the evening he had lost heavily for the second time that day. That thought and pondering the forthcoming meeting with Monsieur Mercier occupied his mind throughout Sunday and on his return to Paris on Monday afternoon. He went straight to his office and was thankful that he did, for he found a note had been left there for him.

Opening it, he saw it was from Lucy and read that her Mother and Mr Newton had invited them to dine on Tuesday evening. He blessed his good luck in meeting Monsieur Mercier. If he had not he would not have returned to Paris until late on Tuesday and he knew how that would have upset Lucy. Fortune had smiled on him there at least; maybe she would smile further when he met Monsieur Mercier.

Chapter Twelve

Philip made sure he was at Monsieur Mercier's on time. He had judged him to be a stickler for punctuality and, mindful of the possibilities that might open up from this meeting, was determined to appear in a good light from the start. The footman showed him straight to Monsieur Mercier's study.

'Good day, my boy.' Monsieur Mercier rose courteously from the chair behind his desk, shook hands with him warmly and indicated an armchair. 'A glass of wine?'

'Only if you are taking one, sir.'

Monsieur Mercier rang a bell and Philip realised it must have been a prearranged signal for within a matter of moments the footman reappeared carrying a tray with two wine glasses and a decanter.

'I presumed Bordeaux would be acceptable,' said Monsieur Mercier, casting a querying glance at Philip.

'Most certainly.'

With glasses charged, Monsieur Mercier leaned back in his chair, raised his glass and said, 'I hope this leads to a pleasant and rewarding acquaintanceship.'

'I hope so too, sir.'

'Now, to get down to business. I have some land in Calais. With its potential as a developing port, I am thinking in terms of building warehouses there and leasing them to firms with export businesses who don't want to build their own. I will therefore require some working capital. At this stage, as I briefly mentioned, I don't want to use my own money; it would need some complicated manoeuvring. Armand Debois told me of the speedy and pleasant way in which you were able to oblige him and so, having checked up on the reputation of your firm, I have come to you.'

'I am pleased you have, sir, and will do all I can to oblige you. I can assure you of the soundness of my family's firm. We have a fine reputation in Switzerland though until now have not offered our services outside that country. I should be delighted if you became our second French client.'

Monsieur Mercier went on to explain his scheme and produced maps of Calais. Philip saw that the land was in an ideal position for development for the purpose the businessman had in mind. 'The land has been in the family for a very long time. With its proximity to the new developments at the docks, I see I can turn it to my advantage rather than leaving it idle.'

Philip had been studying the maps and realised that Monsieur Mercier's proposition had great potential and would make an ideal investment opportunity for his own company.

'Have you any idea, sir, to whom you might lease such warehouses?'

'That is something I am looking into but the matter is at a very early stage.'

'There is talk of factories being built on the northern outskirts of Paris.' Philip made the comment tentatively.

'I've heard so too.'

'It would perhaps be advantageous for you to know what type of factories?'

'Naturally. I'm already trying to glean that information but the people concerned are not saying much at the moment. If you hear anything I would like to be the first to know; it may well affect negotiations between us.'

'I understand that, sir. Also that this is merely an exploratory conversation.'

'It is. I wanted to know about the possibility of raising finances from your firm should I go ahead with my plans. With an understanding between us now, it will save time when and if I go ahead with the project I have in mind.'

'Well sir, I can put your mind at rest. The financial backing will be there if you need it. I will inform head office immediately. I am sure they will raise no objection. If you could give me a little more detail, say the acreage to be developed, the number of warehouses you are proposing to built, whether there will be houses built for workers, the accessibility of the sites for the transportation of the products whatever they are, and access to the docks . . . I am sorry to put you to this trouble but the information can only strengthen my proposals to head office.'

'Quite right. I will see you have all that in the next two days.'

'I look forward to receiving it, sir. I am sure we will then come to an arrangement that will be beneficial both to you and to my firm.'

Monsieur Mercier stood up and extended his hand. The business interview was at an end. Philip knew there would be no social exchanges but ventured to ask, as Monsieur Mercier escorted him to the door, 'Sir, have you heard from Madame Daudet since she returned home?'

'Yes, we have, only this week. She is well and wished to be remembered to you if either my wife or I saw you. I apologise for not mentioning it. It had slipped my mind.'

'Understandable, sir. Goodbye.' He shook hands and left the house.

As Philip walked back to his office his step was light. Blanche had not forgotten him, had even bothered to send him a message; he was pleased by that. And his interview with Monsieur Mercier had proved fruitful. Not only had it resulted in what could be a lucrative deal for his firm, it had also yielded information that could prove useful to Philip personally. If Monsieur Mercier was contemplating building warehouses at Calais then he must know more about the factory developments near Paris than he was revealing. Could there be more land available round Calais that Philip could exploit? Or was he better concentrating on factory sites around Paris? But whichever he followed up, he must move quickly.

As soon as he was in his office he was poring over maps and did so until he had a list of possible areas imprinted on his mind. Now he must try to glean more information about factory projects. Maybe this called for a visit to the Auberon, but he could not do that this evening or would be forced to forego Mrs Wentworth's last evening in Paris.

*

Philip arrived at the Continental to a friendly welcome and, from their reactions, was sure he had chosen well when he presented Isobel with a silk shawl and Arthur with two bottles of a superior French wine.

Five minutes later George arrived, apologising for being late as he gave Isobel a bottle of perfume and Arthur a box of cigars, which they both accepted with delight and profuse thanks.

Though the thought of parting hung over the evening, neither parents nor daughters showed their regrets and the evening passed off in the most enjoyable and relaxed manner, stimulated by good food, fine wine and bright conversation.

Once again Isobel and Arthur were impressed by the two young men and felt they would return to England with easy minds about the choices their daughters had made.

The following morning Marie and Lucy arrived at the Continental early in order to have breakfast with their parents before accompanying them to the station to catch the train for Calais. The uneasiness of the parting was dispelled when Charlotte, Yvette, Gabrielle and Adelina arrived unexpectedly five minutes before the train was due to leave. The departure was turned into a brighter occasion when their joking comments sent laughter ringing round the station.

'We thought Marie and Lucy would need cheering up once you had left,' explained Charlotte. 'We have something planned.'

'What might that be?' asked Marie.

'If I told you it would not be a surprise.'

Though pressed by both Marie and Lucy she would not give way. Then all thoughts of what the four girls had in mind were swamped when the final call to board the train swept along the platform.

Goodbyes were made, kisses exchanged and hugs imparted in the last hasty moments. Doors clattered shut, steam hissed from the engine, a whistle blew and slowly the train moved forward. Words were shouted, some caught, others lost in the cacophony. They watched the train slowly disappear and were aware of a sudden quiet. People turned away and there was a general air of sadness and regret.

Marie and Lucy, looking glum, started towards the exit. Their four friends had moved a short distance away to allow them to make their final farewells to their parents. Now Charlotte glanced at her three companions and gave a little nod. They all moved as one to Marie and Lucy and swept round them, laughter on their lips as they grabbed them by their arms and bustled them along. 'Come on, we're going down to the river. We'll find a waterside restaurant and then laze around.'

Marie and Lucy could not turn down the invitation being extended for their benefit. They threw off their despondency. After all, their parents would not want them to be miserable. They were in Paris and meant to enjoy themselves. Which was exactly what they did for the rest of the day. The four other girls had just received their generous monthly allowances from their parents and each had contributed towards hiring a boat and boatman to take them on the water. The day passed all too quickly for them but all found it relaxing and when they finally came ashore they knew it had prepared them for the new term.

Marie and Lucy insisted that the others should all come round to their apartment where they could eat and plan their evening. Lucy was glad of the suggestion for when they reached the apartment she found another note from Philip awaiting her.

Marie saw an expression of disappointment cross her face. 'What is it?' she asked.

Lucy screwed up her face. 'Philip may be away a few days on business.'

'I'm sorry.'

Lucy gave a little toss of her head and thrust her discontent aside. She should not spoil the rest of the evening for her friends. 'I suppose it can't be helped. Business is business and setting up a branch in Paris for the first time will make its demands on him.'

'I expect it does,' agreed Marie.

'Right, then let us enjoy ourselves. It will soon be work, work, work.'

As the girls mingled with the crowds strolling along the boulevards in the fine evening air, Philip entered the Auberon. After depositing his cape and hat with the attendant in the cloakroom, he ordered a glass of wine and went to the main lounge. He took a seat beside a small table from where he could see most of the room. He was aware of glances cast in his direction. He had expected as a newcomer to draw such attention. He sat down and accepted the drink when it was brought to him.

He had been there ten minutes watching members come and go when he saw a man of about twice his age approaching him. He was slightly built but elegant in a well-fitting evening suit. Philip's immediate thought was that here was a man who looked after himself. There was something undeniably distinguished about his fine head and well-groomed hair, greying at the temples.

'Good evening, Monsieur. A new member, I venture to guess.'

'I am indeed, sir. Philip Jaurès.' He held out his haïd.

'Leon Lorrain.'

'Pleased to meet you, do sit down.' Philip indicated the chair opposite his.

'Thank you.' Lorrain sat down and placed the drink he had brought with him on the table. 'I make it my business to speak to a new member when I see one. Some of the others here, I think, can be a little slow to do so. Jaurès? The name seems to mean something to me.' He frowned as if searching his brain, then almost at the same moment snapped his fingers. 'Yes, you have come to open a branch for your Swiss investment firm. I believe you are a member of the family?'

'You are quite right.'

'It is only what I heard about town. I did not know that you had become a member here.'

'Courtesy of Armand Debois.'

'Ah.' Lorrain nodded. 'An influential member.'

'Then I was lucky to meet up with him.'

'Through business?'

'Yes. If you don't mind my asking, what are your interests?'

Lorrain smiled. 'I suppose you mean in the way of business?'

Philip returned his smile. 'Of course.'

'Ah, well, I suppose that question is inevitable in a club like this. Shipping is my line. And before you ask or offer – no, we

175

do not seek funds for expansion. We are content as we are, with ten freighters plying between France, Britain, Scandanavia, and recently we have branched out into the American trade.

'Sounds as if you are successful.'

'We are indeed. Though there is some controversy within the firm as to which French port should become our main base'

'But don't you use them all?

'I suppose we do, but you do need a busy port from which to conduct your main trading.'

'But wouldn't that have to be Calais?'

'Well, it depends on certain developments . . .'

This conversation was taking a turn in a direction Philip saw could prove useful to him. Unfortunately just then a waiter came to tell Monsieur Lorrain that his table was ready and Philip saw his chance to learn more being thwarted.

Lorrain started to get out of his chair but stopped. 'Have you eaten?'

'No,' replied Philip.

'Care to join me?'

He wasn't going to let this chance slip. 'That is most kind.'

Lorrain looked at the waiter. 'Lay another place at my table.'

'Yes, sir. And I'll tell the chef to delay your meal.' He turned smartly to Philip. 'I'll bring you a menu immediately, sir.'

The fiow of their conversation had been interrupted but a quarter of an hour later, seated together in the dining room, they were able to take it up again, prompted by Philip who said, 'You were intimating that Calais may not be the best base for your company?'

'That is so. As I said, it depends on developments.'

'In Calais?'

'No, around Paris. Surely you've heard of the move to build some factories on the northern side of the city?'

'I've heard rumours.'

'Well, the placing of those factories is the key to which port will be the fastest to develop. Like most other shipping firms, that is where we'll want to be.'

'So the controversy within your firm, that you mentioned, is about that?'

'Yes, there are those who think Calais, because of its nearness to Britain and the shorter distance to Scandinavia, will benefit most. Others favour Le Havre because it is at the mouth of the Seine and could deal with river traffic from Paris. Also it is nearer to America so would benefit from the growing trade with that country.'

'When do you think this debate is likely to be settled?'

Leon Lorrain shrugged his shoulders. 'Who can tell? Schemes come and schemes go. Many rumours are voiced and die a death, but those that are about now are much more substantial. Developments in these two ports depend on the decision-making of the Parisian factory owners, or rather those proposing to build factories, and what is more important than where they intend to site them? Study the maps, Philip, and you will see that certain sites would benefit the trade passing through Le Havre and others would direct trade through Calais. And of course the building of those factories would depend on the availability of land, whether it is suitable for building purposes and its price.'

'Does nobody know what sort of factories these will be?'

'Again there are rumours, but I don't think the choice of goods would have a major impact on which port will be used. It would, however, have a significant influence on expansion, particularly in the way of dock space and warehousing. Whichever way the situation goes there could be many firms seeking money for development. I'm sure if you keep your eyes open, your firm could benefit.'

As he walked home Philip turned this conversation over in his mind. Leon had been right, there would be many opportunities for his firm to finance proposed projects, but there could also be the chance for him personally to speculate on certainties and swell his own bank account.

The following morning he studied his maps again in the light of what he had learned from Monsieur Lorrain. He had previously concentrated on Calais, as indeed Monsieur Mercier seemed to have done, but that might have been because he already had land there. Philip had never really considered Le Havre, but Leon Lorrain had opened his eyes to that possibility. With two outlets for goods from new factories everything would depend on which area north of Paris was designated for industrial use. He scrutinised every possible aspect of the project again and in the afternoon hired a carriage to take him to view all the parcels of land he estimated would be considered for factory-building.

The next morning he was still debating which he thought best to exploit. Realising that it must be linked to developments at Le Havre and Calais, he decide to pay both ports a visit to see for himself the possibilities for expansion in each one.

Four days later when he returned to Paris he realised that if he was to speculate, he had to act soon and do it discreetly. On his way home from his office he called at the Auberon on the off chance that he might pick up a bit of news or gossip.

When he went into the main lounge he saw Leon Lorrain sipping a glass of whisky, clearly in a thoughtful mood.

'You look serious,' Philip said.

Leon, so deep in thought that he was unaware of Philip's approach, started. 'Oh, my goodness. I didn't see you. Do sit down.'

'I hope your thoughts weren't as serious as your expression?'

Leon gave a wry smile. 'Well, I suppose it depends on how you look at it. We had a meeting today to settle which port is to be our main base. Le Havre and America won.'

'And you don't agree with that decision?'

'Well, I'm still not sure. I was just thinking over what was said.'

'But you could switch once further details are known if others favour Calais?'

'Yes, we could, but certain aspects of our plan need to be put into motion as soon as possible. If we then had to switch we would have wasted money. But the decision has been made and we all have to stand by it and do our best to see that it comes good. When I consider all the arguments, I think the right decision was made. The main premise of the argument was that the Seine could be used for transporting goods to Le Havre, and I agree it is an important point.'

Philip now had much to consider. Of his two chief informants, Monsieur Mercier was putting underway the building of warehouses in Calais while Monsieur Lorrain's firm had come out strongly in favour of Le Havre. The more he thought about it and linked their decisions with his own surveys of the land and the two ports, the more confused he became. And then he recalled that because Monsieur Mercier had come to him for funding when he had already put in motion his scheme, he must have had some inside information.

As Philip left his house the next day his mind was made up.

In the office he made one last survey of the maps. Yes, the Seine would provide a water link with Le Havre, and there was land near the river that had looked most suitable when he had visited it. But he saw little real difficulty in transporting goods to Calais by road and the nearest land to the route that would be taken was entirely suitable as far as he could judge. Calais was close to Britain, and Monsieur Mercier . . .

He left the office at a brisk pace and his enquiries soon led him to the small company that owned the land adjacent to the Calais route. The offer he made met no opposition when he said that he could complete all the financial arrangements that morning. His next call was to a small bank, Banque de la Seine, the manager of which was only too willing to open an account in the name of Jaurès Aspect with only Philip himself empowered to deal through it. He then went to the main bank that he was using for the Juarès Investments account and asked them to transfer a substantial sum to the Jaurès Aspect account at the Banque de la Seine. It was, he explained, intended for contingency purposes for a short period of time after which the whole sum would be transferred back to the main account.

Philip returned to his office well satisfied with his morning's work. He was sure that over the coming months he would make a substantial profit by his use of the company's money. That profit would remain in the Jaurès Aspect account at the Banque de la Seine to which he was the only signatory. The company's outlay would be put back into its main account, after Philip had made his killing, with no one but him any the wiser.

Philip smiled to himself, pleased that soon a fortune would be his even though all he had at the moment was a patch of wasteland.

Chapter Thirteen

Edward had set himself a deadline to finish his two commissions by Easter. He would then stay in Whitby to attend the Easter services with his mother and the following week leave for London to deliver the two paintings in person.

'Will you be coming straight back?' Colette asked tentatively the day before he was due to leave, though she thought she already knew the answer. She laid her serviette down and looked across the dining table at her son.

He met her gaze firmly. 'No, Mother. I thought you understood that I might go on to the south coast to make enquiries about my father.'

'Yes, I remember, I just thought . . .' She let her voice trail away.

'No, I haven't given up on the idea. The desire to meet him is as strong as ever.'

'So be it,' sighed Colette, resigned to his determination.

'I may pursue some other possibilities in London before I move on. I will see how things turn out. Have no fear, Mother, I will write regularly so you know where I am.'

Reaching London the next day, Edward went straight to Claridge's where Matthew Robinson had insisted on booking a room for him for a week. Though he had felt embarrassed by Mr Robinson's generosity, Edward realised it would be unfriendly of him to refuse the offer.

Once he was settled in he wrote a note to Mr Fontaine telling him that he was in London to deliver the two paintings he had commissioned. His enquiry with the hotel receptionist about delivery of the note was dealt with immediately and efficiently.

One of the bell-boys was instructed to deliver it and to wait for an answer. He returned with an appointment for Edward at eleven o'clock the next morning.

The next day the same boy took charge of one of the paintings and guided Edward, carrying the other, to Mr Fontaine's home.

On his arrival a butler showed Edward to Mr Fontaine's study. Abbas rose from behind a large oak desk and came to greet Edward with a warm handshake.

'I was so excited when I got your message last night but I had guests so had to curb my desire to see the paintings until this morning. It did at least enable me to invite my friend, Mr Lomax Sotheran, to join us.' He turned to the gentleman who had risen from a leather armchair near the window. 'Lomax, this is the young man I was telling you about.'

'I am pleased to meet you, sir,' said Edward as he shook hands with a smartly dressed man he judged to be in his fifties. Edward saw kindness in the keen eyes that were already making a judgement of this young artist.

'One of the paintings I commissioned is a gift for him. I knew he would like to meet the artist so here he is.'

'I hope I have done justice to the subject.'

'Well, let us see,' cried Abbas eagerly.

Edward carefully unwrapped the first canvas while the two men stood by in silent anticipation.

'Ah, that is mine,' cried Abbas when the picture was revealed. 'Wonderful! Wonderful!' His eyes were bright with admiration for the scene, looking downstream from the bridge in Whitby. 'That ship passing between the two stone piers, leaving the harbour for destinations unknown, will always carry me far across the ocean. The atmosphere you have created around that departure takes me on board for the adventure of a lifetime.' He turned to Edward with a broad smile. 'Young man, that painting will give me untold pleasure.'

Lomax had stood quietly by, delighted by his friend's enthusiasm and wondering what his own painting had in store for him. What subject had Abbas chosen? He was brought out of his reverie by the question, 'What do you think of it, Lomax?'

'Delightful.' He turned to Edward. 'You undoubtedly have talent to get such atmosphere into your painting.' He looked expectantly at Abbas.

'All right, all right.' He threw up his arms in mock surrender. 'I know you are longing to see my gift to you.'

Edward took that as a signal and began to unwrap the painting.

When the final sheet of paper was removed a tense silence descended on the room. The outburst of enthusiasm that Edward had anticipated did not erupt. Disappointment was settling over him when he glanced at the two men. He saw they were dumbfounded, literally unable to speak as they stared unbelievingly at the picture of Whitby from the West Cliff. This was no ordinary interpretation of the scene. The houses climbing the cliffside one upon the other were there but remained subordinate to the main theme, the ruined abbey high on the cliff top. Edward had interpreted that in an eerie way, using moonlight and cloud to special effect. He knew he had created a ghostly atmosphere, and was pleased when he heard Mr Sotheran whisper, 'Ghostly monks shadow those walls,' for that was what he had tried to depict.

Then the grip that the painting had exerted on the two men was broken when Lomax said with all sincerity, 'It is wonderful, just wonderful. Thank you, Abbas, thank you so much.' There was a catch in his voice and he turned and clapped his friend on the back in appreciation of the gift. A moment later he was shaking Edward's hand. 'What I said about your talent a moment ago was inadequate. This painting shows that you have a very special ability. You are indeed very gifted. How is it we haven't heard of you here in London? And what a good job Abbas's friend Matthew Robinson made him a gift of one of your paintings.'

'Well, thank you, sir, for all your kind words but I'm sure I am not worthy of them.'

'My dear boy, don't hide your light under a bushel. You have a great gift that you should share with people. You must exhibit in London. Abbas is the man to organise that. He did it for Mr Robinson's photographs, he can do it for your paintings.' He looked hard at his friend. 'Can't you, Abbas?'

'I can and would dearly love to, if Mr Clayton will allow me?'

'Sir, I don't deserve this praise.'

'Of course you do,' replied Abbas, 'especially if Lomax says so. He is one of the leading, if not *the* leading, art critics in London.'

Edward was taken aback. If he had known beforehand he would have been even more nervous about displaying his paintings than he had been.

Lomax gave a short laugh. 'I am no artist, young man. Couldn't draw or paint to save my life. But I do know about paintings – what makes them good, what makes them bad. I know about composition, the use of paint, brushwork and so on.'

'Then I am privileged that you think highly of my work.'

'I do indeed, and I insist that before you return north you should have Abbas arranging and organising an exhibition for you.'

'I will be only too pleased,' he said, 'and with Lomax's support I think we could find a good venue. With the right publicity, we could attract real attention. When will you be in London again?'

'I am here for a full week now.'

'Then why don't we meet again and discuss the preliminaries, make a date to aim for and discuss what further subjects you should paint and what you already have available?'

'Admirable,' agreed Lomax. 'Tomorrow it is then. Here again, Abbas?'

'Yes, why not?'

'Good. Same time?'

'If that is suitable?' Abbas looked questioningly at Edward.

'It will suit me. And I thank you, gentlemen, most deeply.'

'Think nothing of it,' said Lomax with a dismissive wave of his hand. 'It will be our privilege to bring a new and vibrant talent to the notice of the world.'

Edward was walking on air when he left, and hurried back to Claridge's.

The following morning, over a hearty breakfast, he considered what paintings he already had that might be used in the proposed exhibition, and what subjects he might suggest for new paintings.

Back at his patron's house once more he was shown straight to the study where he found Mr Fontaine and his friend Mr Sotheran already ensconced in comfortable armchairs.

Edward returned their warm greeting with equal enthusiasm and added an apology. 'I'm sorry if I am late, gentlemen.'

'Indeed you are not,' Mr Sotheran reassured him. 'It is I who was early. I had some suggestions about the exhibition's venue to put to Abbas.'

Abbas Fontaine noted the glance of eager anticipation Edward cast at him. 'Nothing has been decided. It will take a little time to consider the various options but Lomax has made some good suggestions. As a critic he gets around more venues than I do but between us we'll come up with the best available place to suit your work.'

'I'm most grateful for all the trouble you are taking. I only hope my work will come up to expectations.'

'If you keep up the standard you've shown in the two paintings I have seen you need not fear,' put in Lomax. 'I stayed up half the night just looking at the painting Abbas so generously gave me.' He glanced questioningly at Edward. 'Tell me, do you know of a painter by the name of Arthur Newton?'

Edward's heart skipped a beat and then began to pound in the grip of an excitement that was hard to keep under control. He must keep calm. 'I have heard of him but have only seen a few of his works. We have three at home. Why do you ask, sir?'

'Newton came from Leeds. I thought you might have come across his work, for he was better known in the North, though he did sell in London. Your painting reminded me of his work.'

'Did you know him?' Edward asked tentatively.

Lomax shook his head. 'No, I never met him. He was a painter of great promise who I firmly believe never really fulfilled himself. I was so impressed by the first paintings I saw that I kept a check on his progress. Sadly his work fell into mediocrity. Oh, it was good enough to sell but eventually it lacked the sparkle and atmosphere of his earlier paintings. It was as if there were other things on his mind . . . trouble in the family, financial problems, whatever else affects an artist's work. It did sparkle again momentarily but then he seemed to disappear. No more of his work, outstanding or mediocre, appeared on the market. It was as if he had stopped painting.'

184

'And that was it?' said Edward. 'Was he living in Leeds all this time?'

'I was so curious about the man that one day when I was there I made enquiries about him. I learned that he had left Leeds for Scarborough but later moved to the south coast. I tried to pursue the matter on one occasion when I was in Southampton but no one had heard of him there, then I received further clues that took me to Plymouth and Winchester where the trail went cold. I could not get another lead. His moving from one place to another seemed to tell me that he'd wanted to disappear and live a quiet life so I gave up, respecting what I thought he wished for himself. It is a great pity because there was tremendous ability in what I saw. I believe he could have become internationally known.'

It took Edward all his willpower so say nothing at this praise of his father. He wanted to tell somebody, shout it from the rooftops, but he knew it would have to wait until he saw his mother. She was the only one he could confide in. His mind was racing. Then he became aware of Mr Sotheran continuing. 'Your picture of Whitby Abbey at night reminded me of Newton's work. You have great potential, don't let it slip as he did. Be careful of the outside influences that can affect your work. Now I must stop pontificating, we have your exhibition to plan.'

'Have you any completed paintings at home?' asked Abbas.

'Yes, half a dozen, maybe more.'

'They could form the nucleus around which we'll plan the show. But we'll need some eye-catching new work too.'

'I am going to York in three weeks to see a new exhibition,' said Lomax, 'why don't you come with me, Abbas? We could go on from there to Whitby to see Edward's paintings.'

'A splendid idea,' agreed Abbas. 'I have a niece, Hester Stevens – you've met her, Lomax.'

'Yes, a charming girl of about your age Edward.'

He was a little bemused at this change of subject.

Abbas laughed. 'Edward's thinking we are trying to be match-makers. No, young man, let me explain. Hester has helped me with a number of exhibitions I have arranged. She has a very good eye for display, especially of paintings, and I take heed of her opinion on these matters. It would be good if she could see what you already have available.'

'Then she is most welcome, sir.'

'Good, it is settled. We'll come to Whitby in three weeks.' They agreed to arrive there the day after Lomax reached York. 'Book three rooms for us at the best hotel for three nights.'

'I will, sir.'

They went on to discuss other possible subjects.

'Get started right away,' instructed Lomas. 'Have one canvas ready for us to see when we come to Whitby. If it is of the standard of the two you brought with you then we have no worries.'

'Any particular one of the subjects we have been discussing?' queried Edward.

'No, suit yourself. And we'll see if there are any further special lines you should take when we are there.'

On his way home Edward counted himself doubly fortunate. The commissions had been a triumph, and now he'd have a London exhibition devoted to his work. It could attract serious attention; he must see that it did by painting as he had never painted before. He offered a silent plea to his father to help him.

That turned his mind to what Mr Sotheran had revealed. His father had gone to live on the south coast but had kept moving around. Would he ever be found if he kept doing that? Who could tell where he might be? Maybe Mr Sotheran was right and his father had simply wanted to disappear. One way of doing that was to give up painting and it would seem that was what he had done. Mr Sotheran's observation that it was a waste of his talent made Edward all the more determined to find Arthur and persuade him to paint again.

'Good gracious!' Colette showed her surprise when Edward walked in. 'I wasn't expecting you back. I thought you were going to the south coast? I was expecting a letter any day.'

'That was my original plan,' he replied as he shook himself out of his outdoor clothes. 'But something happened in London that dictated I should return home to tell you my news in person.'

186

'And I'm pleased to see you.' She smiled as he kissed her on the cheek. 'You look like a cat who's licked the cream,' she added as she led the way into the drawing room.

'I know,' he said with broad smile. 'It has all been so exciting. I've lots to tell you.'

'Sit down, I'll order tea.' She went to a bell-pull beside the fire. By the time she'd reached her chair the door opened and a maid appeared. 'Tea, please, Tess.

'Now what are you dying to tell me?' Colette asked.

He told her quickly, almost breathlessly, about his meeting with Mr Fontaine and Mr Southeran, the only interruption coming when Tess brought in the tea. Colette ignored it, waiting on tenterhooks for him to go on. Her eyes brightened with every sentence until he reached the news that they were going to arrange an exhibition for him.

'Wonderful, wonderful!' she cried when he had finished. 'This is marvellous, that they should think so highly of your talents as to do this. Oh, your father would have been so proud! And so would Bernard. Matthew will be absolutely delighted to learn that he played the initial part.' She regarded her son with pride in her eyes. 'You've a wonderful opportunity here, Edward, don't let anything spoil it.'

Though he made no comment, he knew his mother was referring to his search for his father.

Colette reached for the teapot. When she had poured, he said, 'I have more to tell you.'

She met his gaze as she handed him a plate of cakes. 'Nothing could be better than what you have already told me.'

'It's completely different but it resulted from my painting of Whitby Abbey by moonlight. You know, the one I took with me?' She nodded. 'Well, Mr Sotheran compared it with Father's paintings. Apparently he knew his work quite well, being an art critic. He too had wondered what had happened to him and had even tried to trace him.'

Colette held her breath. 'Did he find Arthur?' she asked tentatively.

'No. Eventually he gave up because Father had moved about on the south coast. Mr Sotheran gained the impression that he wanted to disappear. He has the feeling that my Father wishes to remain anonymous and live quietly.'

'I hope you will remember Mr Sotheran's opinion.'

'I will, Mother. I have already promised you that I will give up the search if I see anyone is going to get hurt.' Edward gave a brief pause and then added with deep feeling, 'But wouldn't it be a fine thing to find him and get him to paint again, with all the life, verve and atmosphere that only he can put into a painting? We have seen it ourselves, a few others have, but the majority will only have seen him as a competent journeyman, nothing more. Wouldn't it be exciting if we could show his true talent to the world?'

'It certainly would,' agreed Colette wistfully, recalling the magic she had seen appear on canvases in the house in Well Close Square where once she had loved with an intensity that had seared her feelings for life. She started, drew herself back to the present and said, 'You mentioned that Mr Fontaine, Mr Sotheran and Mr Fontaine's niece were coming in three weeks and that you were going to book them some rooms for three nights?'

'Yes.'

'No doubt they will come the day after their arrival to see your paintings and make their choice. Invite them to a meal that evening.'

The next three weeks were far from idle for Edward. He chose night paintings from those he already had. Without compromising his usual standard he also completed one painting of a ship tied up mid-river at Whitby and did several other sketches of the town.

A letter gave him the time of arrival of his mentors and he made sure he was at the station ten minutes before the train was due. He was thankful that it was a pleasant day and his visitors would receive a good impression of the town.

As the time for the train's arrival drew nearer his tension mounted. Anxiety gripped him. Would his paintings be good enough? Would Mr Fontaine and Mr Sotheran be impressed? And what of Miss Stevens? How much did she know of the painter's art? Was she an expert? What influence did she have with her uncle and his friend?

He strolled up and down the platform, dwelling on these questions but finding no answers.

A distant whistle drew him sharply into the present. When the train came in view he stood anxiously watching its arrival. Edward searched over the heads of those hastening to the ticket collector notice to hand in their tickets and set out for various destinations. Then he saw his visitors descending from a carriage near the back of the train. Weaving through the passengers leaving their compartments, he hurried in their direction.

'Mr Fontaine, Mr Sotheran.' He greeted them warmly with a welcoming smile and handshake.

'Mr Clayton.' They greeted him with equal warmth.

Mr Fontaine stood to one side and half turned to a young lady who had held back. 'My dear, come and meet Mr Clayton.' As she stepped forward he added, 'Mr Clayton, my niece, Miss Hester Stevens.'

She extended her hand and eyes filled with curiosity met his. 'I am pleased to meet you, Mr Clayton.'

Edward made a small bow as he took her hand. 'Welcome to Whitby, Miss Stevens. I hope your visit will be a pleasant one.'

'If this weather is a portent then it must be! And equally, I hope our visit will be beneficial to you.'

'Thank you.' Edward's eyes had never left her. He sensed an air of confidence about her as if she was saying, Put your trust in the assessment I will make of your work. It will be a true one and made for your benefit.

He saw that her clothes had been sensibly chosen for the journey. Her topcoat was open down the front and revealed a grey ankle-length skirt, tight-fitting at the waist and topped by a patterned blouse. A silk cravat was tied at her throat. The small straw hat with blue ribbon tied round the tiny crown was placed towards the back of her head, resting on thick, coiled dark hair. Miss Stevens was smart and the toil of the journey had done nothing to mar that. She knew she looked good and it showed in the set of her head and in the knowing light in her dark eyes. She could see the effect she was having on Edward.

A little embarrassed by the pause in the conversation, he said quickly, 'I have a carriage waiting.' He nodded to the porter whom he had primed beforehand to collect their luggage and started to lead the way to the exit.

'Have you always lived here?' asked Hester as she walked beside him while her uncle and Mr Sotheran fell into step behind.

'Yes, Miss Stevens.'

'Oh, please call me Hester. I don't like formality and I shall call you Edward. It will make for easier conversation.' She gave him a quizzical look.

Edward felt his embarrassment fade and smiled his approval of her suggestion. 'I agree with you. The old conventions are too restrictive.'

'We are moving close to a new century, one that may bring great changes in social attitudes. I certainly hope so at any rate.'

They had reached the exit. After they had handed in their tickets, Edward ushered them to the waiting carriage. The porter helped the coachman stow the luggage, and once they were all settled he sent the horses forward to the hotel on top of the West Cliff where Edward had booked rooms.

He supervised their arrival. When they had gone through the formalities of registering, he said, 'My mother has invited you to take tea with us. I will return for you in half an hour, if you agree?'

'That is most kind of her,' replied Abbas. 'We will be delighted to accept.'

He made his goodbyes. As he did so he was aware that once again he had come under Hester's close scrutiny.

When she reached her room and the boy who had carried her leather suitcase for her had left, Hester wandered thoughtfully to the window; the first thing she always did when away from home. She liked to appraise any new view. This time she had a corner room with two windows; one gave her a view to the sea, the other a glimpse of the ruined abbey with the town roofs below. Even from here she could feel the atmosphere of the old town, and with what she had seen on the way from the station recognised that this was a painter's paradise. She looked forward to seeing what Edward had made of it.

With that thought her mind turned to him. He had come over as a likeable young man, particularly when he had got over his initial shyness. That she could understand and excuse. After all, he had been faced with three people who may well hold his destiny in their hands. She liked his open manner and the way in which he had accepted her suggestion that they use Christian names, one that some men would have shied away from in their attempt to observe the conventions. She had sensed his manner become more relaxed towards her and had liked that. She smiled to herself at the thought that he was quite handsome too. She looked forward to seeing him again, meeting his mother and assessing his paintings.

Edward entered the hotel to find Mr Fontaine, his niece and Mr Sotheran waiting for him in the lounge.

He spread his hands in an apologetic gesture as he came to them. 'I'm sorry if I'm late.'

'You aren't,' replied Hester quickly, a point noted by Edward. She was not one to hold back as some young ladies would have done. He liked this modern trait in a young woman who was neither conservative nor overpowering in the way she dressed. She had changed into a simple dress that seemed to be anticipating a coming trend yet did not cry out to be noticed. The only adornment was a pink brooch with a single pearl at its centre, worn at the front of her high-collared white blouse. She carried a silk shawl but no hat so that when they went outside she draped the shawl over her head and twirled one end round her neck.

'We haven't far to go and as it is a pleasant day I thought we might walk,' he observed.

'Splendid,' cried Abbas. 'We are in need of some fresh air after that train ride.'

'Delightful,' called Hester who had crossed the road to get a better view of the port and the sea.

When the three men joined her, Edward saw that her eyes were eager. 'Is this a busy port?' she asked.

'Yes, but not as busy as it once was, especially at a time when communications inland were poor. It dealt in many trades then: coal, alum, whaling, iron ore, fishing. It was noted for its shipbuilding in the heyday of the wooden sailing ships, and of course there were all the allied trades connected with that.'

'Sounds an interesting place.'

'It is. If you have time, and your uncle will permit me, I would like to show you some of the town.'

Abbas started to speak. 'It will be . . .'

'Uncle,' Hester cut in, being particular to sound gentle, 'I can make my own mind up.'

He raised a hand in surrender. 'Quite right, my dear. As you have pointed out to me before, you have a mind of your own.'

'And isn't that exactly why you employ me from time to time?'

Lomax chuckled. 'She got you there, old friend.'

Abbas inclined his head in agreement.

'So there you are, Edward, it's up to me,' said Hester, and paused playfully. 'What do *you* think I should do?'

He was taken aback that she had thrown the decision-making on to him. He had glimpsed the modern young woman in her again, someone ahead of time. He knew she had already made her own mind up but by asking him to decide she had put them on an equal footing, something most women at that time would never have attempted to do.

'Er . . . well, I think you should choose to let me show you some of the sights.'

'Well said, Edward,' she cried, laughter ringing in her voice. 'Tell me when you will call for me at the hotel and I will be ready.'

'I will do that before you leave today.' He then directed everyone's attention to a large house, standing in its own grounds, with sea views. 'That is where Mother and I live.'

'What a wonderful position,' cried Hester. 'You could never get tired of that view.'

Edward smiled. 'That's true. The light is ever-changing so the panorama is different every time you look at it.'

'Spoken with the eye of an artist,' commented Lomax.

Colette greeted them with gentle, lady-like warmth, making them immediately feel welcome and at ease. Her charm won all their hearts, especially that of Hester. This was a lady with whom she could easily be friends.

Immediately they entered the drawing room Lomax's eye was drawn to the painting over the mantlepiece.

'An Arthur Newton!' he exclaimed and hurried across the room to view it. Everyone sensed he did not want the study into which he had suddenly immersed himself interrupted so no one spoke. After a few moments he turned round. 'That is one of the best Newtons I have seen.' He looked at Colette. 'You are indeed fortunate to have it. It is wonderful. Such a great pity that he did not paint more of that calibre.' He glanced at Edward. 'Now I know why you were so interested in him. I'm so sorry I was not able to help.'

Over tea Colette made her invitation for them to dine the following evening, which they accepted with grace and delight. She then asked, 'When would you like to view my son's paintings?'

'Tomorrow morning, if that is convenient, ma'am?' Abbas glanced at Lomax who nodded his agreement.

'Shall we say ten o'clock?' replied Colette.

Before that could be confirmed, Hester, who was raging inside that her uncle had not looked at her for confirmation as well as Mr Sotheran, spoke up. She had other arrangements to fit in. 'If it is convenient, I suggest we have a preliminary look at Edward's work now. It will give us time to think about his paintings and then make our full assessment tomorrow morning.' She turned to him. 'Then in the afternoon I can perhaps take up your offer to show me some of Whitby?'

Edward glanced at his mother and saw her almost imperceptible nod. He looked at Abbas and Lomax. 'Is Hester's suggestion agreeable to you, gentlemen?' They both agreed and he stood up. 'Then if you will excuse me, I will get the work ready in my studio.'

Fifteen minutes later he was back to announce he had everything ready for them to see. They all rose from their chairs but before they left the room Hester stopped them. 'Mr Sotheran, Uncle, I suggest we make no verbal comment when we view Edward's paintings. We should keep our opinions to ourselves. In that way our judgement will not be influenced at the time and we will come to our discussion with open minds.'

The agreement made, Edward led the way to his studio.

'What a wonderful room,' cried Hester with great enthusiasm. 'Oh, the light!'

It came from two large windows that faced the sea.

'It's magical,' both men agreed.

'It is special,' commented Edward. 'Northern light.'

He saw doubt in Hester's eyes but held back his explanation when he saw she was going to comment.

'North? How can it be? We are facing the sea on the east coast.'

He smiled. 'That puzzles a lot of people but due to the curvature of the Yorkshire coastline Whitby faces north, although it is on the east coast.'

'You have admirable working conditions,' commented Lomax, having taken in Edward's comment while viewing the room.

'Mother set it up for me.'

'Let us hope her faith in you is justified,' commented Abbas with a glance at the easel that stood in an ideal viewing position. There was a canvas on it but it was covered with a large cloth. Eight other paintings stood turned to one wall, awaiting display on the easel. A table held Edward's equipment but it was obvious that it had been rearranged so that three sketchbooks could be accommodated. At this moment they were closed. Four chairs had been placed from which the best view of the easel could be obtained, taking into consideration the fall of the light.

'Please do sit down,' Edward invited. 'While I display a painting, tell me when you want to see the next.'

When they were comfortable he drew away the covering on the easel to reveal a seascape. They proceeded to view the eight canvasses that had been stacked against the wall. Without making it obvious Edward studied their faces, hoping he could judge something from their reaction, but he gained nothing for their expressions remained blank.

When they had viewed the paintings to their satisfaction their attention was drawn to the three sketchbooks. Each of them took one and started to work through it, but flicked to the end quickly after Abbas commented, 'It is going to take some time for each of us to look through your sketchbooks. May we take them with us? It would enable us to look at them more in more detail.'

'Certainly,' agreed Edward.

Shortly afterwards the three guests left, saying how much they were looking forward to tomorrow.

Edward spent a restless night, wondering what opinions they had formed of his work. He tried to reassure himself by recalling the positive reactions of Mr Fontaine and Mr Sotheran in London. Would the work he had shown them yesterday enhance that view or detract from it? What had Hester thought? How much did her judgement influence her uncle and Mr Sotheran? She was a forceful young lady and certainly not averse to speaking her mind.

He dozed, becoming wide awake again as such thoughts pushed themselves forward once more, dozed again, became semi-conscious dwelling on a vision of an attractive young lady holding his future in her hands, and then finally fell asleep.

He half woke with a start. The clear early-morning light streamed through the tall window from which he had drawn back the curtains before retiring. He reached for the pocket watch on the table beside his bed. Through bleary eyes he peered at the pointers. Six o'clock. He placed the watch back on the table and flopped back on his pillow with a sigh, wishing he had slept better. Maybe now . . . No. He knew sleep had gone. If he lay in bed thoughts that this could be the most important day in his life would only disturb him.

He slid out of bed, carried out his daily toilet, dressed and went quietly downstairs. He shrugged on his waist-length woollen jacket and stepped out of the house into the sharp morning air. The sun had left the horizon but as yet had not won its battle with the chill. He turned away from the buildings that were extending Whitby along the West Cliff and walked close to the cliff edge. Far below a pewter sea lapped casually at the cliffs that swept in a long curve to rise high beyond the tiny village of Sandsend. He always loved this early-morning walk; it gave him time to think, something he had done more frequently since learning who his true father was. But this morning other thoughts preoccupied him. This day could be a turning point in his life. An exhibition in London could bring him to the notice of the art world and that could open up all sorts of possibilities. How he wished he had his father with him to turn to for advice.

Chapter Fourteen

As one young man in Whitby faced an event that could decide his future, another in Paris anxiously watched developments that could make or wreck his life.

Three weeks had passed since Philip had bought the land that he judged would be valuable once the industrial expansion to the north of Paris began. They had been anxious days. He had tried to obtain more information but there were always conflicting reports. Philip had to content himself with waiting while trying to keep his mind occupied with his firm's business.

'What's the matter with you, Philip?' Lucy put the question one pleasant evening after they had cycled four miles out of Paris and she had chosen a quiet spot beside a stream, hoping the trip would relax him. 'You've hardly spoken all the way here.'

'It's nothing,' he replied.

'I don't believe that,' she countered. 'You've been preoccupied during our last few meetings. Is it me? Have I done something wrong?'

'No, of course you haven't.'

'Then what is it?'

'It's work. I'm in the middle of some delicate negotiations. They would result in a big loan for Jaurès Investments which would put me in really good favour with my father, but the people I'm dealing with are taking their time making up their minds. I'm anxious in case they turn down my proposals for the loan they are seeking.'

'Do you think they are playing a strategic game, keeping you on tenterhooks, hoping you'll come up with better terms?'

'Maybe, but I cannot make them any more attractive.'

'Then see them again and point that out. Tell them you need

an answer or else you'll have to offer the funds to other interested parties.'

'But if I try to force their hand it might result in our losing the contract altogether.'

'Better that than having you in this sort of mood.'

He turned to her and smiled, reaching out to take her hand. 'Have I been such bad company?'

'Yes, you have.'

'I'm sorry.' He leaned closer and kissed her.

'I think I can make you do better than that and help you forget your worries.' Her arms came round his neck and her kisses were many.

Philip responded. He knew he would have to be careful. He would not want to risk making Lucy question him again. He could not tell her that the picture he had painted was a lie and that his real worry was about the gamble he had taken in buying land for his own ends with his firm's money. That sum would have to be replaced in the main Jaurès Investments account within the next five months, before the annual audit took place in September.

'Does Lucy still enthuse about Philip?' Arthur asked Isobel as they were reading the latest letters from their daughters.

They had returned from Paris in high spirits and within the week had arranged to get married during the second week in August. Two weeks after their return, with the other preliminaries attended to, they were about to draw up a list of people to invite to the wedding.

'Indeed she does.'

'Then he and George will have to be invited.'

'I expected nothing else.'

'Good.'

'Why did you ask?'

'No reason.'

'Arthur, is there something on your mind?'

'Not really, just an undertone in Marie's letter where she says that Philip was anxious about some of his work.'

'Lucy mentioned it too, remember?'

'Yes.'

'She doesn't seem to set too much store by it. Things can't always go smoothly at work. He must suffer worries from time to time when working with firms wanting big loans.'

'Of course, forget it. Now, let's get on with this list and then we can send out the invitations. You make a list of the people you would like to invite and I'll do the same.'

Arthur placed a sheet of paper in front of him and picked up a pencil. He wrote 'Marie and George' then paused. Who else? Anyone from his old life? No, no one. He had never kept any strong links. His friend Ebenezer Hirst would be too old to travel, if indeed he was still alive. Arthur had been remiss ever to lose touch with the man who had been instrumental in developing him as an artist, he knew, but when he had decided to 'lose' himself he had ceased to paint, except for his own pleasure, and that had meant cutting himself off even from good friends. He had moved to various places on the south coast after Rose had died to cover his tracks.

He stared at the sheet of paper. Only two names! It was no good putting down his sister and her family – he did not even know where they were. He had an American address for his brother and supposed he should by rights invite him though it was very unlikely that he would be able to come. They had been only occasional correspondents but nevertheless he wrote down 'Oswald'.

He wished he could write down 'Edward', but could not. To do so would reveal secrets that were better left untold, and that would also involve having to invite Colette, who still held a special place deep within his heart, locked away, to be revealed to no one.

'How are you doing?' asked Isobel hesitantly.

'Three so far. Marie, George and my brother in America, though I don't expect he'll come. How about you?'

'Two – Lucy and Philip.'

Arthur's lips twitched with amusement and, as their eyes met, both of them burst out laughing.

'It looks like being a very big wedding,' chuckled Arthur.

'Wait a moment – I can double my list. I'll ask my farm manager and his wife. They have been very good to me.'

'There's going to be quite a big crowd!' Arthur went on with amusement.

'There certainly is,' laughed Isobel. 'Let's leave it that way. A nice quiet ceremony will suit me.'

'If you are sure?'

'Of course I am. As long as you are there, I will be happy.'

'You couldn't keep me away.'

'Maybe the girls won't be pleased.'

'Oh, I'm sure they will understand. After all, it's not as if we're in the first flush of youth.'

Isobel smiled wistfully. 'I wish we were, but there's still life in us.'

'Then it's settled. A small wedding with the guests we have just named. I'll ask George to be my best man.'

Two days later the invitations were sent.

Edward returned from his walk to join his mother at breakfast. Realising he was nervous about the coming assessment of his work, she tried to reassure him that everything would be all right, even though she too could eat little.

At ten o'clock Hester Stevens, Abbas Fontaine and Lomax Sotheran were admitted to the Clayton residence. With greetings exchanged, Colette was turning to the drawing room when Abbas stopped her.

'Mrs Clayton, may we use Edward's studio? It would be better to view his work there?'

'Of course.' She turned and led the way.

When they'd entered the room Edward asked, 'Will you need the use of the easel?'

'Most certainly,' replied Abbas.

Edward began to see that the chairs were arranged so as to view the easel when Abbas stopped him. 'Before we look at the individual paintings, pull up a chair for yourself, Edward.'

As he did so the others arranged theirs in an arc.

Once they were settled Abbas spoke again. 'We studied your sketchbooks when we returned to the hotel yesterday and then had a long discussion about them and what you had shown us here.

We exchanged views and were all agreed that your work was worthy of an exhibition in London.'

Mother and son exchanged a glance of delight.

Edward expressed this immediately as the tension drained out of him. 'Thank you, gentlemen. Thank you, Miss Stevens. How can I express my delight in the faith you have shown in my work?'

Abbas raised a hand in dismissal of Edward's words. He went on, 'But we did not all agree on which paintings we should use nor on what we should ask you to do next. So if we could see the paintings again and discuss them . . .'

'Certainly.' Edward was on his feet in an instant.

Over two hours they studied the eight paintings again and discussed them individually. Edward put in his own views but listened intently to what they all had to say and drew on their knowledge and criticism, storing it away for future reference. He valued their opinions and realised that Mr Sotheran, although no artist himself, knew a great deal about techniques and was easily able to read the artist's intentions. He was astonished by Hester's knowledge and her insight into what he was attempting to do in each painting. It was she who immediately voiced her thoughts after they had seen the eighth painting.

'I am still of the opinion that we want only six of these paintings, provided Edward can manage to paint a seventh in the time we have before the exhibition. Knowing the venue, I believe seven will be enough. We will be able to present each one individually – so that no one painting will intrude on another. Each painting will make its own individual impact and will, I believe, be more likely to sell because it will attract the buyer's eye without any undue distraction.' She caught Edward's expression. 'You look a little disappointed?'

He was embarrassed that she had caught his momentary display of doubt. 'No, no,' he hastened to reassure her. 'It was just that I thought maybe all of them . . .'

'Believe me, I am right,' she said firmly.

'I wasn't questioning your judgement.'

Hester did not deem it worthwhile to say any more on the matter. Instead she said, 'It is now a question of the new painting we want you to finish before the exhibition, so that we have one we can list as your very latest work. We decided it had to be based on something from one of your sketchbooks, and choosing one sketch in particular caused us a problem because we could not agree which it should be. We will show you the three we have chosen and leave it to you to make the selection – the one you would be happiest to work into a painting.'

'Very well, that seems the best idea.'

As there was one from each book, Hester was able to lay them out side by side on the table.

Edward saw they were of three widely differing subjects and could be interpreted in a number of ways. One was a close-up of a cliff face seen from above so that the viewer received the impression of looking down that face to the sea below. The second was of a stream cascading over rocks and stones, a moment frozen by the artist but still hinting at the passage of time. The third was a composite of a shipwreck on a wild sea that gave way to the tranquillity of a peaceful ocean on which he had imposed a small sketch of a funeral with a smudged outline of Whitby Abbey behind.

He took a few moments to think about them all and visualise what he'd had in mind when he'd made the sketches. Finally he stabbed his finger at the first one. 'That,' he said.

'Why?' Hester asked.

'The challenge of perspective attracted me. I'd always intended some day to work this sketch into a painting that would give the viewer the impression he or she was standing right on the edge of a precipice. I also see in this subject a wonderful opportunity to work in many colours.'

'Excellent,' beamed Abbas.

Edward glanced at Lomax for his approval. 'It wasn't my choice,' he said.

'Yours, Mr Fontaine?'

'No, Hester's.'

She gave a little smile when she caught Edward's glance in her direction. 'Two minds . . .'

*

When Edward called for Hester at her hotel for their prearranged sight-seeing tour of Whitby shortly after half-past one, she immediately put a question to him. 'The cliff painting that you propose to do, where are the actual cliffs?'

'Ravenscar, down the coast.'

'Far?'

'Seven miles or so, why?'

'I would like to see them but it's too far to walk.'

'I could hire a carriage.' He saw excitement flash in her eyes and did not wait for her approval. 'Come on.' He grasped her hand, set off and escorted her down a path that joined a roadway that ended up by the river. As he headed for the bridge he noted that she made no attempt to loosen her hand from his and sensed her pleasure at having done something on the spur of the moment.

As they hurriedly made their way through the townspeople going about their daily lives he pointed out various points of note and found she took a keen interest in everything he had to tell her about the port.

They crossed the bridge to the East Side and in Church Street entered the stables at the White Horse.

'Good day, Mr Clayton.' The ostler turned to Hester and touched his brow with his forefinger. 'Ma'am.'

'Good day, Ben. Can you fix us up with a horse and trap?'

'No trouble.' Ben gave a shout and a youth appeared. In a matter of a few minutes they had a horse between the shafts of a trap that showed evidence of having been recently polished.

'Thanks, Ben. Tell Mr Powell to put the hire charge on my account.' Edward discreetly passed Ben a coin and tossed one of lesser value to the youth who was holding the horse steady. He caught it deftly, grinned and called, 'Thanks, Mr Clayton.'

Edward climbed into the trap, took the reins and held out a hand to assist Hester who was being helped into the trap by Ben.

'Comfortable?' he asked when she had settled and accepted the rug the ostler offered her.

'All ready,' she called, smiling happily.

Edward sent the horse out of the stable yard and soon they were climbing the road to the cliff-top, leaving Whitby and the abbey behind. He kept to a gentle pace, controlling the horse with care.

'This is fun!' called Hester with glee, shedding her serious art critic image. She unfastened the ribbon from around her chin, removed her small hat and loosened her hair to allow the breeze to flow through it.

Edward smiled at her. He liked this mood of carefree abandonment, so different from the self-contained picture she had presented in the company of her uncle. He made the pace a little faster, bringing joyous laughter to her lips. He wanted to ask questions about what she thought of his work but did not want to spoil the atmosphere of the afternoon. Perhaps on the way home?

They chattered about this and that, moving wherever their thoughts took them, but both avoided mentioning art and the forthcoming exhibition.

Six miles from Whitby he turned on to a narrow track that gradually allowed them a view of the coastline. Hester went silent. A few moments later she placed a hand gently on his arm. 'Please stop,' she said quietly, her eyes fixed on the view. He did as he was asked without saying a word for he saw she was transfixed.

Below them the cliffs swept down towards a long curving stretch of sand before soaring again to a high bold headland. A perfect bay, and across it, nestling under the rising cliffs, were the red roofs of a small village glowing in the sunshine.

'Wonderful,' whispered Hester. 'Truly magnificent.'

'So it looks today,' replied Edward, 'but see it when storms lash this coast and you'd think differently.'

'What is the village?'

'Robin Hood's Bay. A fishing village, once the haunt of smugglers.'

'How romantic!'

'Maybe, but it's seen many a raid by Revenue Men that's ended with bruised heads and broken limbs.'

He flicked the reins and kept the horse to a walking pace so that Hester could enjoy the nuances of the ever-changing scene as they moved along the track that would take them to the cliff's edge. He finally halted the horse close to a broken fence. Climbing down, he tested it and decided it was strong enough for him to tether the horse to it. Once that was done he helped Hester to the ground.

'Just a few yards now,' he said.

She did not speak, but when he stopped walking slipped her hand into his and gripped tightly, for they were on the very edge of the cliff.

'There,' he said, looking down.

Hester followed his gaze. The cliff dropped sheer from their feet, and a few yards to their right turned at right angles to form a small headland so that they were gazing down a wall of rock in many colours: brown, fawn, green and black. Far below the sea broke on an outcrop of rocks that churned its blue and green into foaming whiteness.

Hester gazed in awe for a few minutes before she spoke. 'Unbelievable. Out of this world.'

'Very much of it,' corrected Edward.

'Truly,' she replied. 'You have all the correct proportions and angles in the sketch you did. Oh, it will be so wonderful for you to bring colour to it!'

'I also aim to bring atmosphere. It will be no photographic representation,' Edward said with resolve.

'Good. I do so look forward to seeing it. Can we walk a little?'

'Of course. We have plenty of time.'

'I'll need to return to the hotel to change, remember.'

'I will.'

'I hope this is not giving your mother too much trouble.'

'It isn't. In fact, she's enjoying it. She likes the planning, and I know Cook likes to do something different from our usual meals.'

'Good. That is a relief. I know that none of us would want to be any bother.'

'Rest assured, you aren't.'

'Ah, but what would you have thought if we had turned your work down?' she asked with a teasing twinkle in her eye.

'Well, it would have been a blow but I would have applied myself to doing what I am doing now.'

'And what is that?'

'Enjoying your company.'

'Flatterer!'

'No, I mean it.'

'Then I thank you for the compliment.'

'You are here for another day. May I show you Whitby tomorrow and then take you to Sandsend to walk the cliffs there?'

'That would be very agreeable and will give me more to think of when I am back in London.'

'Have you always lived there?'

'Yes, on the outskirts. It is not long before we are in the country but we don't have views like this.' There was a touch of regret in her voice.

'You must try and come again.'

'Maybe I could persuade Uncle to let me come and see how you are getting on,' she added mischievously.

'How did you come to help him with organising exhibitions?'

'It's only a sideline to his true occupation of antique dealer and came about because of his interest in art. I went along with him to an exhibition, not one that he had organised, and started criticising the way the paintings had been displayed. He realised I had an eye for that sort of thing and I've helped him ever since.'

'That is my gain.'

'And I suppose now you want to know what I think of your painting?'

'Well, I wasn't going to spoil your day out but I *was* going to ask you on our way back to Whitby.'

'It wouldn't have spoiled my day.'

'Then, your honest opinion, please?'

'It is no good giving anything else. If I didn't, I wouldn't be true to myself and nor would it do you any good to be given a false assessment. Edward, you have tremendous innate talent. In one or two of your paintings, while they are still good, I can see you lost interest in your subject before you finished the work. But in others, where your interest has not waned, there is real power.

'Even if you are painting for yourself, you need a purpose for tackling that particular subject, and I can see you have that in most cases. Make sure it is always there whenever you paint in

205

the future. I think your exhibition will be a success. I have seen worse ones that have paid off for the artist, but yours should go beyond that. There is a quality to your work that stands out. I believe knowledgeable people will seek it out.'

Edward had listened intently and realised that Hester was a shrewd judge. He only hoped her prediction would prove correct.

'You flatter me,' he said.

'No, Edward, I don't,' she replied in all seriousness. 'To do so would be wrong. I meant every word I said. Tell me, does your mother paint?'

'No. She's a photographer.'

'Professionally?'

'Yes, she sells locally.'

'I must ask her to let me see some of her work. Please encourage her. Maybe an exhibition?'

'If you can persuade her.'

'I can see where you get your eye for a picture, but your talent . . . no one else in your family paints?'

Edward was caught in a dilemma. What should he do – reveal his true ancestry? If he did, what might it lead to? He had promised he would step back if he thought any harm might result. Was this such a time? He liked Hester but she was a comparative stranger to him. What might she do if he revealed he was the son of Arthur Newton? Might she know something of his father? But how could she know more than Mr Sotheran? He was close to dangerous ground, he knew. He stepped back.

'No,' he replied. 'I don't know where my interest comes from. I used to draw as a child and my mother encouraged me.'

'And then as you grew up you sought out the techniques of other artists. I can see you have studied Arthur Newton's work. You have that painting of his in your house and I think you have probably seen some more. I can see his influence behind some of your techniques, especially in the paintings you delivered to Uncle Abbas and Mr Sotheran. Am I right?'

Edward gave a little smile and nodded. 'Yes, I like Arthur Newton's work. I did not know it was so obvious that he had influenced some of my paintings.'

206

'Only to an expert eye that knows of his work – oh, dear, that sounds as if I am flattering myself. But do be careful not to become a slave to his work; develop your own talent, your own special techniques and way you interpret a subject. Now, I think I have said enough on the subject.'

'And I think I had better get you back to Whitby.'

Edward drove to Hester's hotel. When he'd helped her from the trap she said, 'Thank you so much for such an enjoyable afternoon.'

'It has been my pleasure,' he replied. 'And we have tomorrow.'

'Yes, I look forward to it. But although he puts no restrictions on me, I had better see if Uncle Abbas has anything arranged, although I think he will welcome time with his friend.'

'We can plan something when you come to dinner this evening.'

'We can,' she agreed. 'I am looking forward to it. Goodbye for now, and thank you again for such a delightful afternoon and for your company.' Her eyes intent on his were accompanied by a warm appreciative smile.

It was a thoughtful Edward who drove the trap back to the stable and reserved it for the following day before he walked home.

Hester found her uncle reading a newspaper in the lounge when she entered the hotel.

'On your own?'

He nodded. 'We had a walk and Lomax was feeling a little tired so went for a rest in readiness for this evening. Did you have a pleasant time?'

'Splendid,' Hester replied. The enthusiasm in her voice and the sparkle in her eyes were not lost on her uncle. Had she a liking for Edward Clayton or was it too soon after the recent breakdown of her deep friendship with a young man he had always suspected of duplicity? To be proved correct had given him no pleasure. 'I asked Edward if he would show me the cliff he is going to paint for his final picture for the exhibition.'

'And?' he prompted when she paused.

'It's stupendous. An awkward angle looking down a sheer cliff face – but, oh, the colours. I hope he can do justice to it on canvas.'

'He will, unless I am very much mistaken. Where is it?'

'Ravenscar, about seven miles down the coast.'

'So you won't have seen much of Whitby?'

'No, but if you have nothing arranged for tomorrow, Edward suggested he should show me more of the town and then take me to Sandsend.'

Abbas smiled to himself, wondering what Hester's reaction would be if he said that he did have something in mind. He gave a dismissive wave of his hands. 'The only thing I am going to arrange is for Mrs Clayton and Edward to dine with us tomorrow evening. My dear, you do what you like during the day. Enjoy yourself.' He looked at the wall clock. 'I suppose we may as well take our time over getting ready for this evening.' He pushed himself from the chair and, accompanied by his niece, went upstairs. 'See you in the lounge at six,' he said as they parted company.

Closing the door behind her, Hester did a pirouette in the middle of the room and flung her arms wide in ecstasy. This evening, dinner with Edward. Tomorrow he would show her Whitby, and then tomorrow evening she would share a table with him again. Oh, how she wished her stay were to be longer. Would she have to wait until he came to London before she saw him again?

Abbas, Lomax and Hester arrived at the Clayton residence to a warm welcome. Colette and Edward came into the hall to greet them on hearing the maid attend the front door. After the visitors had disposed of their outdoor clothes, Colette, chatting to Abbas and Lomax, led the way into the drawing room, leaving Edward to escort Hester.

'May I say what a beautiful dress you are wearing,' he remarked. 'The colours suit your complexion so well.'

Hester blushed, but was delighted that her choice had caught his attention and he had thought so well of it as to remark about it. The brocaded silk was patterned with red and yellow roses. It had a square neckline and short sleeves. The neckline was trimmed with dark green velvet matched by a loose belt around the waist. Her hair was taken up from the back and pinned on top with an aigrette of similar material. Around her neck was a silver chain which held a heart-shaped pendant beneath her throat.

'Thank you,' she replied with a demure inclination of her head. 'I did so enjoy seeing those cliffs today.'

'I'm glad. And very pleased you asked me to take you there. Now, when you see the finished painting, you will be able to judge if I've done justice to that scene.'

'I'm sure you will, though I now recognise it is an even greater challenge than I'd judged from your sketch.'

Colette gracefully ushered them to their seats and Edward poured the wine. Friendly conversation ranged wide and was continued during the elaborate meal. With further wine taken in the relaxed atmosphere of the drawing room afterwards, the evening was judged a success by all.

'My niece tells me you took her to see the cliffs that we picked out for you to paint,' remarked Abbas to Edward as he settled into his chair.

'Yes.'

He gave a little chuckle. 'Maybe you shouldn't have done that. She'll be all the more critical of your interpretation.'

'Then it might be a good idea if she keeps an eye on my progress.' The words were out almost before Edward realised what he was proposing so he added quickly, 'But that would not be possible, I suppose. We are so far from London.'

Hester's heart had started racing when she heard Edward's unexpected proposal. Did he really mean it? And was there more behind the suggestion?

'Oh, I don't see that as a problem,' countered Abbas. 'There is an adequate train service and Hester is a self-sufficient young lady who is not averse to travelling alone.'

Hester held her breath. Where was this conversation going? Would it be in the direction she wanted, a direction she had not dreamed of a moment ago?

'What do you think, Hester?' her uncle asked.

She caught a twinkle in his eye that only she could interpret. Had he engineered this? Suspected she had feelings for this likeable young man in spite of their short acquaintance and seen it might alleviate the hurt she had recently suffered?

'It might prove useful to see how Edward is progressing.

Knowing where we are holding the exhibition, I have a place in mind to hang that painting but it will have to be just right. Though I could not presume to tell an artist what he should do, of course.'

'You would not be doing that,' Edward put in quickly. 'Suggestions are always valuable, and in this case knowing where the picture is going to hang is particularly important.'

Colette, who had been listening and watching her son closely during the whole evening without anyone being aware of it, realised there was no polite social barrier between him and Hester. In fact, as the evening wore on, she saw there was a strong bond of affection between them. Her thoughts raced. Hadn't this happened all too quickly? But why shouldn't it, if two persons felt drawn together? They were the only ones who knew their true feelings and how deep they ran. She felt a sharp pang in her heart. Jealousy? Oh, Colette, she chided herself. Don't be so silly, so possessive. Edward has his own life to live. If someone else captures his heart then so be it. You have no God-given right to it.

She found herself coolly saying aloud, 'If Hester thinks it will be worth seeing the painting during its progress and wants to do so then she must not think of staying in an hotel on her own, she must stay with us.'

'That is most generous of you, Mrs Clayton, and would certainly ease my mind. I know Hester is a very independent and capable girl but I am sure that she would be happier staying with someone she knows.'

As he was speaking Hester and Edward had exchanged brief eye contact and each knew the other was pleased with the way this had developed.

'Then that is settled,' said Colette. 'Hester, we shall look forward to having you. Just let us know when it will be convenient for you to come.'

'Thank you, Mrs Clayton, that is most kind.'

'Not at all, we have plenty of room.'

'If Edward keeps me informed of his progress, I think it might be advantageous to see the painting when it is half-completed.' She glanced at him for his approval.

'Certainly, I can do that,' he agreed.

'A good idea, Lomax?' Abbas asked his friend whom he was aware had been taking all this in even though he had not said a word.

'I think it is a splendid idea. It would be no use Edward's pursuing something that Hester thought incompatible with the whole exhibition. What he begins to produce next may be on different lines to what any of us envisage. We cannot interpret an artist's mind. The fact that Hester has seen the real place and can link it with Edward's sketch and interpretation, gives her an opportunity to make useful suggestions. She must, however, be mindful of the fact that a critic should never try to influence a painter to do what he does not wish to do.'

'I am sure Hester understands that,' replied Abbas.

'I certainly do and would never dream of trying to tell Edward what he should do.' She had caught her uncle's almost imperceptible wink and smiled to herself. Her favourite uncle was a romantic at heart.

'Now,' said Abbas in a tone that said that was the end of the matter, 'Lomas, Hester and I would be honoured if you, Mrs Clayton, and Edward would dine with us at out hotel tomorrow evening.'

'That is most kind of you all and I am sure that Edward is in complete agreement when I accept your kind invitation for both of us.'

'Splendid,' said Abbas. 'I hope you won't mind when I tell you that Matthew Robinson will be joining us. When we arrived I sent him an invitation; the hotel organised a rider to take my note so I could get an immediate reply. He accepted and I booked him a room so that he could stay overnight. Strange how things work out. I organised his photographic exhibition in London; he made me a present of a painting done by Edward. I commissioned two more and that has led to an exhibition for Edward and our own delightful stay in Whitby.' He raised his glass. 'To a successful exhibition.'

'The weather looks settled, I believe we are going to have a fine day,' observed Edward as he escorted Hester from the hotel the following morning.

'I bow to local knowledge,' she replied. 'What is the first thing we do?'

'We head for the White Horse to collect the horse and trap, but we'll do it at a more leisurely pace today. I'll drive us to the abbey and then we'll return through the town and head for Sandsend and a walk on the cliffs. I asked the White Horse to pack us a picnic if the weather was good.'

'A picnic! How splendid.'

'It would have wasted time to return for lunch.'

The blue sky was marked by only the occasional white cloud and the sun was driving the cool of the early morning away as they made their way to the riverside and the quays on the West Bank before heading for the bridge.

Hester was buoyed up by the activity that pulsed through the town and along the river. From a few fishing vessels tied up on the West Side fishermen were unloading their night's catch and housewives were buying to feed their hungry families. Sailors were checking ropes, mending nets, painting woodwork or searching sails for tears caused by recent high winds. Edward was solicitous for his companion's welfare as they moved through the press of people hurrying to their work, hastening with messages, seeking an inn, shopping, cajoling youngsters who bumped into them as they raced past. She paused on the bridge to take in the scene up river. Ships at the quays on the East Side were preparing to leave, taking on consignments of goods bound for London or the Continent, while others prepared to unload the commodities they had brought in on the previous evening's tide. Hester took it all in, aware of the multitude of sounds that overlaid the bustle of this thriving Yorkshire port.

Once again Edward was pleased at the interest she showed and struck by the probing questions she asked. This continued during their ride along the east bank of the river and up the winding track to the Abbey Plain. The stark ruin, with its commanding position that overlooked the town but left it exposed to the furies of wind and rain, fascinated her, and Edward was thankful that he knew more than most about its history.

'I have enjoyed this,' Hester remarked as Edward helped her

back into the trap. 'You have a gift for making what could be a dry subject interesting.'

'You flatter me,' he replied, 'but I have always had an interest in local history and I find Whitby has much to offer in that respect.'

'Tell me more.'

Edward kept up the flow of information as they drove back through the town and took the road from the West Cliff to Sandsend. It afforded them views across the sea that today reflected the blue of the sky and was lazy in its contact with the sands that swept towards the high cliffs beyond Sandsend. As they passed by the tiny village that cuddled into the rising land beside a stream, and climbed the twisting track to the high cliffs beyond, Edward regaled her with tales of smuggling and clashes with Revenue Men, of chases at sea and boarding parties.

They reached the cliff-top and he drew the horse to a halt in a shallow dip in the land from which they had a wonderful view looking back along the coast to the piers at Whitby and the landmark abbey.

'Time for our picnic,' he announced.

'This is glorious,' she exclaimed enthusiastically as she settled on the rug he had spread on the ground.

'Let us see what delights they have provided for us,' he said, placing a wicker basket on the ground.

Together they quickly unfastened and swung back the lid. Hester gasped at the array inside.

'That's better than I expected,' remarked Edward. 'They've done us proud.'

'You must be a special customer.'

'Well, I do use them a lot, especially when it comes to wanting a horse.'

They began to investigate the contents more thoroughly. Beautifully carved succulent ham, pickles, three varieties of cheese, brown bread and white – both home-made – two types of jam, also home-made, an apple pie, some cream and two bottles of wine.

'My goodness, will we want anything tonight?' commented Hester.

'That's a long while off,' pointed out Edward.

'I suppose so. And I must say the air has given me an appetite.'

'Whitby air does that to visitors.'

They took their meal at their leisure, enjoying the view, their conversation and each other's company.

Hester drained the last of the wine from her glass and lay on the rug, staring at the sky. Edward sat for a few moments sipping at his wine then he too lay on his back. Each felt the silence between them become charged with interest. She wondered if she was seeking a balm for the hurt she had suffered at the hands of another man with whom she had been in love. In love? Was she experiencing that with Edward or . . . ? He let his mind dwell on the girl beside him. He sensed he was attracted to her in a different way from any of the girls he had previously escorted to parties or the theatre, or with whom he had walked these very cliffs. But . . . He halted the objections that reared in his mind, obstacles he always put in the way of lasting relationships. Why should he raise them now? Wasn't Hester different from anyone else? And didn't that question tell him that what he was feeling for her was unlike anything he had experienced before?

A movement from her interrupted his thoughts. She turned on her side, raising herself on one elbow so she could look down at him.

'Edward, you have been so kind to me. I have enjoyed your company and wish I was staying longer.' Her voice had a quiet huskiness; her eyes were soft and sincere.

'You are coming back.'

'Do you want me to?'

His eyes met hers. 'Yes.'

'Not just to see your painting?'

'No. That is just incidental to your visit now.'

Hester leaned towards him. As their lips met, his arms came around her and pulled her close.

The following morning Colette and Edward were at the station to see their friends leave Whitby.

As they walked home their thoughts dwelt on two of those people in particular. Colette's were on Matthew Robinson. He had been attentive throughout the previous evening without being over-powering or monopolising all her time. His conversation had been bright, intelligent and humorous, ranging over many subjects. She got on well with him and found his company congenial. She knew if she said 'Yes' to a marriage proposal from him, her life would be comfortable and she would want for nothing. Was that the path she should take? After all, she could not expect Edward to remain at home forever; in fact, deep down she wished that he would find a nice girl to marry. Maybe that was nearer happening than she had envisaged a few days ago.

During Hester's visit she had sensed the growing attraction between the two young people. Would she welcome anything closer? Why not? They had only known each other for less than four days, but did that preclude falling in love? Love moved in mysterious ways: could develop slowly or hit sharp and sudden, like an arrow to the heart. In all of this she was certain of one thing – she must not interfere. She could advise if asked but never push nor raise barriers. If anything did materialise between her son and Hester Stevens, what of her own future? Matthew Robinson? Oh, Arthur, if only you had not been married!

Startled by the last thought she diverted her mind to the suggestion that Abbas had made after he had seen some of her photographs: that she should hold an exhibition in London; a suggestion that Matthew had strongly supported.

Edward thought of the girl who had leaned out of the carriage window waving goodbye and finally blowing him a kiss. It took his mind back to their kisses on the cliffs above Sandsend. He realised he had been attracted to her from the moment he had been introduced to her and that the attraction had grown each day she was in Whitby, short though the stay had been. He knew that his feelings had reached a pitch he had never experienced with a girl before. Was this truly love? If not, why was it that he had not wanted her to go and was now dwelling on and looking forward to her visit to inspect his painting? The quicker he got on with it, the sooner she would return. He found himself wishing it could be tomorrow. His thoughts pulled up short at what he was considering.

What about his search for his father? As much as he wanted to find him, Edward would not be able to pursue the quest until after the exhibition. He knew his father would want him to concentrate on that now and only wished he could be there to see it. And what of Hester – what would she say if she knew he was the son of Arthur Newton? She could not have suspected anything even though she had commented on the fact that he showed some techniques adapted from a study of Arthur Newton's work. The future held so many paths and he only hoped he chose the right one. Could Hester be his companion and lover along it?

Chapter Fifteen

Marie and Lucy slit the envelopes open.

'Invitation!' cried Lucy, separating a card from the folded sheets of the letter.

Marie pushed her card, with its bold announcement of her father's forthcoming marriage to Isobel Wentworth, to one side and read the letter. Behind her father's words she could sense his feelings for Lucy's mother and his joy that she had accepted him. She also sensed that it did not diminish his love for her and that she was released from feeling any obligation for his welfare.

'No real news,' she commented when she came to the end. 'Everything seems to be going well.'

'The main news in my letter is that Mother has two people interested in buying the farm. They don't mind waiting to complete the purchase until the beginning of August and both are then prepared to wait until after the honeymoon to move in. So it's a matter of the best offer.'

'Splendid,' said Marie. 'Father doesn't mention it,' she added with a puzzled frown.

'Mother added it as a P.S. so maybe your father didn't know when he wrote to you,' offered Lucy in explanation and then said, 'I wonder if Philip and George have received their invitations?'

'We'll know later. Remember they're meeting us when we leave the studio.'

'I hope Philip is in a better mood than he has been lately,' commented Lucy. 'It's as if he has something weighing on his mind and has to force himself to be the lively person we first met.'

'Have you tackled him about it?'

'Yes, and he says there is nothing the matter. But when I have pressed him further he always says that it's work. I know he has made a success of establishing the firm's office in Paris and that brings greater responsibility as more companies come looking for loans. He says he's hoping head office will allow him to recruit some help.'

Marie, who over the past two months had noticed that Philip seemed to be carrying a load of worry but had made no comment, now wondered if Lucy was trying to convince herself that what she said was true and was avoiding looking for any other reason that might be affecting her relationship with Philip. She knew Lucy was worried and resolved to keep a closer eye on her friend. The last thing Lucy wanted was an unhappy romance after her previous experience.

They left for their atelier without another word on the matter. Their friends were already at work on their paintings and, along with them, Marie and Lucy spent a profitable day. Marie was pleased Lucy could become absorbed in her work and saw it as a good omen for her successfully completing the year.

Only Yvette left early to do some sketches of the carvings on Notre Dame, but Marie and Lucy began to tidy up at four o'clock.

'Dates again?' asked Charlotte teasingly. 'Bicycle ride?'

'No. George has found a new restaurant he wants to try,' explained Marie.

'Where's that?' asked Adelina with interest.

'Let you know when we've been,' said Lucy.

'If it's good you can introduce it to us.'

'That's a date,' replied Marie enthusiastically, wanting to give Lucy a night out to look forward to.

Leaving everything ready to resume their painting tomorrow, they left the atelier in buoyant mood and hurried to a small square with a fountain playing at its centre.

'There they are.' Marie spotted George and Philip sitting on the low wall surrounding the fountain's basin.

The two young men sprang to their feet when they saw Marie and Lucy. Words of greeting and kisses over, they linked arms and set off at George's instigation.

'Where are we going?' asked Marie.

'You'll see,' he replied.

Lucy and Philip, a couple of paces behind, were content to follow.

'Have you had a profitable day?' she asked tentatively, hoping that she would not get the dismissive grunt she had received on a number of occasions lately.

'It was,' he replied. 'The Debois brothers want to negotiate a further loan. They are bent on buying another section of land next to the one they have already purchased. Our preliminary talks were satisfactory. I'm sure it will go through and that will be important when the audit comes up in August.' He knew what he said was perfectly true but his borrowing of company funds on his own behalf still hung over him like the Sword of Damocles, though only he knew that.

There had been times recently when Lucy had posed questions that had made him realise he must be careful in his replies and not let her suspect that anything was wrong. Maybe that would soon be at an end. He had heard a rumour today that the decision on the factories would be taken soon. He had sought a meeting with Monsieur Mercier who verified the rumour but added he had heard, on good authority, that they would be built near the Calais route out of Paris. That had put Philip in a good mood that carried on into this evening in the company of Lucy, Marie and George.

'I'm so pleased,' replied Lucy. 'The Debois brothers seem to have taken a liking to you. But then, who wouldn't?' She squeezed his arm.

'Flatterer,' he grinned.

'No. I love you.'

He gave her a quick kiss.

George led them to the banks of the Seine and after a quarter of a mile cut away from the river towards a short side street. Halfway along it he took two steps down to a door over which was painted 'Restaurant de Fontenoy'. He pushed the door open and led the way in. The walls of the vestibule were painted red and the lighting was dim. A curved counter stood to one side behind which a young couple stood ready to attend to them.

'Monsieur George Reeves – I booked a table earlier today.'

'You did, Monsieur,' said the young man. 'It is a pleasure to welcome you.' His smile encompassed them all.

The young lady beside him extended a similar greeting. Stepping from behind the counter, she said, 'Please follow me,' and took them through a door into a large room filled with tables of various sizes. All were set with cutlery and wine glasses on pristine white table-cloths. Three other young couples were already dining and cast them only a cursory glance. The young lady ushered them to a table set for four in one corner of the room.

'I hope this will be suitable for you,' she said as they sat down, assisted by two young waiters who seemed to have appeared by magic.

'Very much so,' said George. 'Thank you.'

The waiters produced menus.

'You will see they are extensive,' the young lady pointed out. 'We serve any sort of meal all day from ten in the morning until midnight, catering for whatever people desire. We aim to attract mostly students, of whom there are many in Paris, and so you will find our prices reasonable. Hopefully when our reputation grows we will attract other diners as well as students. Before I leave you to enjoy yourselves, may I ask how you heard about us? We have been open only three days.'

'A friend of mine was here on your opening night and recommended me to come,' replied George.

'Thank you, Monsieur, and please thank your friend. Enjoy your evening.' She smiled and glided away. The two waiters hovered discreetly out of earshot.

'What a pleasant reception,' remarked Marie. 'If the meal is as good we'll be here again.'

'I like the décor,' commented Philip, 'though I wondered what we were coming to when we first came in. That vestibule was a bit dim, but this is nice and bright and the tables leave plenty of space for movement and conversation without being overheard.'

'I like the theatre theme in those posters and paintings,' said Lucy, thankful that Philip seemed to have thrown off the worried air that had been hanging over him and marring their recent outings.

'We should have some wine while we study the menu,' he said, and called a waiter over. He was presented with a wine list and a few moments later had ordered a bottle that he knew they would all like. With glasses charged he said, 'George and I decided while waiting for you that we would not tell you this until we were settled at our table. We received invitations to your parents' wedding today.'

'Good,' both girls exclaimed with delight. 'So did we.'

'That was only to be expected.'

'Yes, I suppose so, but it makes it seem real. You'll both be coming?'

'I'll have to,' said George with a grin. 'Your father has asked me to be his best man.'

'What?' Marie exclaimed in surprise.

'You didn't know?'

'No. He hadn't said a word, not even in his letter today.'

'Must have been that he wanted me to give you a surprise. But why me? Hasn't he any close friends? I'll not press him if he wants to change for someone else.'

'He won't. I don't know of anyone else he would ask and his brother is in America.'

'Of course I'll be delighted.'

'You'll be coming?' Lucy turned to Philip.

'Of course.'

'Work won't get in the way?'

'I'll do my best to see that it doesn't.'

'Good.' She smiled in delight; the Philip she had known and had come to love was himself again.

He picked up his glass, raised it and said, 'To your parents.'

Arthur walked briskly in the direction of Cherry Hill. He felt all was well in his world and the bright day raised his spirits. In just over a month he would be married and then he and Isobel could do just as they wished. They had made no definite plans except that with the farm sold she would move to his house, which they would keep. Unless the letter that rested in his pocket produced any other thoughts in Isobel. He had an open mind about its contents and would not wish to impose a decision one way or the other. It held stirring possibilities, but on the other hand to take no action would not bring any dire consequences.

He turned into the long drive that led to the farmhouse and waved on seeing Isobel sitting outside.

She rose from the garden seat and came to meet him.

'I disturbed you,' said Arthur by way of apology.

'I don't mind. You can do that any time you wish,' she replied as she linked arms and strolled towards the house. 'I've had a letter from Philip accepting the invitation.'

'Good.'

'He says Lucy is delighted that he has done so, and she is well.'

'I received an acceptance from George saying he will be honoured to be best man but I have left that letter at home.'

'That sounds as if you have had another one.'

'I have. Shall we sit on the seat and I will read it to you?'

'Certainly. Does this mean it's important?'

Arthur gave a little shrug of his shoulders. 'Depends how you take it.'

They had reached the seat and as Arthur sat down he withdrew an envelope from his pocket, took out a letter and started to read:

> 15 Central Buildings
> Denver
> Colorado

My Dear Brother,

Your letter reached me today and on reading it I sat down immediately to pen this reply to you and offer my congratulations on your forthcoming marriage. Please give your bride-to-be (Isobel, a name I like) all my best wishes. I hope you will both be very happy and find a warm and loving companionship. As regards my attending the wedding, you will understand that it is impossible as I cannot take so much time away from my job with the railway.

Though we have not been regular correspondents you knew I was formerly based in New York. Well, as you will see from the address on top of this page I have been moved to Denver in Colorado, a long way from New York but wonderful country. As an artist I am sure you would love it.

You indicate that as Isobel is giving up the farm you will have much more time to enjoy life together. Why don't you come to America? See for yourself the wonders you could put on canvas. There are artists here – Thomas Moran, an Englishman from Bolton among them – who see beauty in the wild and remote Western landscape. Their efforts are educating the American people away from the idea that the West is nothing but unattractive rugged mountains, desolate desert and scrubland. With this new outlook people are buying their paintings and the men in authority, making money out of the railroads, one way or another, are wanting their portraits painting. You could make a fortune. Think about it.

My thoughts will be with you on your great and important day.

Love to you both. I look forward to kissing the bride.

Yours sincerely,

Oswald

That's kind of him,' said Isobel. 'I'm sorry he won't be here for you, though.'

Arthur shrugged. 'I didn't expect him to come all that way but I'm glad we sent him an invitation. And now he's moved West.'

'He enthuses about it particularly from the artist's point of view.' Isobel looked quizzically at him. 'Are you tempted?'

Arthur smiled. 'Not really.'

'We could go. We'll have all the time in the world and the cost need not deter us when I've sold the farm. It might stir your enthusiasm to paint again if it is as wonderful as Oswald says.'

'I'm not worried about that happening. Besides, I don't think I'd like to leave the greenery of England.'

'Well, we could go just for a visit. We won't have Marie and Lucy to consider. You think about it, and if you wish we can go.'

'We'll see.'

*

Edward painted with inspiration. From the first stroke of his brush he knew exactly what he wanted to show: the vibrancy of the sea in contrast with the solid cliff face, determined not to yield to constant attack and stealthy erosion; the vitality in its surface reflected in its many colours. He would represent all these aspects in a scene that was typical of many parts of the Yorkshire coast and in particular Ravenscar. He would also celebrate the memory of a girl who had fascinated him and on whom his thoughts had dwelt during the intervening weeks since he had watched her train depart for London. But this painting would be no mere physical representation, even if there would be an element of recognition for anyone who knew Ravenscar. Its main theme would be life itself.

He became more and more anxious to know Hester's opinion and whether she thought it would fit in with the other paintings they had chosen for the exhibition. He had written to her last week informing her that he thought the painting was nearing a stage where she should see it. A reply had come by return telling him when she could come. And that was to be today.

He had come into his studio to take a last look before he went to the station to meet her. His fingers itched to take up a brush but to do so now might just spoil what he wanted Hester to see. He glanced at the clock on the mantelpiece. Half-past three. He went into the hall, picked up his hat and put his head round the drawing-room door.

'I'm going, Mother.'

Colette, sitting on a chair beside the window, looked up from her embroidery. 'All right, Edward.' She watched the door close and sat with her needle poised, making no effort to make the next stitch. Her mind dwelt on her son. She had sensed a new vibrancy about him ever since he'd heard Hester was coming. It had confirmed her feeling that he was attracted to the girl, might even be falling in love with her. Now she felt both pleasure and satisfaction that at last her son might be finding a young lady to love.

Edward stepped out briskly as he walked to the station. Life was good. An exhibition in London that could bring him to the notice of a wider world than he had so far encountered in Whitby and its locality; a new energy in his painting, and a new enjoyment of life through the influence of a girl who had unexpectedly entered his life. He silently thanked his father for his inherited talents. His father? He wondered where Arthur was. When would he be able to take up his search again?

The train came to a hissing, clattering halt. Doors swung open; people stepped out on to the platform and started for the exit. Then Edward saw her. His heart missed a beat as, with joy filling his mind, he hurried to meet her. A smile of pleasure lit up Hester's face when she saw him. They came together, each momentarily struck by shyness. He swept his hat from his head; she dropped her small bag on the ground.

'Hester.'

'Edward.'

There was no need for further words. Their eyes expressed their feelings. Then they were in each other's arms, holding tight in a hug that spoke volumes. They eased away, looked into each other's eyes, and kissed.

'It's good to see you again, Hester.'

'I'm delighted to be here.'

He picked up her bag. 'We'll get a cab.'

'Do you mind if we walk? I've been sitting a long time and it's a fine day. The sea air smells so good. My bag isn't heavy, is it?'

'No, I was expecting it to weigh more.'

'I travelled light. I thought if there was anything I wanted, I could get it here. In fact I do want a new dress. Maybe your mother . . .'

'I'm sure she would be delighted.'

'A shopping expedition of that nature will help us to get to know each other better.'

Edward wondered what lay behind that remark but it pleased him that she had made it.

They left the station and he matched his pace to Hester's. She was in no hurry. Though her chatter was light it was interesting, enlarging on his queries about the welfare of her uncle and Mr Sotheran, asking about his mother and commenting on what she was seeing on their way to the West Cliff, while all the time avoiding putting any questions to him about the progress of his painting.

225

That came after Colette had given her a warm welcome, shown her where she would sleep, allowed her to freshen up after her journey and then greeted her with tea and cake in the drawing room.

Hester had taken her first bite of cake and sip of tea when she said, 'How is the painting progressing, Edward? I must say I had not expected you to call me to Whitby so soon.'

'It's come along very well.'

'I'm pleased, that's a good sign. Does it mean you will have it finished in plenty of time?'

'If things continue to go well. And, of course, it will depend on what you think of it.'

'Shall we find out when we have finished our tea?'

'I can't wait.'

'I'm afraid you will have to,' Hester teased. 'This tea is too tempting. And what do you think of the painting, Mrs Clayton?'

'I don't think I should comment.' Colette smiled. 'I'm prejudiced, of course. Another piece of cake?'

Realising that Colette was joining in the teasing, Hester reached for one and cocked an eye at Edward. 'Sorry, it's so delicious I must have another taste.'

He glared in mock annoyance and then everyone burst out laughing. Each of them felt that their friendship had deepened. Colette was especially pleased for Edward.

With tea finished at last he stood. 'Should we?' There was no need to put the full question; the others knew what he meant.

Hester gave a little smile. 'I daren't say no, dare I?' She rose from her chair.

'Coming, Mother?' Edward asked, seeing that she had not moved.

'No. You don't need me there. I'm sure Hester will tell you exactly what she thinks.'

He felt nervous anticipation of just what Hester would think as he escorted her in to his studio. A thin cloth covered the painting on the easel, which was strategically placed to catch the best light. Edward went to it; Hester stood back. He glanced at her. 'Ready?'

She nodded. Edward carefully removed the cloth. He moved away from the easel and looked at Hester, hoping to catch her immediate reaction, but her countenance was inscrutable. He did not speak. She remained still, gazing at the picture for a few minutes. His stomach churned. What was she thinking? Surely there should have been some reaction by now? He detected none. His mind reeled with the thought that she didn't like it. But if she didn't, why didn't she say so? She moved; stepped sideways to view the painting from a different angle. Paused for a few moments then repeated the action three more times. Expecting a fourth step Edward was startled when she spoke. Her tone, though soft, split the silence like glass.

'Splendid. The development of the angle of vision is fantastic. Whatever you do, don't lose that when you move on. The bold lines you have used to emphasise that could be lost in the colours when you intensify them, as I expect you have in mind?'

'Some of them, yes. Others I intend to tone down. In that way I believe I will strengthen the illusion that the viewer is standing on the edge of a precipice.'

'Splendid. I like the tones you are working into the sea. They lend a peaceful atmosphere, which is good, but I do think you should also want the viewer to realise the sea can be a potent enemy. Bear that in mind when working on the water at the bottom of the cliff. Combining both elements in the same picture may seem contradictory, but I can see from the lines you are working along that you don't intend this to be a photographic representation but rather an atmospheric exploration of the sea and land, with the viewer in such a position they can't decide which element carries more power.'

He had taken in every word, surprised by her perceptive analysis. It pleased him and he was about to say so when Hester broke her brief silence. 'I am delighted with this and look forward to seeing it finished. If it is developed in the way I hope it will be, it will form a worthy centrepiece to the exhibition.'

'You think it a possibility?'

'It's up to you. You are the painter, only you can raise it to that category, but from what I have seen here and in your other work, you are capable of doing so.'

'Those are kind words.'

'I am not being kind, I am merely stating fact.' Her expression became even more serious. 'Edward, you may as well know that when I am involved in criticism or passing opinions I don't hold back. I don't believe it is fair to the artist not to give an honest opinion. Looking at your work in sequence, I can see how it has evolved. In your more recent paintings it has progressed rapidly and in this one it has taken a gigantic leap forward. You have drawn new inspiration from somewhere, and I am pleased that this canvas shows none of the influence of Arthur Newton. I'm not condemning what you have done in that respect. As your own work has progressed you have allowed his influence to slip away and put more and more of yourself into your paintings. That is as it should be and this one is all you – keep it that way.'

He nodded, again realising how perceptive her judgement was. Her words 'a new inspiration from somewhere' came back to mind, and with them came the thought that when he had been painting this picture he had been painting it for Hester – he had been inspired by her and it had influenced his painting, just as his father had been inspired by his mother. Arthur Newton's greatest period of work had occurred when he was inspired by Colette, whether in reality or memory.

'You are quiet.' Hester's words startled him.

'I'm sorry. Your analysis made me think.'

'Oh, dear, have I been too critical?'

'No, no,' Edward was quick to reassure her. 'You are very perceptive and your thoughts about my painting are just what I wanted. I am indebted to you and extremely grateful.'

'It is my pleasure. And I thank you and your mother for having me to stay. I hope you both will stay in London for the whole of the time of the exhibition.'

'Mr Robinson is anxious to fix that and is hoping that you will give us the dates of the exhibition.'

'Uncle Abbas received confirmation of those the day before I left. The venue will be in Bond Street and the dates are the fourteenth to the twenty-eighth of July.'

'Good. That will give me time to finish this and sketch out

some ideas which might be displayed separately from the main exhibition.'

'Splendid! Often preliminary sketches lead to commissions. Make a wide variety, but whatever you do, don't concentrate on those at the expense of this painting. I see this as the masterpiece, the talking point of the exhibition.'

When they rejoined Colette she anxiously awaited Hester's verdict and was more than pleased to hear it. With the dates fixed she could plan ahead. Although she had reservations about Matthew's generous offer to accompany them, she was also flattered by his attention, and, realising that much of Edward's time might be taken up with Hester and the exhibition, knew she would be grateful for an escort during her stay in London.

When they had finished their talk of dates and arrangements, Hester gave a message to Colette. 'Uncle Abbas told me to remind you about the possibilities for an exhibition of your photographs and ask if you have given any more thought to it?'

'Well, it has crossed my mind now and then but I have not thought seriously about it.'

'I think you should.'

'So do I, Mother,' put in Edward enthusiastically.

'From the few photographs I saw when I was last here, there is potential for an eye-catching exhibition. Maybe you could show me more?'

'Oh, one exhibition in the family is enough,' Colette demurred.

'These would be completely different exhibitions at completely different times,' Hester pointed out.

'Come on, Mother, let Hester see more of your photographs.'

'Please do, Mrs Clayton.'

Colette gave a little chuckle. 'I can see I'll get no rest until I do. After this evening's meal then.'

'Edward, this has been a wonderful week.' Hester stood by the open carriage door of the train which was about to leave Whitby. 'Thank your mother for her hospitality again, won't you? And I am so grateful to you for your company and for being my escort.'

'It has been my pleasure. I have enjoyed having you here and hope you will come again.'

'I would love to.'

Their eyes held each other's and both of them realised something special had passed between them. They moved closer. His hands took hers and their lips met.

'Think of me,' she said huskily.

'You'll never be far from my thoughts.'

They kissed again. Their lips lingered, expressing their desire to be together. That was broken only by a shout along the platform, 'All aboard.'

Hester trembled, gave him a last kiss, and with damp eyes stepped into the carriage. He closed the door. She opened the window and leaned out, reaching her hand towards him. He entwined his fingers with hers. A whistle blew. The engine hissed. Wheels gripped the rails and started to move. Edward walked beside the carriage, still with their fingers linked in loving contact. The train picked up speed. His steps faltered and their hands slid away from each other. His dropped to his side in resignation at the parting; hers still reached out as if the gesture would bring contact again, one that would hold them together. Resigned that that could not be so, finally she raised her arm and waved. He waved back. They watched each other as long as possible.

With Hester finally lost to sight he turned and reluctantly trudged towards the exit. She sat down heavily, sighed and wiped away a tear that had spilled from her eye and run down her cheek.

On the twelfth of July Matthew Robinson arrived in Whitby, booked a room for the night at the Angel, ordered dinner for three for six o'clock then walked to the Clayton residence on the West Cliff where he was promptly admitted by the maid and shown to the drawing room.

'Are you ready, all packed for tomorrow?' he asked brightly after he had greeted Colette and Edward.

'A few odds and ends to throw in at the last minute,' replied Colette.

'Edward?' Matthew raised a questioning eyebrow.

'All ready, Mr Robinson, except for one painting that I couldn't send with the others. If you'll excuse me, I'll just go and finish wrapping it.'

'Of course. Dinner is at six. Tomorrow morning the carriage will be here at nine for the nine-thirty train.'

Edward nodded and left the room.

'Thank you, Matthew,' said Colette as the door closed. 'You are so considerate and far too generous. It is embarrassing for me.'

'My dear Colette, please don't worry. You are a friend.'

'But I feel obligated.'

'You shouldn't. There is no need. I think a lot of you but I don't want to embarrass you or have you feel under any undue obligation. I don't seek to interfere in your life. What I do, I do out of friendship and a great respect for you. I hope I've done nothing to mar a friendship that means a great deal to me?'

'And I hope I've done nothing to hurt you? You are a dear man and it is good to have a friend who cares.'

Hester stepped out of the cab and hurried into King's Cross Station. Aware of all the activity that made this the beating heart of the capital's connection with the North of England, she enquired about the arrival of the train from York.

'It's due in ten minutes. Platform three,' she was told.

Relieved that she was in time, she strolled through the crowded concourse. A distant whistle, a rumble which grew louder, and then the hiss and clatter as the sounds of the train overwhelmed the chatter of the people who thronged the station.

Doors swung open, passengers alighted and hurried to leave the platform and be on their way. The crowd thinned. Hester became anxious. She could not see them. Had their plans changed? She strained to see over and beyond the bobbing heads that still surged towards her. What should she do if they hadn't come on the train Edward had mentioned in a letter? Then she saw them. Relief swept over her quickly to be replaced by pleasure. Her eyes on them, she felt sure they must have seen her. She waved but there was no answer. Then they were there in front of her, their faces breaking out into smiles.

'Welcome to London,' she said brightly with a special smile for Edward.

'We didn't expect . . .'

'I couldn't let you arrive without a welcome.'

Greetings over, she escorted them from the station and found a cab that took them quickly through the busy streets to Claridge's.

'Wait for me, I'll be down in a minute,' Edward suggested as they watched their luggage being taken care of. Once he had been shown his room, he hurried back downstairs and found Hester sitting in the lounge. She smiled warmly, her eyes fixed intently on him as she rose from her chair. As he had entered the room he had taken in the fact that she was the only person there. He held out his hands to her. No word was spoken as they embraced then kissed, each knowing that they both wished they could linger.

'I was so pleased to see you at the station,' he said as they sat down.

'I had to be there, especially as I was unable to get back to Whitby again. As I told you in my letters, my uncle thought it wasn't necessary.' She gave a mischievous little smile. 'Maybe I shouldn't have given such a glowing report of your painting.'

'Maybe not, but I enjoyed your letters. And now I am here.'

'And I am more than delighted.' She pressed his hand. 'Everything is ready, except for the one painting you have brought with you. I look forward to seeing how you completed it. Can we do that between tea and dinner this evening?'

'I am entirely in your hands.'

'Your mother and Mr Robinson have something planned for this evening?'

'No. I took it that we would be dining here. You are most welcome to join us.'

'Ah, no.' She gave a little shake of her head. 'That is another reason I was at the station, to extend my uncle's invitation for you all to dine with him and Mr Sotheran at Simpson's in the Strand at seven.'

'That is most generous of him. I am sure my mother and Mr Robinson will be delighted.'

'It will give them plenty of time to have a rest and get ready, unless they have any other plans.'

'I am sure they had nothing in mind.'

'Right. Then suppose I call for you in an hour? We can take the painting, see it hung and return here for your mother and Mr Robinson before we go to meet my uncle.'

'That sounds an ideal plan. I shall tell them when I go to my room.'

'Good.' Hester rose from her chair and he followed suit.

When they reached the door he stopped and kissed her again. 'It is wonderful to see you.'

Exactly one hour later Hester walked into Claridge's to find Edward waiting for her with his painting. She had retained the cab in which she had come. As they drove down Bond Street the excitement between them mounted; she was anxious to see the finished painting, he to hear her opinion. On reaching the venue Edward paid the fare and on his query she dismissed the cabbie.

Edward viewed the building and was impressed with its imposing façade. He was even more impressed when he walked inside. A curving staircase with an intricately executed, wrought-iron banister dominated the large hall. Hester was known here and when the doorman behind his large mahogany desk greeted her, replied in a friendly tone and accepted the key he had taken from a drawer on seeing her arrive. She led the way to some large double doors on the right, unlocked them and pushed one open.

They stepped into a long room where Edward's paintings were displayed on the wall. He stopped and gasped, his first impression one of awe. He had never expected to see his work shown in such elegant surroundings, but it was an elegance that did not detract from but rather enhanced it.

He turned to Hester. 'This is wonderful. I never thought . . .' He let his words trail away and instead said with all the heartfelt expression he could muster, 'Thank you so very much for all this and what you have done.' He kissed her on the cheek. His eye roved quickly across the display. He immediately realised that

Hester had applied much thought to what should be placed where, for the greatest effect.

'That is where I thought the painting you have brought should go.' She indicated the wall opposite the door at the far end of the room. 'From what I remembered of it, I realised it would make the most impact there.' A teasing twinkle came to her eyes as she added, 'As long as you haven't spoiled it.'

'We'd better see,' he said, and went to the wall on which it was to be hung. He was about to pose a question when it was answered by the opening of the door through which they had just entered. Two men appeared carrying steps. He glanced appreciatively at Hester. 'You've thought of everything.'

She smiled but hung back at a suitable point from which to view the picture. 'Tell me when,' she said and turned so she could not see it. She could hear Edward unpacking the painting, and as the men were hanging it, was tempted to turn round.

She heard Edward approve of its positioning and the men step out of the way. There was a pause and then they passed her, carrying the steps from the room. Once they had closed the door Edward said in an expectant tone, 'All right – now.'

She spun round and stood there speechless, transfixed by the magic that emanated from the painting to embrace her.

Edward watched her, wondering what she was thinking, wanting her to speak, wanting to break the silence himself yet knowing from her expression that to do so would ruin something for her. He had to wait for her to assimilate the effect of the painting.

When it came a few minutes later it was expressed in one word spoken in barely above a whisper. 'Edward!'

Though the initial tension was broken he knew from the way she was looking at the picture that she did not want to make further comment yet. When that came it was undiluted praise. 'This is simply wonderful. People will stand in awe before it. Not only is it a magnificent depiction of coastal scenery, it is also an interpretation of two forces in opposition, the strength and security of the land and the changeability and power of the sea. Opposing forces, each determined to triumph, and yet in each there is respect for the other and a sort of union in this celebration of life, with all its troubles and its harmony. Edward, it is magnificent. It is sure to sell. Nothing is more certain.'

'It is not for sale,' he said quietly.

For a moment Hester did not take in what he had said and then the words struck home. 'What?' she cried. 'It must be! It will sell. You'll have many people wanting it. I'm going to put a high price on it.'

'It is not for sale,' he said again, but this time though the words were just as quietly spoken, they were filled with determination.

She recognised it but stared at him in challenging acknowledgement. 'Why?'

'It is for you.'

She stared in disbelief for a moment. 'Edward, I couldn't . . .'

'You can and you will.'

'But . . .'

'No buts, it is to be a reminder of your visit to Whitby and also my thanks for all you have done. If anyone wants to buy it, I'll take commissions for similar paintings, but in that one there are sentiments I wish only you to see.'

She stepped close to him. Her deep kiss expressed her thanks. She prolonged it by slipping her arms round his neck and holding him tight.

When they had finally examined each painting in turn Edward was amazed by the thought and expertise she had put into displaying each canvas to its best advantage.

As they were about to leave the room they stopped at the doorway and looked back at the end wall.

'It's a tour-de-force, Edward.'

'Your sense for display makes it so.'

'No, it is all in the painting. You were inspired.'

'By you. You were in my mind every time I put brush to canvas after you left Whitby.'

'Edward.' A tear ran down her cheek.

When she had composed herself she said, 'We have plenty of time to enjoy a stroll back to Claridge's, don't we?'

'I'd like nothing better.'

There were a few moments of silence as they started to walk.

It seemed that each was searching for a way to open the conversation.

'I owe you a great deal, Hester, not only for what you have done to organise this exhibition,' began Edward.

'It was my uncle's idea.'

'But once he mooted it, I think you had a great deal of influence. And from what I understood in Whitby, he left the display mainly to you.'

She gave a little shrug of her shoulders as if to dismiss the matter.

'But I owe you for more than that. Your visit to Whitby influenced my painting, probably more than you were aware.'

'But I did nothing in that respect.'

'Yes, you did. In your analysis of my work.'

'I'm pleased if it was influential to you in producing the painting you brought with you today. That is truly splendid work, and all the more so because it is so innovative. I am pleased that you have thrown off the mantle of Arthur Newton – not that I am deni-grating his work which I like very much. His influence is very evident in some of your earlier painting and it's none the worse for that. Most artists are influenced by others at some point, but it is essential that influence does not become a template and stifle the disciple's own creativity. I could see that you drew on his tech-nique and his particular liking for night scenes, but in this latest painting you move boldly into your own light. When did you first become aware of him? What drew you to him?'

Edward hesitated. How much should he tell her? The urge to pour out his secret was strong but he held himself in check. Some day he may tell this perceptive young woman the truth but this did not seem the right time. There was too much to be done.

'I was drawn by the fact that he painted Whitby, my home town,' Edward said.

She nodded. 'He wasn't a Whitby man, you know.'

'No, he lived in Scarborough.'

'Did you ever meet him?'

'No.' There was only a fractional hesitation before his reply but Hester was aware of it and wondered why it had been there.

236

Chapter Sixteen

Monsieur Bedeaux stood back and viewed each of the students' latest paintings. The six girls were on tenterhooks but could not help but make the odd knowing smile at each other as their tutor muttered to himself, grimaced and grunted. They knew from experience to read nothing into these noises but nevertheless were edgy as they awaited his verdict. Their whole lives might rest on his opinions; certainly their immediate futures would. Four of them had been given a second chance by him, they could not expect a third.

Marie and Lucy saw that their friends, even though they were trying to adopt a couldn't-care-less attitude, were anxious.

Monsieur Bedeaux gave one last explosive grunt, swung round to face them and said, 'Mesdemoiselles, your work shows improvement. You have applied what I have taught you as individuals to your work and that pleases me – but what pleases me most is that I will have the pleasure of your company for another year! *Bien!*'

Their faces were instantly wreathed in smiles; they shouted for joy and crowded round him, almost sweeping him off his feet in their exhuberance.

'Mesdemoiselles! Mesdemoiselles!' he spluttered, trying to fend them off though they knew he liked the fuss.

They showered him with thanks, saying how much they looked forward to returning and expressing their determination not to let him down. When he had calmed them he held them in a further moment of suspense and then said, 'Though there are another ten days left of this session, I will reward your hard and diligent work by allowing you to go home now, but please return with full sketchbooks of ideas to start work on September the tenth.'

With more calls of thanks ringing in his ears Monsieur Bedeaux left the room, pausing only at the door to smile back at the young people to whom he had brought such pleasure with his decision. He sighed and wished he were their age again.

As the door clicked shut six excited students embraced each other, showered themselves with congratulations and decided that they should celebrate.

After a most enjoyable evening at the Restaurant de Fontenoy, Marie and Lucy faced the next question. 'When are we going home?' Marie asked.

'We won't be expected yet, but I think it had better be as soon as possible with the wedding not far away. Do you want to wait for George?'

'I'll see what he says tomorrow, but I think it would be best for us to go as soon as possible.'

When Marie saw George he told her that he could leave whenever he liked; his work was completed and he was sure he could get permission to leave early. It suited him, for it meant he could go home before the need to be in Deal to act as best man to Arthur. Philip, of course, could not leave until he came to England for the ceremony.

Isobel and Arthur received a pleasant surprise when their daughters arrived home sooner than expected. Though the main preparations for the wedding had been made, the girls' early arrival would make the three weeks or so before the wedding even more pleasurable.

Two days after seeing Lucy, Marie and George off at the station, where they had jokingly reminded him not to be late for the wedding, Philip was surprised to receive a visit from Monsieur Mercier at his office. He rose quickly on his feet to welcome him warmly.

'This call is part business and part pleasure,' explained Mercier as he sat down.

Philip cocked one eyebrow questioningly, 'Whichever, sir, it is always a pleasure to see you.' Business? Could it be that the gentleman wanted to borrow more money and, if so, did that signify further developments in Calais that would affect Philip's own investment? But pleasure? That aspect of the visit puzzled Philip, although only for a moment.

'I'll get the pleasure out of the way first,' said Monsieur Mercier. 'Madame Daudet is with us again, arrived yesterday. She asked after her friends in Paris and made a special mention of you.'

Philip, though surprised that Blanche was in Paris again, was flattered that she should have made a special enquiry about him. If pressed he would have had to admit that the news sent a flutter through him and brought a vision to his mind of a beautiful, sophisticated woman whose smile, lit by her wonderful eyes, always set his pulses racing.

'Thank you for the message, sir,' he replied automatically while his thoughts dwelt on temptation.

Monsieur Mercier cast him a knowing smile as he said, 'I rather think she has a special interest in you – and who can blame her? You are a handsome young man and seemed to get on well with her when she last visited us. So you are invited to dine with the three of us tomorrow evening. That is, if you are free?'

'I certainly am, sir.' He wondered if he had answered a little too quickly.

'Tomorrow then, six-thirty for seven.'

'Thank you. It is very kind of you to extend this invitation, sir.'

'Now, to business.' Mercier's expression and tone of voice became more serious. 'Have you heard any more about the site for these proposed factories?'

'Rumours, sir, only tittle-tattle that a decision will be made soon. I did hear that the factories were likely to be placed near the route to Calais, but it is beginning to look as if there was no substance in that.'

'I've heard a date has been fixed for the decision. I wondered if you had heard that too?'

'No, sir. I haven't.'

'Have you had anyone recently wishing to invest in land north of Paris? It might be an indication.'

'Well, sir, that is really privileged information.' Philip saw a scowl beginning to come over Monsieur Mercier's face so quickly added, 'But, knowing that you will be the height of discretion and that what passes between us in this respect will go no further, I will tell you that I have had one company enquiring, though nothing has come from it yet. I think they too are waiting for a decision from the department concerned.'

Monsieur Mercier, his scowl gone, nodded. He gave a little grunt and said, 'Look here, Philip, I'm anxious to find out if the date has been fixed, and no doubt it would help you with your dealings if you knew it too?'

'It certainly would, sir.'

Mercier looked thoughtful. 'I have an idea from whom I might find out.'

'You have, sir?'

'Yes, but it's better if you don't know who.'

'You think you can get it, sir?' asked Philip hopefully.

'It's possible, but even if I can, we will have to be very careful about how we use the knowledge.'

'You can rely on me, sir. No word will pass my lips.'

'Good.' The visitor eyed him even more seriously. 'If I get this information, you realise that it will be privileged and I will only be passing it on to you because of your friendship with Blanche who has hinted that she might like to make some investments through you. If she does, and you act on my information, she must never know your source. I have a certain position to maintain and cannot afford for it to be sullied in any way. Remember, people talk and tongues slip.'

'I understand, sir.'

'I hope I will know everything by tomorrow evening.'

The following night Philip passed through the gateway to the Merciers' residence on rue de Chaillot and walked briskly to the house, anticipating a memorable evening. He could soon be in possession of valuable information that would dictate the course of his future, and there was the lure of Blanche besides. He was drawn by the thought of seeing her again, feeling a mysterious conviction that she was part of his destiny, and yet how could she be? He recalled her previous visit when he had first met her and realised there'd been a special empathy between them then. Would it still be there?

240

He was admitted to the house by the footman who obviously had been instructed as to his arrival. As they crossed the hall to the drawing room the clock chimed six-thirty. Philip felt a little glow of satisfaction at his timing.

The servant announced him and he passed into the room to be welcomed warmly by Monsieur Mercier.

'Ah, Philip, so good to see you and welcome you once more to my home. The ladies aren't down yet so that gives me the opportunity to tell you I have received that information we spoke of. The date fixed for the decision is the sixth of August.'

This information sent a cold chill to Philip's heart. The date of Lucy's mother's wedding . . . he should be in England! But he couldn't be. He must be here in Paris, to act quickly once the announcement was made. Any delay would cost him dearly, one way or the another. He had to force himself to show no adverse reaction to the information. Monsieur Mercier must have no intimation that the news had distressed him. Well, there was only one thing for it. He would have to write to Lucy and her mother, apologising for being unable to attend.

'The sixth of August,' he found himself automatically repeating.

'Yes, at ten o'clock in the morning. You should have everything in place to act quickly, without making it appear that you had inside information.'

'I will be extremely careful, sir, and am indeed most grateful to you for confiding in me.'

Mercier waved away his thanks and nothing further could be said on the subject for at that moment, Madame Mercier appeared.

'Madame, it is a great pleasure to meet you again,' said Philip, giving her his most charming smile. He took her proffered hand and raised it to his lips.

She smiled coquettishly at such a greeting from a handsome man and maybe wished fleetingly that her years were not what they were. 'We are delighted to have you, Monsieur Jaurès.'

'Philip, please, Madame.'

She inclined her head in acknowledgement and moved towards a chair. Monsieur Mercier went to a decanter and glasses that had been placed on a small table, above which hung a painting.

'A new work, Madame? I don't recall it from my previous visit. A Tissot, if I am not mistaken,' Philip observed.

'You are right. I took heed of your advice.'

'I'm glad you found it useful.' Philip was glad that Lucy had insisted he continue to learn about art in case he should ever be challenged by anyone about the subject again, but was glad that any further pursuit of the topic was halted when the door opened and Blanche came in.

The whole atmosphere changed with her arrival. She was Philip's idea of perfection. Her eyes were bright and drew his gaze to them. She knew the effect she was having on him and was pleased. She had taken great care with her appearance tonight. There was not one strand of her copper-coloured hair, piled high on her head, out of place. Her beautiful face was framed by the turned-up collar of her white dress. Its slightly flared cut emphasised the tightness across her breasts and at her waist. Blanche held herself erect with an easy grace that compelled attention.

'Philip.' Her voice was soft and low, caressing, inviting. Her smile openly expressed her pleasure at seeing him again. 'I am pleased to see you and must thank my host and hostess,' she turned her gaze on them, 'for giving us the opportunity to meet again.'

'It is a pleasure that I will always remember,' responded Philip, wondering who could ever forget the exquisite creature who stood before him.

For one moment, as they sat down and accepted the drinks that Monsieur Mercier had poured for them, the date the sixth of August flashed through his mind again but he instantly dismissed it. Nothing should intrude on time spent in the presence of such a charming person as Blanche.

The evening passed all too quickly for him and as he made his departure, Philip sensed that it was the same for Blanche. But they had tomorrow to look forward to because during the evening he'd invited her to accompany him to the races at Chantilly.

It was a thoughtful Philip who went to bed that night.

The following morning he was up early; before he left for the races there was a letter he must write. It was no good putting it off.

*

242

My dear Lucy,

It is with the deepest regret that I put pen to paper to tell you that I will not be able to be with you at your mother's wedding on the sixth of August. An important business transaction has been rescheduled for that date, one that I must attend to personally. I have sought ways to get out of it, but as it deeply concerns my future I feel I must be here.

I am so sorry. Be assured that my thoughts will be with you all on that day.

I am sending separate letters to your mother and to Mr Newton.

My love,

Philip

He re-read the letter, signed it and then wrote the other two letters. Now he felt free to be in Paris on the day he saw as vital to his future.

He posted the letters on his way to meet Blanche who appeared before the coach he had hired for the day drew to a halt at the door of the Mercier residence. Philip was flattered to think that she must have been watching for his arrival.

'You look exquisite,' he commented as he greeted her.

She acknowledged his compliment with a smile, pleased that her sand-coloured silk dress with its bright red stripes had attracted his attention. Its high neck clung to her ivory throat from which hung a diamond pendant. She wore suede gloves and carried a bright, multi-coloured parasol with a frilled edge. Her hair was taken to the top of her head again but in such a way as to emphasise the wide-brimmed red picture hat she wore tipped back so that it did not hide her face.

They had started their ride when Blanche began to speak. 'I may as well tell you that I need some investment advice,' she gave a slight pause, 'but my real purpose in coming to Paris was to see you.'

His surprise at this admission was evident.

She gave a little laugh. 'Shocked, Philip?'

He brushed that aside with, 'What am I to read into your statement?'

243

'My luck deserted me. I lost at the races, at cards, and a couple of speculations have failed. I wondered if it would have happened had you been with me?' She half turned towards him on the seat so that she could look directly into his eyes.

'And what did you conclude?' he prompted when she paused.

'You were my talisman. We won when we were together. We made a good partnership.'

He gave a little smile of remembrance. 'We did, didn't we?'

'Maybe we could be again?'

'And that is what you are hoping today will prove?'

'We shall see. What about you? How has your luck been since I left Paris?'

'Not good.'

'There you are then, doesn't that prove something?'

'Could be just coincidence.'

'I believe there's more to it than that. I think our paths crossed for a reason. Think about it. Weren't we good together?'

'We were,' he had to admit. And since then, things had not been the best for him. But that might all change on the sixth of August. In the meantime . . .

'There you are, it's true – we *are* good together!' There was laughter on Blanche's lips as she grabbed Philip's hand and they hurried back with the lightest of steps to their waiting coach.

'A win on every race but the first!' He laughed heartily. Was this an omen for the future? Was his land speculation going to pay off? Had his luck returned together with Blanche?

Their spirits were high as they drove back to Paris and, after a pleasant meal, tested their skill and luck at the gaming tables.

Nothing went wrong for them. When they finally drew up outside the Merciers' residence it was with feelings of regret that the evening was at an end.

Blanche looked at Philip quizzically. 'Was I right to come back to Paris?'

He smiled. 'You certainly were, Blanche.'

'We have something, Philip.'

'How long are you staying?'

She gave a little shrug. 'I hadn't considered that. It depended whether we forged our luck again together. I think we have and I'm afraid if I go home I may lose.'

'Will you be here on the sixth of August?'

Puzzled, she looked at him questioningly. 'Why then? What's important about that date?'

'It concerns a speculation I have in hand.'

'And the sixth is the day you'll know the result?'

'Yes. If you are here I'll win. I must, you are my talisman.'

'Tell me about it? If I am to weave my magic I must know what it is.'

'Tomorrow, Blanche. It's a long story, and one that can't be told standing here. I'll call for you at twelve and tell you over lunch.'

She knew she could not persuade him otherwise and kissed him on the cheek. 'Tomorrow,' she whispered.

She started to turn away. Philip stopped her and pulled her into his arms. Their kiss told them how strongly the desire between them ran.

She walked into the house, pausing briefly at the door to raise her hand in thanks. He was a few years younger than she, but would such a difference cause a barrier? It was their feelings that mattered. And they were good together, lucky together. That counted for everything with Blanche.

Philip watched her go into the house, his thoughts aflame. He enjoyed the company of this beautiful woman who filled his mind. Blanche's beauty turned heads wherever she went. Aware of this, he felt proud to be in her company. Above all, for him at this moment she was a lucky emblem.

Such thoughts occupied his mind as he walked home, but he also found that mercenary considerations crept in – Blanche was a rich widow. But why was he thinking like this? There was Lucy. What would she think when she received his letter?

The next evening, once they were seated comfortably in an exclusive restaurant not far from Notre Dame where Philip had booked an alcove table so that their conversation could be private, Blanche looked expectantly at him. Philip said nothing until the wine waiter had retreated after the wine was approved.

He raised his to Blanche. 'To us, may our luck continue.'

She inclined her head in acknowledgement and he saw a flash of speculation in her eyes.

'So, the sixth August is an important day for you. In what way, might ask?'

'I'd better tell you everything, but before I reveal what I have done, I must have your promise that what passes between us will never be revealed to anyone, and I mean anyone?'

Blanche's expression became grave. 'This sounds serious.'

'It is. I could be in deep trouble if ever I was found out.'

'Then why tell me?'

'Every time you have been with me you have brought me luck, and I want you with me on the sixth. If my telling you the full story keeps you in Paris with me on that day, then I'll do it. If you are not going to be here there is no point in telling you and it would be better that you did not know.'

'But I can't guarantee to bring you luck with whatever it is.'

'That I'll have to risk, but I will feel more comfortable about the gamble I have taken if you are here. On that day there will be an announcement that will make or break my future.'

'This sounds serious. You really think I will make a difference?'

'I feel sure of it.'

'Then I'll stay.' She saw relief in Philip's face and reached out to place her hand over his. 'I'm sure everything will turn out right, whatever it is.'

During the meal he told her all the details of his land speculation. She listened without questioning him and when he had finished, said, 'I can see why you are worried. You have taken a huge gamble on someone else's decision and only have a fifty-fifty chance of winning. If it goes against you, you are in terrible straits.'

'I know. All I can do is to sit tight, but with you beside me I think the chances have swung in my favour.'

'Oh, Philip, I hope you are right but I cannot influence the outcome. Betting on the horses, the cards or at the roulette tables is a different matter, a different sort of gambling where you can use judgement and observation.'

'I know, but you said yourself that your own luck had run out after you left Paris. See what happened yesterday once we were reunited.'

Blanche smiled. 'Your faith in me is touching but don't expect too much. I think the best thing I can do between now and the sixth is to take your mind off things. Please let me do that, Philip.'

As she made this request her eyes were fixed on his. He met her gaze, feeling relaxed and light-headed at the thought of spending time with this exquisite lady who had cast a spell on him. With Blanche he felt drawn into a new world where only the two of them existed. It was as if he had never met Lucy.

'A letter for you, love,' Isobel called up the stairs and Lucy came rushing down. 'I have one in the same writing,' she added as she handed over the envelope to her daughter.

'Philip!' explained Lucy and tore the envelope open. Full of excitement, eagerly anticipating news of his life in Paris, she pulled out the sheet of paper. The joy on her face, the brightness in her eyes, faded quickly when she took in the meaning of his words.

'He's not coming!' she gasped. The shock was overwhelming. Her eyes began to burn as they filled with tears. 'Oh, no!' She sank onto a chair as her joyous world collapsed around her. She barely heard her mother's words.

'I've got a letter too. He apologises for having to be in Paris on our wedding day.' Isobel let her words fade away. Realising her daughter was in shock, she fell to her knees beside her and took her into her arms. 'It can't be helped.' The statement sounded lame but that was the only attitude to take in the face of Philip's poor explanation for having to stay in Paris.

'But he said he would come,' wailed Lucy.

'I know it's hard, love, but we cannot stand in the way of important business. Whatever that means.'

Sobs racked Lucy. 'But why does it have to be on that day?'

'Who knows, love? There must be a perfectly good reason. I don't think Philip would have missed the wedding unless it was

247

something very important,' Isobel sought to reassure her, though privately she had her own worries.

'I suppose not,' muttered Lucy grudgingly.

'Come on, dry those tears and let's walk over to see Marie and Arthur. We must tell them. They've probably had word also, but let's go and see.'

Lucy nodded and continued to dab at her eyes as she left the room. A few minutes later she came down the stairs to join her mother who was waiting in the hall.

Isobel smiled when her daughter reached her. 'That's better,' she commented with affection, having noted that Lucy had wiped away all evidence of her tears. The subject was not mentioned again until they reached the Newtons' residence where they found that Arthur had received a similar letter.

He and Marie expressed their regrets and tried to salve Lucy's disappointment.

'I'm pleased Marie is going to be with you until we return from our honeymoon,' said Isobel to her daughter. 'Try and put this setback behind you and have an enjoyable time together.'

Hester watched Edward talking to two visitors at the exhibition standing in front of the painting he had given her. She had engineered it so that she was alone, ignoring the guests milling around the room viewing the paintings during this preview evening. She admired Edward's poise, his amiable manner particularly when dealing with strangers, his innate sense of style that always made him appear immaculately turned out, his handsome features. But more than that she was struck by other attributes that remained hidden from others because they were directed only at her. He had a special thoughtfulness, a tenderness that was only for her. His touch meant more to her than anyone else's; a light would come into his eyes when they met. She recalled these things and so many more as she stood watching him and realised she was in love.

'Hester, you shouldn't be alone.' She started as a voice broke into her thoughts and destroyed the magic spell that had drawn her into another world.

'Oh, Mr Sotheran! I was miles away.'

'I was aware of that.' He gave a knowing little smile for he had followed her gaze before he spoke and realised at whom it was directed. Oh, to be young! he thought.

'You like the exhibition?' she asked, trying to hide her embarrassment.

'It is truly magnificent. I shall say so in my newspaper column but enlarge on my praise too with specific comments about the paintings, especially the one in prime position.'

'You especially like that?'

'I do indeed. There is something extraordinary about it, and I don't mean the colouring, or the interpretation of a coastal scene, or the power Edward has given to the sea and its many moods.'

'I'm glad you see all that,' she put in.

'Ah, but there is so much more. There is true inspiration behind that painting which has come from someone other than himself. Someone inspired Edward and I hope they will go on doing so.'

Hester made no comment but as he walked away whispered to herself, 'I hope so too.'

The room was finally empty except for Hester and Edward. Her uncle, his mother and Matthew Robinson had discreetly left them to themselves, saying they would meet them later at Claridge's to toast the success of the exhibition.

The young couple stood in the centre of the room. Silence filled it, all the more intense because it had followed on so quickly from the noise of many conversations. Now all was still. They were alone in a roomful of Edward's finest creations. Their hands met lovingly. In the moment that followed Edward pulled Hester close to him and kissed her without a word.

When, reluctantly, their lips drew apart, he said, 'Thank you for this splendid exhibition and for all you have done to make it special.'

'It was you who painted these masterpieces.'

'But they would not have been noticed in the way that they were without your flair in exhibiting them. I am sure that had a lot to do with drawing people's attention to individual works. It's resulted in six sales and three commissions.'

'And there may be more before the exhibition finally closes.

I'm so pleased for you, Edward.' She raised herself on her toes and kissed him on the cheek.

He grasped her round the waist and kissed her again.

As their lips parted she gave a little smile. 'I could do this all night but I think we had better go and join the celebration.'

'I suppose we must.'

Holding hands, they left the room, pausing to look at the picture hanging at the far end of the room. 'Thank you for that,' she said quietly, her voice full of emotion, recalling what Mr Sotheran had seen in it.

All celebration over, Edward had retired to his room when there was a knock on the door. He opened it.

'Mother.'

'I just wanted to have a word with you alone.' Colette stepped into the room and he closed the door. His mother's eyes were damp with joy, he saw. 'I am so proud of you,' she whispered, holding out her arms to him. He came to them and hugged her.

'Thank you for all your encouragement,' he said as they sat down.

'For what little I did I was more than rewarded tonight, seeing your talent recognised.'

'I wish Father could have been there.' He caught her quizzical look. 'I meant, both of them,' he added.

'That recognition pleases me.'

'I mean it. The man I knew as my father all my life will always be that. I would not have grown into the person I am without Bernard's influence. My talent I have inherited, and I am grateful to my real father for that. Some day I hope he and I will share an exhibition such as we have had this evening.'

'You still mean to find him?'

'I must. We have so much to share. I don't think I would feel complete unless I was able to do that. Our common dedication to art is a strong bond.'

She nodded, knowing that after his success this evening he was more determined than ever to find Arthur.

Chapter Seventeen

During the early part of August Philip saw Blanche every day. He found her company not only stimulating but also comforting in his anxiety. She did her best to divert his mind from entertaining thoughts of the dire consequences he might shortly have to face. They drew closer and their attraction deepened.

But in the darkness of his bedroom Philip's conscience was troubled. Betrayal of Lucy haunted his mind in the still hours of the morning. He tried to thrust these thoughts away by thinking of the beautiful woman he was seeing every day. Apart from her physical attraction he found Blanche easy to talk to, someone in whom he could confide.

For her part Blanche found herself drawn closer than ever to this handsome young man whose confidence she saw being daily undermined by worry, even though to anyone else it was far from evident. One evening in his apartment they gave way to their mutual attraction and lost themselves in love for a few hours.

'When shall we know tomorrow?' Blanche asked, bringing him back to reality finally as she lay quiet in his arms.

'Ten o'clock. The announcement will be made at the offices of the Regulator. All interested parties will be informed at nine just before the public announcement so no one can manipulate their investments accordingly.'

'You'll call for me at nine-thirty? That is, if you want me to be there?'

He twisted over to face her. 'Want you to be there? Of course, I could not face it without my lucky charm.'

She ran a finger down his cheek and looked seriously into his eyes. 'Don't pin too much hope on me. But I'll be there for you.'

At nine-thirty Philip was at the Merciers' to collect Blanche.

'Is Monsieur Mercier coming with us?' he asked as she joined him in the hall.

'He's already gone.' Her eyes twinkled as she added, 'I think he thought we would want to be on our own.'

When they reached the Regulator's office they found the room set aside for the announcement already teeming with people. The buzz of speculation was rife and only stilled into a charged silence when a clock struck ten and the Regulator himself walked into the room to take his place behind a desk on a dais.

He gazed across the crowded room, cleared his throat and said, 'Good day, gentlemen, and also to those few ladies who have graced us with their presence. I must apologise for the protracted decision-making process, but let me assure you it would have been most unwise for us to make a hasty decision. I am sorry that you were kept waiting for so long but there was much to consider.

'It has not been easy to reach a decision for those concerned. I must assure you that they took everything into consideration, debating long and hard, for they wanted the final outcome to be unanimous. Arguments were prolonged and involved many visits to the sites under consideration. I think it became general knowledge that these were reduced to two, one not far from the Calais road and the other close to that leading to Le Havre. Both ports had much to recommend them but it was not that which chiefly concerned us. It was felt that both could more than cope with the upsurge of trade that would come with the factories, so our chief concern was with the possible benefits to Paris. Our decision has favoured the placing of the factories in a site that can make use of river transport as well as roads, so the site used is to be that near the Seine.'

Pandemonium broke out; excitement and disappointment charged the air. Laughter and curses mingled as speculators counted up their gains or losses.

Blanche gripped Philip's hand. She hoped her touch would give him the confidence to face the future. She saw he had gone deathly pale and knew he was seeing his world collapse around him. The knowledge that he had illicitly borrowed money from his company with which to speculate haunted her as she said, 'Let's go.'

He did not speak but turned at her bidding and automatically followed her, guided by her touch, as she led the way through the milling crowd to the exit. Once outside she paused and squeezed his arm. 'Philip, I'm so sorry that luck ran out for you.'

He gave a wan smile and shrugged his shoulders. 'I'm done for, Blanche. I borrowed money I shouldn't have. The consequences will be disastrous.'

'Come, let us find a seat by the river and talk about it.'

They walked in silence, each turning over the problem in their mind. It was only when they found a seat that Blanche posed a question. 'Couldn't you throw yourself on your father's mercy. Surely he wouldn't see his own son disgraced?'

Philip gave a little grunt of derision. 'You don't know my father. Everything has to be straightforward with him. He built up the reputation of the firm founded by my grandfather on honesty and straight dealing.'

'But . . .'

'Not buts. He'll be ruthless in his punishment so that the outside world will see that he and the firm grant no favours to anyone. The name Jaurès must not be sullied. I'll just have to take the consequences of a gamble that did not pay off.'

'That could mean prison.'

'Yes.' He let out a wail. 'Why, oh, why, did they have to choose that site?' He shook his head. 'I'm finished, Blanche, finished. Go, walk away from me now and forget you ever knew me.'

She gripped his arm more tightly. 'Look at me, Philip, look at me.' There was steel in her voice, a command he had to obey. He looked up slowly and met a gaze of piercing determination. 'I can't do that. You have come to mean a great deal to me. Walk away? Never!'

'But I'll be branded an embezzler. I don't want that stigma affecting you.'

'It won't.'

'It's bound to, through your association with me.'

'Not if . . .' Her voice trailed away and a compelling light came to her eyes.

'If what?' he prompted.

'How much did you borrow?'

Blanche looked startled when he told her but was so quick to compose herself that she hoped he had not noticed her astonishment. 'That's a large sum. You certainly gambled with high stakes.'

'And would have made a considerable fortune if the decision had been in favour of the Calais route.'

'Forget that, it's done with. There's nothing we can do about it, but we can do something else.'

He was puzzled. 'It is I who must solve this. I don't want you involved.'

'Not even if I loan you the money?'

For one moment he could not believe what he had heard. 'What?' The pitch of his voice was filled with incredulity. The implications rushed in on him. Here was his way out but . . . 'I couldn't borrow from you.'

Blanche smiled. 'I put it that way to test you. I'd hoped that was what you would say. I read much more into that refusal than mere words. I detect in it your loving concern for me.' She intensified her gaze and challenged him not to look away as she went on: 'I love you, Philip. Marry me.'

He stared at her in disbelief. His mind spun, hardly able to grasp what she was saying. 'Does this mean you will not loan me the money unless I married you?'

'No, Philip, it does not. You should know I'm not that kind of a person. Blackmailing someone into marriage does not augur well for a relationship and its outcome. I will still lend you the money, though it would have to be on strictly commercial terms. But I think since my return to Paris your feelings for me have grown stronger. Marriage is the answer. We will be in this together, but your reputation will not be sullied. From what you told me of the arrangements you made, your father need never know. We will be united and our luck will remain intact; we'll look back on this as a mere setback in what we'll achieve.' He was struck by the enthusiasm, excitement and promise in her voice. The future beckoned with renewed possibilities.

Then thoughts of Lucy penetrated his mind and a contest between the two women battled within him. Lucy, gentle Lucy, who wanted nothing more than to be a good artist and to fall in love, as he knew she had with him. He had respect for her and deep feelings – but love? Was he in love with her? Had he ever been? With her inheritance gone, had his feelings changed? True, he had enjoyed being with her, though had always thought it wise to keep his gambling instincts from her. But with this other gorgeous creature sitting beside him, who could send his pulses racing, life took on a different aspect, becoming ever more exciting and tempting. He did not have to keep his gambling tendencies from Blanche for she had the same leanings. They were good together and she had stolen most of his heart. Now that she was offering him all her love and an escape from his problem he was sure he could give her his undivided love.

Philip took her hands in his and drew her slowly to him. 'I love you, Blanche, not because of the escape you offer me but because you are you. I know that life for me will be full of joy and excitement from now on because we will be together, making our luck work for us.'

'Good. You have made me very happy,' she said. A moment later their lips met, sealing a shared future.

That night, alone in his apartment, Philip put pen to paper and wrote:

Dear Lucy,
I hope the wedding went well today. I thought of you at the ceremony and afterwards. I hope that Mr and Mrs Newton, as they now are, will have a happy future.

I do not know when you intend to return to Paris and your studies but I must tell you that I am going to be out of the capital for a considerable time. Possibly I won't be back until after the start of your term. I thought it best for you to know so that you can make plans accordingly.

Philip re-read his words and nodded. They would do. He paused with his pen poised above the paper. Was he being a coward? Shouldn't he have told Lucy the truth? He gave a slight shake of his head – regret was there for taking the cowardly way out but he could not face doing it any other way. She would learn soon enough when she returned to Paris. He hesitated just a moment longer before finishing his letter as he had done the others: 'My love, Philip'.

He sat staring at it for a few minutes before folding it and sealing the envelope, knowing that he had embarked on a course which had already been turned to his advantage by arranging for a considerable sum of money from Blanche's account in Marseilles to be transferred to clear his debt in Paris. Blanche had secured his future which would now be spent with her.

'Be gloriously happy.' Marie hugged her father, expressing all the love she had for him.

Arthur's eyes were damp as he eased her away and, still holding her round the waist, looked into her eyes. 'You looked beautiful today. Your mother would have been proud of you. Thank you for your blessing on this marriage.' He hugged her and then let her go to Isobel.

The bride welcomed her with arms open wide and, as they closed round her, the girl felt their loving protection. 'Be happy, Marie. You have a wonderful young man in George.'

Marie smiled back at her. 'It is I who should be wishing you every happiness.'

'I have that with your father. I am privileged to have found a love I never expected to find again but have done in Arthur. Don't worry about him, his happiness is paramount with me.'

'Thank you. You have my love too.'

They hugged each other with affection, kissed then stood apart, knowing that similar sentiments had passed between Lucy and her stepfather.

The stepsisters watched the coach that was taking the newly-weds to the station disappear then walked slowly back into the house. The farm manager and his wife stayed twenty minutes and then left, hoping their new employer would be as pleasant and as considerate as Isobel had been.

George left the next morning for Norfolk, and Marie and Lucy planned what they would do until the honeymooners returned. Three days later Lucy received the letter from Paris.

Marie saw her face cloud with disappointment. 'What's wrong?'

'Philip will be out of town until after the start of term.'

'On business?'

'He doesn't say.'

'I expect that's it. Probably linked to the reason he did not get to the wedding. I know it's disappointing but some things can't stand in the way of business, especially if it's important.'

Lucy grimaced. 'I know,' she agreed despondently. 'But . . .' She stopped herself. 'Well, we'll still return early to Paris and do the things we planned.'

Four days after writing to Lucy, Philip knew that everything was secured. It was as if he had never borrowed his firm's money and the special account was closed as if it had never existed.

'That is a great relief,' he confided in Blanche as they enjoyed a glass of wine outside one of the most fashionable restaurants. He reached out and took her hand. 'Thank you for what you have done. I will replace it all and more one day. I have been giving the future considerable thought.'

'I thought you might.'

'The only ties I have in Paris are through the company. Though I say it myself, I believe I have placed the Paris office on a sound footing. I have heard murmurings to that effect coming out of head office, especially from my father. I think that Paris could be run by someone else and I could move elsewhere, say to Marseilles.'

'Ah.' Blanche gave him a knowing smile. 'So that is why you kept quizzing me about my home town.'

He returned her smile. 'That and something else. If I can persuade my father that it presents a good business opportunity, we could move there.'

'But . . . Paris?'

'I am not bent on staying here. If we do, we will have to think of buying a house whereas in Marseilles you already have one. But,' he added quickly, 'if you would rather stay here . . .'

'No,' she interrupted him. 'I would prefer to stay in the home I already have. It is in a wonderful position five miles out of Marseilles, overlooking the sea. I would miss it terribly if I had to leave, but I was prepared to if your business commitments meant you had to stay in Paris.'

He smiled and pressed her hand lovingly. 'You are a charming and considerate person. All I have to do is to persuade Father that my proposition is one that will benefit the firm. I am sure after what I have accomplished here in Paris, coupled with news of your knowledge of trading in the Mediterranean, he will be persuaded.'

Philip hoped he was right and knew he would do his utmost to get his father to see that the proposition was a good one. He wanted to be away from Paris as soon as possible, certainly before Lucy returned.

'I'll do all I can,' Blanche reassured him.

'Good. Do you want a big wedding?'

'No. What about you?'

'The quieter the better. I suggest we go to Marseilles and get married there as soon as possible. But what about your family?'

'I have no one. What about yours?'

'If we are married already there is nothing they can do about it.'

'Are you sure? Might it not not jeopardise your father's attitude to your proposal?'

'He is adept at keeping personal matters and business dealings apart. He may disapprove of my marrying without the family knowing but it won't colour his attitude to a business proposition. Besides, when he is met with your beauty and charm he'll be won over immediately on both accounts – my father still has an eye for the ladies.'

Two days later, after a hectic day of packing and tying up loose ends during which Philip appointed someone to take charge of the Paris office on a temporary basis, he and Blanche left for Marseilles. Philip was astounded by her home and its position.

'It is truly wonderful,' he commented after she had shown him round and they had come to stand at a window that gave them a magnificent view of a tranquil bay. It was like a promise that this was what they could expect from now on. 'No wonder you didn't want to leave.'

'I would have done if it had been necessary. I'll return to Paris if your father insists that you should be there.' His hands clasped her waist. 'It is you who matter, not the place.' She studied him seriously. 'You are not uneasy at being in the house I shared with my first husband?' She sensed a moment's hesitation and got in before he could speak. 'He has left traces of himself behind but I can assure you he will not haunt my feelings for you nor the life we will share here. I know he would approve of my finding happiness with you.'

His hands tightened on her waist. 'Then I thank him for his understanding, and for the gift of you.'

A week later they were married in a quiet civil ceremony.

'They're home!'

Marie and Lucy had both heard the rumble of the approaching coach. Leaping to their feet, deserting their drawing boards and letting their pencils roll to fall from the table, they rushed from the house. They were waving vigorously, their faces wreathed in welcoming smiles, as the coach drew nearer and nearer.

Isobel and Arthur reciprocated the excitement. As soon as the vehicle stopped Arthur was on to the ground and helping his wife from the coach. Everyone fell into each other's arms, exchanging kisses and hugs. They left the coachman and servants to see to the luggage and went into the house busily exchanging questions and answers.

It was not until outdoor clothes had been cast off and Isobel and Arthur had tidied themselves and settled down in the drawing room that calm returned. The girls were eager to hear about Scotland and Isobel and Arthur to know what their daughters had been doing.

It was only then that Isobel posed the question to Lucy, 'Have you heard any more from Philip?'

'Yes, Mother. He wrote to tell me he is out of Paris until after the start of term, but Marie and I will still return early as arranged and be well prepared for the new session.'

Chapter Eighteen

'You are sure they'll be here?' Even the usually serene Blanche confessed to being a little apprehensive about encountering Philip's family now that the meeting was drawing nearer with every turn of the coach's wheels between Interlaken and Spietz on the shores of Lake Thun.

'The family always spend August and the first two weeks of September at our house in Spietz,' Philip reiterated what he had told her before. 'They'll be here.' He gave her a reassuring smile. 'You'll be all right. They can't help but be charmed by you. Just be yourself.'

She tried to calm herself as the coach climbed towards a large house situated on a hillside above the lake. The village was high on a slope against a backcloth of tree-covered mountains. But when she alighted from the coach in front of the house it was the view back down the lake that took Blanche's breath away.

Philip saw her reaction. 'Wonderful, isn't it? And the weather is just right for our visit.'

Blanche was lost for words. The mountains beyond the lake and its companion, Lake Brientz, were snow-capped peaks of awe-inspiring magnificence.

'Fiescherhorn, Eiger, Mönch, and glorious Jungfrau,' said Philip, close to her ear as he pointed them out.

Blanche said nothing but drank in the beauty that touched her soul. She felt confidence rising in her. What could go wrong for her amidst such splendour?

'I think we had better make our presence known,' said Philip, gently taking her arm.

She started. 'Of course.' Only then was she aware that he had dismissed the coach and it was rumbling back down the curving drive. He began to lead her towards the six steps that led up to a paved veranda running the full width of the house. They reached the large double doors and Philip gave a good tug at the metal door-pull. The nervous tension that gripped Blanche was broken when the door opened.

'Monsieur Philip!' A slight girl, neatly dressed in mauve with a chiffon scarf tied neatly at her neck and a small white cap holding her hair in place, showed her surprise.

'Hello, Teresa. Where's the family?'

'All out in the garden, sir. Should I announce you?'

'No, I want to surprise them. But you can get someone to bring our luggage in.'

'Certainly, sir.' She cast Blanche a quick glance and then looked at Philip so that he could read her thoughts.

'Put it all in my room.' Before she could say any more he had taken Blanche's hand and was leading her away. 'That'll give cause for speculation downstairs,' he whispered with a grin. He took her through a door at the back of the large hall, and along a passage to a rear door.

Blanche saw a large garden as wide as it was long, tree-lined, with magnificent flowerbeds bordering a well-manicured lawn. But she saw that the lawn wasn't kept merely as a showpiece. Four people were lounging there in comfort, enjoying the sun, while children raced in play despite the heat.

'Mother, Father, my sister and her husband, and their three children,' Philip explained quickly and quietly. Standing in the shadow of the house, no one had noticed them. He gripped her hand tightly. 'Come on.' He led her into the sunlight.

The movement caught the eye of the older lady. She sat up, her eyes widening in amazement. 'Philip!' she gasped.

Immediately everyone's attention was drawn and they were out of their chairs in a moment. Philip's mother came to greet them with outstretched hands, his father only a step behind. His sister and her husband held back a little so that the older people could make their greetings first, but all eyes were unmistakably on the

261

lady who was with him, and he saw that those eyes were filled with curiosity and admiration.

'Mother.' He let go of Blanche's hand and she stayed half a step behind him. With close contact gone she suddenly felt vulnerable.

She saw a slight person, beautifully dressed in the lightest of attires as befitted the hot day. Already she could sense a strong personality, a person who ruled but did not impose, who knew how to get her own way with her husband without his knowing, who would never interfere in his business unless asked for advice and then it would be carefully thought out. She saw affection and a mother's love for her son as she took Philip into her arms. He kissed her on both cheeks and then turned to exchange a warm handshake with his father, a tall man who still retained an athletic figure, well groomed and dressed in clothes chosen for comfort in the privacy of his home on a hot day.

'This is an unexpected pleasure, Philip.' His voice was sharp and clear without being overbearing or commanding, but Blanche sensed steel in it too and presumed that his wife was the only one who would get the better of this man thanks to a love match of mutual adoration and understanding of each other's strengths and weaknesses.

'Mother, Father, I want you to meet Blanche, my wife.'

The announcement brought a shocked silence in its wake. Eyes were turned on Philip in disbelief.

'What? Married?' The words exploded from his father's lips.

Blanche wasn't sure whether he was angry or not but she had no time to consider that point for she heard Philip explaining.

'We met in Paris and immediately fell in love. Blanche was a widow and has no family so we wanted to avoid a big formal wedding. There was a quiet civil ceremony yesterday in Marseilles where Blanche has a wonderful house on the coast. Then, without further delay, we came here. We hope you and all the family will give us your blessing.'

Seeing her husband still looked annoyed, Madame Jaurès took charge. She stepped closer to Blanche who knew that this attractive woman had been busily summing her up with a shrewd judgement that went a lot by first impressions. She was glad that she had dressed elegantly for this meeting and now summoned all her grace and charm to her aid. She saw Madame Jaurès open her arms. Without hesitation Blanche stepped into them and received an embrace that spoke of warmth and welcome. Each knew that the other had Philip's interest and happiness at heart, and in that moment they were united in love and friendship.

'Welcome to the family, Blanche.'

'Thank you, Madame Jaurès.'

As they parted Philip's mother turned to him. As she hugged him to her she said quietly, 'Be happy, my son. She's lovely.'

Blanche had turned to Philip's father who had still not taken his eyes off her. 'Monsieur Jaurès.' She held out her hand to him.

He took it and raised it to his lips. When he looked at her she saw all animosity had disappeared in the wake of his wife's attitude. 'I think, now that you are a member of the family, I am permitted a kiss,' he said with a mischievous twinkle in his eyes.

Blanche smiled. 'I think you are.' She stood on tiptoe with her hands on his shoulders to kiss him, allowing the embrace to linger a long moment for she had recognised that this man would enjoy flirting and a kiss would please him. She knew she had scored when he said quietly to her, 'Where did my son find such an exquisite creature, and why did he keep you hidden until now?'

They were aware then that Philip's sister and brother-in-law had come forward, eager to offer their congratulations.

Philip made the introductions. 'My sister Camille, her husband Julian.' Kisses and congratulations were exchanged and the children were called to meet their new aunt. Blanche showed a keen interest in them for she knew that winning the children's trust would go a long way to accomplishing her own acceptance within the family.

'Maurice,' Madame Jaurès addressed her husband, 'I think this occasion calls for champagne.'

'Of course, Marcelle.' He hurried away to return a few minutes later with two bottles and one of the maids carrying a tray of glasses.

Once they were charged and the toast to the newly-weds made, Madame Jaurès said, 'Now, you must tell us all about it, Philip. And you too, Blanche.'

By the time the tale was over, with no hint about Philip's illicit dealing, Blanche felt more comfortable with his family and they were delighted with the new member, recognising her charm, elegance and friendliness. Maurice saw that his son had married into money but also knew that this had not been the sole reason behind the match.

He said as much later, after the evening meal, when he and Philip, on his instigation, were alone in his study.

'See you make that marriage work, my son. You have a most beautiful and charming wife, and one who is rich too. You say she has a home overlooking the Mediterranean, not far from Marseilles?'

'Yes, that is where we would like to live, Father.'

This announcement caught his father unawares. 'But what about Paris?'

'I have been giving that a lot of thought. I think I have done well in establishing a firm base there. I have made many good contacts and we are getting known. I feel sure that a flow of clients will continue now that our honesty and competitive terms are known in the city.'

'I grant that you have done well. Only the other day I was looking at the Paris books and found that they were better than I'd expected in the short time you have been there. It gave me hope you could build on what you have achieved.'

'I am sure that someone else could do that just as easily. I have not left the office unattended to come here but engaged someone trustworthy to take over while I am away. I was hoping you might see clear to appoint him to a permanent position and allow me to open an office in Marseilles.'

'Ah, I see.'

'I think after our first experiment outside Switzerland, we should expand further. Marseilles, with all its Mediterranean trade, could be an ideal place.'

'But it would be an entirely different enterprise from that in Paris.'

'True but many of the same basic principles will apply. Trading patterns would be different but I have a knowledgeable ally in

Blanche. She knows a great deal from the business she and her husband set up, in which she played an important role.'

His father looked thoughtful. 'It is not something we can undertake lightly. I know you would like it because of wanting to live in Blanche's house.'

'That is not the reason I put forward this suggestion. I do honestly believe it would benefit the firm to open an office there.'

'Though I said this to no one else, I will admit that I had the Paris office opened as a test case. It has succeeded, but opening another in Marseilles needs careful thought.'

'That's all I'm asking, that you give it some consideration.'

Two days later Philip strolled hand in hand with Blanche beside the lake.

'You have made a hit with all the family, my love.'

'With everyone?'

'Yes. They all adore you.'

'How did they take the prospect of your moving to Marseilles?'

'No one has expressed any objections, but really the only person it concerns is my father.'

'I presume you have put your proposals to him?'

'Yes. He's thinking them over.'

'When are you likely to have his answer?'

'He has not said but he can't keep us waiting long. After all, the business is involved and he won't want that to stagnate. I enthused over the potential of a Marseilles branch and told him of your experience in Mediterranean trade. No doubt he will have a word with you.

'Mother and Father have suggested we should go to visit relatives in Geneva for a couple of days to tell them of our marriage. It will be better coming from us personally rather than their hearing of it for themselves. I said we would. Is that all right with you?'

'Of course, it's the right thing to do.'

'We'll leave tomorrow and be back here three days later. I expect Father will have an answer about Marseilles then.'

*

When they visited the house in Geneva to see his uncle and aunt, Philip knew that there was every chance Adelina would be there for she was very close to his cousins and spent much of her time in Geneva with them. He was not wrong, and though he and Blanche were swamped in the family's heartfelt congratulations he detected a little frostiness in Adelina's words. It came as no surprise, therefore, when she sought him out alone.

Blanche was changing for the evening meal while he strolled among the flowerbeds in the large garden.

'Philip, when did you meet her?' Adelina came straight to the point.

'A short while ago, at Longchamps. You do like her?'

'Well, she's charming, most gracious, and wants to be loved by all of us, but I had no idea you . . .' She left the words unfinished and said, 'What about Lucy?'

'We are good friends.'

Adelina gave a little snort of derision. 'I don't think she sees her relationship with you like that! In fact, I would go so far as to say she's madly in love with you. You must have realised?' A thought struck her. 'You've just got married while Lucy was in England for her mother's wedding. You were supposed to be there.'

'Business kept me in Paris.'

'Oh, yes,' she mocked, 'personal business! So Lucy doesn't know?' She could see the answer written all over Philip's face. 'Oh, my goodness! Poor Lucy. You have a painful encounter in store when she returns.'

'When is that?'

'I don't know her plans. I'm going to friends in Grindelwald and not returning to Paris until the start of term on the tenth of September.'

As he walked back to the house Philip wondered if that would be the date when Lucy would return to Paris. If so, maybe he would have left the city for Marseilles by then. It depended what his father had decided.

'You seem a little anxious,' commented Blanche as they neared the residence in Spietz.

'Just wondering what Father's decision will be.'

'Don't worry about it,' she replied. 'If we have to be in Paris, so be it. All that matters is that we are together.'

He gave a wan smile. 'I know, but I also realise how much it means to you to live in your wonderful house.'

'Well, there's nothing we can do about it. You made a good case for opening an office in Marseilles and I painted a glowing picture of the potential for trade there, drawn from my experience. I think your father was impressed by my knowledge.'

'And hopefully will see it as an asset if he agrees to open a branch there.'

They were heartily welcomed back by all the family but it wasn't until after the evening meal that Monsieur Jaurès called his son and Blanche to his study. He was pouring wine when they came in, and as they sat down in front of his desk handed each of them a glass. He took his own seat behind the desk. This house was primarily a holiday retreat but when the family's sojourn there was long Maurice needed somewhere quiet in which to conduct his business. That world did not stand still because he was on holiday.

Watching his father closely, Philip tried to read his expression but could deduce nothing from it. His mind was anxious and he felt a hollowness in his stomach.

Maurice raised his glass. 'To you both, and welcome to the family, Blanche. I am pleased that my son chose such a beautiful wife and one with an astute mind also.' He raised his glass and watched her over its rim as he sipped at the wine. She met his gaze with a gracious acknowledgement of his compliment.

He set his glass to one side and leaned back in his chair. 'Well,' he said, 'I have thought about your proposal, Philip, and taken into consideration what you have already accomplished in Paris.' He paused and looked searchingly at them across the desk-top. 'I have decided that you shall open an office in Marseilles.'

The tension that had mounted in Philip and Blanche evaporated in the joy of this news. Their beaming smiles told everything. Then they were on their feet.

'Thank you, Father, you'll not regret this.' Philip shook hands firmly with his father and then turned to Blanche and received her excited congratulations. He hugged her tightly, and when she pushed him gently away turned back to Maurice who had come out from behind his desk.

'Thank you, Monsieur Jaurès,' said Blanche. 'You have made your son and me very happy, and in the happiness we share there will be success for the firm of Jaurès. And may I say how delighted I am to be able to stay in my home?'

He took her hands as she kissed him appreciatively on the cheek. 'My dear, it is an added pleasure for me to be able to ensure that. I detected your love of the place, and from Philip have learned how beautiful it is. I hope one day I shall see it.'

She held on to his hands. 'Monsieur, there is an open invitation to you and all the family. Please visit whenever you wish.'

'Thank you, my dear. Philip is a very lucky young man to have found you.' He turned to his son. 'Take good care of this very precious young lady.'

'I will,' he replied. As he escorted them to the door, Philip shook his hand. 'Thank you for your trust, Father.'

'I know you'll not let me down, Blanche will see to that.'

In the privacy of their room they let out a whoop of joy and flung themselves into each other's arms. They spent another idyllic week in Spietz then left for Marseilles. As they entered Blanche's house beyond the town she took her husband's hand. 'Welcome home, Philip.'

He saw deep sincerity in her eyes. 'Those words mean a lot to me,' he replied, a lump coming to his throat. How much the use of the word 'home' meant to him was evident in the tender kiss he gave her that sent a shiver down her spine.

'We'll be happy here,' she said huskily.

During their meal that evening Blanche brought up the subject of Paris. 'Tomorrow we'll find business premises for you in a suitable quarter of Marseilles, and then we'll have to consider your removal from Paris. What will there be to do there?'

'Well, there'll be my apartment to clear.'

'Do you have a lot there?'

'No. It was rented until I saw how the situation was developing, so I have only a few clothes and the odd personal item.'

'What about the office?'

'Nothing of note there, I kept personal and office lives separate.'

'What about the man you left in charge?'

'Father agreed he should stay and will consider employing him permanently.'

'Then there is really no necessity for you to go to Paris. Your time could be better spent here.'

'I suppose so. What are you getting at?'

'I want you to impress your father, so the sooner things are established here the better. I think I should go to Paris to see the Merciers and inform them of our marriage. After all, I was under their roof when we decided all this. I think they ought to hear about it from me. So if I am going there I could see to packing your belongings.'

'I suppose so, but wouldn't you rather I came with you?'

'Of course I would, but it will be more advantageous for you to get the operation here underway. Besides, I'm used to travelling alone and nothing could keep me away from you longer than is necessary.'

'Very well, if you think that is best.' Philip agreed. Already he had seen that this arrangement would enable him to avoid a meeting with Lucy. Breaking the news of his marriage could now safely be left to Adelina.

The following day, with her knowledge of local property owners and their premises, Blanche was able to advise and help with the negotiations for Jaurès' new office. Satisfied with the property, she took Philip to the people who would decorate and furnish the offices for him. Their next visit was to the most important bank in Marseilles which handled Blanche's own account. The manager was only too pleased to open a new one for a leading Swiss investment company, especially when he heard the amount that would be transferred to open the Marseilles account.

As they left the bank Blanche said, 'Now the basics are established, you can organise the rest to your liking. I'll introduce you to one of the best restaurants in town so you'll be well entertained while I'm away and then we'll make arrangements for my trip to Paris.'

They returned home in the middle of the afternoon, highly satisfied with what they had accomplished. Two days later Blanche left for Paris.

Having written to George to tell him that she and Lucy were planning on returning Paris on the twenty-third of August, it was no surprise to Marie when his reply informed her that he would return with them for she knew he wanted to have a word with her father. However, knowing that Lucy was disappointed that Philip would not be there when they reached Paris, she was quick to have a word alone with George when he arrived.

'Please wait to ask Father about marrying me.'

'Why?' George expressed surprise and disappointment.

'Lucy's heard from Philip that he won't be in Paris for a while. She was expecting to be able to spend more time with him before the start of term. I think it has raised some doubts in her mind about him. Seeing us so happy when Father agrees might upset her all the more.'

'*If* he agrees.'

'Oh, he will!' insisted Marie with all the certainty of someone who could use her charm effectively.

'But . . .'

'Please, George. It only means waiting until the end of term.'

'All right. For you, my love, if that is what you want.'

On the fifth afternoon after their return to Paris, Lucy and Marie were hurrying back to their apartment to get ready to meet George at the Restaurant de Fontenoy when Lucy stopped in her tracks. Marie swung round and saw amazement mixed with excitement on her friend's face. She followed her gaze and saw it focused on a door that stood ajar. It was only then that she realised they were in the street where Philip lived.

'He's back!' cried Lucy, and rushed for the apartment.

Not wanting to spoil the moment of reunion, Marie held back a few paces.

Just before Lucy reached the door, it opened wide, a woman stepped out and turned to put a key into the lock.

'Philip? Where's Philip?' Lucy's joy turned to bewilderment as the questions poured out. 'What are you doing here? Why the key? Who are you? What's happened to Philip?'

The woman stared in amazement at Lucy's reaction to what she was doing but at the same time there was curiosity in her eyes. 'And who are you?'

'Lucy Wentworth.'

The woman's expression showed that the name meant nothing to her.

Marie stepped forward. 'And I am Marie Newton, Lucy's friend.' The way she imparted that information demanded some explanation from the stranger.

'And I am Blanche Jaurès.'

'Blanche Jaurès?' Marie repeated the name.

'Yes, Philip's wife.'

Blanche saw shock register on Marie's and Lucy's faces. The colour in Lucy's cheeks disappeared.

'No!' Her wail was heart-rending. 'It's not true. It can't be!'

'It certainly is true. We were married in Marseilles during the second week of August,' replied Blanche coolly.

'Oh, no.' The truth hit Lucy hard. She began to swoon and would have fallen but for Marie.

Blanche realised there was a tale to be told by this reaction. 'I think you had better come inside,' she said. She opened the door and led the way into a room on the right. It was strewn with boxes, packed and half-packed.

Marie stared aghast. 'You're moving? Why?'

'Philip and I will be living in Marseilles. He will not be coming back to Paris.'

Marie realised that this woman knew nothing of Philip's relationship with Lucy. She glanced at her friend, who had sunk on to the only chair in the room. Her body was racked with sobs and Marie knew Lucy could not speak for herself. Philip's wife deserved an explanation.

'We have known Philip for about a year. Lucy struck up a special relationship with him and . . .'

'Who are you to steal him away from me? 'she cut in with venom

271

in her voice and hatred showing through her tears. 'He was mine! Mine!' she screamed. 'He loved ME!' She eyed Blanche with hatred and contempt in her eyes but nevertheless noted the expensive dress she was wearing. 'Look at you . . . he could only have married you for your money! He must have! You witch. You stole him from me with promises of riches.'

Blanche's mind reeled under the accusation. Riffles of horror prickled her neck. Philip and Lucy must have had an intense love affair but how far had it gone? What had he promised her? Was this girl right? Had Philip married her for her money? Her heart cried out even as doubt entered her mind. Philip had declared an undying love for her that had nothing to do with her wealth, but . . .

'You can't deny it!' screamed Lucy.

'I can and I do,' countered Blanche. 'He never hinted that he had anyone else. Never even mentioned you. Never!'

'I don't believe you!'

'Believe what you like but the plain fact is that he chose me.' The sting in the words silenced Lucy as they brought home the fact that Philip had married this woman.

'How long have you known him?' asked Marie, wanting to support her friend.

'Not long, since earlier this year. I met him at the races.'

'Races?' Marie and Lucy gasped together, and in their sharp exchange of looks each realised the other had no knowledge of Philip's interest in gambling.

'Yes,' Blanche confirmed.

'The cheat!' hissed Lucy, turning her fury on Philip. 'That explains why he made so many "business" trips. He deceived me about that and he's done the same over you. And I thought we had something special.'

'Special? How special?' asked Blanche, fearing the answer might be that this girl had been jilted. 'Did he propose marriage?'

Lucy did not answer. Blanche looked at Marie who gave a slight shrug of her shoulders to indicate she did not know.

'Did Philip ever ask you in so many words to marry him?' Blanche asked forcefully.

Lucy did not answer but Blanche knew she had heard the

272

question. She waited patiently, willing this girl to give her the answer she wanted to hear.

Slowly Lucy's eyes settled on her. For one moment she considered saying yes, but knowing that would only cause a rift between Philip and his wife, and realising she could never have him now, she found she could do nothing but tell the truth. She shook her head slowly. In hardly above a whisper she said, 'He never did.'

Relief surged through Blanche; she knew her marriage was safe, her future secure. For Lucy it was bleak. There seemed little point in continuing to live.

Chapter Nineteen

Lucy felt completely hollow. Her mind had ceased to register what was happening. It was minutes before she realised she had left Philip's apartment and was back in the street walking alongside Marie who had solicitously taken her arm.

Lucy stopped in her tracks. 'Have I been dreaming or did that really happen?'

Marie said gently, 'Yes, love. We're going home now.'

The sympathetic expression on her friend's face confirmed that Lucy had not been dreaming. 'Oh, no!' she moaned, and clung on to Marie's arm.

'I'm sorry. So sorry,' said her friend.

'Why? Why did he do it?'

'Only he knows.'

'I loved him!' Lucy's cry was filled with anguish.

'I know,' said Marie gently. 'But there's nothing we can do about it. The sooner you come to terms with what has happened the better. You still have a life to live and . . .'

'It's not worth it. I'd be better out of it.'

'You mustn't talk like that, Lucy,' said Marie sharply.

'Why not? What is there to live for?'

'Plenty if you put your mind to it. Your art for a start, our friendship, the love of your mother and my father. What do you think they would say if they heard you talking like this? Come on, let's go home.' She started walking and Lucy had to fall into step beside her. 'You can start thinking positively now – we are meeting George for a meal, remember?'

'Oh, no! I couldn't,' cried Lucy.

Marie did not reply to that. Though she tried to divert Lucy's

274

mind she realised that her friend had retreated into her own thoughts as a result of the shock she had experienced.

They had been back in their apartment for an hour during which time Lucy had merely sat in a daze, lost to what was happening around her.

'Lucy, it's time we got ready. We don't want to be late,' Marie gently reminded her.

'I don't feel like going.'

'Come on, it will take your mind off things.'

'I'm not hungry. I'd be miserable company. You go, Marie, you can't leave George on his own.'

'Nor can I leave you.'

Lucy jumped from her chair and stared defiantly at her friend. 'What's that supposed to mean? You think I'll do away with myself?'

'Well, you said . . .'

'It doesn't matter what I said, I'll be all right. I'll still be here when you get back.'

Though she was worried, Marie recognised the danger in allowing Lucy to think she could not be trusted. 'Are you sure? I'll stay if you would like me to?'

'I told you to go. I'll be all right,' she said forcefully. Lucy came to her friend and, putting her hands firmly on Marie's arms, looked her in the eye. 'I want you to go. While I have been sitting here, I have been remembering Giles's betrayal. I got over that through my art and my friendship with you, I can get over this in the same way. But not here in Paris, it will hold too many memories. Please, go to George. You can't leave him at the restaurant wondering where you are.'

'Very well, but I shan't be long.' Marie was a little mystified by this quick change in Lucy's attitude and worried that reaction might set in, but she had to give her the benefit of the doubt.

'Lucy not with you?' asked George when Marie arrived at the restaurant.

'George, I'll tell you everything in a minute but I don't want to be here long so if you could have a word and speed things up, I would be grateful.'

Seeing the concern in Marie's eyes and accepting the need for urgency, he went to have a word with the Head Waiter.

The result was that their meal was served more quickly than usual and during this time Marie acquainted him with what had happened.

As the story unfolded George's expressions of disbelief grew stronger and stronger.

'I thought those two were certain to marry.'

'So did I,' replied Marie, 'and so did Lucy.'

'But Philip had never indicated as much?'

'Apparently not. It seems he had only known his wife a short while before he was swept off his feet. I could see why – she's a beautiful woman with the aura of wealth. Maybe that's why he married her.'

'But he comes from a rich family himself, he can't be short of money.'

Marie shrugged her shoulders and looked thoughtful. 'Did he ever tell you he was interested in horse racing?'

'No.'

'Apparently he is. His wife told us that's where they met.'

'So a common interest drew them together?'

'Could be, or else he had run up a gambling debt he didn't dare reveal to his family and saw marriage to a rich woman as a way out.'

'Don't you think she would have seen through that?'

'Maybe she did. Maybe she wasn't bothered. Philip is a handsome man and she obviously fell in love with him.'

'So he used his charms to that end?' George mused. 'If that's right, Lucy's well rid of him.'

'Whatever the reason, we can do nothing about it except give her our support.'

'What is she going to do?'

'For a moment I thought the shock was going to turn her suicidal but I think that has vanished. I wanted to stay with her this evening but she insisted I should come and not leave you waiting.'

'But you fear for her?'

'Naturally it is in the back of my mind, though she sounded

more stable and reasonable as I left. The last thing she said was that she would turn to her art but she would not stay in Paris.'

'That's natural, but where does it leave you?'

'I don't know and at this stage I cannot say. She could easily change her mind again, the situation is so volatile.'

'I think it would be wise to get you back.'

She nodded. 'I'm sorry.'

Outside the apartment he gave her a goodnight kiss and said, 'We must meet tomorrow so you can tell me how Lucy is and what is happening. I'll be at Jean-Jacques' for coffee at eleven. Bring her with you. Maybe I can help.'

Marie entered the apartment quietly. She heard no sound but the lights were on in the main room. Expecting to find Lucy there, she was alarmed to find it empty but immediately chided herself for overreacting. She tiptoed quietly to Lucy's bedroom. Though it was in darkness, the curtains were drawn back and allowed sufficient light into the room for her to see that Lucy was asleep. She started to turn out of the room but stopped and moved silently to the bed. She looked down at her friend and felt a surge of relief. Lucy was breathing.

The next morning Marie was up first. After making some tea she took a cup to Lucy whom she found just waking. Her immediate enquiry was, 'Did you sleep well?'

'Yes, in a way. I had a horrible dream in which someone, I don't know who, was urging me to kill myself. I must have walked in my sleep because I woke up to find myself in the bathroom with a bottle of pills in my hand.'

'What pills?' asked Marie in alarm.

'They weren't mine. I haven't any.'

'Good grief – mine! The ones I got last term when I wasn't sleeping very well. You didn't take any?'

Lucy shook her head. 'No. The top was still on the bottle.'

'Thank goodness for that.' Marie felt relieved but at the same time alarmed that the suicidal tendency had reappeared. She would have to be extra-vigilant.

'How was George?' Lucy asked as she sipped her tea.

'He was fine but shocked to hear what Philip had done. We are going to meet him at Jean-Jacques'.'

Lucy screwed up her face. 'I don't think I want to face him, not just yet.'

'Now that's silly, Lucy. You've got to face your friends sometime and the sooner the better. Besides, George wants to help if he can. So finish your tea, get up and I'll have breakfast prepared by the time you're ready.' From the authoritative tone in Marie's voice, Lucy knew it was no use arguing.

Lucy showed no sign of wanting to talk during breakfast and Marie respected that, thinking it better to let her come to terms with meeting George in her own way. Her morose attitude had diminished somewhat by the time they reached Jean-Jacques' where he was already waiting. Realising that Lucy would still be under strain, George tempered his usually effusive greeting and ordered coffee for them.

'I don't know what to say, Lucy,' he said finally. 'The news came as a terrible shock to me and I want you to know that I'll help in any way I can.'

She gave him a wan smile. 'Thanks, but there is nothing any of us can do about Philip. He's married and is not coming back to Paris. I've got to try and forget him, drop those threads of my life and pick up others. With my art and the support of Marie, I can do that.'

'I'm sure you can,' George replied with conviction. 'I'll do what I can, too, and I'm sure your other friends will give you all the support they can.'

'Yes, if I stay in Paris.'

Alarm flickered in George's eyes. 'Surely you aren't thinking of leaving?'

'It's the only thing for me to do. There would be too many memories here.'

'But that would mean giving up your art course?'

'Yes.'

'But you've completed one year successfully. You can't throw that away.'

278

'I won't be throwing it away. I've learned a lot and can build on that elsewhere.'

'But . . .' He shot a plea for help in a glance towards Marie.

'Don't make any hasty decisions,' she advised. 'You would lose so much if you left. Monsieur Bedeaux spoke highly of your work at the end of last term. The individual tuition he will be giving from now on will be most valuable. Please, think it over seriously before you finally decide.'

'I have thought it over.' The words caught in Lucy's throat. Despondency flooded back and with it an intense hatred of Philip. Tears rose in her smouldering eyes and she could not hold them back 'Why? Why did he do it?' Her cry was heart-rending.

'I don't know,' replied Marie. 'I wish I did.'

'Help me! Please help me, Marie!' The intonation of each word was so piercing that it frightened her, raising doubts in her mind that she could pull Lucy round.

Marie placed a comforting hand on her friend's. 'I'll do anything I can.'

'Take me home!' The cry was that of a lost soul.

'I don't think that's the answer,' replied Marie.

'Nor do I,' put in George.

Defiance made Lucy unreasonable. 'Of course you can't understand,' she screamed, her eyes flashing. 'You two are all right. You've never . . .' She bit at her quivering lip. Anger started to crease the corners of her mouth and glow in her eyes. 'Why should everything be right for you two? Why should I be the one who always gets hurt? Why? Why?' She banged the table so fiercely with her fists that a coffee cup fell from it to shatter with a crash on the pavement. The noise and Lucy's screams drew the attention of others who glanced over with curiosity. A waiter, showing displeasure, rushed forward to attend to the debris.

'Calm down, Lucy, please,' requested Marie embarrassed by the attention that was being directed at them.

'Calm down? Is that all the help you can give?'

Marie was perturbed by her friend's response. Upset as she was, she had to remind herself that this was not the true Lucy speaking, the one she had come to know and love. She shot George a glance that indicated she thought she and Lucy might be better on their own so that when she said to Lucy, 'I think we had better go,' he agreed. They both rose but Lucy remained seated, looking up at them defiantly. Marie met her gaze, not wavering at all. 'Come on, Lucy, we can talk elsewhere.' She held out her hand to her friend. The gesture dissipated any defiance Lucy still felt. She gave a long sigh and, taking Marie's hand, got to her feet.

They walked slowly away from the restaurant, leaving George to apologise for the disturbance. When he caught them up, Lucy said quietly, 'I'm sorry.'

He brushed her apology aside. 'Let's find a seat.'

By the time they found one Lucy appeared calmer. Her face was drained and there were red rims round her bloodshot eyes but the tears had ceased. As they sat down George said, 'I have some personal tuition in ten minutes, I shall have to go.' He looked at Marie with concern. 'Will you be all right?

'Of course,' she replied reassuringly. 'We'll sit here and have a chat for a while.'

'I'll meet you in two hours?'

Marie nodded, and from his side long glance knew he hoped they would be alone then. They watched him stride away.

'You are very lucky to have found George,' Lucy commented with no hint of jealousy in her voice now.

Marie noted this and hoped that the rancour had been driven from her friend's mind. She wanted to avoid harping on Lucy's misfortune but the situation had to be confronted and the best solution for her found. 'What do you really want to do?'

Lucy made a determined effort to control herself. She realised there was nothing to be gained from harbouring hatred of Philip. She needed to dismiss the association as an unfortunate episode in her life. She knew it would not be easy; hers had been a deep love, not something she could forget lightly. The hurt would remain and its ugliness would torment her. She knew that on those occasions she would have to be strong, but with Marie's help was determined eventually to win.

'I'll go home,' she said.

'But, Lucy, the course. You are doing so well.'

'There are too many memories.'

'But Philip will no longer be here.'

'To me he will always be here.'

'Immerse yourself in your work. Enjoy Paris.'

Lucy shook her head. 'I don't think that's the answer.'

'You won't know until you give it a try.'

'And torture myself with memories of Philip? I would see him in all the places we shared together.' She shuddered and her expression darkened. 'I need to get away. I must! We'll go back now and I'll pack.' She pulled herself up sharply. Distress clouded her eyes. 'I will lose you too if you stay here!' A low moan escaped her lips. Her thoughts were jumbled and she found nothing but confusion when she tried to sort them out. She saw a life bereft of the friendship she cherished most, more so than ever now she had lost Philip. She needed Marie, but Marie was staying in Paris.

'Then stay with me.'

'I can't.' She shook her head wildly. 'I just can't. But I need you, Marie. You are such a good friend. Please don't sever our relationship?'

Her pleading could not be ignored but even as she said, 'I won't, Lucy, I won't,' Marie wondered how she would manage. Had she committed herself to leave Paris? What would her father think? Was she giving up her best chance to become a serious painter? What would Monsieur Bedeaux say? And how would George take it if she were to leave Paris and him?

As they walked back to the apartment Marie tried her best to make Lucy see she could benefit from staying in Paris, but no matter what argument she presented for doing so, Lucy was adamant that the best thing for her was to leave. That was the position when they reached the apartment but Marie held on to a glimmer of hope, even though she hadn't mentioned it to Lucy, that their parents might get her to see things in perspective.

As she went to meet George, Marie determined to come clean with him. 'Lucy is packing,' she said as soon as they met.

'So she is determined to leave Paris?'

'Yes. And I'm going with her.'

281

'What?' George exploded before she could offer any further explanation. 'You can't.'

'I have to.'

'You have not,' he countered.

'I can't let her go on her own. She is distraught. Says she would be devastated if I severed our friendship now.'

'But it is she who is severing it, not you,' protested George angrily.

'That isn't how she sees it. I daren't risk what she might do if she believes I am deserting her. I've got to see her to England.'

'But if she says she'll never return, what then?'

'I'm not dwelling on that possibility. I'm hoping that our parents will persuade her and then I'll return with her. Why not come to England with us? There'll just be time before the start of term.'

'I've arranged private tuition until the start of term and it's important to me. If I come to England I'll have to forego it.' Her expression of disappointment tugged at him but he said, 'Marie, our whole future together is at stake. Can you jeopardise that for a friend who is acting unreasonably? Can't she see she's better off without Philip?

'She loved him. Can't you understand what this has done to her?'

'She'll have to get a grip on herself sometime, and the sooner the better. She shouldn't wreck your life.'

Marie could see that it was no use carrying on a conversation in this vein so put the question to him starkly. 'You won't come with us then?'

'No. Why should I give up my special tuition?' replied George with a frankness that hurt her though she kept that well hidden.

When she reached the apartment Marie saw two suitcases on Lucy's bed. They were half-full. 'I would have finished by now,' she explained, 'but I went out and got our train tickets for tomorrow morning.'

Taken by surprise and still smarting from George's attitude, Marie said haughtily, 'You were sure I would come then?'

'I knew you wouldn't desert me,' replied Lucy.

Her flat tone disturbed Marie. She wondered if Lucy was adopting this attitude because she had lost Philip and wanted her friend to lose George. Maybe she had already got her way but Marie wouldn't give her the satisfaction of knowing it, so she said nothing. She realised the situation would have to be handled delicately if she was to return to Paris. She hoped she would have allies in her father and stepmother and that their added voices would persuade Lucy to act sensibly. With a sigh, she went to her bedroom and started to pack.

With her bags beside the door, Marie stood in the middle of the apartment, regret in her heart, hoping and praying that she would be returning.

'What are we doing about this place?' Lucy asked as she came from the bedroom.

'We have no time to deal with it now,' replied Marie coolly. 'I will have to come back and see to it, or write to George and ask him to inform Madame Foucarde.'

Lucy merely nodded and headed for the door.

They spoke little on the way to the station. Marie's resentment was palpable as she watched Parisian life pass them by. She was going to miss this, but more than anything she was going to miss George and couldn't help fearing that this might be the end of their love affair. She glanced at Lucy and saw that she was not looking out of the window – it seemed she did not want to see anything that would remind her of Philip. She stared straight ahead, eyes unseeing. It was the absence of life in them and the apathy in Lucy's entire attitude that troubled Marie most. One wrong word, one wrong gesture, might send her friend over the edge of reason. Though she had realised the devastating effect Philip's betrayal had had on Lucy, Marie had thought she had eased that by agreeing to leave Paris with her. She now realised that the battle was far from won and that it would take very little to unhinge her friend entirely. She was thankful then that she had decided to accompany Lucy to England.

In the hustle and bustle of the station she kept close to her, found them seats facing each other beside the window, and got her settled. Marie sank back in her seat and tried to let the tension drain from her, but found it impossible. Thoughts of what she herself might be giving up crept back. Was she doing the right thing? She clenched her fist and pressed it hard against her mouth in an attempt to stem the tears that threatened.

Their train journey was uneventful and the sea crossing to Dover invigorating. Lucy seemed brighter and it made Marie hope that she would be more receptive to a return to Paris.

When the coach that Marie had quickly hired in Dover pulled up at the Newtons' house, the front door opened and an astonished Isobel and Arthur stepped outside.

'This is a surprise,' called Isobel as she and Arthur came down the path to meet them. The smiles on their faces vanished when Lucy rushed at them, visibly distraught, tears streaming down her face.

'Mama! Mama!' Her cries were rent by an anguish that Isobel associated only with a broken heart.

She took her daughter into her arms in a gesture that held all the comfort a mother could give. 'What is it, love?'

'Philip!' Lucy spat the one word out but could not bring herself to explain.

Arthur greeted Marie and asked, 'What's happened?'

'Philip got married while we were away.'

'What?'

'Oh, no!' exclaimed Isobel, and led her daughter into the house, her arm protectively around Lucy's shaking shoulders.

With home comforts around her once more Lucy calmed down. Over a soothing up of tea, Marie related events in Paris. She knew it was a trial for Lucy to hear them but she was pleased that her friend showed no adverse reaction.

Isobel insisted that Lucy retire to bed early and take a sedative. She stayed by her until her daughter was asleep and then returned to join the others. As soon as she sat down she expressed her concern. 'Lucy tells me that she is not going back to Paris. That's understandable, but I'm not sure it's the right thing to do.'

'I tried to persuade her to stay,' Marie explained, 'but she was

284

adamant that she wanted to come home. She said she wanted me with her and I couldn't let her come alone. I am hoping you can persuade her to return to Paris, though.'

'All we can do is try,' said Isobel.

'You'll have to get back or you'll be taken off the course,' said a worried Arthur. 'That would be a great pity. Marie, you and Lucy both received excellent reports. You are at an important stage of your development. We have to try to make Lucy see this and understand what she would be giving up if she doesn't go back.'

'We'll try our utmost tomorrow,' soothed Isobel. 'For now my poor girl needs rest and our understanding.'

When she came down the next morning Lucy announced that she had slept well, and everyone drew hope from the fact that her attitude was more lively. Nevertheless the topic of the future would have to be brought up after breakfast.

Isobel was the first to break the idle conversation. 'Lucy, we must discuss what you intend to do.'

'Do, Mother?' she said, just a shade too casually. 'I'm here.'

'I know, dear, but when are you going back to Paris?' Isobel thought it best to put the query directly to her.

'I'm not.'

'But your course?'

'I'm giving that up.'

'But you were doing so well!'

'I don't care. I couldn't bear to go to Paris ever again – too many memories.'

'That may be, but you could be jeopardising your artistic future,' insisted Arthur. 'Monsieur Bedeaux sees real promise in you. That would all be lost. Someone else may not see your talent as he does.'

'And don't forget, Arthur used his influence to get you accepted by Monsieur Bedeaux in the first place,' Isobel pointed out.

'I am not going back!' A determined note had come into Lucy's voice

'You'll be alone here,' countered her mother. 'Marie will have to return otherwise she will be dismissed from the course too.'

285

Lucy drew herself up. 'Marie promised me she would be with me.' She looked hard at her friend, defying her to deny it.

Marie looked embarrassed. 'What I meant by that was that I would not let you travel home alone.'

'You didn't!'

'Lucy, you can't expect Marie to give up now,' Isobel admonished.

A wild expression came into Lucy's eyes. 'Why not?'

'But I can't . . .' Marie started.

Lucy gave a grunt of derision. 'Oh, I know, it's George. You want to get back with him just to show me that *you* can hold on to a man!' Her voice had risen as she flung the accusation at her friend.

'It's not like that, Lucy,' cried Marie.

'It is!'

'No, it's not!'

'You're no friend if you go back and desert me.'

Marie felt guilt and despondency weighing her down.

'Don't talk like that, Lucy!' snapped her mother.

'Well, she won't be. She said she would be with me!' Lucy jumped to her feet and fled the room, banging the door behind her.

'I'd better go to her,' said Isobel, showing concern. As she crossed the room she called over her shoulder. 'We'll talk again when I've got her calmed down.'

As the door closed, Marie turned to her father and with anguish in her voice asked, 'What are we going to do?'

He gave a slight shake of his head. 'It's difficult. Make the wrong decision and Lucy's mind could be affected.'

'And if that happens, I could be the cause?'

'Philip's to blame, not you.'

'True, but I would have contributed to it. And that could damage your marriage, Father, by causing a rift between you and Isobel. I can't let that happen.'

'Does that mean you intend staying? You can't jeopardise your career,' he said hastily. 'We've got to persuade Lucy to return with you.'

286

Just as he was saying that the door opened and Isobel caught his words. 'I don't think you'll do that. Lucy is adamant, even threatening what she might do if she is forced to go back.'

'No one's talking of forcing,' said Arthur irritably.

'She'll see it like that,' replied Isobel coolly.

Marie was torn. She could already see what might happen between these two kindly people. 'I think we have to find something that will divert Lucy's mind utterly and completely from what she has experienced at Philip's hands. There has to be something . . .'

The minutes ticked away and no one seemed capable of finding the solution. Ten minutes later Arthur rose from his chair and excused himself. When he returned he held up a sheet of paper. 'This might be the answer to our problems, but it will mean sacrifices by the young ones.'

They stared at him with curiosity for his words and serious tone indicated that what he was about to divulge was something momentous.

Chapter Twenty

'Lucy needs to be diverted, and I think this piece of paper may do the trick. I think Isobel will recognise it and have an inkling of what is in my mind.

'Marie, this is a letter from your Uncle Oswald in America. He sent it to congratulate us on our wedding and offer his regrets that he couldn't be here. He also mentioned the visits of artists to Western America, especially with the expansion of the railways. They have thrown open many more opportunities to depict the American landscape, especially that of the West, and men of industry there are wanting portraits of themselves and their families. Oswald's trying to encourage me to go out there to paint. I wasn't keen initially, but Isobel suggested we might take a holiday. Now I wonder if it could help Lucy.'

'You mean, take her there on a trip?' asked Marie.

'Well, Lucy has indicated that she does not want to be separated from you . . . As I see it, your staying together could be vital to her welfare, which is what we are really discussing here.'

'But what about my studies in Paris? I was hoping you could persuade Lucy to change her mind about going back.'

'From what I know of my daughter, how she has taken Philip's betrayal and is obstinately saying she won't ever set foot in Paris again, trying to persuade her will be hopeless,' put in Isobel.

'So where does that leave me?' The despondent note in Marie's voice worried Arthur. He realised his daughter was faced with a terrible choice: sacrifice Paris or leave Lucy without the prop she seemed to need with the dire consequences that might entail.

'I am all for you finishing your course, but not at the expense of Lucy's health.'

Isobel appreciated his consideration.

'How would it be if you came with us, Marie?'

The suggestion brought a momentary silence. Even Isobel was taken aback by this unexpected proposition but she quickly saw that it could be the answer, not only to Lucy's problem but to getting Arthur painting again. 'Why not?' she said to lend support to the idea.

'But there's George . . . we didn't part on the best of terms and I don't want to lose him,' said Marie, biting her lip.

'Why not invite him to come as well? All expenses paid,' said Isobel. 'I wouldn't want my daughter to be the cause of separating you two, and it would relieve you, Marie, of the necessity of making a choice which I know would be extremely hard for you.'

'George seems set on completing his course,' she replied. 'All I can do is ask him.'

'If he wants tuition, tell him I will don my teacher's hat and oblige,' offered her father. 'You and Lucy are welcome to it as well.'

'Splendid!' cried Isobel, for that would certainly mean Arthur taking up his paintbrush again.

'You'll do that while we're travelling?' Marie queried.

'Why not? It will add another perspective to the journey which may prove valuable to us all. Now, the first step is to get Lucy's reaction. If she takes to the idea then you must return to Paris and see what George says. What you do after he has heard your proposition, I leave to you.'

'Very well.' Marie had little doubt what Lucy's response would be; any reason not to return to Paris would be more than acceptable to her.

When Isobel and Arthur raised the prospect of the American trip her immediate response was, 'Is Marie coming?'

'More than likely,' Arthur reassured her. 'Maybe George too. I will take up your tuition. I can't pretend I will be as good as Monsieur Bedeaux but you will still be learning.'

'I'm sure it will be as good, if not better,' replied Lucy in a voice that was tinged with excitement. Marie saw how her anxiety had dropped away and knew that she expected her friend to come to America. Marie dreaded to think what effect it would have on her if she returned from Paris to say she was not going. That would all depend on George's reaction to her father's offer and how determined he was to complete his course in Paris.

With the matter settled for the moment Arthur said, 'We must not waste time. Marie. You should return to Paris as quickly as possible. I'll go into Dover immediately and arrange for your journey tomorrow.'

Marie's anxiety about George's attitude heightened the nearer she drew to Paris. When she hired a cab at the station she instructed the cabbie to go via George's atelier. Telling the cabbie to wait, she hurried inside only to find George was not there. She scribbled a note to him and left it, hoping he would be in later that day. Then she went to her apartment, still not sure of what she was going to do. Should she start packing or should she wait until she had seen George?

Half an hour of soul-searching got her nowhere and she was becoming more and more irritated. What if George had left Paris for a few days? What if he had had an accident and was lying incapacitated in hospital? What if she had so upset him that he had turned to someone else?

Her agitated mood was interrupted by a knock on the door. She knew it couldn't be George; the strict rules for tenants of the apartments forbade that. Nevertheless she rushed to the door.

Madame Foucarde confronted her with the news that a young man awaited her.

George! It must be George! She grabbed her bonnet and rushed out.

'Marie! You are back!'

She was gratified by his evident pleasure at seeing her though she detected a touch of wariness too, as if he feared she might disappear again. 'I've a lot to tell you and we've a lot to talk about. Let's go to Jean-Jacques'.' She grabbed his hand and set off.

'What's this all about?' he asked.

'I'll tell you over coffee.'

'Is Lucy with you?'

'No.'

'You got her home without any bother?'

'Yes.'

'How is she?'

'She seems to be her normal self but is still easily upset.'

'Is she coming back?'

'She is adamant that she will not return to Paris.'

'Your parents couldn't persuade her?'

'No.'

'But you are back for good?'

They had reached Jean-Jacques'. 'Order the coffee and I'll tell you all.'

George listened but made no comment or query as Marie informed him of her father's proposals. Her heart was sinking by the time she reached the end of her story for she thought she detected a refusal in his subdued expression.

When he did not speak she said with a touch of irritation in her voice, 'What do you think?'

George replied with a question. 'Are you going?'

'I'm asking you!'

'My extra tuition is going well. My next term's course is all planned out. I can't throw that up.'

'My father said he'll tutor us.'

'As much as I admire your father's work, his tuition would be along different lines and might be wrongly directed for me. Here my course is set. So is yours. I think it would be silly for you to give it up. I'm surprised your father doesn't see it that way too.'

'He was anxious for me to return, but when Lucy was adamant she would never come back to Paris he thought this compromise would suit everyone and hoped you would be agreeable to it.'

'I think it would be a backward step for me.'

'Don't be so intransigent,' snapped Marie. 'Can't you see the opportunities? A new land, new horizons, new subjects to paint, landscapes and portraits that my uncle says will readily sell. You've got the basics, you can develop them in your own way.'

'My path is set. I would be a fool to give it up.'

'And what about us?' Marie's eyes were beginning to dampen.

'Stay with me.'

Her lips tightened. This was the dilemma she had feared.

'I love you, Marie. I want you to stay.'

'Please don't put me in this position,' she pleaded.

'It's of your own making.'

'It's not,' she snapped.

'This would never have arisen if you had been firm with Lucy from the start. It was stupid to let her think that you would stay with her, no matter what.'

'She was a friend in trouble, and remember, she's now my stepsister.'

'But you can't tie yourself down like that!'

'I couldn't desert her now.'

'But you are willing to desert me?'

'Come with me.'

'No. If we've got to be true to our beliefs, then so be it.'

'Don't walk away from me, George. Please don't force me to make a choice.'

'It's up to you.' He stood up, looking down at her with angry determination.

She was distraught. He had put up a barrier between them and she couldn't surmount it. To do so might waken all the devils in Lucy's mind, bringing upheaval to a marriage in which two people she loved dearly had staked their whole future.

'I can't stay,' she said, scarcely above a whisper.

The anger in George's face darkened. He swung round and the depth of his disappointment was evident in every step that took him further away from her.

Marie buried her face in her hands and wept.

How long she stayed like that she did not know. When she looked up she saw several people giving her concerned glances. She quickly wiped her eyes, stood up and shuffled between the tables, almost stumbling in her eagerness to get away and be alone. Once clear of the restaurant her footsteps became slow and heavy. Tears flowed again in spite of her efforts to hold them back. By the time she reached the apartment block she had wiped her eyes and composed herself. She slipped across the enclosed yard without Madame Foucarde seeing her.

In her apartment she closed the door behind her and leaned back against it with a heartfelt sigh. The hurt of George's desertion would remain with her for a long time.

She pushed herself from the door with renewed determination to get on and be away from Paris as soon as possible. She packed her things quickly, leaving only sufficient for her one-night stay. She wrote a letter to Monsieur Bedeaux expressing her regrets at her decision to leave but saying that personal matters gave her no other choice. She thanked him for his help during the year that would always mean so much to her. She left another letter for the girls at Charlotte's lodgings. After buying her ticket at the station and ascertaining the time of the train, she called on Madame Foucarde to tell her that she was leaving tomorrow and would not be returning.

The following morning Madame appeared to bid her a tearful goodbye and Marie had to steel herself not to break down. She reached the station with twenty minutes to spare, settled herself in her seat and took out a book to read to drive away the thought that she was leaving Paris and George.

She had been reading for ten minutes when she heard a knock at the window. She looked up, wondering who was causing the disturbance. Her eyes widened in surprise and her heart started to thump. George! Immediately he was gone. She reached out as if to stop him, wanting to know why he was here. Then there he was, in the carriage with her. He grabbed her two cases. 'Come on,' he said, and was swiftly on his way out of the carriage. Marie could do nothing but follow. Once on the platform she protested, 'I'm not staying, George.'

He dumped her cases and swung round to face her. 'I know you're not – I'm coming with you. I have to ask your father something, but I can't leave until tomorrow.'

There were tears in Marie's eyes again, but this time they were of joy. She flung her arms round his neck and kissed him. 'Oh, George, that's wonderful!'

He held her tightly by the waist. 'I couldn't lose you.'

'How did you know I would be on this train?'

'I guessed you would be leaving as soon as possible. I knew you would have to tell Madame Foucarde so I went to see her and she told me you had already left for this train. The only thing to do was stop you, so here I am. We'll change your ticket for a train tomorrow.'

'But I've nowhere to stay tonight.'

'We'll get a room at a hotel.'

The implication behind that statement only struck her as they left the station, but Marie made no protest.

The love they made for the first time that night was tender and passionate and set a seal on their future.

Arthur was pleased to see them, and expressed sincere gratitude to George for escorting Marie home.

'I was pleased to,' he replied. 'Besides, sir, there is something I want to ask you.'

'Ask away,' said Arthur as he led the way into the drawing room.

George took his time closing the door behind them, trying to give himself a few moments to pluck up his courage. 'Er . . . I . . .' He dampened his lips during the pause. 'I want to . . . er . . . I would like to marry Marie, sir.' The words finally came out in a rush.

Arthur thought of teasing George by playing on his nerves but decided that would be cruel. 'Your request does not surprise me. I have no need to ask what your prospects are. I know where your ambitions lie, and with diligent work and application I am sure you'll realise them. Of course you may marry my daughter.'

For one moment there was a bewildered expression on George's face.

Arthur laughed. 'Did you expect it to be harder than that?'

'Well, I . . .' George's words faded away as Marie rushed to her father and flung her arms round his neck.

'Oh, Papa, thank you, thank you!' Tears of joy came to her eyes as she kissed him.

'Thank you, sir.' George held out his hand.

'Mind you look after her, young man.'

'I will, sir.'

Marie threw herself out of her father's arms to embrace George. 'I love you,' she whispered.

'When are you thinking of sailing to America, sir?' he asked.

Before Arthur could answer, the door opened and Isobel and Lucy came in.

'You are back! And George too!' cried Lucy. She rushed to her stepsister and hugged her then turned briskly to George, her face clouded with suspicion and defiance. 'You're not taking her back to Paris, away from me?'

'Lucy, that is not going to happen,' said Marie gently. 'George is going to come to America with us.'

Lucy immediately lost all hostility. 'Thank goodness,' she said with a great sigh.

'That is, if it is all right with you, Mr and Mrs Newton?'

'That was the offer we made,' said Isobel. 'I am pleased to hear you accept.'

'We have one more thing to tell you,' said Marie. 'George has asked me to marry him, I have accepted and Father has approved!'

For a second their silence conveyed surprise then Lucy let out a cry of 'Wonderful' that opened the flood gates to a round of congratulations, kisses and more hugs.

'When?' she asked.

Marie laughed. 'We haven't had time to decide. Besides we have this American trip to think about.'

'George was just asking me when we intended to go,' explained Arthur. 'I think we should aim for two weeks tomorrow, if that suits everyone? But you, George, will want to see your parents.'

'Two weeks will suit me,' he replied. 'I'll leave for Norfolk tomorrow, and be back in plenty of time. I'll have two pieces of momentous news to tell them. May I take Marie with me?'

'You must. She should meet them before we leave for America.'

The wind blew hard across the north Norfolk flats sending grey clouds from the north, portents of rain, scudding across the sky. Marie shuddered in the sharp air as she dismounted from the coach in front of an imposing house that looked as if it could withstand any such buffeting. She hoped that it did not herald a dark reception.

Ushered into the hall by George, she found herself facing a slim woman whom she feared might use her elevated position, as she came down the curving staircase, to impose an imperious atmosphere on the situation. Mixed with her surprise at seeing her younger son, Mrs Reeves's eyes were sharply assessing the girl who stood beside him.

'George, what on earth are you doing here? I thought you were in Paris.' With this observation came a heightening of the suspicion directed at Marie.

'It's a long story,' he said as he came forward and embraced his mother when she reached the bottom of the stairs, 'but first I want you to meet Marie Newton.'

Nervously, Marie came forward too. 'Mrs Reeves, I am pleased to meet you.' She hesitated and then held out her hand.

Mrs Reeves's gaze was penetrating but she took the hand. 'Marie,' was all she said.

'Where's Father?' George asked.

'In his study scrutinising the estate accounts.'

'I'll bring him to the drawing room.'

His mother nodded and while George went off to summon his father, she led Marie to the drawing room.

'Are you one of the two young women George told us he had met in Paris and whom he accompanies on the crossing?'

'Yes, ma'am,' replied Marie. 'My father is extremely grateful to him. It eases his mind that we have such an escort.'

'I'm delighted that my son is of some help.' Mrs Reeves's voice had softened into a more friendly delivery. 'But what are you doing here now?'

'I think George wants to explain that himself,' replied Marie. She was thankful that at that moment he appeared so she could avoid any more embarrassing questions.

His father, a stocky red-faced man, blustered in behind him. 'A young woman, George tells me. Where is she? Ah, it's you.' He eyed her up and down then glanced towards his wife. 'What's this all about, Ellen?'

'I don't know, Horace.'

He swung round on George. 'Well?'

'First of all, Father,' replied George, 'I want you to meet Marie Newton.'

Horace grunted and nodded.

'I'm pleased to meet you, Mr Reeves,' said Marie, and held out her hand. When he took it she felt the hard palm and broad fingers of a man who was not afraid to do physical work alongside his farm workers.

He grunted a greeting – an attempt to appear casual, Marie thought, but she knew his brown eyes were busily making judgements. He looked at his son. 'Well, why aren't you in Paris?'

'I've left, Father.'

'Left? What do you mean?'

'What I say,' replied George firmly. 'I've resigned my position on the course.'

'What?' His father exploded again.

'Oh, George.' His mother's admonishment was more gentle. 'Why?'

'When, as my son, you showed no interest in the estate I agreed to your pursuing something you wanted to do. I did not expect you to be faint-hearted about it. You wanted to study art so why this decision?' his father demanded.

'Just sit down and hear me through, please.'

His parents sat down on the sofa and George and Marie sat in chairs opposite them. George leaned forward, feeling more comfortable delivering his story that way.

At certain points Horace mumbled as if he was about to say something but recognised the signals his wife gave him, a gentle tightening of her fingers on his arm, an advice to say nothing yet.

'So it was a choice,' concluded George, 'stay in Paris and most likely lose Marie or accept the offer to accompany her to America and still receive tuition from her father. I chose the latter course. I hope you will understand.'

'America? Too far away. Wild country,' Horace blustered.

'You know nothing about it, Father.'

'I don't think you do either or you wouldn't be going. What possibilities are there for art there? Very little, I expect.'

'There must be or Marie's uncle wouldn't have suggested our going.'

Ellen, who had sat very still throughout this exchange, said quietly but in a tone that demanded to be listened to, 'You must think very highly of this young lady to give up Paris for America.'

The statement brought a moment of tense silence to the room that was broken by George's charged reply. 'I do. So much so that I have asked her to marry me. Marie has said yes and her father approves. I hope you both do too?'

His parents were stunned. The unexpected announcement found them lost for words for a moment or two.

'Any more surprises?' was all that Horace could say, his usual blustering delivery gone.

Ellen's eyes grew wet. She rose from the sofa and held out her arms to George. He got quickly to his feet and came to her. As she held him tight she said quietly, 'Be happy.' She eased him to one side but still held him with one arm while she held out the other to Marie whose heart had been racing from the moment she had realised George was going to tell his parents. She came and found the warmth of acceptance in Ellen's embrace.

'Horace,' Ellen said over her shoulder, 'come and give your future daughter-in-law a kiss and then break out a bottle. There's something to celebrate.'

Marie knew there would be no more objections from George's father.

Horace grasped her by the shoulders. 'Welcome to the family, Marie. No time to get married before you leave for America, I suppose?'

'No,' she replied, and accepted his kiss.

'Then we'll have to wait for your return,' he said, and went off to get the wine.

Ellen took them both by the hand and looked at them with love. 'You've given us two momentous surprises but all I can say is, make each other happy.' She gave then both a kiss. 'How long are you staying now?' she asked. 'I want to get to know Marie better.'

'Is five days all right?'

'As far as I'm concerned,' replied his mother.

He looked quizzically at Marie who nodded.

By the time she returned to Deal she was glad they had stayed that long for she'd learned much more about George and his background in Norfolk, and knew she had won the approval of his parents.

When they reached Deal they were immediately swept up in preparations for America. Lucy excitedly announced that they were booked to sail on the steam ship *North Star*, leaving from Liverpool in seven days' time. Arthur had been to London to see the agent for the shipping line and had returned to announce the sailing date and inform them they were travelling as saloon passengers so would have their privacy and be away from the noise and motion experienced in the after-part of the ship. The agent had also booked them rooms at a Liverpool hotel and assured them a company representative would meet them on their arrival there and another would meet them in New York to ease their way through arrival formalities, escort them to an hotel where rooms would be booked, and advise them on their onward visit.

The succeeding days were busy with many decisions about what to take, cases to pack and unpack and repack to satisfy changes of mind, new purchases to be made, items cast aside. Life was a whirl of excitement which heightened as the day for departure drew nearer, but there were also moments of apprehension, spoken and unspoken. Yet once they were in the train for London where they would stay overnight, the spirit of adventure took over as they anticipated the wide new world awaiting them.

When they reached Liverpool the next day Arthur was relieved to find that the shipping company was as good as their word. A pleasant young man met them on the platform. Why he should have had any doubts about the arrangement Arthur didn't know, after all it was only good business sense to offer such services and carry them out efficiently. Which was exactly what the representative did. Three porters were immediately summoned to see to their luggage and he kept up an easy flow of conversation as he escorted them from the station to a cab that he had already hired. Within fifteen minutes he was booking them into a first-class hotel and assuring them that he would see them again at ten o'clock the following morning.

The representative walked into the hotel just as the clocks were chiming that hour the next day. Two hours later he was bidding them a safe journey and a pleasant crossing, having seen them aboard *North Star*.

'Mother, I have finished the second painting that was commissioned as a result of my exhibition,' announced Edward as he came into the drawing room.

'Are you happy with it?' she asked.

'Yes.'

'May I see it?'

'Of course! You know I value your opinion.'

They went to his studio. The seascape was still on the easel, his brushes and paints just as he had left them five minutes ago.

Colette stood to consider the painting. She took a pace back, nodding as if to say it was a better viewpoint. Edward stood beside her, looking critically at his own work.

She moved to the painting and pointed to the crest of a wave. 'A little more highlight there,' she said, and returned to her former position.

Edward picked up a brush and made the slight alteration suggested by his mother. He moved back beside her, assessed what he had done and glanced at her. 'Well?'

'It has made a big difference. Even though it was a small adjustment it has put more life into that wave and emphasised its all-embracing, destructive power.' She turned her eyes from the painting to look at him. 'Don't you think so?'

'Yes, I do,' he said emphatically. 'You are a genius, Mother.'

She gave a little laugh of pleasure at this but shook her head, 'No, it was just that you have been so near to the picture throughout its creation that a small point like that was easily overlooked. I sometimes saw the same in your father's work.'

A moment's silence at this mention of Arthur came over them.

300

'Mother, I am thinking that next week I will personally deliver the two paintings that are ready.'

She gave a knowing little smile. 'A good excuse to see Hester again,' she teased.

He returned her smile. 'Why not?'

'Exactly, why not? She's a nice girl. You could do a lot worse.'

'Mother! It hasn't got to that stage, but I would like to show her my appreciation of what she did during the exhibition.'

'Quite right.'

'While I am down in London I might take a holiday. The other commissions are not wanted until December as they are to be Christmas gifts'

'Again, why not? You worked hard for that exhibition, and afterwards. You deserve to have a break from painting and to relax for a while. You'll come back to your work refreshed. No doubt you'll be writing to Hester?'

'I have already done so,' Edward replied a little sheepishly.

'Good.'

'And I've had an answer this morning,' he added. 'Hester's parents have invited me to stay with them.'

'Ah,' she said knowingly. 'I met them at the exhibition, nice people who seemed to take to you.'

Edward ignored that and said instead, 'Hester asks if you have thought any more about your photographic exhibition?'

Colette tightened her lips in momentary exasperation. 'What with Hester and Matthew keeping on about this, I suppose I had better give way.'

'Good.' Edward did not disguise his own enthusiasm. 'I'm pleased and I know Hester will be. Matthew has never disguised the fact that he thinks highly of your photographs and their interpretation of Whitby life and landscape. It will get you taking more pictures and be good for you to work towards something like this during the winter. You can get Aunt Adele and Susan involved again. I'm sure they would be delighted. They still talk a lot about the photography you used to do together. I don't suppose the exhibition will take place until the spring or early summer of next year.'

'All right, don't go overboard. Just tell Hester I'll do it.'

Edward went immediately to write to her and tell her the day and time he would be arriving in London. He ended the letter by saying how much he was looking forward to seeing her again.

Edward allowed the other passengers spilling from the train to precede him until they'd thinned out and there was less likelihood of his well-wrapped paintings being damaged in the crush. He would not allow them to be handled by a porter but relinquished his two bags instead.

His face creased into a beaming smile when he saw Hester craning to catch a first sight of him. Their eyes met and hers shone with pleasure.

'Hello, Edward,' she said pleasantly, and because his hands weren't free slid her arms around his neck and kissed him. 'Welcome to London. It's so good to see you.'

'And you.'

'I have a cab waiting.' She turned to the porter and told him where it was.

Once they were settled in the cab she said, 'I'm so glad you are staying a few days. Mother and Father said I was to tell you that you can make it as long as you like.'

'That is extremely kind of them.'

'I suggest we go straight home and that we deliver these paintings tomorrow. Unless, of course, you would rather we delivered them on our way now?'

'No, tomorrow will suit me.'

'Good. How is your mother?'

'She is well. By the way, she has agreed to have an exhibition in London.'

'Marvellous.' Hester's eyes brightened with enthusiasm. 'I look forward to organising it. My uncle will be pleased.'

Edward was given a warm welcome by Hester's parents and quickly settled in. When he stepped out of his room he heard a door open a little further along the corridor. He glanced in that direction and saw Hester beckoning him. He looked askance as he went to her.

'I was listening for you. Come, see.' She opened the door wider and allowed him to step inside but did not close the door. 'I wanted you to see it.' She indicated an alcove. Edward saw the painting he had given her at the exhibition. 'Perfect setting, isn't it?'

'Perfect.'

'You must have known just where it was going to hang.'

'Seems like it.' He smiled.

She kissed him on the cheek. 'Thank you so much for your gift. It reminds me of you every night before I go to sleep.'

He swept her into his arms and kissed her then and she responded with equal ardour. 'I have no need of a painting because the lovely vision of you is always with me.'

'Oh, Edward. It is so good to have you here.'

'I think we had better go down.'

Hester gave a reluctant smile. 'I suppose so.'

When they reached his door Edward stopped. 'Wait a moment, I have something for you and for your parents.' He went inside to reappear a few moments later with two packages of the same size.

'What are they?' asked Hester, a touch of excitement in her voice.

'Wait and see,' he teased.

'Oh, Edward!'

He laughed and hurried down the stairs.

When they entered the drawing room he presented Hester with her package and handed the other to her mother.

'There was no need for this,' said Mr Stevens while his wife made her thanks and started to open the wrappings.

'It is just something to thank you for your hospitality.'

Hester had her package undone. 'Oh, Edward, it's delightful.' She stared at the small portrait a moment longer and then held it so that her parents could see it.

'Hester, it's you!' Her father's words were laced with surprise and her mother just stared in wonder at the picture of their daughter, sitting in a window seat looking out at a garden beyond.

'What a wonderful way to deliver a portrait of someone,' commented Hester. 'What is your painting, Mama?'

She held it for her daughter to see.

'Ah, Whitby by moonlight. Edward's favourite time.'

After they'd delivered the paintings the following day, Hester suggested that, as it was a pleasantly warm morning, they should take a walk in Hyde Park.

They were strolling at their leisure among the promenaders in the park when she brought up the subject of the two gifts he had made her family.

'When did you do them?'

'The canvas of Whitby ten months to a year ago. Your portrait very recently.'

'The influence of Arthur Newton is strong in the Whitby scene but I also see it has crept into your painting again in the study of me.'

'Is that a bad thing?'

'Not necessarily, but as I said before, I strongly advise you to find your own way, be you, Edward Clayton.'

'That may not be so easy.' For a brief moment he wished he could take the words back when he saw the curiosity in Hester's expression.

'Why?'

He hesitated a few moments before answering, 'It's a long story. Let's find a seat.'

No other word was spoken until they sat down. Edward took Hester's hand then and his expression was serious. 'What I tell you must never go any further. It involves a secret that spans more than my lifetime, and I promised my mother I would never breathe a word about if I thought that any ill would result from it. She believes that what I am about to tell you could hurt certain people deeply and does not want that. But I think you should hear it because of the number of times you have seen the influence of Arthur Newton in my painting. It is true that I have made a serious study of his work, but there is more to it than that.' He gave a little pause. 'The influence is inherited!'

'What?' Hester gaped at him. 'But you are Edward Clayton.'

'That's my name but . . .'

He poured the whole story out and Hester listened without questioning him. When he had finished he added, 'Obviously I experienced a strong desire to find him, especially after the brief encounter I had with him. It helped me realise from whom I had inherited my artistic ability.'

'I think you should give your mother some credit for that. Her ability to judge a picture has been passed on to you and enhanced by what you've inherited from your natural father.' Hester still found herself struggling to take in what she had been told.

'I have an intense desire to find him,' Edward went on. 'I feel I need to.'

'Have you tried?'

'Yes.' He went on to acquaint her with the enquiries he had made. 'They led me to the fact that he was at one time living on the south coast, a fact borne out by Mr Sotheran who told me, not knowing of my relationship, that some time ago he had tried to find Arthur Newton himself. It seemed my father continually moved house and had given up painting. Mr Sotheran, who has other more pressing affairs, has given up his quest.'

'Do I take it that you still want to find your father?'

'Yes.'

'What does your mother think about that?'

'She is wary because of his marriage and the fact that he has a daughter.'

'She is frightened of the wounds that might be opened, no doubt.'

'Yes, but I promised her that my enquiries would be discreet and that if I ever found they were leading to upheaval and hurt, I would cease to pursue the matter.'

'If you promised that, why go further now?'

'My intense desire to get to know him.'

'I can understand that, but why take the risk of hurting other people? You are happy, you have your work, you are on the verge of becoming a sought artist. Why threaten that?'

'Because of this, Hester.' He tapped his heart.

'But you might break other people's hearts. What about his wife? What about his daughter? You must consider them.'

'I do and will. I would drop everything if I saw that happening.'

'But how can you tell that unless you get close to them?'

'I don't know. I will just have to see how and which way my enquiries are going.'

'I think you are taking the risk of upsetting, maybe even destroying, many lives.'

'It won't come to that.'

'You can't be sure.'

He shrugged his shoulders.

Hester had seen the steely determination in Edward's eyes all the time he had been speaking. She realised that nothing would put him off. 'So you think your father is still somewhere on the south coast?' He nodded. 'When are you taking up your enquiries again? I know you have commissions to fulfil and I think you should be working towards another exhibition.'

'The two commissions that I still have are not required until near Christmas; I have them sketched out already, and thought that while I was here I would make some enquiries on the south coast before returning north. Why not come with me?'

'My heart says yes but all my better judgement goes against it.' Hester looked stricken. 'I'm sorry, Edward, but if you are to pursue what I consider a foolish quest, you will have to do it on your own.'

Chapter Twenty-one

Edward looked out of his hotel window in Deal and sighed. The day looked as miserable as he felt. The sea was pewter-grey under dismal clouds that couldn't make up their mind whether to rain properly or keep dispensing the fine mist that looked like nothing but soaked to the skin in no time at all.

Edward's search for any information about his father had produced virtually nothing. One art dealer in Folkestone knew of his work but had not handled any of his paintings for some time; he knew nothing of Arthur's present whereabouts, and in fact had never met him. The paintings he had handled had been brought in by various customers. He had had no luck in Dover but had attached some significance to the fact that two art dealers there had referred him to one in St Margaret's at Cliff. It was with high hopes because of this double mention that he finally ventured out to visit the little village.

'Arthur Newton?' A white-haired man with stooped shoulders peered at Edward over the rim of his glasses as he savoured the name. Then he added wistfully, 'If only.'

'If only what?' asked Edward cautiously when the man offered no further explanation.

He did not answer but shuffled to a drawer at one end of the oak chest that ran the full length of the wall behind an equally long counter. He opened the drawer, and when he turned back placed two paintings covered in soft paper on the counter. He uncovered one of them. Edward's heart skipped a beat. There were unmistakable signs that this was his father's work but he did not recognise the scene.

'Walmer Castle,' said the man, giving a name to the depiction of stern military walls painted in greys and purples to bring out the atmosphere of a dour construction built to defend and resist.

'Where is that?' asked Edward.

'Between here and Deal.'

Edward felt a little surge of excitement. So his father must have been in this area at some time. He peered at the date: 1893. Two years ago, maybe even less if there had been any indication of the month.

'I wouldn't say that it is Newton at his best,' commented the man, 'but this one,' he folded the paper back off the second painting, 'now this is a gem. Newton at his glorious best.'

Edward found himself looking at a painting of Whitby with all the hallmarks of his father painting with inspiration. Without looking at the date he knew it must have been done when his father and mother were together in Well Close Square.

'Wonderful,' he agreed, his voice scarcely above a whisper.

Both men stood looking at the painting, neither of them speaking, as if to do so would break the magic it was casting over them.

Eventually Edward said, 'I would like to buy them both.' The two men agreed a price and shook hands on a deal that satisfied them.

'I know Newton was from the north,' said Edward, 'but he must have been to Walmer Castle to do that one?'

'Yes. He came to live on the south coast but his popularity was waning at the time because his painting, as superb as you see it in that one,' the dealer tapped the Whitby painting, 'was slipping into mediocrity. I think he realised it and gave up. There is little new work since he came south.'

'May I ask where you got the painting of Walmer Castle?'

'Certainly. There is no secret about that. It came to me from an estate of a Miss Eastry. When she died everything went to her nephew, Mr Vincent Reculver, who lived close by.'

'Where was that?'

'Kingsdown, between here and Deal.'

'I wonder if he has any more of Newton's paintings?'

'I would doubt it, but you never know. You are a collector of Newton's work, sir?'

'Yes. I'm interested in it. I'd be obliged if you could furnish me with Mr Reculver's address?'

'Certainly. I keep meticulous records of all the paintings I handle. That one,' again he tapped the Whitby painting, 'came from a dealer in Leeds a few years ago.'

'Mr Ebenezer Hirst?'

'You know the man?' The art dealer's surprise was marked.

'Indeed I do. Alas, he is no longer with us.'

The other man showed sorrow. 'I am sorry to hear that. I dealt with him from time to time. He was a great admirer of Newton also.' While he had been speaking he had opened a big ledger. Flicking its pages open, he found the one he wanted, ran his finger down the entries and said, 'Ah, here it is.' He took a pencil and a sheet of paper, wrote quickly and handed the information to Edward. 'The address you want.'

'Thank you for your help,' he replied, and after a further hand-shake left the shop with his two paintings.

He hired a coach to take him to Deal with instructions to stop at the address in Kingsdown on the way. Though he was politely received by Mrs Reculver, he was informed that her husband was in London until the day after tomorrow. In answer to his enquiry she told him she knew of the painting to which he referred but no more than that; her husband was more likely to be able to help. Edward left after making an appointment to return.

He had found a hotel in Deal and had to be content to wait there. He had hoped for fine weather for his stay but at the moment it looked as if he would not get the walks he'd hoped for. His thoughts turned to Hester. The day would have seemed much brighter if she had been with him. He wondered about the work she was doing. If the other exhibitions she was organising were half as successful as his, she would be doing well and success always brings in more clients He wondered if he had received special attention and if so hoped it would extend to his mother also when Hester came to organise Colette's photographic exhibition next year.

Standing in the hotel in Deal, looking out at the shingle beach on a dreary day, with nary a soul in sight, he began to feel pangs of homesickness. Was he really being foolish in his pursuit of Arthur Newton? Was Hester right?

He shook himself to clear such thoughts from him. He had made progress. There was no guarantee he would get further, that Mr Reculver would know any more, but he had to try. He must be patient and wait for three o'clock tomorrow afternoon.

At exactly that time he was shown into the drawing room of the house in Kingsdown where he reacquainted himself with Mrs Reculver.

'It is a pleasure to see you again, Mr Clayton. My husband got back just half an hour ago. He will be with us in a few minutes. Please do sit down. You are not from these parts?'

'No. Yorkshire. To be more precise, Whitby.'

'It's on the coast like us, I believe?'

'Indeed.'

'I hope my husband will be able to help you with your enquiry. Ah, here he is.'

The door opened and Edward was met by a man whom he judged to be maybe five years older than himself. His hopes were raised for this man had an open face, a pleasant smile and firm, friendly handshake.

Edward, who was quickly on his feet, introduced himself and thanked Mr Reculver for seeing him.

'Jack, please,' returned Mr Reculver. As they sat down he glanced at his wife. 'You ordered tea, dear?'

'It will be here in five minutes, Jack.'

'Good.' He turned his eyes back to Edward. 'Alice is so efficient, I'm such a lucky man.'

She blushed. 'Don't embarrass me, Jack.'

'Well, you are, dear. It's good to be back. I don't like London, and the sooner I'm back on this coast the better.'

Edward read love in the couple's banter and wondered if he could ever be like this with Hester.

Their tea arrived.

'I'm ready for a good cup after that journey,' sighed Jack, settling himself more comfortably in his chair. 'Now, Edward,' he added as Alice started to pour the tea, 'my wife tells me that you have an interest in a painting you have just purchased?'

'Yes. It's of Walmer Castle, dated 1893 and signed Arthur Newton. I am a collector of his paintings and like to find out a little of their history if I can. The subject leads me to believe that Mr Newton painted it while he was living on the south coast. He might still be living here for all I know. It would be wonderful if I could meet him. The dealer from whom I purchased the work told me that you had sold it to him as part of your aunt's estate?'

'Perfectly correct,' Jack answered as he gave a nod of thanks to his wife for the tea. 'We aren't interested in art. We already had what we wanted on our walls so decided we would sell this painting.'

'Do you know where your aunt got it?'

'It was a Christmas present from a dear friend.'

'So that friend either bought it or commissioned it from Newton?'

'Your aunt said it was 'specially commissioned,' put in Alice. 'She was quite proud of that.'

'I didn't know that,' said Jack, pulling a surprised expression.

'She told me one day when I visited her. You weren't with me, probably at work.'

'Yes, I do a bit of that,' Jack said jocularly.

'Do you know who your aunt's friend was?'

'Yes, Mrs Darnel.'

'So if she commissioned it direct from the artist, she might know where he is?'

'I suppose so.'

'You wouldn't have Mrs Darnel's address by any chance?' asked Edward hopefully.

Jack started to shake his head but stopped in surprise when his wife said, 'It is highly possible.' She rose from her chair but paused before making for the door. She looked teasingly at her husband and cocked her head as if to say, with pleasing pride, I told you so.

'Your aunt's address book, the one you wanted to throw out, saying it would not be wanted . . .'

'You kept it?' He raised his eyebrows. 'There you are, Edward, I told you she was efficient.'

When Alice returned a few minutes later she was carrying a leatherbound book with a brass clasp. 'It was too beautiful to throw out.'

'And now proving to be useful also,' commented Jack, admitting he should have given it a second thought.

'Let me have a look.' Alice turned the pages. 'D. Darnel . . . Ah, here we are. Pencil and paper, Jack, please.'

He got out of his chair, went to a small desk and returned to hand her a notepad and pencil.

She wrote down the details. The address meant nothing to Edward but he didn't have to ask for Alice was already explaining. 'Not far to go. At the other end of Deal from here you'll find three houses, each standing in their own grounds. This one will be the first you come to.'

When he left, Edward's thanks were profuse for he had a feeling that he was on the verge of meeting his father.

He lost no time in reaching the house in question. His knock was answered by a smartly dressed maid who took his request to Mrs Darnel then returned to tell him that she would receive him.

He was shown to a room that looked on to a well-kept garden of immaculate lawn and flowerbeds. An elderly lady was sitting in the window. She greeted him with a smile and eyes filled with curiosity.

'It is good of you to see me, Mrs Darnel.'

'From the north I suspect from your accent, Mr Clayton?'

'You are very perceptive, ma'am.'

'To be more accurate, I would say, Yorkshire. That intrigues me. What does a gentleman from Yorkshire want with an old lady in Deal?' There was a twinkle in her eyes as she added, 'I like mysteries, Mr Clayton.'

He had taken the seat she had indicated to him. 'Two days ago I purchased a painting in which I was particularly interested. The dealer told me it was sold to him by a Mr Reculver. That painting, I believe, was given by you to Mr Reculver's aunt.'

'Ah, yes, to dear Nell. She and I were at school together. When she moved to be near her nephew in Kingsdown I had this painting done as a welcoming present for her.'

'So you actually commissioned it from the artist?'

'Oh, yes. It was very convenient, he lives next-door.'

Edward had to stifle the excitement that threatened to burst from him.

'Oh, my goodness! I am particularly interested in this artist, Arthur Newton, and had hoped you could tell me about him, but to find he lives next door . . . well . . . do you think it would be possible to meet him?'

'I'm sure it would be if he were here.'

Edward's face dropped. 'Doesn't he live here any more?'

'Oh, yes, but the family have gone to America.'

'America?'

'Just a short while ago.'

'How long for?'

'I don't know. Nothing was decided. They have gone to visit his brother. If they like it they may stay out there. On the other hand, they may be back in months.'

Edward was filled with disappointment. So near and yet . . . If only he hadn't had those commissions he would have been on the south coast sooner! But, he reminded himself, if he had been he might not have got the leads he had done during these last few days; may only have found blank walls. As it was, he was next to the house in which his father had lived.

'It's most disappointing for me, Mrs Darnel. I have a particular interest in this artist and am a collector of his works. If you receive any indication when he will be returning, would you let me know?'

'I will, but I am not certain to hear until the last minute so that I can open up their house. And, as I say, if they like it out there they may stay.'

It was this latter statement that worried Edward on his way back to London the next day. But he also wondered what Hester's reaction would be and how his mother would view this news.

Reaching the city, he sent a note to Hester and arranged for her to dine with him that evening.

On seeing her again he wondered if the decision he had made

on the train to London had been the right one. He was in awe of her beauty and personality. He realised what he had long suspected was true: she was ambitious for him. With her by his side, suggesting new directions to take, where to exhibit and when to do so, which galleries to cultivate, who was likely to buy his pictures, he knew he could become a sought-after painter.

'Well,' she said as she settled in the cab, 'did your search bear fruit?'

'Wait until we settle over our meal,' he replied.

'Ah, I can tell it did,' she said with a knowing smile. 'You look so pleased with yourself.'

'That is because I'm seeing you again,' he replied, trying to divert her attention and not give any more away.

'Flattery won't disguise the pleasure you have derived from your visit to the south coast.'

'And you are not going to wrest any more out me until we have had our first taste of wine.'

The alcove in Simpson's in the Strand was cosy and comfortable and the menu offered them a wide choice of succulent and tempting dishes. Edward chose the wine but ordered that the first glass should be poured only after they had placed their order.

With that out of the way, Hester took her first sip and said, 'Now you have to tell me.'

Edward raised his glass in acknowledgement and went on to relate how near he had been to seeing his father.

'So that is that,' Hester said with marked finality when he had finished the tale. 'Now you can forget all about what I thought was completely the wrong course for you.'

'No, I can't. I've decided to go to America.'

For a moment Hester was dumbstruck. She stared at him in disbelief then exclaimed: 'What? You can't!'

'I can and will.'

'But it is ridiculous! Do you even know where he has gone?'

'No.'

'Then it's even more ridiculous! How on earth do you expect to find him?'

'I only missed him by a week or two on the south coast.'

She gave a snort of derision. 'America is rather bigger than the south coast.'

'I'll find him.'

'And what if you do and realise other people are going to be hurt by your revelation?'

'Like I told you before, I'll not pursue it.'

'And how long will you be gone?'

He shrugged his shoulders. 'Who knows?'

'What about us?'

'Come with me.'

'Edward, you make it all sound so easy but I've responsibilities here. I've my family, my work. Exhibitions planned, including your mother's. I can't just walk away from them. People are relying on me. To some it's their livelihood. I think it's you who should consider staying here and giving up this foolish idea of finding your father. He has made no attempt to contact you after all.'

'Maybe for a very good reason – he's married and has a daughter.'

'All the more reason for you to give up this idiocy! What do you hope to gain from it?'

'Peace of mind. If I don't follow this through now, I will always wonder.'

'But going to America . . . Why not wait until he returns?'

'Mrs Darnel indicated that it wasn't certain he ever would.'

'You are determined to do this?'

'Yes.'

Hester tightened her lips. She was hurt by what it would mean, and it appeared that Edward thought more of finding his father than he did of her. She steeled herself not to break down. The love that she thought they shared lay in ruins about her. She folded her napkin carefully and laid it down precisely on the table.

'Take me home, Edward.'

'But . . .'

His protest got no further for she had started to rise from her seat.

'Please.'

There was nothing he could do but comply unless he made a

scene. He followed her from the room, pausing only to pay the bill.

Hester was overcome by the dilemma that faced her. She had made her decision immediately on hearing Edward's, but as she waited for him she was almost on the point of reversing it. She would have been overwhelmed by love and regret but for the steeliness she summoned to control her emotions.

Edward joined her but she did not speak until they were settled in a cab.

'If you are intent on this quest, I see no future for us. I will not come to America, for the reasons I have given you, and I will not wait for your return – goodness knows when that will be, if ever! Should you return, I will be your friend and my business relationship with you and with your mother will not be affected.' Her voice was cold, matter-of-fact. She sensed he was going to protest, even attempt to change her mind, so added quickly, 'Nothing will make me alter my decision. I will not embark on any expedition that I see as jeopardising our future. I thank you for your friendship and will always have fond memories of our time together.'

Edward recognised the finality of those words, and, as much as he admired Hester, realised that if either of them had given way a barrier would have been raised between them and then the loving, sharing relationship of a successful marriage would never have been possible between them. Hester was now his friend and that was all she could ever be.

Chapter Twenty-two

The misgivings that Edward had had on his journey from London to Whitby intensified as he walked up the path to the house on Whitby's West Cliff. He regretted compromising the love he and Hester had shared but foremost in his mind at this moment was how he would break the news to his mother of the trip to America.

When her maid announced, 'Mr Edward is back,' Colette hurried into the hall to take her son in her arms and welcome him home. He shed his coat and she linked arms with him as she escorted him to the drawing room, calling over her shoulder to the maid, 'Tea, please, Tess.'

'How have you been?' she asked solicitously.

'Very well, Mother.'

'And Hester?'

'She was in good health when I left her.'

Edward's reply had no enthusiasm about it. Colette sensed all was not well between them and it troubled her, for she liked Hester and had hoped that the relationship would develop into love.

'Is that all you have to say about her?' she prompted while he hesitated. She recognised he had more to tell her and that he was wondering how to begin. 'Sit down and start at the beginning.'

He settled himself in a chair opposite his mother. 'When the exhibition closed, I informed Hester of my proposed visit to the south coast.' He glanced down at his hands, which he rubbed together, and then with a contrite look at his mother, said, 'I told her the reason. I'm sorry, but under the circumstances I could do no other.' He saw displeasure flicker across her face and quickly added, 'But before I did, I got her to promise that it would never be revealed by her.'

317

Colette's relief was evident in her remark, 'I believe Hester will keep her word, she is trustworthy. So, what did she say?'

'Well, naturally she was more than surprised, but as you know she had previously wondered why it was that some of my work was a lot like Arthur Newton's. My revelation made her realise it was as a result of more than my close study of Newton's technique. I told her I was trying to trace him and that was why I was going to the south coast. I even asked her to come with me.'

Colette looked surprised. 'Did she?'

'No. In fact, she tried to talk me out of it. Thought it was a foolish idea and that I might hurt people. I told her of my promise to you.'

'So you made your search?'

'Yes.' He went on to recount what he had found out.

'America!' Colette received the surprise with mixed feelings. Questions rose in her mind but she voiced only what she hoped was true. 'So, that is that. Well, having this out of your mind will make it easier for you to concentrate on your painting.'

Edward did not hold back. 'It is not the end. I'm going to America!'

This bold announcement came as such a shock that, for a few moments, Colette could only stare incredulously at her son, wide-eyed. 'You don't mean it?'

'I do, Mother. This is the first important lead I have had. I can't just let it go.'

'But America? It's impossible.'

'It's not.'

'Edward, what about your work here?'

'I'll be back.'

'But where will you start? America is such a big place.'

'Mrs Darnel said he had gone to visit his brother.'

'But where is that?'

'I will make enquiries. Look how my questions led me from one person to another on the south coast until I contacted Mrs Darnel. I just missed my father. A few days earlier and going to America would not be necessary now.'

Colette realised how determined he was. She could argue,

318

condemn his idea, put all sorts of obstacles in the way, but she knew she would be the loser in the end. It would be far better to agree to his plans; he would respect her all the more if she gave him her blessing. Above all, she must hide her own hurt. But first she had to make one more attempt. 'What does Hester think of this?'

'I asked her to go with me but she refused, saying she had family, work and so on to consider, and it was therefore impossible to join me. She expressed the view that now my father had gone to America my quest was even more foolish.' He paused for a moment. Colette, realising he was about to say more, made no comment. 'She said that because I did not know how long I would be, she would not wait for me.'

'Oh, Edward! I'm sorry. You are prepared to lose her over this?'
He bit his lip and nodded.

'Please, do think it over. You will be losing a wonderful girl.'

'I know, but if I don't try to find my father there will always be this yearning and regret inside me, and I daren't risk that.'

'So there is no hope of a reconciliation? I had hoped you two . . .'

'None, Mother,' he broke in. 'She said we would always be friends and that she would still handle exhibitions for me and for you.'

Colette felt tears rising but fought them and controlled her own emotions, holding them to herself.

Two weeks later her son sailed to America.

'I have made the train bookings, Mr Newton.' The shipping company's agent in New York who had been instructed to see to the Newton party's requirements handed over an envelope.

'Thank you, Mr Fisk. And may I add the thanks of all my family for your help since we arrived a fortnight ago? When the ship docked we were anxious to be on our way to Denver but we are glad now that we took time to see New York. It has broken us in to a completely new way of life.'

Mr Fisk gave a little smile. 'As you say, you have seen a different way of life, but remember – this is New York, nowhere else is the same. You will be moving away from city life, and a very individual

319

city I might add. Denver will seem so much smaller, and you will feel and see a Western influence there.'

'Just what I expected,' replied Arthur. 'We all look forward to the opportunities the West will present for our painting. New York has enabled us to expand our subject matter – I am pleased with the way the younger ones have interpreted city landscape and life. Now we look to achieve something different.'

'And I'm sure you will find plenty to keep you drawing and painting out West. Now, Mr Newton, I will be here at nine in the morning to escort you to the train. If you could all be ready then?'

'We will be.'

Arthur passed this message on to the others when they sat down for their evening meal in the hotel. A new excitement pervaded the atmosphere around their table. The voyage across the Atlantic had been uneventful. Everyone except Isobel found their 'sea-legs' straight away. She suffered for two days but, after recovering, enjoyed the sea air and luxury accommodation. New York, pulsating with life and peopled with every different nationality so that there were times when they did not know if they were truly in America, fascinated them all and they were not slow to realise its potential for an artist.

Immediately on landing, with the help of the shipping agent, Arthur had despatched a telegram to his brother in Denver informing him where they were and when they would arrive at his home town. The reply had settled their minds about their arrival in Colorado's leading city.

Now the next step in their adventure was upon them.

Already Isobel and Arthur were pleased with its results, particularly as far as Lucy was concerned. A new light had come into her eyes and her attitude to life as soon as she left the house in Deal. She seemed to have shed her troubled past and was looking to the future with keen anticipation.

Marie was pleased to see that her stepsister was coping much better than she had expected so soon after the shock of Philip's betrayal and felt relieved that her own obligations towards her were lessened. She was able to devote more attention to George about whom she was apprehensive in case he felt like an outsider in the party. She need not have worried. George was strong enough to deal with that and put behind him the upset of curtailing his course in Paris. Arthur, realising that such minor tensions might exist, had put his tuition plan into operation immediately they were on board the liner bound for New York, had continued it in that city and was not about to let it drop on their train journey to Chicago, then onward to Kansas City and through to Denver. Isobel too was thankful for this aspect of their visit to America because it had made him take up his paintbrush in earnest again, albeit at the moment for teaching purposes but hopefully reviving his own artistic ambitions in the future.

As with the sea voyage, they were all thankful that they had decided to travel first class throughout when they boarded the train and settled in to their luxurious carriage with dining facilities readily available, unlike the other passengers in second and third class where conditions were far from salubrious through over-crowding, and dining to be had only at certain stops in facilities offered on the station platforms.

They were fascinated by the ever-changing landscape they travelled through. Though they found the prairies seemingly endless and relatively uninteresting, as artists they revelled in the changing light that brushed the grassland and plains with delicate colour, especially in the early morning, and in the magnificent sunsets that set the western horizon ablaze. Even distant gathering storms brought a new perspective to their artistic eyes and were eagerly recorded in drawings and notes in their sketchbooks.

The train clanged and hissed to a jolting stop in Denver where the station was packed with people for whom this arrival was a highlight. Citizens came to watch and revel in the activity that broke out immediately the train stopped and would continue until it left on the next stage of its journey West.

Arthur, peering out of the window, wondered how he would recognise his brother, whom he had not seen for over thirty years.

The car attendant was beside them to help with their luggage. With practised efficiency he had soon deposited it on the platform and organised a porter to take over from him, not easy among all the people milling around, some set on their jobs, others meandering or standing around simply satisfying their curiosity about who and what the train had brought to town. Passengers were greeted by relatives or friends or else hurried to engage one of the many cabs that had appeared in the vicinity once word had spread that the train was nearing the town.

Arthur marshalled his group around their luggage as he tried to pick out Oswald. He spoke briefly to the porter, informing him of the situation and asking him to wait.

'Arthur!' A booming voice set him swinging round and everyone else's eyes turning towards the newcomer.

They saw a well-dressed man in a grey hip-length jacket and exquisitely cut matching trousers. He carried a cane and at that moment was doffing a wide-brimmed slouch hat of brown felt in deference to the ladies. He was slightly taller than Arthur, his build and demeanour giving the impression of power.

'Oswald?' Though he knew this must be his brother, for he knew no one else in Denver, the name came out as a question.

Oswald let out hearty, deep-throated laugh. 'Don't remember your little brother? Maybe it's my beard.' He gave his short, pointed, neatly trimmed beard a little stroke. With its flecks of grey, matching those beginning to appear in his neatly groomed hair, it gave him an imposing look. 'Ah, well, it has been a long time and I can't say I would have recognised you immediately, but I had an advantage. I knew how many there would be in your party, and seeing your group looking lost I guessed this must be you.' By the time he had finished speaking the brothers were shaking hands and exchanging an embrace. 'Now, Arthur, tell me who's who?' said Oswald as they stepped apart.

He made the introductions and immediately everyone was put at ease by the warmth of Oswald's greeting. He held Isobel's hand a moment longer as he surveyed her and said in all sincerity, 'I can see my brother has married a beautiful lady, and from his letter, I know you have made him very happy. For that I am grateful to you, and I look forward to becoming better acquainted with my sister-in-law.'

'And I with you,' returned Isobel.

Oswald did not allow any more to be said for he turned to the porter. 'That's my carriage over there,' he pointed to it, 'and I have hired the one behind it.'

'Very good, sir.' He immediately called to a second porter who was by his side in a flash and, with a glance at Oswald, touched the peak of his cap and said, 'Sir!'

The two porters scooped up the luggage and hurried off towards the carriages.

'Seems you have them at your beck and call,' commented Arthur.

Oswald gave a little smile. 'They know me. Should do, I make it my job to know all the staff in my territory. I have a good memory for faces and names and they know that too.'

'Your territory?'

'Yes. Didn't I make it clear that I am in charge of the Union Pacific Railroad operation in a large section of the South West?'

'I thought it was just Denver station.'

Oswald laughed. 'Much greater responsibility than that! The station master here is one of the railroad's employees under my jurisdiction. Come on, we can't stand here chatting. You'll hear all about me and I about you when we are at home.'

He ushered them to the waiting carriages where the luggage had already been stowed. Arthur tipped the two porters generously and then climbed into Oswald's private carriage with Isobel while Marie, Lucy and George occupied the hired vehicle.

As they drove away from the station Isobel commented on the variety of dress among the people around the station and on the streets.

'There is still an element of the frontier here, and with Denver the biggest town for a wide area we get all manner of people: miners, cattlemen, cowboys, gamblers, hangers-on, railroaders, as well as the well-to-do who have made fortunes out of the various trades. It is a booming town and will continue to grow. There are those who follow convention and fashion and those who don't so you get a mixture of both.'

'And those? Are they the Rocky Mountains?' There was a touch of awe in Isobel's voice as she peered from the carriage.

'Yes, ma'am,' Oswald replied with pride as if they were his personal belongings. 'I love that view as I drive home.'

'They seem so near.'

'Well, that's the effect of the light. The foothills begin about twelve miles away but the majority of the range is in the region of thirty miles away.' He glanced at Arthur. 'There's plenty of subjects for you out there.'

'That's just what I was thinking,' he replied.

Isobel was pleased at the enthusiastic anticipation she saw in his eyes.

Nearing the outskirts of the town they had come to a row of big houses, each in its own grounds, set back from the dirt road. They turned through the gates of the third of seven, all of individual design. The drive swept in a gracious curve to the long frontage of an imposing building of wooden construction. A wide veranda ran the full width of the three-storied house with each floor having large sash windows that matched those on the first floor. The house faced west and so took advantage of the wonderful view of the mountains.

Isobel took Oswald's hand as she stepped from the carriage but she staggered and raised her free hand to her forehead. 'Oh, my,' she muttered.

'Light-headed?' asked Oswald with concern.

'Are you all right, love?' Anxiety gripped Arthur.

Isobel swallowed hard, trying to regain her composure.

'I should have warned you,' said Oswald apologetically. 'It's the height. We are just over five thousand feet above sea level here and it does affect some people until they get used to the more rarefied atmosphere. You soon will. Just take things easy for a few days. Now, let me help you inside.'

He escorted Isobel up the four steps to the veranda and then into the imposing hall with its finely carved mahogany banister curving beside the stairs. He led her to a chair at the bottom. 'Sit for a few minutes, and then you'll be all right. Ah, here is my wife. Dolores will take care of you.'

They all looked at the woman who came down the stairs with an easy grace that seemed to make her glide over each step as if it wasn't there. Her smile was warm and full of pleasure, enhancing her beauty that immediately entranced them all. Thin black eyebrows

324

curved above dark eyes that were vivacious and at the moment full of delight. Her oval face was ivory-like, a feature highlighted by her straight black hair drawn tightly back. She wore a chiffon frock in a pastel mauve that suited her complexion. It was tight across her breasts and came in to a slim waist before widening slightly as far as her ankles.

Oswald held out his hand to her as she neared the bottom step. 'Dolores, my dear, come and meet my family.'

His voice drew Arthur's attention away from her and he was pleased at the adoration he saw in his brother's eyes. He had previously only mentioned his wife's name in his letter; now Arthur wanted to know more about this beautiful woman who held his brother's heart, and who he reckoned must be nearly twenty years younger.

'First, Oswald dear, this lady is in distress. She should have my immediate attention. You must be Isobel,' said Dolores gently and took her hand.

Isobel gave a wan smile and nodded.

Dolores reached for a bell set on a small table next to the chair on which Isobel was sitting. She shook it and almost instantaneously two maids appeared, each immaculately dressed in a black skirt and white blouse with a small white apron tied at the waist. They were dark-haired like their mistress.

'Yvonne, get me a glass of water. Conchita, help me assist Mrs Newton into the drawing room.' As they crossed the hall she said over her shoulder, 'I'll meet you all in a moment.' She glanced at Arthur and said reassuringly, 'She'll be all right in a few minutes. The altitude has made her short of breath, but it will pass.'

They reached the drawing room and a few moments later Dolores reappeared. 'I have left Conchita with Isobel.' She embraced everyone with her smile. 'Now, who is who?' She turned to Arthur. 'Oswald's brother, of course!' She held out her hand. When Arthur took it he felt the warmth of a welcome that said, This is your home for as long as you like.

'Thank you for your attention to Isobel, and may I say how wonderful it is to meet you?'

She went on to greet Marie, Lucy and George with an interest that quite won their hearts. They knew instantly that they were going to like it here, and that coupled with the painting prospects made them certain that they had made the right decision in coming to America.

'Now I will have you shown to your rooms, and after you have recovered from your journey we will have tea in the drawing room.' Dolores was about to reach for the bell again when Conchita appeared.

'Ma'am, Mrs Newton is much recovered.'

'Thank you, Conchita. I will see to her now. Will you show our guests to their rooms?'

'Yes, ma'am.' Conchita hurried away.

As Dolores crossed the hall to the drawing room, Isobel appeared. Dolores and Arthur were quickly by her side. She gave a small smile and in a low voice said, 'I'm sorry for being so stupid.'

'You weren't,' Dolores hastened to reassure her. 'It happens to a lot of people when they first come to Denver unaware of its altitude.'

'Are you feeling better, love?' asked Arthur, still concerned.

She patted his hand. 'Much, thank you.'

'Just take things steady until you get used to the change.'

She nodded. Any further conversation was halted as the maids appeared and the guests were shown to their rooms.

Half an hour later, feeling much fresher and easier after their long journey, everyone was relaxing in the drawing room when Dolores and Oswald joined them.

'Now, a good cup of English tea to make you feel at home,' announced Oswald briskly. 'That's something in which I had to educate my Spanish wife.' He smiled at her with affection.

She returned his smile, slipped her hand from his and came to sit beside Isobel. 'Are you feeling better?'

Isobel nodded. 'Yes, thank you. I am so grateful to you.'

Dolores gave a dismissive wave of her hands. 'It's nothing.' Her eyes included everyone in her next announcement. 'This is your home so please be at ease here. The staff have all been briefed to see to your needs so treat them as your own and ask for anything you want.'

The tea arrived and they enjoyed the conversation that accompanied it and enabled the new arrivals to get to know Dolores and Oswald.

'You've done well for yourself,' commented Arthur to his brother indicating the opulence of the spacious room that overlooked a large lawn and well-kept garden with unimpeded views of the snow-capped Rockies in the distance.

'Leeds training, Arthur! As you know, I wasn't too happy when Mother and Father packed me off to the railway offices, which meant my moving at an early age to York, but it paid off, taught me a lot, and when I came out here I saw the opportunity to be in on the expansion of the railroads. I played my cards right, got to know the people who mattered, and was not shy of coming West when that was suggested by head office in New York. But let me tell you, it wasn't all plain sailing. There was a lot of hard work but it paid off and here I am. I found my beautiful wife in Denver while negotiating to buy land for the railroad from her family.'

'Are they still in Denver?' asked Marie.

'They have a big ranch north-east of the town. We shall take you to meet them. Now, yourselves?'

Before long Oswald and Dolores were in possession of all the facts relating to their reason for coming to America, though Arthur and Isobel toned down Lucy's reaction to her broken romance with Philip.

'We thought after that it would be good for us all to get away. There was nothing to hold us there,' explained Arthur. 'Isobel had sold her farm, I was free and could continue the tuition these three had given up by leaving Paris.'

'And I hoped it would get Arthur painting again,' added Isobel.

'What made you stop?' Dolores asked him.

He shrugged his shoulders. 'Circumstances. Other concerns had dimmed the inspiration in my painting so I gave up.'

'Well, there are plenty of new subjects out here,' Oswald assured him. 'The landscape is truly magnificent. At one time the West was regarded as mere wilderness with no redeeming features, but artists saw it as more than that. Through their paintings they have educated the American people in its beauties. There are lots of opportunities here for you. Apart from the landscape there are so many people – miners, cowboys, gamblers, lawmen, ranchers, anyone and everyone. And there is a ready market for portraiture, all the tycoons want themselves and their families to be remembered.'

'Oswald,' put in Dolores, 'if our visitors are going to paint, why don't we set up the spare room on the first floor as a studio for them?'

'A splendid idea,' he boomed with enthusiasm.

'We couldn't put you to that trouble,' Arthur demurred.

'It's no trouble. The room is virtually empty at the moment because we have had it decorated recently and not yet decided on the furniture we want. We may as well set it up for you. It's big enough to accommodate the four of you. We'll show it you when we introduce you to the rest of the house.'

'These past two weeks have been wonderful,' said Isobel as she and Dolores strolled in the garden enjoying the sunshine. 'But I'm sure we are being a nuisance and intruding on your privacy.'

Dolores linked arms with her. 'You are neither a nuisance nor an intruder. I enjoy having you all, and so does Oswald. I know how much he appreciates having his brother here and making up for all the years when he had no family of his own here.'

'But he had you.'

Dolores smiled wistfully. 'Ah, yes, and there is a great love between us but we both regret having no children: I was unable to have any after a riding accident. That is why he dotes on Marie and Lucy. They are fulfilling a need. So, please, never think that you are in the way.'

'Thank you.' Isobel was touched by the welcome she'd received from this generous woman.

'Dolores, Isobel!' His call brought them turning round to see Oswald hurrying towards them with a sheet of paper in his hand. 'Look at this, just look at it!' Excitement filled his voice as he held out the paper to them. 'Isn't that just wonderful?'

They were looking at a pencil sketch of Dolores. Apart from its being a good likeness, her character had been brought out in many subtle ways that made the sketch come alive. The head was tilted in a pose Dolores often adopted, but the artist had brought out much of her character by that attitude and by the way the eyes, with their slightly downward aspect, were concentrating on the viewer. One hand was raised to her white mantilla. The position of the long delicate fingers enhanced the lovely face.

'That is just beautiful.' Isobel was the first to break the silence.

Dolores stared at herself in wonder. 'Who did this?' she asked quietly.

'Marie,' replied Oswald proudly.

Dolores looked amazed. 'But I never sat for her.'

'There were times when Marie quietly sketched you without your knowing, and she drew on her memory too.'

'Remarkable,' said Dolores.

'Apparently she wants to concentrate on portraits so I have commissioned an oil painting of you. Now, I want you to come to the studio and see what Lucy and George have been doing during this past fortnight.'

When they reached the studio Dolores went straight to Marie. 'This is wonderful, Marie, you have such a great talent.' She kissed her on the cheek.

'Thank you,' she replied. 'Uncle Oswald has probably told you that he has commissioned a painting? I will need you to sit for that.'

'It will be my pleasure.'

'Isobel, come and see this!' Oswald directed her to Arthur's easel.

She saw a painting of a view towards the Rockies and squeezed her husband's arm. 'I am so pleased you have taken up the brush again.'

'It's not my best work, but I will get there. Just have a look at Lucy's.'

Lucy had dramatised a mountain scene, and though it had been drawn from imagination Oswald could detect the influence of her close observation of the local countryside. 'I love the drama you have created in this scene and hope you will retain some of that when you see the mountains close to.'

George had chosen to use some of the sketches he had made on the train and used them for his depiction of Denver railway station, aided by a visit to town a week ago. His canvas was alive with activity. The hustle and bustle that surrounded a train's arrival could be sensed in the painting.

When the general admiration of the work had died down, Oswald called out, 'Listen, all of you. I am so impressed by what I have seen that this is what I propose. First, that we go to my lodge closer to the Rockies. It is near enough for me to get into work in Denver and will give you the opportunity to paint the wild landscape in its many aspects and present it in your own individual styles.

'Now what I want next is for Dolores to sit for Marie, and I too will sit for her. We can't have one of us on the wall and not the other! Arthur, Lucy and George, I want you to keep in mind an exhibition I will organise in Denver. I believe many people will be interested in attending but apart from that I will invite railroad people and local businessmen who I feel certain will readily be forthcoming with commissions.' He looked round them all. 'Now, what do you say to that?'

They all gaped at him. Was his enthusiasm running away with him? Was he seeing their work from partisan eyes? Or was he presenting a real opportunity, one they should take advantage of?

Arthur spoke for them all. 'Oswald, that is a wonderful gesture. I am sure all of us will be delighted to bear it in mind. It will give us something to aim for.'

'Good. I will have everything arranged to leave for the lodge a week today, if that is all right with you, Dolores?'

'Of course it is. I love it close to the mountains and I'm sure you all will too.'

Edward was pleased when the American coast came in sight. He had been confined to his cabin for two days when the heaving, rolling ship encountered a violent storm in mid-Atlantic. He had never felt so ill and lay in his bunk wishing death would release him from this awful malady. But survive he had and soon regained his 'sea-legs', thankful that he had at least been able to travel first class with its attendant luxury and privacy.

Now, on deck, he was enjoying the glorious morning whose crisp air brought the vista of Long Island and New Jersey into sharp relief. It was a welcoming sight, one which he thought must surely give hope to the many emigrants in steerage seeking a new life. He wondered what this country had in store for him in the course of his search.

He stayed on deck, marvelling at the huge Statue of Liberty that dominated the entrance to New York, a symbol of hope for all who came to her country. His first sight of New York dispelled all the mental images he had had of the city. It was much larger than he'd expected, spreading along the banks of the Hudson and East Rivers, the spires of its many churches rising above houses and commercial buildings.

The waterways teemed with shipping: steamers and sailing vessels, discharging or receiving cargoes at their docks; small craft of every description, and ferries plying their everyday trade bringing life to the city.

Port officials and a doctor came on board and quickly cleared the way for the disembarkation of the steerage passengers. This was much quicker and easier, Edward understood, than in former days when there had always been a lengthy delay. Once again he was thankful that his first-class passage meant he was dealt with quickly throughout the landing formalities.

As he took his first steps on American soil a voice greeted him. 'Help you, sir?' He glanced round. A youngster of about twelve years old, barefoot, with tattered trousers and grubby shirt, looked up at him from under the peak of a flat cap perched on his forehead with little success in hiding a mop of ginger hair. In spite of his unkempt appearance Edward saw a round open face lit by a tentative smile that carried, along with the hungry look in the eyes, the hope of earning a coin or two.

'Sure,' replied Edward. 'You can carry one of these cases and direct me to a cabbie to transport me to the best hotel.'

'Yes, sir. Old Dan's your man. Follow me.' The youngster took a case and set off. 'From England, sir?'

'Yes. What's your name?'

'Roger, sir. First time in New York, sir?'

'Yes.'

'Going to be here long, sir?'

'Don't know.'

'Why not?'

'It depends.'

'On what, sir?'

Edward smiled. 'You're full of questions, aren't you?'

'Weighing up whether I should offer any more help,' Roger replied brightly.

'And should you?'

Roger grinned and pursed his lips as if giving the question careful consideration. 'I think I should. You appear trustworthy, not someone who would send me packing without rewarding my service.'

'And what might that be?'

'I know New York like the back of my hand. You don't. I could be your guide for as long as you like. Show you the sights, tell you the places to avoid, warn off the pickpockets, thieves and the girls only after one thing – your money.'

'You, at your age, know all these things about this city?'

'I do.'

'What do your parents think?'

'Ain't got any. My dad left us when I was five, Ma died two years later. I ran off before the authorities could put me in a home. Wasn't going into one of those places when I could fend for myself on the streets. Here we are, sir.'

Edward was faced by an elderly man slouched on the seat of his cab, his horse seemingly asleep as well.

'Dan!' Roger shook the man's arm.

He started and, seeing Roger with a stranger, was immediately wide awake.

Edward saw that Dan was not as old as he had first appeared.

'Sorry, sir.' He touched his forehead. 'Taking the opportunity to catch up on sleep. Where to?

'This gentleman wants the best hotel in town,' piped up Roger. 'That's the Astor.'

Dan looked Edward up and down. 'Looks like it. Thanks for bringing him to me. Climb aboard, sir. Roger, see to the luggage.'

332

In a few moments Edward was seated comfortably in the cab, his luggage beside him. About to close the door, Roger paused. 'See you in the morning, sir. I'll be outside the front door of the hotel at nine. If you want a guide, I'll see you right. If not, well, too bad for me.' He shut the door and stood back.

The cab moved off and ten minutes later was stopping outside a large solid-looking building with an imposing entrance above which lettering announced that this was the Astor Hotel. A commissionaire in impressive burgundy livery was immediately at the door. 'Good day, sir. Welcome to the Astor.' Edward noted how he accentuated 'the'. Seeing the two suitcases, the commissionaire looked round and snapped his fingers at two boys in similar livery. They rushed forward to haul the luggage from the cab and take it inside.

Edward paid the cabbie who said, 'Have a good stay, sir. You'll find Roger a big help if you are a stranger here.' He touched his forehead and sent the horse on its way.

The commissionaire escorted Edward into the hotel and in a matter of minutes the formalities were over and he was in his room, pleased that he had been directed to such an opulent and comfortable place. Then he realised it was not home; such places, no matter how good they were, never could be. He suddenly felt alone and homesick. If only Hester had agreed to come with him. He flopped into a chair, feeling sorry for himself. After a few minutes he shook off his mood. This was no way to be thinking. He had come to America with a purpose, and intended to fulfil it. He banished his lethargy, unpacked, changed and went in search of the dining room. He was presented with an extensive menu, made his choice, and while he waited to be served started to consider where he should begin his search.

Chapter Twenty-three

The thoughts of the previous evening were still with Edward the next morning but in the cold light of day, with his feeling of loneliness accentuated by all the sounds of a city coming awake to purposeful life, they seemed inconsequential.

When he analysed the leads he had, he realised they were very slender and that he would have to rely on intuition and luck. The only concrete fact he had was that his father was in America to see his brother and must have arrived via New York. By now he could be anywhere in this vast country. As he ate breakfast he reconsidered his thoughts of last night.

He recalled that his mother, when telling him of his father's early life, had mentioned that he had worked in the railway offices in Leeds. A job there would be well regarded and no doubt he had been encouraged to take it by his parents. Could they have done the same with his brother? Could he too have found employment with the railways? If so, could he have used this experience when he had come to America, where new frontiers were being opened up by the railroad industry? The more he thought about it, the more Edward convinced himself that his was a distinct possibility. In fact, he saw it as the only lead he had at this moment. It was one he would have to exploit.

He paused in front of the hotel to watch as motor-cars vied with horse-drawn carriages and carts for space in the road and pedestrians hurried along the pavements, a new nation forging ahead towards its destiny as if there wasn't any time to waste. Had this tide of change swept his father beyond his reach?

As he took his first steps Edward was aware of a sharp movement to his left and a familiar figure appeared beside him.

'Morning, sir! Said I'd be here.' Roger grinned at him. 'Where do you want to go, sir?'

The commissionaire who had been strolling in front of the hotel saw the confrontation and, with a dark scowl on his face, hurried over to intervene.

'Of with you!' He waved Roger away. 'I've told you about pestering hotel guests before. Now, git!'

'Hold on,' broke in Edward, 'I told him to be here this morning. I need someone to show me around this town.'

The commissionaire, surprised, pulled himself up short. 'Ah, very well, sir.' He looked hard at Roger and cautioned him, 'Mind you look after this gentleman.'

'I sure will.'

Edward turned down the street. Roger fell into step beside him. 'Thanks, sir. You saved me from a clip round the ear.' His ready grin had turned to one of appreciation and hope. 'Do you really want my help?'

'I wouldn't have said so if I didn't. Learn that right away, Roger. Never say what you don't mean.'

'Yes, sir. Right, where do you want to go?'

'Well, I don't really know. I'm looking for someone, you see.'

'What? In New York, and you don't know where they are?'

'Might be anywhere in America.'

Roger stopped in his tracks. 'I ain't walking round America!'

Edward laughed. 'I don't intend doing that either, but I've got to start somewhere and it'd better be here. Now, take me to the offices of the railroad companies.'

'Which one?'

'I don't know.'

'Does the person you want work for one of them?'

'I don't know.'

'You don't know much, do you?' grumbled Roger.

'So let's start with the nearest one.'

'That'll be the Northern Pacific.'

'Right, lead the way.'

Five minutes later they'd reached an imposing building. 'This is it, sir.'

'You wait here until I return,' Edward instructed him.

As he entered the building he saw Roger sitting down on the pavement, his back to a wall.

Ten minutes later Roger leaped to his feet as Edward reappeared. 'Any luck, sir?' he asked brightly.

Edward shook his head. 'No. A clerk who had only been working there a month looked up some records but could find no name to correspond with the one I am looking for.'

It was the same story over the next two days and Edward was beginning to despair. His visit to Union Pacific was thwarted because the man he was told could help him was away but would be back in a week.

Coming out of the offices of one of the minor railroads, his final hope, Edward informed Roger that once again he had been disappointed. 'Now that I am here in New York, though, I may as well wait until I can see the man at Union Pacific.'

'Why don't you try some of them again, sir?' asked Roger. 'Try and find somebody different to help you?'

'I suppose it's worth a try.'

'So where would you like to start?'

'What about the first one? The clerk there was new to the job.'

'Northern Pacific.'

When Edward entered the building for the second time he saw that the clerk who greeted him was different from the man he had previously seen. This one was older; in fact Edward thought he was possibly more than twice the other man's age.

'Good day, sir,' the man greeted him pleasantly.

'Good day,' returned Edward. 'I am trying to trace someone from England who I think might have emigrated to America many years ago and may well have been employed by one of the railroads.'

The man gave a small smile. 'Not a lot to go on, sir! But if you have a name I'll see what can be done to help you. I have worked all my life for various railroad companies.'

Edward's hopes rose a little. 'His name is Newton.'

'Newton.' The employee savoured the name thoughtfully. 'Do you know a Christian name, sir?'

Edward gave a shake of his head. 'I'm afraid not.'

'That makes it more difficult. But let me make a search.' He took a key from his pocket, turned to a filing cabinet and unlocked it.

Ah, thought Edward, I've got someone with more authority than I did on my first visit. He waited hopefully as he watched the man flick through the contents. He plucked something from the drawer and turned back to Edward.

'We have a Gerald Newton employed in Chicago. Might he be the person you are looking for?'

'Could be. Do you have any other information about him?'

'Seems he came from England but there is no exact date. He has been employed by Northern Pacific for five years.'

'Do you have his address in Chicago?'

'Sorry, sir, we haven't. And if we had I would not, by company rules, be allowed to divulge it. If you do want to follow this up it would be best to contact the Chicago office.'

'A personal visit, I suppose?'

'It would be best, sir.'

Edward hesitated a few moments, considering this option. The man behind the desk closed the file with a thoughtful expression, as if he was digging back into his memory.

'Thank you, you have been most helpful.' Edward smiled and turned for the door.

'Just a moment, sir.'

Edward stopped and returned his attention to the clerk who had laid the file on the counter.

'The name Newton has jangled something at the back of my mind. I was employed by Union Pacific for a short while, way back, and feel sure there was a Newton employed by them too. If I remember right he was highly thought of, but what happened to him I don't know. I wasn't with the company very long. Maybe you have already been to their offices?'

'I have, but the clerk I need to see is away for a week.'

'Ah. Then I'm sorry, I can't be of further help.'

'I appreciate what you have done.'

'I wish you success, sir.'

'Thank you.' Edward's step was a little brisker when he emerged from the building.

'You've done better there, sir.'

Edward eyed Roger. 'How do you know?'

'I can see your face, you can't.'

He grinned. 'You're right. I have two possible leads but one is in Chicago.'

'Chicago? I ain't going there!'

'Maybe I'm not either.'

'Why not?' Roger was astonished. If Mr Clayton had a lead, why wasn't he going to Chicago immediately? 'Ah.' An explanation struck him. 'You said two leads.'

'Yes, though one will have to wait.'

'So you won't require my services any more.'

'I have a week to wait in New York and don't really know my way around. Want to be my guide?'

'Sure do, sir,' gasped Roger, delighted that his association with this Englishman should continue for it had paid him well so far.

'Good. Be outside my hotel at nine in the morning to start a guided tour of the art galleries.'

'Art galleries?' Roger screwed up his face. 'Who'd want to look round those fusty old places?'

'I do, and maybe you'll learn a thing or two.'

'Isn't it just wonderful?' Isobel slipped her arm through Arthur's, startling him for he had not heard her footsteps in the meadow that sloped gently away from the lodge before plunging steeply down to a foaming river that swirled over many boulders strewn along its bed. Arthur saw it as a wonderful living picture created in many shades of brown, blue, white and green, and itched to put his impressions on to canvas. The far bank rose cliff-like at first and then flattened into a small forest-bearing plateau that, half a mile away, began to rise steadily towards the great fortress of the solid mountains behind.

Every morning of the fortnight they had been at the lodge he had come out here to drink in the peace and absorb the ever-changing light that made the scene different every day. It had brought thoughts of Colette, and how she would have loved to photograph this view in all its changing moods. Such thoughts pricked his conscience still. He had a wonderful wife in Isobel; why should his mind turn again to Colette after all this time? Each morning he felt guilty and chided himself for entertaining such thoughts.

'You were far away?' Isobel commented with a questioning smile.

'Lost in this beauty and my desire to paint it, but my feeble efforts would not do it justice.'

'Don't belittle your ability, Arthur.'

He gave a wry smile. 'In my glory days I wouldn't have had second thoughts about attempting it. I would have tackled it fiercely and done it justice. Now I'm frightened I wouldn't.'

'You won't know unless you try.'

'Ah, but I do.'

'Your old flair is coming back. Marie, Lucy and George all say so. They can see it happening as you teach them.'

'It isn't the same.'

'I don't understand all the niceties but surely, if they can see the development, it only needs you to exert yourself again and you will be the Arthur Newton whose work was once sought after. Try, Arthur. I know you can do it. Do it to please me?'

Could he deny the interest, encouragement and pleading he saw in her eyes? Wouldn't the granting of her wish purge the thoughts of Colette that had haunted him each morning and wipe away the feeling of guilt? He put his arm round her waist and turned her to him. He looked deep into the hope in his wife's eyes and kissed her long and tenderly, expressing not only his love but also his thanks to Isobel for being who she was.

'For you.' he whispered. Enormous pleasure swept over him when he saw the light in her eyes change from uncertain pleading to joy. He kissed her again and hurried back into the house.

She stood watching him, her heart filled with song and certainty in her mind that the outcome would be a painting that would restore the name of Arthur Newton.

Isobel waited where she was. She thought she knew why he had gone to the house and a few minutes later was proved correct. He reappeared carrying his easel, canvas, and a compact box holding his paints, brushes and pencils.

Isobel hurried briskly towards him. 'Let me take that,' she said, reaching for the box.

'I'll set up over there.' He indicated a flat piece of ground. She did not take a lot of notice as her mind was busy forming a question.

'Are the others coming?'

'No. I've told them what I want them to do and have sent them further downstream to where there is a relatively easy path to the water.'

'Didn't you want to go there too?'

'No. This is the scene I want to paint, in memory of this particular morning. I believe that because of you I am going to rediscover what I thought I had lost. This painting is to be special and it's for you.' Arthur gave a teasing smile. 'Besides, I wanted us to be alone.'

She smiled too at the implication.

He set up position close to the edge of the bluff so that his view would take in a particularly pleasing aspect of the river. 'What about this?' he asked.

Isobel came up beside him. She nodded but at the same time he saw a thoughtful light in her eyes.

'Well?' he asked. 'You don't look certain.'

Isobel stepped away from him, paused then took three steps forward. She paused again and with a slight shake of her head moved to her left, closer to the edge of the plateau.

'Careful of the overhang!' called Arthur, but his warning came too late. A large crack appeared in the earth and simultaneously a huge piece of ground fell, taking Isobel with it.

Horrified, Arthur was shocked into immobility. Then, as a piecing cry rang out, he leaped forward as if to prevent the disaster. He pulled up short, on the very brink of destruction, and stared down at the river that crashed over a fresh fall of rocks and the body that lay among them.

Horror lay heavily on him, then an unearthly cry broke from his lips. 'NO!' It reverberated from the cliff across the river and was flung back at him in a mocking echo. He clamped his hands to his ears as if that would shut it out but still it rang in his mind.

340

He screwed his eyes tight in an attempt to erase the visible horror but nothing worked. Finally he turned and ran to the lodge. In disarray, his face contorted, eyes wild, he burst in. He never knew what he said or what was said to him, but a few minutes later he found himself sitting on a chair in the kitchen with the cook trying to calm him. He looked up at her pleadingly.

'Help has been sent for, Mr Newton. Someone has ridden to Denver for your brother.'

'The children?' he gasped.

'A servant had gone to ask them to return to the house immediately but without giving a reason.'

He nodded, grateful that Oswald's staff had taken matters into their own hands.

'Drink this, Mr Newton.' The cook handed him a glass.

Without looking at it, he drained it. The fire of the brandy hit the back of his throat and then his stomach. He spluttered and coughed but the shudder that ran through him cleared his mind. He caught his breath and nodded his thanks to the cook who would have poured some more but he stopped her.

'I must get to her.' He started to get up.

'No, please, Mr Newton. It would be dangerous. Wait until your brother comes.'

'But I must go to her, she might still be alive!'

'One of the men who knows the best way to reach Mrs Newton is already on his way.'

Any further idea he'd had of going was driven from his mind as Marie, Lucy and George rushed in, concern on their faces. Alarmed at seeing her father so dishevelled, his face creased in agony, Marie was by his side immediately, her arm around his shoulder. 'What is it, Father? What's happened?'

'Oh, Marie, Marie!' Tears welled in his eyes. 'Where's Lucy?' He looked beyond his daughter and, seeing her, held out his free arm.

She came to him. She felt that the arm he put around her was seeking to comfort her and knew that whatever had happened affected her deeply. 'What's wrong?' she cried. 'Where's Mama?'

'Oh, Lucy!' He held her tight. 'She fell from the cliff into the river.'

For a moment silence saturated with disbelief filled the kitchen, then Lucy let out a long wail and cried, 'Where? Where?' She looked round desperately and accusingly. 'Why isn't anybody doing something?'

'They are, Lucy. They are. One of the men has gone to the river and someone has ridden to Denver for Uncle Oswald. We can only wait.'

George, whose face had lost its colour from shock, stepped forward. 'Can I do anything, Mr Newton? I feel helpless just standing here.'

Arthur looked up at him and nodded. 'Go into the meadow. You'll be able to see if the man has reached the river; you might be able to bring us news.'

George hurried from the house. His steps were leaden when he returned with the news that he had seen the man down at the rock-fall, but when he had called to him the other man had shaken his head in indication that Mrs Newton was dead.

The news renewed their shock and devastation; it brought fresh tears, fresh seeking of comfort and a stronger response to it. Arthur, bemused by the tragedy, was constantly expecting to see Isobel walk in. Marie sought to comfort him amidst a natural desire to ease the loss for her dear friend also who had now suffered three devastating blows in her life. In spite of her own suffering at the loss of Isobel, who had become a second mother to her, Marie knew she would have to draw strength from somewhere to help them both. She was thankful she had George's support for a deep sense of loss had seared her own mind. She had always seen kindness in his eyes but now, in the midst of tragedy, there was strength as well.

Lucy was shattered; her whole world had altered forever. Why had this to happen? Why me again? she wondered. What else has fate in store for me? The questions haunted her but there were no answers. She clung tight to Arthur, as if by leaving go she would be consumed by her own grief. She had no feeling and yet she had; her mind was numb, oblivious to anything outside herself, yet she ached with hurt and loss and a desire to see her mother again, just to hear her laugh and speak.

They were still sitting like this when Oswald and Dolores arrived from Denver. They brought a new perspective to the situation. After all the appropriate enquiries, commiserations and expressions of sympathy, they took control. Oswald organised the recovery of the body and its transportation to Denver. Dolores saw to everyone's comfort and soon had the staff going about their daily duties in an attempt to give the impression of normality. Though no one expressed a desire to eat, she insisted that they had something.

It was after they had dispersed from lunch that Oswald saw his brother walking towards the site of the tragedy. Concerned, he hurried from the house, his eyes intent on Arthur, fearing what he might be contemplating.

Arthur reached his painting equipment, still standing exactly where he and Isobel had put it. His body tensed. His gaze wandered from it to the view he had been going to paint; the painting Isobel had been certain would revive his career. Why, oh, why, had he listened to her? Tears started to roll down his cheeks. If he hadn't complied he wouldn't have gone for his equipment, then they would not have set it up and this tragic loss would never have shattered his life. Even when they had found the position, why had he asked her if she thought the viewpoint was right? If he hadn't Isobel would never have walked where she had and would still be alive. Grief and guilt pounded at him, bringing anger at himself and at this view that just begged to be painted. It rose in him until it became unbearable. His cry of vengeance was flung at the heavens; he grabbed his paint box and hurled it over the cliff. Sweeping the easel aside, he threw it after the box, cursing at the top of his voice.

Oswald was shocked at the sight and ran as fast as he could, fearing that his brother would fling himself over the edge. Reaching Arthur, he grabbed him by the arm. 'Stop it! Stop it at once!'

Arthur was only aware of someone trying to restrain him. He tried to shake himself free. Unable to do so, he swung round, his eyes wide with such malevolence that Oswald was frightened and responded automatically in an action that was part defence and part attack. He punched Arthur hard in the stomach, causing him to double up and gasp for breath. Oswald seized his chance and hit his brother again, this time to the side of his head. As Arthur staggered away with a bemused expression on his face, Oswald knew that sense had been driven back into his tortured mind. He grabbed his brother and marched him back to the house where he flopped him into a chair.

Arthur looked penitent. 'I'm sorry,' he whispered.

'I'm sorry too,' replied Oswald, 'but I had to do it.'

Arthur nodded, and Oswald knew his brother held no grudge.

He patted him on the shoulder. 'Come on, get tidied up. We have some talking to do with everyone. There are many things to be settled but we'll not mention this incident to anyone.' He took his brother to his room and stayed with him until he had made himself respectable again, then they went to find the others.

Dolores had taken charge. With the help of Marie, who was showing strength in spite of her personal loss, she had calmed Lucy and brought a degree of stability to the terrible situation.

When they had all gathered together Oswald asked, 'What do you want to do?' Though his remark included them all he was really directing it at his brother. 'Stay here until the funeral or return to Denver? If you wish to stay, Dolores will be here with you. I will have to be in Denver.'

'I would rather return. This place will have too many memories,' answered Arthur.

Everyone else murmured their agreement.

'Very well, we still have time to do so today. We shall leave as soon as you have your things packed. Dolores love, will you inform the staff?'

She nodded.

'I suggest, therefore, that we continue this discussion in Denver but I will say one more thing. I was coming here today with news that I hoped you would all be pleased to hear. I have a venue for your exhibition. You may not want to go ahead with it, but think about it. We can talk about it in Denver.'

Everything for the journey was prepared quickly. As they drove away Arthur did not look back. He wanted to obliterate forever any memory of the place that had taken his second wife from him. Lucy, though her heart was torn in pieces, stared at the scene, imprinting it on her mind so that she would see forever the beauty of the place where her mother had died.

Back in Denver, when Oswald judged the time right he went to Arthur's room where he expressed a desire to arrange everything as his brother wanted.

'It can't be just my wishes you hear,' Arthur responded. 'Marie, Lucy and George are all adults. They are entitled to discuss it too.'

'Will you do that together then and let me know what you decide?'

Arthur gave a brief shake of his head as he replied, 'No. I want you and Dolores to be there. Your suggestions wil be of great value. After all, this is your country; you know the right procedures. Apart from that, we cannot make any suggestions that might impose on you.'

Oswald was pleased to see that his brother had his emotions under control and was taking the realistic view that life had to go on, no matter how many waves of hurt and regret kept sweeping over him. 'Very well, we'll meet in the drawing room in ten minutes. Will you tell the others?'

Arthur nodded.

Ten minutes later they were all together. When Oswald saw them seated comfortably, he gave them all a glass of wine and said, 'First things first. As reluctant as I am to bring this up, it is something we all must face. As soon as we got back I wrote a note to the leading undertaker in town and despatched one of my men with it. He returned a few moments ago with the answer. If you wish, the funeral can be the day after tomorrow.'

'So soon?' Arthur's voice was scarcely above a whisper.

'You can delay it if you prefer,' replied Oswald, 'but is there any point in doing so?'

'I will abide by your wishes, Father,' said Lucy, looking at her stepfather, 'but I agree with Uncle Oswald. What is the point? I know Mama would not want us to delay. I remember her once telling me, "When I die, bury me quickly and get on with life. Miss me but don't mourn."'

Arthur looked with admiration at his stepdaughter. As much as she must be hurting, she had held her emotions in check with great strength. Isobel would have been proud of her. He knew he must respond with equal bravery. He glanced at Marie and saw her nod of agreement.

'Very well! The day after tomorrow.'

'I will send word to the undertaker.' Oswald rose and left the room to return a few minutes later and find Dolores had taken over his role.

'I have been telling them that they are welcome to stay here as long as they like.'

Oswald looked to Arthur for his response but it was Marie who spoke. 'We appreciate your offer but don't want to impose on you further.'

'Dear Marie,' said Dolores with quiet firmness and deep affection, 'you will not be doing that. This is your home for as long as you like. Take your time deciding what direction you wish your lives to go in. I know there was some uncertainty about it when you arrived. Now you may be looking at things differently.'

'I concur with what Dolores has said,' put in Oswald. 'I told you that I had a venue for your exhibition. Why don't you go ahead with it? I am sure Isobel would want you to.'

Arthur looked at Lucy who responded with, 'I'm certain she would.'

'Very well,' said Oswald. 'I'll arrange it for . . .' He glanced at Arthur who would know the state of the paintings and drawings they had been working on.

'You've been painting for two weeks at the lodge. You had some pictures completed before we went there so you have a good basis for selection. If we say three weeks' time, you will have more completed,' replied Arthur who saw the others nod at his decision. 'But only you three will exhibit, I won't.'

He rode the outbursts of protest then said, 'I was about to start the one painting I would have exhibited when Isobel fell. I can no longer paint it and if I attempted anything else it would only be mediocre. Isobel wanted to see new life in my paintings, and I am sure I could have restored it in her presence. But not now.'

No one spoke. They knew it would be no good trying to alter his mind. They let the matter drop and were thankful when Arthur

346

spoke again, 'I think you should start on your work immediately, then after the funeral we will assess what new subjects you should add.'

Oswald, realising that his brother wanted to get them absorbed in painting immediately so that their minds would be diverted from the tragedy, added his approval.

Though the atmosphere lightened a little as they reset their studio and started their painting again, it was not until after the funeral that any of them felt a decided enthusiasm for what they were doing.

As they walked away from the graveside the three younger ones felt that their old lives lay behind them and that new ones stretched ahead. They all sensed Isobel willing them to seize their chances.

Arthur felt nothing but despair, though he was strong enough to hide it from the others. He had lost the person who had brought new exhilaration to his life, who had loved him and inspired him to see that he could regain lost artistic heights, only for that promise to be blighted before it had blossomed. The future held nothing for him in that respect, but in another he had a responsibility to see that Lucy, Marie and George achieved their ambition to become recognised artists. Besides that he knew Isobel would want him to see that Lucy achieved personal happiness too.

They set about their new projects with enthusiasm and under Arthur's guidance, not forced but subtly suggested, their work became more appealing. Marie's portrait of Dolores, whom she had persuaded to sit for her, became no mere outward representation but completely captured her personality so that by the time it was finished Dolores herself seemed to be about to step off the canvas and speak.

Oswald arranged for George to stay at a friend's ranch for three days so that he could sketch the cowboys at work and leisure, an experience that he turned into vibrant sketches and paintings. A desire to develop her landscape painting meant that there were times when Lucy needed to be outdoors. On these occasions Dolores accompanied her, with the result that they came to know each other much better and by the time of the exhibition they had become very close.

Their days had become full, and Arthur was pleased with the way everything was progressing. His three charges had flung themselves into their work with zest, though there were still times when he detected sadness in their eyes and voices. Isobel's death haunted him and he knew, though they tried not to make it obvious that they were all concerned for him. Knowing this helped to strengthen his resolve to face life positively and give them support in return.

The day of the hanging was full of excitement. Everyone was up early. The paintings were loaded into wagons by Oswald's staff, supervised by Arthur, and transported to the hall where they were met by Oswald. There followed a day long hanging, arranging and rearranging until they were all satisfied that the display was such that the works would make the maximum impact. Then it was home to get ready for a celebratory evening meal at the Windsor Hotel, courtesy of Oswald and Dolores.

'I'm going to miss Lucy when they return to England,' commented Dolores sadly as she and Oswald were changing.

'So am I,' he agreed. 'I'll miss them all, but especially Lucy.' He put his arms round his wife. 'She's become the daughter we never had.'

Dolores, her eyes damp, nodded. Wanting comfort, she laid her head against his chest.

They stayed like that for a few moments, each with their thoughts on the young woman to whom they had both become attached. Then he eased her away so that he could look into her eyes. 'Dolores, she has no one so . . .'

'She has Arthur.'

'I know, and I realise how responsible he feels for her, but I wondered if you would like for us to have her here with us?'

Her eyes widened at the unexpected suggestion. 'You mean, permanently?'

'Why not? Of course it would depend on whether she would like it too and if she has any ties in England.'

Chapter Twenty-four

Impatient to be continuing his search, Edward found that every day dragged by in spite of his finding much to interest him in New York. He had an expert guide in Roger and marvelled at such knowledge of the city in one so young. Edward's natural interest lay first in the Metropolitan Museum of Art. By making it known there that he was an artist he was directed to the Natural Academy of Design, and to societies and clubs that in turn opened doors to smaller galleries and private collections. The art of a comparatively young nation intrigued him, and he was interested in how it was linked with exploration and the gradual movement West. Apart from an existing interest in the work of Frederic Church and Winslow Homer, he became fascinated by the paintings of the American West by Albert Bierstadt, but it was Thomas Moran who really charged his desire to emulate these masters of their craft. He realised he had to curb that desire until he had completed his personal quest one way or another. Successful or not, he hoped he could see and paint the magnificent Western landscape before he returned to England.

This hope was thrust to the back of his mind as he approached the offices of Union Pacific on the date he had been given.

At the reception desk he put his query to a young man who greeted him with a friendly smile and enquiring eyes.

'When I visited your offices a week ago I was told that the man I needed to see was away until today.'

'Indeed, sir, and what might your query be about?'

'I am trying to trace a man by the name of Newton who may or may not have worked on your railroad.'

'Ah, the man you need is Mr Jepson, sir. I'll see if he is available.'

A few minutes later he was back and asked Edward to follow him. 'Your name, sir?' he enquired.

'Mr Clayton.'

The clerk nodded and led the way along a corridor. He knocked at the second door on the right, opened it and announced, 'Mr Clayton, sir.'

Mr Jepson, a thin-faced man with a neat pencil-line moustache, rose from behind his desk, shook hands with Edward and indicated a chair to him. He inclined his head in a query as he asked, 'What can I do for you, sir?'

Edward repeated his request. The man looked thoughtful and flicked his moustache with the forefinger of his right hand. 'It is not the policy of this company to disclose matters concerning their employees.'

'That sounds as though you do have someone of this name working for the company.'

Mr Jepson ignored the comment and asked, 'May I ask why you require this information, sir?'

Edward's mind worked quickly. 'He is my uncle,' he replied. 'We knew he emigrated from England and worked here on the railways, but have not heard of him for many years. I need to contact him and took the chance that he would still be on the railways here.'

'You've come all the way from England to find a long-lost relative?' The question was more of a statement and Mr Jepson did not wait for a reply. He nodded, seemingly satisfied with Edward's explanation. 'In that case I think I can oblige you. Yes, we have someone of that name working with the company. A gentleman by the name of Mr Oswald Newton runs our South West operation from Denver. I worked with him for a while before he went out West many years ago. I believe he came from . . .' He hesitated as if searching for a name. 'Er . . . oh, what did he call it?' He tightened his lips in exasperation, and then beamed all over his face. 'Got it, Leeds! But I believe he worked for the railroad in York over there.'

'That will be him!' cried Edward, eyes widening with excitement. 'That will be him. Denver, you say?'

'Yes, sir.'

'I'll be able to find him through the offices there?'

'Yes.'

By the time he left Edward was in possession of the train timetable to Denver.

Roger, who had waited patiently outside, showed his disappointment when Edward told him that he thought his search would end in Denver but, used to life's vicissitudes, he cast that aside and wished Edward well and was profuse with his thanks when the Englishman gave him a generous tip.

On arrival in Denver Edward found a cab and directed the cabbie to take him to the best hotel in town.

'That'll be the Windsor, sir.'

He was amazed by the spread of new buildings in the town, their complexity and the variety of architectural styles. He had not known what to expect of this Western town but had pictured it as being a conglomeration of roughly erected wooden buildings from the wild days of expansion. Instead here were large brick-built structures, many with the hallmarks of grand English architecture. The long wide main street, which he saw was labelled 16th Street, cut straight towards the South Platte River. Horse-drawn vehicles were still prominent but a few motor-cars were parked outside offices and emporiums. Even though there was an orderliness about the city it still held a slight atmosphere of the days when it was a rip-roaring frontier town.

When the cab stopped the driver said, 'The Windsor Hotel, sir, the most magnificent in town.'

Edward had no doubt that it was for he found himself outside a large four-storied building of elegant design. The main entrance was under a stone canopy and when he walked inside he was faced by unexpected opulence. It appeared that no expense had been spared to make this place attractive even though, to his English eyes, it seemed to have been overdone. However, he realised if this was the way to attract customers in a fledgling nation, who was he to condemn it? He had no doubt that the grandeur would be carried on throughout the hotel and was proved correct when he saw his room. It was large, with the bed and other mahogany furniture in the latest style and everything laid on for his comfort.

Refreshed, he enquired of the hotel receptionist where he could find the offices of the Union Pacific Railroad.

Reaching his destination, he was greeted pleasantly but his request to see Mr Newton brought a negative reply. 'I'm sorry, sir, Mr Newton is not at his desk today. He is on an inspection tour and won't be back in the office until the day after tomorrow.'

Disappointed, Edward had to accept the situation but asked if he could make an appointment then.

'Certainly, sir. If you will follow me I will take you to his secretary.'

Within a matter of minutes an appointment was set for eleven o'clock. Leaving the building, Edward calmed his frustration at the delay by telling himself that he had achieved much more than he had expected when he first set foot in New York. He would take advantage of this delay to explore Denver at his leisure. He strolled in the direction of the river and found that the town had developed around the river's confluence with the lesser Cherry Creek. The backdrop of mountains entranced him with their snow-capped peaks shimmering in the sunlight. From the paintings he had seen in New York he knew they were a painter's paradise and his fingers itched to be holding a paintbrush. He had pencil and sketchbook in his luggage at the hotel. Tomorrow he would wander Denver with them.

As he passed a building on his left a notice caught his eye. It announced that this was the venue for an art exhibition, something he had never expected to see here. Out of curiosity, he entered the building and was directed by a second notice to a room on the right. He stepped inside and paused to get his bearings. A quick glance revealed paintings and drawings, all framed and well presented, on three walls. Several people were viewing them. As his eyes settled on a group of five people he saw a young lady, who seemed to be the centre of attention for the other two ladies and two gentlemen, glance in his direction as if curious to see who had entered the room. Their eyes met briefly but in that moment a spark passed between them. Edward felt the shock of excitement course through his veins. He stepped towards the first painting but the stranger's attractive face, so expressive as she talked, still filled his mind.

As he moved from one painting to another he was conscious of her eyes constantly drifting in his direction while she continued talking to the other people who seemed to be interested in the paintings. He half turned his head and their eyes met. She looked away quickly, as if trying to hide her embarrassment, under pretence of resuming her conversation. He found he could no longer concentrate on the paintings but stay he must, no matter how long it took.

At last the four people to whom the young lady was talking made a final comment and the group broke up. Edward turned to look at her openly. She stood stock still as if trying to hold on to a moment in time that would end if she moved. Their eyes met and the space between them did not exist; this meeting was meant to be.

She smiled and stepped towards him. 'Good morning. Welcome to the exhibition. I hope you find it interesting and maybe see something that you cannot resist.'

Edward, his eyes fixed on her, was tongue-tied even though his mind said, I am looking at it now.

She laughed aloud at his reaction. 'You expected to meet an American, I suppose?'

'Yes. Now you are triggering a whole new batch of questions.' He laughed in his turn to see her reaction to his words. 'I can tell you too are baffled to hear an English accent. It seems we are both far from home.'

She raised her eyebrows and inclined her head. 'It would appear so.' She held out a hand. 'Lucy Wentworth.'

When he took it he thought he felt something more than politeness pass between them but at the same moment he chided his own overactive imagination. 'Edward Clayton.'

'Do you live in Denver or are you just visiting?'

'I have just arrived this morning.'

'And you've come straight to our exhibition?' There was a touch of teasing in her voice that he liked.

353

'I was passing and saw the notice. And you? When I came in you gave the impression that you had every right to be here.'

She smiled. 'Yes, I am one of the exhibitors.'

He raised one eyebrow. 'You are an artist?'

'You'll have to judge that for yourself.'

Three ladies had just entered the room and Lucy immediately recognised them as people Oswald had pointed out when they had dined at the restaurant attached to the Windsor Hotel. They had been with their husbands who, according to him, were among the richest men in Denver. Lucy was not going to miss such an opportunity. She said to Edward, 'Excuse me, I must see these ladies.'

He glanced in the direction of the newcomers and from their dress immediately concluded that they represented affluent patrons. As much as he wanted to keep Lucy to himself, he could not deny her the opportunity of talking to potential clients. 'Of course,' he said.

She glided away, already putting on a friendly smile. Edward glimpsed it and saw that it was different from the one she had given him when she first saw him.

He looked at the pictures, paying particular attention to those initialled LW and giving the others little more than a passing glance. He kept looking in Lucy's direction and willing her to be free but she was deep in earnest conversation. He caught her glance in his direction a couple of times, though, and saw interest in her eyes.

The three ladies seemed to be in no hurry to leave and Edward finally thought he should not be seen hanging about any longer. He wanted to break into their conversation but it was not etiquette to do so. He neared the door and was aware that Lucy was hurrying in his direction.

'I'm sorry, I did not expect them to stay so long. I was going to suggest that you should come home with me, meet my family and have some luncheon. I know they would like to meet anyone recently arrived from England.'

'That is kind. I would love that, if I won't be intruding?'

'Be back here in twenty minutes. I'm sure they will have made up their minds by then.'

'You are close to making a sale?'

She nodded, gave him a smile and hurried back to her three potential customers.

For twenty minutes Edward strolled, not really taking any notice of Denver's life which teemed around him. His mind was fixed on the young woman with whom he had felt an instant rapport. There had been that indefinable look in her eyes as they met his, and in that moment time had stood still for him as he was sure it had for her. It was as if he had found something that he had been looking for all his life; something he'd once thought he had found with Hester. But this was different, this brief contact had affected him differently. The desire to be with Lucy was so intense it tested his patience. These twenty minutes seemed an eternity. He found it impossible to analyse his feelings completely but only knew he was longing to be with her again.

As he approached the door of the hall he felt relief sweep over him when he saw the three ladies emerge deep in animated conversation. As he passed them he heard one of them say, 'She has a true talent.' Another agreed. He slowed his step. Could he hear more? 'I was very impressed. She will revive interest in the early painters of the West if she continues to produce work like that. I am so . . .' Edward had passed beyond the point of hearing more but liked what he had heard so far. He too had been impressed by LW's paintings of the mountainous landscape, something he hoped to attempt himself. It seemed they had a common artistic ambition. He felt a special delight that these ladies, no doubt influential in Denver society, thought so highly of her work.

He entered the exhibition hall. Lucy had been watching out for him. As soon as she saw him she hurried towards him, her face wreathed in pleasure, a new excitement in her eyes that had driven from them the sadness he thought he had seen on their first meeting.

'You did well?' Though he put the question he already knew the answer.

'Wonderfully! Each of them bought a painting. They are foremost members of Denver society so I'm sure word will spread, which can only be good for my two friends and me. Now let us away, I want you to meet them all.'

She had a quick word with the attendant who had been employed to be on duty while the exhibition was open and then led Edward from the hall with quick purposeful steps.

Outside she hailed a passing cab, informed the cabbie where they wanted to go and climbed inside.

As he settled beside her Edward said, 'Are you sure it is all right your taking me home without any notice?'

'It's not necessary.' Her eyes twinkled.

'But back in England you would not have . . .'

Her amused laugh broke into his words. 'You are in America now. Things are different here.'

'But you know nothing about me.'

'I know you are interested in art otherwise you wouldn't have come to the exhibition, and that you are an Englishman. I know my family will be keen to have news from England. As for knowing anything else about you, it can wait until you meet everyone. We'll soon be there.'

Edward was astonished by the size of the house where the carriage stopped. He helped Lucy to the ground and she waved aside his offer to pay. She led him to the front door and without any preamble went straight in.

'I expect some of them will be in the drawing room. Come on.'

Edward followed her through a door. He was surprised that he felt immediately at home here and put it down to Lucy's friendly ability to put him at his ease, creating the impression that she had known him all her life.

They entered a large room, flooded with light from its long windows. It was tastefully furnished, with paintings of rugged mountains, bathed in sunlight or covered in snow, hanging on the walls. They were very atmospheric, particularly one with mist rising from a lake into which a stream cascaded with a final heart-stopping plunge.

A young woman and man, sitting in chairs close to a window, turned to make their greetings and immediately expressed curiosity on seeing a stranger.

'Hello, you two, I've found an Englishman,' Lucy said brightly. 'This is Edward. Edward, my stepsister Marie and her fiancé George.'

356

They were on their feet. Marie, pleased to see the sadness had been banished from Lucy's eyes, guessed that Edward must have made an impression on her. As she shook his hand she admitted to herself that there was something attractive about him. George too shook his hand and both men sensed warmth in their exchange.

'He came into the exhibition,' Lucy explained. 'And when he spoke I knew you would like to meet someone recently arrived from England.'

'I'm sorry to intrude,' said Edward.

'You are not doing that. You are most welcome. Has Lucy invited you to lunch?'

'I have,' said Lucy. 'And I think Edward brought me luck. I sold three paintings!'

Excited congratulations burst from Marie and George.

'Who to?' they asked eagerly.

'Mrs Hill, Mrs Sheedy and Mrs Byers.'

'Wonderful! You've moved into society.'

'And you are likely to as well. Marie, I overheard them discussing your portraits and saying they thought their husbands ought to have theirs painted. George, they were taken with your cowboy sketches and want to talk to you about them. I made an appointment for you for eleven o'clock, the day after tomorrow.'

Marie and George hugged each other in their excitement.

'Father will be delighted,' cried Marie, eyes brightening as she anticipated his reaction.

'Where is he?' asked Lucy.

'He was walking in the garden,' replied George. 'I'll go and get him.'

'No. We'll all go to him,' said Marie firmly. 'If you go alone you are sure to tell him what has happened. You won't be able to resist.'

George laughed. 'Probably not.'

As they set off, Edward hung back.

'Come on,' said Lucy, glancing over her shoulder at him.

'You'll want to break the news of your success without me there.'

'Nonsense!' she said. 'Come on!'

357

Edward followed her into a well-kept garden, at the far end of which stood a rustic summerhouse; a touch of England, he thought. He could see the outline of a man sitting there.

'Father, Lucy's sold three paintings,' cried Marie.

'And there could be commissions for Marie and George,' added Lucy.

Arthur was filled with delight at these announcements. 'Wonderful! Marvellous! Congratulations!' The words poured excitedly from his lips but died away on seeing a stranger standing a little way behind them. He puckered his brow. A stranger. Why was he here? There was something familiar about him. No, he couldn't have seen him before. And yet . . .

Edward had been swept along on the general enthusiasm but when the man rose to face them, something had lurched in his chest. A strange sensation gripped him. This man . . . no, it couldn't be, and yet why did he feel transported to a day six years ago in Whitby? He saw a puzzled expression in the older man's eyes that he knew was matched in his own.

'Father, I would like you to meet Edward Clayton. He has just arrived in Denver and came into the exhibition. As soon as I heard he was an Englishman I invited him to meet you all. Edward, please meet my stepfather, Mr Newton.'

Lucy immediately sensed an unusual tension between them. She felt excluded from a common bond these two men shared, but how could that be? They had never met before. The way they stared in disbelief at each other mystified her, Marie and George.

'What is it, Father?' asked Marie.

He appeared not to hear. Still looking puzzled, he stepped closer to Edward. 'You can't be . . . can you?'

'Have I altered so in six years?'

'Hardly, but our meeting was brief and I didn't expect to see you in Colorado. You know how it is when you see people out of context – doubts come to mind, you think you must be mistaken. What on earth are you doing here?'

'I came to find you.'

'Find me?'

'After Mother told me who my real father was, I had to.'

'Father, what's this all about?' Marie needed answers after what these exchanges implied.

Arthur turned to his daughter and took her arm reassuringly. 'Marie, it's a long story. Let us go into the house.' When they were in the drawing room he said to her, 'Meet your half-brother.'

'What?' The information struck her like a heavy blow.

'It's true, love,' he replied. 'I'll tell you everything soon. For how, please welcome your brother with love.'

Marie was bewildered by her attempt to grasp what this meant. Bemused, with doubt in her eyes, she half turned to Edward.

He saw confusion and sensed hostility so took the initiative. 'Marie, I am more than delighted to meet my half-sister.' He held out his hand.

She ignored it. Her mind whirled, trying to grasp all the connotations this new relationship brought with it. As they assailed her, her heart thudded hard with shock at what the past had held hidden from her. Before her stood living evidence that her father had betrayed her mother! Her thoughts flew to a visit to Whitby many years ago when she was still very young. She'd seen a strange lady in her father's house there and her mother had been angry, she knew. She'd not understood the implications then. Now they loomed large.

As much as her love for Arthur tried to dominate cold reason, the shock of this meeting between father and son was overpowering. She fought the rage that threatened to explode and, giving her father an accusing look, hurried from the room.

'Marie!' Arthur's plaintive cry was lost in the crash of the door as Marie slammed it shut behind her. With pleading in his eyes, he looked at Lucy. 'Go to her, please.'

Lucy gave him a quick kiss on the cheek 'Don't worry, she'll be all right,' she said as she started for the door.

Dismayed, Edward said, 'I'd better leave.'

'You'll do no such thing,' replied Arthur forcefully.

'I promised Mother that if anyone was going to be hurt, I would give up. I've hurt Marie, I should go. I should step out of all your lives immediately.'

'Never!'

'But Marie?'

'It's been a shock to her, but she'll get over it.' Arthur, wanting to ease the turmoil of the moment added, 'Your mother, how is she?'

'She was well when I left England.'

'She approved of your coming?'

'She knew it was inevitable after I discovered who my real father was.'

'How did you find me?'

George, who had been a silent witness, rose to go. 'You have much to talk about, I'll leave you.'

'No, George,' Arthur stopped him. 'You are one of the family, you should know what happened.'

George sat down again and he and Arthur listened in admiration to Edward's tale of how he had taken up the task of finding his father. But as deeply interested as he was, Arthur's mind kept drifting to Marie, hoping that Lucy could make her see that her world was not shattered but could be enriched by the acquisition of this half-brother who, in a short time, Arthur had come to admire for his kindly disposition and thoughtfulness. And, if he was not mistaken, Lucy had shown a special feeling for him when they had arrived together.

Lucy could hear sobbing when she tapped on Marie's door but had no hesitation in going into the room. Seeing her friend lying face down on the bed, body racked by sobs that came from the depths of her heart, she crossed the floor quickly and sat down beside her. 'Marie, Marie,' she said compassionately, stroking her back gently with the palm of her hand. 'I know you have had a shock, but nothing can alter the fact that you have a half-brother. We just have to face it.'

Marie twisted round to face Lucy. Her cheeks were streaked with tears, her eyes wild. 'Why should I? Why should I accept him? Why should I condone what my father has done – betrayed my mother?'

'I am sure he regrets that, but what is done is done. He needs your love more than ever now.'

'Why should I give it?'

'Because he is still your father, no matter what he has done.

360

Don't let one indiscretion from so long ago destroy the love that is between you. If you do, you'll live to regret it.'

Marie flung herself into Lucy's arms. 'Oh, what am I to do?'

'Forgive him with all your heart. You have told me how devoted he was to your mother throughout her illness; there must have been love there. Concentrate on that, and accept Edward as your brother. I'm sure you'll come to love him.'

'I don't want to hurt Father.'

'There is only one way to avoid that.'

Marie nodded but still held on to her. How long they stayed like that neither of them knew. Marie found comfort in Lucy's arms and solace in her advice, fearing what might happen if she broke away. Lucy was reluctant to move, dreading that if she did so Marie's more reasonable reaction might be abandoned.

Eventually they were disturbed by a knock on the door. It opened slowly and Arthur's voice said quietly, 'May I come in?'

Marie sat up, straightening her dress as she did so and wiping her eyes.

'Can I speak with you, tell you what happened?'

She nodded.

Lucy stood up. 'I'll leave you.'

'No!' It was almost an order from Marie. Then she toned down her voice as she looked at her father. 'I want Lucy to stay here.'

Knowing how close these two had become, and realising that to refuse this request would be counter-productive, he nodded. 'Of course.' He came to the bed and sat down beside his daughter to take her hand in his. He held out his other to Lucy who took it and sat beside him.

Slowly and quietly, he told his story. They listened without interrupting. When he had finished silence filled the room in the few moments that Marie and Lucy took to absorb what they had been told.

Then Marie looked straight at her father as she asked, 'Did you love Colette?'

He hesitated. This answer could mar the whole future for him but he knew Marie was one who valued honesty. 'I did.'

She hesitated only a moment and then stood up. She took one

361

step towards the door then turned and held out her hand to her father. As he stood up her glance caught Lucy's who smiled her approval.

'One moment, Father.' Marie went to a closet and emerged a few moments later with all signs of tears eradicated, her clothes straightened and her hair in place. 'I must let my half-brother see me at my best.'

Arthur smiled. 'So like your mother.' He kissed her on the cheek and took her hand. They walked slowly down the stairs with Lucy behind them. Arthur led them to the drawing room where he had left Edward and George discussing the exhibition.

Not a word was spoken when they entered the room. The young men stood up, Edward's face wreathed in hopeful expectancy.

Marie let go of her father's hand and held out her arms to him. He returned her smile and stepped into them. They hugged each other and felt the connection between them.

'Welcome,' she said, close to his ear.

'Thank you,' he returned as he hugged her harder.

As they released their hold he turned to his father. 'When Lucy introduced us she called you stepfather?'

'That is correct. Marie's mother died in England five years ago.'

The information struck Edward like a blow. Five years. If only he had found his father sooner. Now he had a stepdaughter!

He heard his father continuing to speak. 'I married a widow, Mrs Isobel Wentworth, a charming person. Sadly, she died in a tragic accident in the mountains a few weeks ago.' His voice faltered momentarily but he steeled himself to continue. 'Lucy is her daughter, now mine.'

As Edward started to make his commiserations, Arthur interrupted. 'Thank you, Edward, Lucy and I appreciate your thoughts. We are coping in the way that we know her mother, my wife, would have wanted us to.'

Edward nodded then asked, 'Have you moved to America permanently?'

Arthur gave a small laugh. 'You presume that because we are living in this house? It is not mine. It belongs my brother Oswald. We came here at his suggestion. He thought we might find it conducive to our art, and the invitation came at a time when Lucy was distressed over a broken love affair. We thought it might help her get over it.'

'And it has,' put in Lucy quickly, wanting Edward to know that there was no rival for her affection.

'My brother and his wife are away,' offered Arthur in further explanation.

'He is due back in his office the day after tomorrow,' said Edward.

Arthur looked surprised. 'How did you know that?'

'It's all part of the story of my trying to find you, some of which you have heard. Now I think everyone should hear it all.'

By mid-afternoon everyone was in possession of all the facts that had brought about this reunion far from home.

'It was most fortuitous that you had arranged an exhibition at this time and I saw the notice announcing it and there met Lucy,' concluded Edward.

'And she had the foresight to bring you here,' added Arthur. 'Now, there is a spare room here and I am sure my brother would want his nephew to move in.'

'But I couldn't . . .'

'Of course you could,' chorused Marie and Lucy.

'They are right,' confirmed Arthur, 'Oswald will be very put out if he returns tomorrow to find I have left you in the hotel.'

'If you insist.'

'We do.'

'I'll come and help you with your things,' offered George.

'Uncle Oswald is going to get a monumental surprise when he and Aunt Dolores arrive tomorrow,' laughed Marie, her demeanour indicating that she had got over the initial shock of learning that she had a half-brother.

Lucy, delighted at the way things had turned out, gave Edward a mischievous wink as he was leaving.

Chapter Twenty-five

The following afternoon, from her bedroom at the front of the house, Lucy was the first to hear the crunch of carriage wheels on the drive.

She burst from her room shouting, 'They're here! They're here!' She was still shouting as she flew down the stairs and crossed the hall to the front door. She was eager for Dolores and Oswald to meet Edward and hoped that both, but especially Dolores, would approve of him.

The rest of the family were hastening to join her as she opened the door. The crisp autumnal air and clear atmosphere made the mountains seem much nearer today. They gathered on the veranda at the top of the steps. Edward, with a feeling of intruding on a family scene, hung back until Arthur took him by the arm to stand alongside him.

Excited greetings expressed their pleasure at seeing Dolores and Oswald home again. Handshakes and kisses were exchanged before Arthur silenced them. He could see his brother and sister-in-law wondering about the stranger in their midst. 'Dolores, Oswald, I want you to meet my son Edward.'

They stared at him dumbfounded.

'Son?' A puzzled frown furrowed Oswald's forehead.

'Yes,' replied Arthur. 'It's a long story.'

'I'll bet it is,' his brother commented tersely.

It was Dolores who eased the tension by coming to Edward, taking his hands and kissing him on the cheek. 'Welcome to the family.'

Tight nerves slackened and there was no mistaking the relief in Edward's voice as he said, 'Thank you, ma'am.' He turned to Oswald. 'I am pleased to meet you, sir.'

For one almost unnoticeable moment Oswald hesitated but he knew he must follow his wife's example. He held out his hand. 'Welcome to our home.' His grip was firm and there was friendship and acceptance in it that Edward returned.

'Thank you, sir.'

'No more of the sir. Uncle if you must.'

His statement brushed aside any anxiety that Arthur still retained.

Oswald turned to his brother. 'It seems you have quite a tale to tell us. I can't wait to hear it.'

As they went into the house Dolores linked arms with Lucy. Brief though the moment was she had noticed a special disquiet about the girl, different from that she had sensed in the others. It had melted into joy when Oswald had accepted Edward. Dolores reckoned Lucy had special feelings for this young man; now she felt in her touch an unmistakable vibrancy that could only mean one thing. Dolores longed to have Lucy on her own, to hear what she thought about Edward. Instead, for the moment, she could only test her theory out. 'Isn't he handsome?' she whispered, and noted the glow that brought to Lucy's cheeks as she replied with a nod.

A few minutes later they were all gathered in the drawing room and between them enlightened Dolores and Oswald about Edward's history, his search and the final confrontation in Denver.

When the story was finished Arthur added, 'I hope you don't mind but I invited him to move in with us?'

'You did the right thing,' approved Oswald. 'He can stay as long as he wishes.'

'Of course,' agreed Dolores. 'You all have a lot to sort out. Futures to think of, your art to consider . . . oh, so many things! Take your time.'

'Nobody will want to leave until after the exhibition,' said Oswald. 'We've been so busy listening we have not asked about it. What has Denver's reaction been?'

'A little slow at the start. I believe people first came out of mere curiosity, but then when word got around that it was worth seeing the audience began to be more consistent. That is how matters stand now. I expect visitors will taper off but we'll probably get some folk reappearing, hopefully to purchase the works that attracted them in the first place.'

'There's still a fortnight to run.'

'Yes.'

'And have you sold any?'

'Lucy has sold three landscapes.'

'Wonderful.'

Dolores smiled affectionately at her and clapped her hands as she mouthed silently, 'Well done.'

'They were bought by Mrs Hill, Mrs Sheedy and Mrs Byers.'

Oswald raised one eyebrow. 'Three very influential ladies. Other sales or commissions could easily come from them when their friends see what they have bought.'

'They also showed interest in Marie's portraits.'

'No doubt thinking of capturing their husbands for all time,' Oswald commented with a knowing smile. 'Already this exhibition is proving worthwhile. What about you, George?'

'Sold one to the owner of the Circle C where I did those sketches of his cowboys. He put a reserve on four more and indicated that other ranchers could be interested.'

'It seems to me that you could easily make a future here with your art.' Oswald turned to Edward. 'What do you paint?'

'Anything, but I'm chiefly concerned with landscapes and seascapes.'

'Ah, seascapes, of course, coming from Whitby. I'm afraid we are a long way from the sea here.'

'I can do plenty from my sketchbook. Maybe some people might be interested to learn what lies beyond those mountains, but at the moment it's the mountains that attract me.'

Dolores saw Lucy's face brighten at that.

'Well, there's plenty of scope for you. Maybe you could get your father interested in painting again.' Oswald was aware he was treading on dangerous ground here for he knew that Arthur still abhorred the memory of the day he had been about to take up his brushes again.

366

Edward nodded but made no comment. He would work on that in his own good time when he had assessed the situation. Besides, he had to consider returning to England. At that thought he felt a tug at his heart. He wanted to get to know Lucy better. Even in this short time the spark struck by their first meeting, so different from anything he had ever felt, seemed to be intensifying. How long could he delay returning to England? He had not promised his mother a specific date so he would say nothing yet. He would not even tell her he had found his father; if he did, she would expect him to return immediately. But a time would come when difficult decisions would have to be made.

'Edward!' Lucy's call stopped him as he was crossing the hall to the dining room for breakfast.

He looked up to see her hurrying lightly down the stairs, her face warm with smiles. She wore a plain dark blue dress that fitted her perfectly, emphasising her slim waist, and carried a cape and an artist's bag.

A sensual impulse surged through him, taking him into mysterious realms. He felt an intense desire to be with her, on her own or in company; it didn't matter so long as Lucy was there. He wanted to be close, wrapped in the joy of her presence, but if others were there he wanted to be there too, able to watch and admire her.

'Have you anything planned for today?' she asked as she reached the bottom of the stairs. Her question broke the spell but it carried a promise that made his heart race.

'No.'

'Then why not come with me? I am going to work on my latest landscape. You expressed a desire to paint the mountains.'

'I'd like nothing better.'

'Good. Meet me on the veranda ten minutes after breakfast. There'll be a carriage. Uncle Oswald always has one of his hands take me; he stays around as escort, fishes the creek within sight of me, but if you are with me he can fish further afield.'

Edward didn't think he had misread the twinkle that came in to her eye then.

'What about Marie and George?'

'George is busy on another painting of cowboys at work and Marie is going to seize the chance to go with him to start a portrait of the ranch owner.' She gave a little smile. 'It's quite convenient how our various interests have fitted together, isn't it?'

He read her inference and knowingly returned her smile. 'It has worked out rather well.'

'We'll have a picnic with us for midday,' she said as she opened the dining-room door.

Dolores, Oswald and Arthur paused in the middle of their breakfast to make their greetings.

'Marie and George have left already,' Dolores informed them. 'Have you two any plans?'

'I'm going to continue my landscape,' replied Lucy. 'Edward is going to come and start one.'

'If you can fix me up with materials, Father?' he said.

'Take what you want from my room, I shan't want anything again.' The touch of bitter regret in Arthur's voice did not go unnoticed by Edward who made no comment, merely said, 'Thank you.'

They drove at a fast pace for nearly an hour with the mountains exerting their pull more and more powerfully the nearer they came. Lucy's early chatter lapsed into silence when she recognised in Edward the same symptoms she had experienced on her first venture towards this awesome, inspiring and uplifting landscape.

They left the main trail and drove for another fifteen minutes into a world that seemed to resent the intrusion of horse's hooves and the clatter of wheels on a stony trail. They intruded on a silence that usually only permitted the cry of a bird or tinkle of water. The scenery grew more enchanting the deeper they journeyed. When the river finally came in sight the driver pulled the horse to a halt. He was quickly to the ground and helping Lucy from the carriage.

'I'll be all right today with Mr Clayton with me, Al, if you want to fish that pool you're always telling me about.'

Al's eyes brightened at the opportunity presented to him. He could achieve something he had always wanted to do since he had discovered a particularly promising place the first time he had brought

Lucy here to paint. He tethered the horse, hoisted his rods and asked when he should be back.

'Five hours,' said Lucy.

Edward had been busily unloading their stools and painting gear from the carriage. As Al left them he straightened up and eyed the scenery. 'This is magical,' he said, awe in his expression. The stream foamed over rocks and swirled beside banks that rose from their stopping place to form a low cliff on the right side of the water, while on the left the ground swept away into a rounded, conifer-laden hill. This vista formed the ideal frame to the mountains that rose behind, layer on layer, to majestic peaks touched with a mantle of snow. 'So, so wonderful. How on earth can I ever do justice to it?'

'Be yourself,' said Lucy quietly. 'The painting has got to be in your idiom.'

Edward's mind flew thousands of miles across land and sea and he heard another girl saying the same thing to him in England. He knew what he had to do then and banished all thought of using his father's techniques to reproduce this landscape. This was to be entirely his representation.

'I have never seen your work in progress,' he said as he erected Lucy's easel for her

She was busy taking the protective wrapping from her canvas. As she placed it on the easel Edward stood back to view it.

He was in awe of what he saw. 'This will be far better than any you have in the exhibition. You have dispensed with any attempt at reproducing this particular scene. Instead you have brought out the special atmosphere here, the magical luminosity of the light. The gradations of tone on this part of the mountain make it particularly alive. Are you going to do the same on the part you have still to do?'

'Yes, but in darker tones because of the way the light falls there. What about you, how do you see this scene?'

'In the dramatic vein,' he replied, recalling the paintings of Bierstadt and Moran. 'Those mountains have an unseen drama in them, a grandeur that I feel I must put on canvas. See the cleft over there?' She looked in the direction he was pointing. 'I'm going to make that my focal point.'

Excitement and a desire to achieve what he had in mind were combined with the joy of being with Lucy. He grabbed her round the waist and pulled her to him. His lips met hers, eager yet soft with love. She did not resist but, pliant in his arms, met kiss with kiss.

'This is marvellous country to paint,' she said teasingly as she leaned back into his embrace.

'It is,' he agreed, 'but it is an even more wonderful place to remember as the place I first told you that I love you.'

'Edward!' Her whisper was charged with the wonder and joy of accepting a love she would treasure to her dying day. In that moment their two souls were one.

During the rest of the exhibition, Arthur knew he would have time to get to know his son better. He had to cement relationships, not only his own with Edward but his son's standing with everyone else, especially Marie. He rapidly realised that other people's attitudes would take care of themselves. With joy he witnessed an easy settling of relationships with Edward within the family. Arthur found that he was able to concentrate on his own feelings.

He observed Edward carefully but unobtrusively. He liked this young man; his demeanour, his thoughtfulness for others, his kind words, the way he never wanted to impose himself. Arthur regretted that he had played no part in his son's upbringing and, although he had never known the man who had brought him up, was thankful that Colette had found someone who must have exerted a good influence on Edward. But there was one thing only he and Colette could have given their son – his artistic talent and eye for a picture. In recollecting that union of so long ago, Arthur felt an intense desire to see Colette again. By finding him, Edward had dispelled his wariness that he would upset lives by revealing the truth. That banished uncertainty was replaced by a different one: would Colette want to see him? With this question in mind, and knowing the exhibition was nearing a close he felt it was time to talk seriously with his son. He chose a time one morning when he was able to stroll in the garden with Edward.

'Tell me more about your mother,' he prompted.

'What do you want to know that you don't know already? She's a wonderful person, but you already know that. She was a good wife and is a good mother. She is a talented photographer and due to exhibit soon in London.'

'How did that come about?

Edward explained about Matthew Robinson and how that had led to his own exhibition of paintings in London. He mentioned Hester and how his own desire to find his father had brought about their break-up.

The inevitable questions followed. Has your mother got over her husband's death? Has she formed any other relationships? What about this Matthew Robinson?

Edward gave a little smile because from the way the questions poured out he detected that some hidden depths had been stirred. 'The answers are, yes, no, and Matthew is just a very good friend. At one time he might have had other ideas but Mother put the relationship on the basis of friendship and he accepted it.' Edward paused a moment then in all seriousness added, 'The time is coming when I will have to go home. Why don't you come with me and see her?'

Arthur made a wry face and asked, 'Would she want to see me?'

'Of course she would,' replied Edward without hesitation. 'I have no doubt about it.'

Arthur nodded. 'We'll see,' was his non-committal answer, and Edward knew better than to press him at that moment. Arthur went on quickly, 'There are a lot of decisions to be made. This exhibition has been so successful it makes me wonder if there is a future here for the young ones.'

'If they see it that way, would you stay?'

Arthur gave a sad smile. 'No. It holds a very bad memory for me.'

'As it does for Lucy.'

'Yes, but she has established herself here as a painter, and she gets on so well with Dolores and Oswald.'

'Your painting would become equally well known if you took it up again.'

371

'I would never do such subjects justice. Maybe if Isobel had lived . . .' His voice faltered and he controlled it again. 'Besides, you will be returning to England and I've only just got to know you. I want to know you better so I'll return with you.'

Edward made no comment. He saw a dilemma arising. He had to return to England; he owed his mother that, and his father expected him to do so. But he wanted to be with Lucy too and she had strong reasons for staying in Denver. He decided he must have a word with her now, but when he returned to the house he found that Dolores and she had gone shopping in town.

It presented the opportunity that Dolores had been looking for. With so many people in the house it was not always easy for them to have a conversation face to face but today she was able to take Lucy to lunch at the Windsor. It was when they were having dessert that Dolores brought up the subject that had become dear to her heart.

'What do you intend to do when the exhibition closes?'

Lucy gave a small shrug. 'I haven't really thought about it. I have some commissions to fulfil but . . .' She let her voice trail away.

'You are wondering about England?'

'Yes.'

'Do you have to go?'

Lucy looked thoughtful for a moment. 'I suppose not unless . . .'

When she hesitated Dolores put in, 'Your relationship with Edward comes to something?'

Lucy blushed. 'Has it been so obvious?'

'To me, yes. Maybe to Marie. The men . . .' She gave a wave of her hand. 'Poof, no, they go around with their heads in the sand.' She eyed Lucy seriously. 'If you don't want to return to England, if you want to build on your success here, Oswald and I would be more than delighted for you to stay with us. We have talked about it and, having no children of our own, would love you to remain with us. You and I have got on so well, Lucy, there is a life here for you, if you want it.'

Tears of gratitude welled in her eyes. 'I don't know what to say except . . . thank you.'

372

'Of course a lot will depend on Arthur but we would discuss it fully with him. And there is your relationship with Edward to think about.'

Edward did not stray from the house but kept an eye open for Lucy's return. As soon as she arrived he asked her to come to the summer house with him. Once they were seated he came straight to the point. 'You know how much I love you, Lucy, but what is the future for us? You have a successful life here and I can see that would continue if you were able to stay.'

'I am,' she put in so quickly that it halted him from saying more.

'What?' he gasped. 'Are you?'

'Yes. Aunt Dolores has said that if I see my future here, I can live with them.'

'What does my father say to that?'

'He doesn't know yet. Dolores has just put the proposition to me over lunch.'

'I see.'

'Will you be returning to England?' she asked.

'I will have to. Mother will be expecting me.'

'Would you consider coming back here?'

Edward looked thoughtful for a moment and then said, 'Marry me, Lucy.'

Taken aback a little by the suddenness of the proposal, all she could say was, 'And live where?'

'Who knows? Let's take that as life presents it. I don't want to be separated from you but . . .'

She reached out and caressed his cheek with her fingertips. 'And I love you.' She paused briefly and then continued, 'But there is something I must tell you. I have been married.' He registered surprise. 'You are shocked?'

Edward quickly gathered himself. 'You are a widow?'

'Yes, but there is more you should know. He was an Army officer. Unfaithful with an Indian woman. There was scandal . . .' Her voice faltered.

'Say no more, my love. It is you, as you are now, that I

373

love, nothing from your past can influence that.' He kissed her gently.

There was deep love in her smile of appreciation. 'Let's not announce our intention until we know what everyone else is going to do.'

That came sooner than expected for as they were finishing their evening meal Oswald announced, 'I would like you all in the drawing room in ten minutes, after Dolores and I have had a word with my brother.'

She led the way to Oswald's study where he indicated they should be seated.

'Arthur, I do not know what your intentions are but we want you to understand that if you want to make a permanent home with us, you can do so,' his brother announced.

Dolores added her approval.

'That is most kind of you, but I would rather return to England,' he replied with a slight shake of his head.

'Understandable,' agreed Oswald. 'Do you know what the others want to do?'

'It is entirely up to them. They have the prospect of what might result from a successful exhibition. On the other hand, they would be tearing up roots at home. I don't want to influence them in any way, but I know Edward wants to see his mother.'

'Naturally. He always had the idea of returning to England.'

'There might be another influence at work there,' pointed out Dolores. 'I think Lucy and he are in love.'

'What?' Both men stared at her in amazement.

She gave a little grunt of derision. 'You men never see what is under your nose! I am more certain of Lucy than of Edward, however.'

'But surely they would have said something to me?' objected Arthur.

'Maybe they wanted to wait, to make certain of their feelings. And Oswald and I may be testing that.'

'How?' Arthur looked at his sister-in-law with curiosity.

'Only today, with Oswald's approval, I told Lucy that if she wanted to stay, she could live with us.'

'You mean, you'd give her a permanent home?'

'Yes. But I did say it would depend on whether you objected or not.'

'I have no say over her. She must decide for herself. But now there will be another factor to take into consideration if what you say is true about her feelings for Edward.'

'That is so, and we will stand by whatever she decides.'

'So,' concluded Oswald, 'Arthur, you are definitely returning to England and Edward, more than likely, will be doing so too. But beyond that we don't know.'

'We might in a few minutes,' said Dolores, rising from her chair.

The two men followed her to the drawing room where they found everyone already assembled.

Oswald took centre stage. 'I hope you have all been happy with us, in spite of the tragedy of Isobel's death. Now, with the exhibition nearing its close, I expect you all have decisions to make. Dolores and I want you to know at the outset that we would love any of you to stay on here as long as you like. We are not rushing you into any decisions but . . .' He paused.

Edward sprang to his feet before Oswald could continue. 'You may as well know that I have asked Lucy to marry me and she has accepted. I really didn't know who to ask for her hand in marriage so I spoke to her first.'

There were smiles, laughter, hugs and kisses once again.

'Well,' said Arthur, 'as you know Marie and George are engaged so there will be two marriages. Where? When? There's so much more to decide.'

'But first I'll raid the cellar for some champagne,' said Oswald.

He returned to a happy atmosphere and much excitement about the future. After glasses had been charged and the health and happiness of the newly betrothed had been drunk, Oswald called for order. 'While I was in the cellar and while we have been enjoying these last few moments I've been putting my mind to all the possibilities. The only thing that we definitely know is that my brother is set on returning to England, but now we need to consider where these marriages will take place.'

'It would make sense for us to marry in England,' said George. 'My parents are there, and Marie's father will be.'

'Agreed,' said Oswald. 'We would like Lucy to be married from here but totally understand that Edward will want her to meet his mother before the marriage so it would be right for that marriage to take place in England as well.' He glanced at his wife. 'Dolores, how about we go to England with them?'

Her eyes brightened and her lips curved into a smile. She flung her arms round her husband's neck. 'Can we? Can we?' she asked with the enthusiasm of an excited child.

'I have plenty of time off due to me. I have a good deputy and staff here, I see no reason for head office to turn down a leave of absence. I'll contact them tomorrow.'

Amidst the excitement that charged the room, Marie came over to her father. 'Are you happy about this, Papa?'

'Of course, my love. You have chosen wisely, I have every faith in George.'

'But what if he wants to come back here to pursue his painting?'

In spite of expecting this, Arthur's heart gave a lurch. 'What about you? You too have a great opportunity here. Do you want to take it?'

'I would love to, but I don't want to leave you on your own.'

'You must not consider that. You have your own life to live. You cannot be tied to me forever. Take your chance while you can. I know George will look after you and you will be near your uncle and aunt. I'm sure you will be able to turn to them if necessary. You have my blessing. Now let me have a word with Edward and Lucy.'

He drew them to one side. 'I had no idea that you two . . .'

'It happened as soon as we saw each other when I walked into the exhibition,' replied Edward, 'and since then our love has just grown and grown.'

'I'm pleased for you both, and I know your mother would have been, Lucy.' The catch in Arthur's voice brought a tear to her eye but she held it back as she hugged him.

'Thank you,' she said quietly in his ear. 'I'll always be grateful for the happiness you brought Mother.'

'She brought me happiness too. Now, what do you intend to do after you are married?'

'It's a problem that we haven't solved yet. Lucy could easily build on what she has achieved here. From what Oswald and Dolores have said, we would have their support. I've had a successful exhibition in London, and you and Mother will be in England. We have decided to let things take their course and see how they turn out when we are there.'

'A good idea. Don't forget you could have exhibitions on both sides of the Atlantic. I know the crossing takes time, but does that matter?'

'I suppose not. We'll have to see. After all, you and I have really only just met. There is a lot of ground to make up.'

Arthur nodded his appreciation of the thought. 'I know, but I don't want to stand in the way of your future. I have just spoken with Marie; she and George are tempted to return here and I've told her that I will be all right. I can visit you both at the same time if you decide to come back to America.'

'Thanks for being so understanding,' said Edward. 'If only you would paint again.'

'Mother wanted you to,' put in Lucy. 'I'm sure she'd still want that.'

Arthur patted her arm. 'We'll see.' His tone was non-committal

Edward made no comment but recalled his father's outstanding works when he'd seemed to be inspired. If only that inspiration would come again.

Chapter Twenty-six

When Oswald came in from work the following day he announced, 'I have arranged with head office to take two months' leave, starting a fortnight today. I've booked train seats for the following day and sea passages from New York five days later.' With general excitement breaking out, he continued, 'That should give you time to complete any commissions you are working on and make provision for the others.

I hope that suits everyone but I thought it best to get on with the arrangements once head office had approved my leave of absence. It means we will avoid the worst of the winter and be back in early spring.'

The next fortnight was frantic. No one thought they would ever be ready but they all were. Dolores gave final instructions to the staff to keep the house open and have it ready for their return.

'How many rooms?' queried the housekeeper.

'I don't know.' Dolores pursed her lips thoughtfully. 'Better prepare all of them.'

They relaxed on the train where Mr Oswald Newton's party received special treatment. The accommodation on the liner was magnificent and everyone was thankful for a relatively smooth and uneventful crossing.

As they sailed into Southampton, chosen by Oswald as being reasonably convenient for reaching Arthur's home, he was filled with nostalgia after all these years. Beside him at the rail, Arthur was pleased to be back. He had left tragedy behind him in the mountains of Western America and, though distance would not dim his memories of Isobel, he knew he would feel closer to her on the south coast. Dolores was excited at seeing a new country and chatted incessantly to the young ones who were seeing England with mixed feelings for they knew that in spite of the euphoria of the coming weddings they would have to make serious decisions about their future soon.

They disembarked in fine weather but by the time they reached Deal the rain was lashing down. Arthur was thankful that he had cabled Mrs Darnel, giving her the date of their return, for she had opened up the house, given it an airing, prepared some food, and as soon as she saw the carriage arriving at the door, put the kettle on.

'Not the best welcome,' commented Arthur as they laughingly shook themselves out of their wet clothes, 'but that is countered by your thoughtfulness, Mrs Darnel. Thank you for what you have done.'

She greeted him and Marie and remembered Edward from his enquiries. She received quite a surprise when Arthur introduced him as his son. Being a woman in strict control of herself she did not express it. Instead she extended a welcome to the newcomers.

'Mr Newton, when you told me in your cable how many were coming, I realised you would not have the bedroom space. I have two spare rooms you can use.'

'That is most generous of you,' replied Arthur, 'but we couldn't impose.'

'You won't be. I would not be comfortable knowing you were crushed in here while I have space.'

'My wife and I are prepared to go to an hotel,' said Oswald.

'Nonsense! That's a waste of time you could spend with your brother.'

'Thank you, Mrs Darnel, we accept your generosity. We will not hinder you for long as we will be going north.'

'Use my rooms for as long as you like, and again when you return if necessary.'

Two days later they all headed for Yorkshire, stopping first in Norfolk where Arthur, Edward, Lucy, Dolores and Oswald took rooms at an hotel not far from George's home, leaving the way clear for George and Marie to break the news of their intended marriage and new home to his parents.

Once the excitement of their homecoming was over, George's father with his customary abruptness asked, 'What do you intend to do now you are back?'

'Get married and return to America,' replied George.

'What? Why?' both parents gasped at the same time.

'We can do well with our painting there.'

'Can you live on it?' his father demanded.

'Yes.'

Horace grunted in disbelief.

'There will be two of us painting. We've already had a successful exhibition in Denver. I sold two paintings of cowboys at work and have commissions for five more. Marie sold two landscapes, but her greatest success was through her portraiture. She painted one of her aunt and one of her uncle to tempt others to have their portraits painted. It worked. She now has commissions for portraits of three very important men in Denver and there is every reason to believe that more work will come from them. They all pay well.'

'Enough for you to live on?' Horace still showed concern.

'Yes.' George firmed his voice so that his father need have no doubts.

'Does this mean you will be living in America permanently?'

'Well, we will have to live in Denver,' replied George gently. He saw tears coming to his mother's eyes and went on quickly, 'We hope we will be able to exhibit in London as well.'

'But how will you manage that?' asked Horace in a tone that instantly threw a dampener on the idea.

'The modern liners make it easier.'

'What does Marie's father think of this?'

'You will be able to ask him yourselves.' George went on to explain who was staying in the nearby hotel.

'Then get them here!'

George and Marie started to get to their feet but Ellen stopped Marie. 'Let George go. Stay here and talk to me.'

'Of course,' replied Marie who realised that Ellen felt that she was losing a son not only to his new wife but to America as well. She must take this opportunity to reassure her.

Once introductions of the visitors were over and they had all

380

been given a glass of wine, Horace eyed Arthur. 'Do you approve of George and Marie living in America?' he asked bluntly.

'It is not for me to approve or disapprove,' replied Arthur quietly. 'They are adults and capable of making up their own minds. If they need my advice, I am here. If not then that is that.'

This attitude took the wind out of Horace's sails so he asked instead, 'Do you seriously think they can make a living from painting out there?'

'If they work hard and build on their success at the exhibition. No doubt they have told you about that?'

'They have, Mr Newton,' put in Ellen. 'It is reassuring that you, with your expert knowledge, think they can.'

'I do, and see no reason why they can't exhibit in London as well. My son has a friend who I am sure can arrange that. Just as you and your husband want to see your son, Mrs Reeves, I too want to see my daughter.'

'That is very heartening, Mr Newton. Isn't it, Horace?'

The way his wife had manoeuvred this he could do nothing but agree.

'Now that the American question seems to have been settled and Marie and George are proposing to live in Denver, I would like to say something,' said Oswald. 'I have a considerable acreage of land near my house. As a wedding present I will build them a house on some of that land. The same applies to Edward and Lucy, though that must not influence their final decision.'

There were gasps of disbelief at this generosity. Marie shook her head. 'Uncle Oswald, you can't. It's too much.'

He smiled. 'What I do with my own land and money is for me and Dolores to decide. She knew what I was thinking and heartily approved.'

'Oswald, you are too generous,' said Arthur.

'Dear brother, Dolores and I were not as lucky as you, we have no children. I speculated in land and made a lot of money from early investments in various Colorado mines as well as from my job. What is going to happen to our land and money? Let us enjoy benefiting these young ones while we can. Let us live to see our money being put to good use. There is only one thing, though I

381

do not insist on it. The youngsters want to marry in England. Dolores and I would dearly love to see them married before we return to America, whether they return with us or later.'

'This is more than generous of you,' said Ellen. 'It is comforting that George and Marie will be near you, and Edward and Lucy if they too return to America. I am sure that their wedding can be arranged before you return home.'

'Don't forget we have similar arrangements to make in Whitby,' Edward reminded them. 'And we have to persuade my mother that it is in our best interests to pursue our art in America.'

Immediately further plans were discussed: George would stay in Norfolk to arrange his wedding; Marie, who felt she needed to support her father and be with him for as long as possible, insisted she would go to Whitby with the others. They would return to Norfolk for her wedding and continue on from there to sail back to America with Dolores and Oswald.

Arriving at the house on Whitby's West Cliff by coach from the station, Edward went to the front door on his own.

Hearing the maid's gasp of surprise on opening the door, Colette hurried from the drawing room. 'Edward!' She took him in her arms. 'It's so good to see you. You seem to have been away such a long time.'

'It's good to see you too, Mother.'

'I got your cable saying you were starting out for home but it gave no information as to when you would be here, nor if you had been successful in your investigations.' She started to lead him to the drawing room.

'Wait a moment, Mother, I have a surprise for you.' He moved towards the front door.

Her heart missed a beat. There had been no mention of his father. Was this the surprise? Nervous tension filled her and she chided herself for allowing such stupid speculation.

Edward reached the door. He opened it and stepped outside, half closing it behind him so that the surprise was hidden from Colette. She stood stiffly in the centre of the hall, her eyes fixed on the door.

As it opened Edward stepped back inside. 'Mother, I would like you to meet Lucy Wentworth.'

A young lady whose smile was so endearing it set Colette smiling back came over to her with outstretched arms. 'I am so pleased to meet you, Mrs Clayton. I have heard so much about you from Edward.'

Colette, with a look at Edward, sought an explanation even as she accepted Lucy's embrace.

'We met in Colorado and immediately fell in love,' he explained. He embraced them both and at the same time turned them so that Colette's back was to the front door. 'There's so much to tell you, Mother.'

'Such as how you found an English girl in Colorado?'

'Now that *is* a story, but there is someone who can tell it better than I.'

The door had opened quietly and now Arthur stood inside the house. 'May I do so?' he asked.

Even after all this time she recognised the voice. Eyes widening, gasping with the shock, Colette swung round. 'Arthur!'

He came forward, his hands held out, eyes fixed on her. She took his hands in hers and they looked at each other, wondering what to say.

Edward took Lucy's hand and, unnoticed, they moved quietly to the front door. As he slipped out after Lucy, Edward glanced back. His parents still hadn't moved.

Arthur broke the silence between them. 'You haven't changed at all.'

Colette gave a small smile of contradiction but said, 'Thank you for the painting. I never got a chance to tell you myself.'

The uneasiness between them was only partially helped by these remarks. Their past was laced by betrayal and they were unsure how to handle this meeting after so long.

The front door opened again and Edward reappeared with Marie, who as planned had just arrived with Dolores and Oswald.

'Mother, I want you to meet Marie, my half-sister.'

Colette glanced uncertainly at Edward but then held out a hand to Marie. 'Welcome,' she said, her mind a jumble of emotions. This young woman knew of her relationship with Arthur. What must her thoughts be, facing the woman with whom her father had betrayed her own mother?

Marie, who had doubted the wisdom of this meeting but had kept that to herself, took her hand, betraying nothing with her polite gesture. This woman had once been part of her father's life. She almost felt she was betraying her mother by meeting Colette like this but there was a deep desire in her not to hurt her father.

'Thank you,' Colette replied quietly.

Their eyes met but there was no instinctive rapport, only a touch of suspicion about what the other might be thinking.

Colette knew there was a barrier to be stormed here, and storm it she would, for Edward's sake, even if she never gained the real love and respect of this young woman. Marie sensed a wish in Colette to make amends and knew this called for a response on her part but was unsure whether she could give it. It would all take time, if it was ever attained.

'Come, tell me all about yourself,' said Colette, trying to melt Marie's icy gaze.

'There's not a lot to tell,' she replied tersely.

'I'm sure there is. Did you too inherit artistic skills from your father?'

'I like to think I did but other people must be the judge of that.' They had reached the drawing room. Marie pulled up, staring at the painting over the fireplace. 'One of Father's! One I've never seen, but without doubt one of his best. I wish he would paint like that again.'

'Doesn't he?'

'He hardly paints at all; hasn't done very much since we moved to the south coast, and certainly not since Mother died.'

Colette's heart lurched. Arthur was free . . . but her mind halted the fanciful thoughts that had appeared unheralded in her mind. Any further conversation between her and Marie, stiff as it was, was ruled out when Edward and Arthur appeared, accompanied by Lucy and two strangers.

Edward smiled at the bewilderment on his mother's face. 'I

promise you there are no more, but you have to meet Uncle Oswald and Aunt Dolores.'

After greetings were exchanged, Colette looked at Edward. 'I think you have a lot to tell me and I get the feeling everyone here is involved. We had all better sit down.'

Edward explained how he had gone about his search and how he'd accidentally encountered his father in Denver.

Arthur took over at that point and told Colette of his second marriage, of their reason for going to America and its tragic outcome.

When he finished Edward was about to take up the story again when his mother stopped him, looked gravely at him and said, 'You are going to tell me you want to marry your father's stepdaughter.'

Surprised by this statement, he hesitated but it was for only a moment. 'You are very perceptive, Mother. I hope you will approve?'

The tension that had come over the room was banished when she said, 'From what I saw when you two arrived, what you said then and what I have heard since, you have my blessing.'

Without any inhibitions, Lucy leaped from her chair and flung her arms round Colette's neck to kiss her. 'Oh, thank you so much, Mrs Clayton. You have made me so happy,' she said.

Colette patted her gently on the back, a gesture of loving confidence as she replied so that only Lucy could hear, 'Make sure you love him.'

'I will.'

With congratulations over, Colette said, 'I think there is more you want to say?'

'I want to tell you of how I met Lucy and about an art exhibition in Denver.'

When he had done so his mother said, 'You told me a few moments ago that I was a perceptive lady. I think I am now right in believing that you wish to return to America?' There was a catch in her voice at the thought of losing her son. There was a small pause and then she said, 'You can do no other. Lucy has obligations through the commissions she has gained.'

385

Arthur caught a fleeting moment of doubt and disappointment on her face and knew it had nothing to do with the fact that Edward would be parting from her. He said quickly, 'I know about Edward's successful exhibition in London and that it is a wonderful base to build on. I see no reason why such exhibitions in London cannot continue.'

'You really see that as a possibility?' she asked hopefully.

'Of course.'

'And you must visit America,' put in Dolores kindly.

'Do you intend to marry over there or here?' Colette asked her son.

'We thought here, as soon as possible. Then we'd all go on, you too, to Norfolk for Marie's wedding, and from there to Father's home ready to sail for America from Southampton.'

Colette nodded to Marie. 'I hope you will be very happy and look forward to meeting your future husband.'

'Thank you,' she replied, though there was still some coldness in her voice.

'And when you are in America, keep an eye on my son,' said Colette. She turned away without waiting for a reply, and found herself thankful when they all, except Edward, left for the Angel to prepare themselves for an evening of celebration.

'Has it been too much for you?' asked Edward with concern.

'It was rather more than I'd expected but I think I have absorbed it all now. I'll be sorry to lose you.'

He took her hands in his. 'You won't be, Mother. I am not going to allow the impact of my London exhibition to be wasted. Get Father painting again and we could have a joint one.'

Colette made no comment but asked, 'Where will you live in America?'

'The connections are with Denver. Uncle Oswald and Aunt Dolores are there and have promised to build us a house as a wedding present, just as they will for Marie and George.'

'What?' Colette could not disguise her surprise. 'What generosity!'

'Apart from his good job with the railway, Uncle Oswald made some shrewd investments. Theirs is a wonderful house with lots of land. Having no children of their own, they took to the four of us.'

'You are very lucky.' Colette drew comfort from the fact that her son and his bride would not be alone in a strange land. 'Don't let anyone down.' She looked him in the eye lovingly. 'Do well, as I know you will. Go with my blessing, my thoughts will be with you.'

'Thank you.' Edward's voice faltered. He kissed her and they held each other tight.

Arthur left the Angel before the others. He walked up Skinner Street and paused at Well Close Square, allowing the memories to flood back. Nostalgia filled his mind and he allowed the love that had lain hidden deep in his heart for so long to surface, but only for a moment. Thoughts of that could only hurt. He walked on to the West Cliff above the piers and looked out to sea, allowing his gaze to drift across the harbour with East Cliff and the old church and ruined abbey above. The whole scene was gilded by the light of the late-afternoon sun. His mind drifted back to other times when he had painted this very scene . . . but, no, of course he never had. The light was different then; always was, every day. He felt an itch in his fingers and suppressed it. He could not do this justice if he tried. The view of the ever-changing sea entranced him. He had never felt this way on the south coast and as this thought hit him he realised Whitby was where he belonged, no matter how other things turned out.

He walked on, deep in thought, his steps slow.

Reaching Colette's, he was shown into the drawing room and told by the maid that she would inform Mrs Clayton he was here.

A few minutes later she appeared. 'Arthur.' She kissed him on the cheek as he took her hands.

'I'm early, I know, but I wanted to say I'm sorry if we overwhelmed you earlier. If there is anything more you want to know or discuss, I am here.'

'Thank you, Arthur, that is considerate of you.'

'Not at all. It is our son who is getting married.'

Colette inclined her head at the word 'our', pleased that father and son could be so natural together.

'You have done a good job of bringing him up.'

'With the help of Bernard.'

'Of course. He must have been a wonderful man?'

'He was.'

'I wish I had known him.'

'I wish it too.'

There was a moment of charged silence that was broken when Colette said, with a lump in her throat, 'I'm going to miss Edward terribly.'

Arthur nodded. 'I know. And he's off to America before I've got to know him properly.'

'Children can bring heartache but they bring a lot of love. We must know when to love them and let them go, no matter how hard it is.'

'And this is when we must do it?'

Colette nodded. 'It will be even harder for you, you have two to let go at the same time.'

'Yes, though I draw some comfort from the fact that they will be near each other.'

'I hope Marie will let me share in that comfort too?'

'I'm sure she will. I knew it would be a difficult meeting for you both, and I saw it was, but I'm glad it has happened.'

They heard the maid crossing the hall to the front door.

'Oh, my goodness, they are here.'

The evening passed in a joyful mood. Though the relationship between Colette and Marie was subdued no one noticed it. They each realised that the other was trying to establish a closer bond but did not really know how to manage it.

The following day was hectic as arrangements were made for the wedding of Edward and Lucy. A special licence had to be obtained, the vicar consulted, the church booked and a time settled. Because the newly-weds would be leaving to live in America there was not the usual trousseau and list of household goods to be organised. The main guests were already there so it only required Colette's sister Adele, long-time friend Susan, and Matthew Robinson to be invited. Colette arranged for an intimate reception to be held at her house after which Lucy and Edward would spend the night in Scarborough where the following day they would be joined by those bound for Norfolk.

During the simple ceremony, when the vicar in his short homily said directly to the bride and groom, 'The love you have for each other now should be allowed to grow into a love that will sustain you throughout your lives,' Arthur and Colette, sitting next to each other as parents of the groom, unexpectedly touched hands, a gesture that took each of them back many years.

The rest of the arrangements went according to plan and when they arrived in Norfolk they found that all preparations had been made for Marie and George's wedding to take place the following week.

The days leading up to the wedding which, because of the Reeves' position in North Norfolk was to be much bigger than the one in Whitby, were hectic. Marie found that she was expected to get a new dress especially for the wedding and, not wanting to upset George's parents, complied. It was arranged that the following day the Reeves' carriage would take her into Burnham Market to make her choice.

Marie sought out her father immediately and told him what had been presented to her as an ultimatum. 'You'll have to come with me,' she concluded.

'I can't advise you on dresses. Get someone else to go with you.'

Marie's lips tightened. 'I can't! Lucy and Edward have gone to Blakeney; George has taken Aunt Dolores and Uncle Oswald to Hunstanton. He didn't want me along, I suspect they are up to something.'

'There's Colette. I saw her strolling in the garden.'

Marie scowled. 'If she's the only one, I suppose . . .' She started for the door with annoyance in her brisk step.

'Be kind to her.' Arthur's quiet words carried a wistfulness that Marie caught as she opened the door. They occupied her mind as she went to the garden. She would be civil, but how could she be expected to be kind to the woman who had tried to steal her father from her mother?

'Colette!' she called.

She looked round, wondering what Marie wanted of her. She smiled, hoping that the ice that remained would crack. She looked enquiringly at Marie when they were level with each other.

'I have to go to Burnham Market to get a dress for the wedding. I need to take someone with me but everyone else is out and I can't ask the groom's mother.'

'Of course I'll come,' replied Colette amiably. Though Marie had made it obvious that she was her last choice, Colette saw this could be a chance to get on more friendly terms with her.

Horace soon organised for one of his grooms to prepare a carriage and drive Marie and Colette to Burnham Market. Marie's silence and stiff posture bore all the hallmarks of protest at having to be alone with her.

After a short while Colette could stand it no longer. 'I am glad Edward found his father and you,' she began, hoping that she would start breaking down the uneasiness between them. 'I was unsure about his search at first but I realise now that for him it was a good thing.'

'I don't know if it was such a good thing for me,' replied Marie haughtily.

'I realise it must have come as a shock to you to find you had a brother, but is it not pleasant too to have someone who will always love and support you fraternally?'

'I suppose it is. I like Edward. It is not the relationship with him that I resent so much as the fact that it led to my meeting the woman who tried to steal my father from us!'

These words thundered in Colette's mind. She turned to look directly at Marie. 'You think I tried to take your father away?'

'Well, didn't you?'

'Marie, believe me, I never did that. I did not even know he was married until the day your mother appeared in Whitby with friends and you.'

The sincerity on Colette's face was unmistakable. Marie found echoes of that day reverberating in her mind. She could see and hear her own mother's grief and shock, and that of another woman too . . .

'If I had wanted to take your father away from your mother, would I not have told them both about Edward?' added Colette.

'You kept that to yourself?'

'Yes.'

'No one ever knew?'

'No one.'

'Father never told you he was married?'

'No.'

There was no time for more. The carriage was pulling to a halt in the small market town of Burnham Market. When they dismounted they found themselves a few yards from a bow-fronted shop.

As they looked at what was available and Marie tried on dress after dress, the conversation she had had with Colette kept coming back to mind. Her father had kept quiet about his marriage so Marie's idea that Colette had tried to steal him away from her mother was false. No blame could be attributed to her.

With a dress chosen, they left the shop. As they walked back to the carriage, Marie adjusted her cape. In doing so the brooch pinned to it became loose. It fell to the ground and bounced into the road in front of a coach pulling to a halt. Its rear wheel ran over the brooch, breaking it in three.

Marie cried out in alarm as she saw the brooch shatter. She stooped to pick up the pieces and when she straightened tears started to stream from her eyes. She looked at the pieces in her hand. 'Oh, no!' she wailed.

Seeing her distress, Colette asked, 'It meant something special to you?'

Marie nodded and swallowed hard. 'It was my mother's. My father gave it to her. I was going to wear it at my wedding.'

'I understand,' Colette said gently. She flipped her own cape back and unpinned a brooch from her own dress. 'Marie, your father gave this one to me. I know it won't mean the same, but please have it and wear it at your wedding in memory of your mother.'

Marie gave only a moment's hesitation and then took the brooch. 'Thank you,' she said. 'It will be an honour to wear it.' She hugged

Colette and both women realised then that hostility was at an end between them.

On the day of the wedding, when Arthur recognised the brooch on Marie's dress he knew that all was well between his daughter and the woman he had loved so many years ago.

Marie and George, Edward and Lucy, all thought it best if they travelled to America with Dolores and Oswald and so passages were arranged on a ship from Southampton. In spite of the sadness of parting, all was excitement as those bound for America cleared officialdom. Arthur and Colette were allowed on board until the final announcement warning those not travelling to leave the ship brought last-minute kisses, hugs and tearful goodbyes.

The travellers lined the rail. Colette and Arthur found themselves a position on the quay, ignoring the bustle around them, trying to lip-read last-minute messages, starting when the ship sounded its horn, and smiling and waving and wiping tears from their eyes as the gap between ship and dock grew wider and wider. Colette slipped a hand into Arthur's. They drew comfort from each other's touch.

They watched until the ship became smaller and smaller. Other people had dispersed and the activity on the quay had died down. They were alone.

They stood stock still, neither wanting to break the moment for to do that would mean there was a new life for them to face.

Without moving Arthur said quietly, 'While we were in Whitby I bought back my old house in Well Close Square. I want to paint again, inspired by the woman who was my only inspiration.'

Colette's hand tightened on his and now there was more than comfort in it.

'Welcome home,' she whispered from the depths of her heart.